C000226297

BRYAN ALDERSON

NEST

A novel based on the life of the
twelfth century Welsh Princess

HEDGEHOG PUBLICATIONS

I would like to thank all the people who have helped me with this book:

    Ruth who suggested the subject and who tirelessly proof read the text;

    Katy, who gave me a great deal of help with ideas for improving the book;

    George for technical assistance;

    Julian and **Glen** for help with the cover;

    Julia who provided access to source material long out of print;

    Diana, Fran and **Brenda** for critical reading of the text;

    and the small army of people who have helped along the way, for example **Paul** who researched maw worms for me!

My thanks also go to Chris Powell for permission to use a detail from his wonderful painting of Twelfth Century Carew Castle on the cover of the book and also to John Evans of Pembrokeshire Coast National Park.

I would also like to thank Helen Davies at Carew Castle for all her kind assistance.

About the Author

Bryan Alderson is of Shropshire stock and received part of his secondary education at Bridgnorth Grammar School. He took his degree at Keele.

Roaming the wild and beautiful country round the Welsh border led to an enduring love of Wales. He spent much of his free time in his early years climbing, walking and camping in the Welsh mountains.

Another strand in his development was five years working in Kenya where he built a boat which he and his wife Ruth sailed to Southern Mozambique together with baby Kate and the ship's cat Freddy.

For the last thirty years he has made his home in Pembrokeshire attracted by the magnificent coastline, unspoilt sailing ground and the warm welcome of its people.

He has become very interested in Welsh history which appears to have been overshadowed by that of its larger neighbour. For the last few years he has been trying to bring it to life in the form of historical novels which are as historically accurate as possible. His first book about the bizarre landing of the French Army at Fishguard in 1797 quickly sold out and is due to be reprinted.

Nest is his second novel and makes an honest attempt to discover the real nature of this remarkable Princess, said to be the most beautiful woman of her time, together with her devastating affect on the men around her. These included the King of England, the Lords of Pembroke and Cardigan, and most of all, her besotted cousin, Owain Prince of Powys, who was hunted to death for raping and abducting her.

Bryan's interests include writing, sailing and walking. He spends part of the year in his small cottage in the Dordogne. He sees no incongruity in an Englishman writing about Wales in the depths of the French countryside. However explaining the doings of a twelfth century Welshwoman to curious French neighbours - that's another matter!

Copyright © Bryan Alderson 2004

Published by
HEDGEHOG PUBLICATIONS
54 Port Lion, Llangwm,
Haverfordwest,
Pembrokeshire SA62 4JT

First Edition May 2004
Second Edition September 2004

This book is sold subject to the condition that it shall not, by way of trade or otherwise, be lent, resold, hired out, or otherwise circulated without the publisher's prior consent in any form of binding or cover other than that in which it is published and without a similar condition including this condition being imposed on the subsequent purchaser.

ISBN: 0 - 9530141 - 1 - 8

Printed in Wales by
Withybush Printers Ltd.,
17 Hill Street, Haverfordwest
Pembrokeshire. SA61 1QQ
Tel: 01437 769181

INTRODUCTION

NEST

Wales at the time of the Norman Conquest was a turbulent country with each Prince vying with the others for power.

Into this violent and disunited land rode the Normans who with brutal efficiency exploited the differences between Welshmen.

Wherever they were able to make inroads they built castles to establish permanent control, subduing the population by force.

Amidst this chaos was growing up a most beautiful and unusual woman - PRINCESS NEST - daughter of the last King of South Wales.

Many men loved and desired her, including the King of England, and one died because of his obsession for her.

Her immediate descendants conquered Ireland, and founded many of the great families of both countries. Later one married into the Tudor family and her son Henry seized the throne of England and became Henry VII.

Also by Bryan Alderson

Red Shawls and Black Bonnets
A story based on the bizarre landing of the
French Army at Fishguard in 1797.
Published 1997. ISBN 0 9530141 0 X

The Haven
The life of a family living on the shores of
the Milford Haven Estuary throughout the ages.
(due to be published in 2005).

*The cover painting is based on a detail from a painting by
Chris Powell. The artwork is by Ruth Alderson*

PROLOGUE

THE YEAR IS AD 1109

Desperate events
in Carew Castle
Pembrokeshire

Gerald hung by his fingers above the long drop to the cesspit. If he hesitated a moment more Owain and his men would succeed in breaking down the door to their bedroom and would certainly kill him. His death would be incidental. Owain had broken into the castle to rape and abduct his wife, Nest. Gerald could not bear to think what Owain would be doing to her in a few minutes time.

Nest was begging him to escape, to save his life and to organise rescue for her and the children. In a minute or so, Owain and his men would have the door down and it would be too late.

They had heard nothing of Owain's daring break-in to the Castle until the attack had started on their barred door a few moments ago, accompanied by shouts, threats and the strong smell of smoke. It was her idea that he could escape by sliding down the garderobe* into the cesspit, and thence to the moat.

When he released his grip, the unmeasured fall might break his legs or his back. The stench from the cesspit below was choking his lungs and his fingers were aching with the strain of supporting his weight. There were further crashes on the door.

Nest's anxious face, as she peered down at him, was lit by the flickering light from the tapers. The children were sobbing with fear behind her.

'Go now my love, there is not a moment to lose. I will try to distract Owain long enough for you to get safely away.'

'What sort of man am I, to leave my wife to be raped and my children at risk? I should die like a man, defending you.'

'Go while you can,' shouted Nest. 'What is the use of a dead husband to me? I want a live man to spend my nights with. Save yourself, the better to plan my rescue and your revenge. I will cope with what is to come if I know you will soon be back to make me your own again.'

Further battering, and the splintering of wood, signalled the final collapse of the door. Nest determinedly prised Gerald's fingers from the edge of the garderobe, and he found himself sliding faster and faster down the chute towards the stinking morass below.

The door crashed down into the room and Owain, with several other armed men, clambered in over the wreckage, weapons at the ready. Nest

---

* *Norman castles were equipped with long chutes built into the walls called 'garderobes', which acted as primitive toilets, emptying into cesspits, or directly into the moat.*

pulled the three, terrified children to her, as Owain prodded her with his bloodstained sword.

'Where is your cowardly Norman husband, cousin? You belong to me now, and I am going to kill him.'

Without waiting for an answer, Owain pushed her to one side and frenziedly began to search the room. Finding no one, he seized Angharrad, aged two, and held his sword to her throat, while she screeched in fright.

'I repeat, cousin, where is the Norman dog? Speak quickly or his brat will die.'

Drawing herself up more bravely than she felt, Nest spat back at him, 'I believed that you were a brave and worthy member of my family, a true future Prince of Powys, but now I see you threatening little children. How brave, Cousin! How noble! As for my husband, he is long gone. You will never catch him now. You can be sure, however, that he will be back with his knights ere long, to avenge me.'

Owain laughed. 'See what a wild cat she is, men, but she will sing a different song when she has had a proper man between her legs. Now go all of you. Search the grounds and kill the Norman when you find him. Except you Madog, and you Ithel! I need you here.'

Moving quickly, Owain dragged the traumatised children from their mother and handed them to Ithel and Madog.

'When an old lion dies, the new lion kills the cubs and sires some more. Take them outside and kill them.'

Nest sprang into a corner and seized a knife, which was lying on the table. She held it to her breast.

'Unless you swear on the Bible to return these innocent children unharmed to Pembroke, I will kill myself here and now. If you do so swear, I will give my body to you willingly. Is it really worth being hanged by Gerald to possess the corpse of a lifeless woman?'

'What a wench,' thought Owain. 'She really means to do it. It is about time that she got a good rogering.' He snatched Nest's Bible from the table and swore a foul Welsh oath that he would return the children to Pembroke.

'Safe and alive,' insisted Nest.

'Yes, safe and alive,' snarled Owain.

'If I find at some future time that you have broken the oath, you can be sure that I will find some way to kill you,' she shouted. 'You will have to sleep sometime.'

Pushing Madog, Ithel and the children out of the room Owain ordered, 'take the brats to the Bishop's house at Lamphey and return here quickly. Do not tell the Bishop our plans. Welshman or not, I do not trust him. Return here immediately. We have to make our getaway before bloody Gerald comes back with some Knights. Now, cousin, it is your turn.'

10

Owain swung a powerful blow at Nest, knocking her off her feet and sending her knife spinning away across the room. He seized Nest by her long, blonde hair and dragged her to the bed. He then started to rip the clothes from her body.

She tried to pretend it was not happening to her. He might be forcing himself into her, invading her most private places, but, despite the horror, she knew that the core of her being was somewhere else. Her innermost self was somehow detached, free from his violence. As he raged above, thrusting and gasping, she made herself mentally stand back from the pain and the violation and see that Owain had really lost, and she had won. She would live, her children would live, and so would her beloved Gerald. She had outwitted Owain. This was just a nightmare that would pass. By keeping her nerve she had ensured that, one day soon, Owain would pay with his life for this rape.

She must concentrate all her efforts now on enduring long enough to escape from the clutches of this odious, violent oaf who called himself her cousin. Although it sickened her soul, she must pretend to enjoy Owain's primitive assault. She must force herself to beguile him long enough for Gerald to get safely away. She started to moan and to clutch Owain's bloodstained body to her.

She found that the actress in her could sustain the performance enough to convince Owain that he was arousing her. In the meantime she withdrew into her real self, the deepest part of her being, where such as Owain could never reach her. She thought of other things, long ago - worse times than this - when it seemed that she and all she loved would surely perish.

the main characters

King Rhys ap Tewdwr King of Deheubarth (South Wales) died 1093

PRINCESS NEST Daughter of Rhys ap Tewdwr c1080-1136
Nest's children - Henry (by King Henry)
William, Maurice, David, Angharad (by
Gerald), Robert (by Stephen)

Bethan servant and companion to Nest
Gelert servant and guard to Nest.

Prince Gruffudd son of Rhys, brother of Nest
Prince Cynon son of Rhys, brother of Nest

King William I 'The Conqueror', King of England and
Duke of Normandy 1066-1087

King William II 'Rufus', King of England 1087-1100,
son of 'The Conqueror'

KING HENRY I 'Beauclerc', King of England 1100-1135, later
also Duke of Normandy and Count of Flanders
son of 'The Conqueror.'
Count Robert de Meulan advisor to King Henry.
Robert, Bishop
of Salisbury Justiciar to the King.
Captain Thomas master of King's ship 'The Raven'
Captain Jack master of the King's ship 'The White Ship'

Robert, Duke
of Normandy 1087-1107 (followed by 28 years in
captivity) eldest son of 'The Conqueror'.

GERALD de WINDSOR Lord of Pembroke c1067-1116 son of Lord Walter Fitzother (advisor to King Henry).

Gerald's children
John and Llinos (by his concubine Myfanwy)
Hait sometime secretary to Gerald.

Arnulph de Montgomery Gerald's Overlord, brother of Robert de Montgomery and son of Roger de Belesme, (Earl of Shrewsbury)

STEPHEN Constable of Cardigan (Aberteifi)
Son Robert (by Nest)

RICHARD FITZGILBERT Stephen's Overlord.

Robert Fitzmartin Lord of Newport.

Robert Fitzhammon Lord of Gloucester.
Lady Aelgifu his wife.

OWAIN Prince of Powys d. 1116 son of Cadwgan, Prince of Powys.
Ithel and Madog, servants to Owain.

Muirchertach King of Munster.
Princess Siobhan, his daughter.
Niambh, servant to Princess Siobhan.

Waldo joint leader of the Flemish settlers (with Wizo!)

Magnus Viking King of the Isle of Man.

Ranulph Flambard Bishop of Durham, advisor to King William Rufus, famous for spectacular escape from the Tower of London.

13

BOOK ONE

NEST AND HENRY

Starting many years earlier
when Nest was still a child

chapter one

Many years earlier, Pembroke Castle
AD 1092

'Castle' was hardly the right word for it, thought Gerald, as he stared gloomily at the Welsh tribesmen teeming round the foot of his wooden stockade. He knew they were trying to tempt him, yet again, to waste some of his men's precious arrows, to further weaken his power to resist.

The Welsh had arrived at Pembroke two weeks ago, sweeping all before them. Their leader, King Rhys ap Tewdwr, despite his advanced age, was personally leading his forces, and Gerald could only presume that he was the cause of the siege being conducted with such vigour. Gerald, after some years of campaigning in Wales, had found the Welsh to be brave and ferocious opponents, but hardly persistent. That was not their style. They would surge through a district burning and pillaging and would attack any opposition with great courage and energy. If, however, they met determined resistance, say in the form of a stockade resolutely defended by Normans, they would normally pass on after a couple of days, seeking easier prey. Why then were they still there after two weeks?

The sudden assault had taken him by surprise. The news had hardly reached him of the attacks on distant St Dogmaels and Llechryd, when he found his own people were pouring into the stockade seeking refuge, hotly pursued by Rhys' men.

Because of the suddenness of the attack, there had been no time to stockpile supplies to withstand a siege, and food and arrows were nearly exhausted. However, that was not the only thing that Gerald de Windsor was worried about. He did not have complete confidence in the fifteen knights that his liege lord, Arnulf de Montgomery, had left him. They seemed resentful of Gerald's recent promotion to Castellan, and this was combined with an intense dislike of their remote posting so far from civilisation.

As Gerald paced round the stockade, reinforcing the weak points and trying to give encouragement to his men, he tried to put together a plan to survive the next few days. It would be especially difficult after the supply of arrows was used up. However, Arnulf de Montgomery, brutal scion though he was, of a brutal family, remained a good judge of men, and Gerald, as he paced the ramparts, found himself quietly confident despite the odds against him. Far from buckling under the strain he found he knew what he had to do. This was, after all, an opportunity for him to prove himself equal to Arnulf's confidence in him. If he could hold out for the next few days, that would be a great achievement. His father,

Walter Fitzother, Castellan of Windsor Castle, would be forced to take his youngest son more seriously. Even the King might get to hear of it. He just had to survive the next few days.

Two hundred yards away, just out of effective arrow shot, Rhys ap Tewdwr, King of Deheubarth (South Wales) was also studying the situation. His men were restive. Besieging castles was boring and ill-suited to their temperament, and actually trying to storm castles was definitely risky against well-armed Normans. It seemed self-evident to Rhys's soldiers that it was far more productive to harry the remaining farms in the area, carry off some livestock and rape some women. There might even be some women young and healthy enough to be worth taking back home.

Rhys however, had larger designs: this land of Penfro used, after all, to be part of Deheubarth, until recently seized by the Frenchmen. It should be part of his domain again. He had returned from exile in Ireland, defeated his Welsh rivals Cadwgan, Madog, and Rhirid, killing the latter two and driving Cadwgan into hiding. He was determined to complete the task of rebuilding his Kingdom by getting rid of the Norman enclaves at Penfro (Pembroke), and Rhyd y Gors (near Carmarthen). He had the insight to realise that the Normans were potentially far more dangerous than Cadwgan and his brood. He was certain that, before he could hand on Deheubarth as a safe inheritance to his sons, he had to totally destroy all Norman power in the area.

Rhys was a very old man* and weary of war, but he was determined to make one last effort to clear South Wales of all his enemies, Welsh and Norman alike. He would govern wisely and well, so that the Cymry would remember his fame in their ballads alongside his great ancestor, Hywel Dda, he who had studied in Rome and made just laws for his kingdom. For this purpose Rhys had fought many battles and had lived in exile for many weary, long years.

When William the Conqueror had made his rather political pilgrimage to St Davids in 1081, and offered an annual subsidy in return for Rhys recognising William as his Overlord, Rhys had deemed it expedient to accept. After all, at that time, Norman power seemed far away and the agreement seemed the best way to keep the Normans from interfering in the future. However, when The Conqueror's son, William Rufus, had succeeded to the throne in 1087, he had maintained neither the subsidy nor the royal protection, and the Normans had soon started to establish

---

* *The historian Laws, says that this siege, 'the Siege of the Pigs', took place after Rhys's death (1093), in 1094, but it seems more likely to have been conducted by Rhys himself, then nearly 90, in 1092. Whatever the truth, he must have been a very active ninety year old to have a twelve year old daughter, and at least one younger son, apart from the various older sons.*

themselves in Deheubarth. They had established a Royal castle at Rhyd y Gors, and the castle he was now besieging, here at Pembroke, built by Arnulf de Montgomery only last year.

No, the Normans must be prised out of their castles, and it did not seem to Rhys that the Red King had the same drive and persistence as his terrible and clever father. Men said that Rufus was more interested in boys than women, and Rhys calculated that such a pansy would have little stomach for battling to retain his remote outposts in Western Deheubarth (West Wales).

Rhys wanted to win this final battle and so be able to return in peace to enjoy his old age in his Court in Breicheiniog (Brecon). His bards would then sing of his glorious victories, his Teulu (Military Retinue) could glory in so great a King, and he could relax and enjoy it all with his wonderful sons, his wife, and not least with his already beautiful twelve year old daughter, Nest.

He was sure that one day bards would sing of Nest's beauty, and great Princes would seek her hand in marriage. When that day came he would be proud, but also very sad to lose her. She made him happy with her love for him and her wit and humour. He would sorely miss her. However he had noticed that she was going to be a force to reckon with. She could already silence her unruly brothers with just a glance from those piercing green eyes. He was sure she would soon break many hearts. He must make certain that she married a strong man whom she could respect: she would make mincemeat of a weakling.

His reverie was broken by his son, Prince Gruffudd, a tall dark haired twenty year old, who was already proving his worth as a soldier, and as his heir.

'Sire, a man has been brought to me who claims to bring a message from restive Knights in the Castle. He says that they are weary of the siege and propose to abandon it and their Castellan, Gerald de Windsor, to their fate.'

'Bring this man to me, my son. It would seem that our persistence here might now bring its reward.'

The messenger, Cadell, when he was brought before Rhys, proved to be quite informative. The King detested any Welshman in the service of the Normans, but forced himself to listen to what this thickset, unappealing man had to say. Apparently Gerald's knights wished King Rhys ap Tewdwr to know that they were planning to escape by boat from the castle that very night, leaving Gerald de Windsor dangerously exposed. In addition, in exchange for unmolested passage to the royal castle at Rhyd y Gors, they were willing to give Rhys information about the state of matters within Pembroke Castle.

'Tell these 'brave' knights, your masters, that they can depart free of molestation by my men. As for information, I can get that from you, base Cadell, by poking my spear in your guts until you tell me.' The King now seized a spear from one of the Teulu and brought it dangerously close to Cadell's stomach.

'There is no need for that, dread Lord,' quaked Cadell, 'I am a good Cymro, and pleased to serve my King in ridding this land of these French devils. Be pleased to know, Lord, that there is very little food in the Castle, and their supply of arrows is nearly exhausted. The Norman Lord will have no choice but to surrender if you maintain your siege a little longer.'

'Give this man some hot cawl,' ordered Rhys. 'Go back then to the Castle the way you came, and tell your traitor knights that they may run away in peace this night. However, if any of my Lords behaved as they have, I would have them torn limb from limb by wild horses.'

****

Later that evening when Gerald had made his last tour of the ramparts and was preparing to turn in for the night in the little cubby hole that was all the little stockade could offer its Castellan, he was disturbed by Gilbert, one of the Knights' Squires. He had previously impressed Gerald as a young man worthy of future promotion. His role was Armour Bearer to Richard de Hoda, Gerald's most senior knight.

'Sir, forgive me disturbing your rest. I have been struggling with my conscience as to where my true loyalty lies. There is a matter that will wait no longer.'

Gerald studied Gilbert's face keenly. This nervous young man clearly had much on his mind. He realised at once that the matter was not a minor one.

'Sit down, Gilbert,' he said kindly, 'and unburden yourself. I know you to be a man of honour.'

'Sir, I have sworn loyalty to my master, Richard de Hoda, but I know him to be a traitor to you, and therefore to our liege lord, the King. He and the other knights have parleyed with Rhys ap Tewdwr and plan to flee the castle within the hour, abandoning you and your men to your fate. Even now they are waiting for me to join them.'

Gerald knew that his knights were seriously disaffected, but he had not thought for a moment that they would betray him to the Welsh. Even so, he did not doubt that Gilbert was telling the truth. He must do something very quickly to save the situation.

'Where are these traitors now?'

'They are sitting in a boat in the cavern and plan to leave as soon as I return. I made the excuse that I have some food hidden in the wood store

20

and that it would give us strength for the journey. There is no room in the boat for the other squires, and they will have to be left behind.'

'You have done well, Gilbert, and shall be rewarded. Come quickly! I will call out the guard. We will arrest these so called knights while they are unprepared.'

Seizing his sword, Gerald ran to the guardhouse and ordered the sleepy men to arm themselves and form up outside. Gilbert followed him, dreading what was going to befall his fellow squires.

The castle was built over a cave, which gave direct access by boat to an arm of the estuary. The rebel knights were obviously using the cave as a concealed assembly point for their escape. Access to the cavern from the stockade was down a stout wooden ladder through a hole in the roof.

Having quickly been informed of what was afoot, the startled soldiers scrambled down the ladder, with Gerald and Gilbert in the lead. The flickering tapers in the cavern lit up a small boat, still secured by its painter, loaded deep in the water, with the fifteen knights and their armour jammed into it.

The noise of Gerald's arrival, was, for a few vital seconds, taken by the deserters to be Gilbert returning with the food, and Gerald clearly heard the abandoned squires urging the knights not to break their knightly oaths.

By the time the knights had realised their mistake, Gerald's men were down the ladder and had their spears at the knights' throats. Tight in the boat as they were, the knights had no chance of resistance. Gilbert had quickly secured the boat's painter, preventing it moving from the quay.

'What a sorry day is this when Norman knights stoop so low as to betray their Lord and a King's castle to the Welsh,' shouted Gerald.

More soldiers now crowded down the ladder into the cavern and became enraged by the knights' betrayal. The traitors were roughly dragged from the boat and hurled on their knees in front of Gerald.

They looked a sorry sight in the flickering light, as they knelt in the sticky red mud begging for their lives.

'What reason can you give me, Richard de Hoda, for this base treachery?' demanded Gerald.

De Hoda tried to bluster it out. 'Your situation is hopeless. What is the point of staying here to face inevitable torture and death at the hands of Rhys ap Tewdwr. With my greater experience, if I had had the command, I would not have allowed myself to be in the desperate situation that you find yourself...

'Silence,' shouted Gerald. 'All can see what a sorry state you base knaves are in, because of your treachery. You have all betrayed your knights' oaths. You are not worthy to be called knights. On behalf of our liege lord, Arnulf de Montgomery, and through him our dread sovereign, King

William the Second, and acting as Castellan of this castle, under siege by the enemy, I do now strip you fifteen traitors of your rank of Knight, and condemn you to be hanged for desertion and treason.'

There was a shout of angry approval from the soldiers and groans of disbelief from the knights.

'Spare us,' cried one. 'Without our help you are lost.'

'You have already proved by your actions that I cannot trust you. Therefore you must die.'

Meanwhile the abandoned squires hung back in a group fearing what Gerald would next announce as their own fate.

'Bring rope, and let us get this vile business completed,' ordered Gerald, grim faced.

Soldiers climbed on barrels to throw ropes over the beams, which reinforced the roof of the cave, and one by one the knights were dragged forward to have nooses placed around their necks. They were then hauled brutally into position under the beams and forced to stand on boxes. At this point Gerald's priest appeared in the cavern, attracted by the clamour, and asked to give absolution to the knights.

'Do it, good priest, but quickly. Rhys ap Tewdwr may chose this very moment to make a new attack, and with so many of our men missing from the ramparts we might be overwhelmed.'

One by one, after a quick confession by the knights, and absolution by the priest, the boxes were kicked away, and the traitors were left dangling, their lives slowly choking out of them.

'So may all traitors perish,' mouthed Gerald, retching at the barbarity of what he had had to do. Pulling himself together, he ordered that the fifteen squires should stand before him. With the flickering tapers lighting their frightened faces, Gerald addressed the whole company, the gurgles of the dying knights making a ghastly refrain to his speech.

'I do not need to tell you that our situation here is perilous. Our supplies are nearly exhausted and the enemy seems ready for a long siege. I have, however, a plan. If it works, Rhys will give up his siege and march away to his inevitable fate at the hands our powerful forces in East Wales. In the meantime I need loyal knights to help me lead our brave and proven soldiers. I have decided to trust my judgement by raising you fifteen squires to the rank of knight, to replace your former masters, the traitors who are dying on the ropes behind you. When this siege is over, you shall be confirmed in your new rank, and the estates of your former masters shall be given to you.'

There was a low murmur of gratified amazement from the squires. One by one they knelt in the mud before Gerald, who, drawing his sword, lightly tapped each one on the shoulders saying, 'arise, Sir Knight.'

Hardly had they finished when there was a cry from the roof opening warning that the Welsh were again trying to scale the walls.

The new knights immediately proved their mettle by leading the soldiers up and out onto the battlements just in time to repel the enemy. Gerald breathed a sigh of relief. It had been a very near thing. He thought of the gruesome, twisted, fellow Normans that he had been forced to kill, and shuddered again at the thought. His new Command had brought responsibilities he had not dreamed of when Arnulf had appointed him so short a time before.

After the last man had disappeared up the ladder back into the Castle, the Welsh *'friendly', Cadell, crawled out of his hiding place at the far end of the Cavern, and ran quickly to see if any of the knights still lived. Moving down the ghastly line, he found that the man at the end, protected by the lack of light there, had somehow got a foothold in a cleft in the cavern wall, thus taking some of the weight off his neck. He was still struggling weakly.

Cadell ran to get a box, and climbing up, cut the knight down with his knife, trying to ease his fall at the same time. The stricken man, who Cadell recognised as Simon de Leia, fell to the ground, and Cadell started to revive him.

'Come Sir Knight, do not die now. I have need of thee,' he murmured in Welsh.

As the Norman struggled to a sitting position, gasping and clutching his throat, Cadell gave him a few drops of water from his leather bottle.

'Someone will be back soon. Let me help you to the boat,' he whispered.

The heavy dory, which was so recently the focus of the knights' escape attempt, still lay alongside the quay. The high tide, which de Hoda had planned to use, was dropping now, but Cadell thought he could still get away if he hurried.

Taking Simon under the armpits he half carried, half dragged the stricken man to the quay. Leaving the knight there, he slowly dragged the dory into the deeper water at the cave entrance. When he went back for De Leia, he found that he had revived sufficiently to stagger to his feet. Cadell helped him wade through the water to the boat and lifted him bodily over the gunwale. Pushing the boat a little further to keep it afloat, he scrambled in himself, seized an oar, and started to punt it out of the cavern into open water.

'It will be light soon, Sir Knight, we must hurry.'

* *'Friendly', a modern term, which describes an age old situation, that of a man who eases the path of his country's enemies in some practical way such as acting as a guide, translator or intermediary.*

Gerald was considering his Steward's report: the situation was just as bad as he had expected it to be. His supplies of food and arrows were virtually exhausted. A decision on what to do about it could wait no longer. He had forty-nine arrows left with which to defend the castle (these could easily be used up in half an hour) and, as far as food was concerned, all he had was a pile of rotting turnips - and four live pigs!

He had briefly considered evacuating the castle by sea, but the abortive escape attempt by the knights had shown the limits of that course of action. He had about a hundred people in the castle, and his only seaworthy boat would carry less than twenty - and that had disappeared mysteriously, together with the body of Simon de Leia, whom he had hanged last night, and a Welsh 'Friendly' named Cadell. Matters were now too pressing for him to devote much thought to that puzzle.

A larger craft, normally used to bring supplies from the royal castle at Rhyd y Gors, had been badly damaged when she broke from her moorings in a storm last month, and was presently beached, awaiting repairs, in the Cavern. The sudden arrival of Rhys' army had meant that Gerald had been cut off from the timber that would be needed to repair her.

As there was still no hint that Rhys was about to abandon the siege voluntarily, Gerald was sure that his only hope of survival was to encourage him to do so. But how could this be achieved?

The sun was now well up over the estuary and Gerald, from his vantage point on the battlements, could see that Rhys' men had eaten their breakfast and were moving forward for a fresh assault on the walls. Most of Gerald's men were already in position, having been urged to use their dwindling stock of arrows only in extremis. It was time to try to outwit Rhys.

'Gilbert de Hoda, (Gilbert's heart thrilled to hear his new rank publicly proclaimed), bring me a flag of truce and a trumpeter. I will speak with the enemy. Bring me also a man who can speak the Cymric tongue. Steward, bring the four remaining pigs here, onto the battlements, together with nets and ropes.'

'My Lord, do you want the pigs slaughtered before I bring them?' asked the puzzled man.

'Certainly not. The more lively the better.'

When all was in place, and Gerald had explained his plan to those who would be carrying it out, the flag of truce was raised. Gerald now ordered the trumpet to be sounded.

A sudden silence fell on both sides. The Welsh King and his chieftains were gathered together, looking up, waiting for the parley. A base thought crossed Gerald's mind. They were within arrow shot, and close together. He had marksmen who could probably hit them, perhaps a better plan, than the one he was going to try. He put the thought behind him: it was ignoble to break a flag of truce - and they might miss anyway!

Rhys thinks we are going to parley for our lives was his next thought.

He stood on the highest point of the battlements and started to shout his message in Norman French, pausing to allow it to be translated into Welsh, by Jestyn, the 'Friendly' who stood at his side in the mysterious absence of his countryman, Cadell.

'My Lord Prince,' he began politely. 'We have had the company of your army here at Pembroke for some two weeks now. I have noted lately that your men have been eating very poor fare, and must be very envious of our own provisions. Our own supplies come of course by sea, which is very convenient in the circumstances. Yours come by land, and your base is far from here over many long, dangerous miles. I have therefore decided, good King, that I will share my own abundant supplies with you as it grieves my heart to see your valiant men fare so badly. I will start today by sending you four fat pigs, which should improve your diet mightily.'

The struggling pigs were then lowered in nets over the Gatehouse wall to the ground below, accompanied by taunts from the Normans.

'Fear not good King. Your servants may retrieve them in safety. We will not harm them when they come beneath our walls.'

There were shouts of astonishment from the Welsh Army, when Jestyn translated the announcement. Nevertheless, two of Rhys' men ran forward, to free the pigs from the nets, which then ran wildly through the Welsh soldiery, bowling men over to the accompaniment of jeering applause from the Normans above them.

Consternation reigned amongst the Welsh. Rhys' worried chieftains gathered around him trying to gain his attention. Meredydd ap Merfyn spoke for all of them.

'Sire, it seems we have been deceived. The man Cadell, who brought the Norman knight to us, is a lying traitor. He told us that the Normans are on the point of surrender due to lack of supplies. That is plainly false. He should die.'

'The Norman Lord may be occupying our army here, while his master, Arnulf de Montgomery, is marching deep into our lands, despoiling our women and our cattle,' exclaimed another.

Rattled for a moment, Rhys ap Tewdwr ordered Cadell to be brought before him. Adding an element of farce, one of the pigs broke loose again and ran under the King's legs, felling him to the ground. All this was in full view of the Normans, who laughed in derision.

25

Prodded brutally by spearmen, Cadell was brought before Rhys shaking with fear.

'It is a trick, dread King. The French have no food left. I have seen nought but rotting turnips in the castle.'

'And fat pigs,' snarled Meredydd ap Merfyn.

'They were the last food left,' cried Cadell desperate to convince them. 'Gerald will starve now if his trick fails.'

'Bring the French prisoner,' ordered Rhys. 'Let us see how his tale compares.'

Simon de Leia had recovered to some extent from the ordeal, but still cut a sorry figure as he stood before the Welsh King, clutching his swollen, purple neck.

'The truth, Sir Knight, or you will die painfully here and now,' threatened the old man. When this was translated, Simon de Leia decided that his only hope was to try to convince Rhys of his sincerity.

His answer, when it came, was in strangled gasps.

'There is no food in the castle, sire. Gerald de Windsor's situation is hopeless. That is why we Knights tried to leave, and why fourteen of my friends were hanged last night by Gerald.'

'If I find you base creatures have lied, you both shall die praying that you never were born. Take them away and guard them well.'

Muttering and complaining, the Welsh chieftains reluctantly accepted Rhys ap Tewdwr's decision to besiege the castle a little longer.

In the meantime Gerald de Windsor was having troubles of his own. The Welsh Army was showing no sign of departing, and he had seen Cadell, and the amazingly resurrected Simon de Leia, being questioned by Rhys, and they had plainly given the lie to Gerald's desperate ruse. He must think of something else, and in the meantime keep up the spirits of his men. He would have to try hard as no one in the castle had had any breakfast that morning, and no one was going to eat again until Rhys could be persuaded to march away.

He called his new knights around him and explained his desperate plan for saving their lives.

26

The Bishop of Tyddewi (St. Davids)* had a very comfortable house at Lamphey. Although it was at least twenty five miles to his Cathedral on the windswept St. Davids peninsula, he had found it helpful politically living only four miles down the road from Pembroke, the seat of their new Norman masters. Lamphey was also a much softer, more pleasant place to live in, than bleak Tyddewi.

As he lay in bed eating the breakfast of cakes and ale brought by his servant, Wilfred congratulated himself on not having to get up early for Mass, as he would do normally at Tyddewi. It had all been very fine until Rhys ap Tewdwr had brought his army to Penfro (Pembroke) two weeks ago.

Although Wilfred was really a Welshman whose real name was Gruffudd, he had deemed it expedient to change his name to Wilfred when his position, as Bishop, had been recently confirmed by the Archbishop of Canterbury. In fact things had been going rather well for Wilfred politically until King Rhys had appeared on the scene, threatening the delicate balance between Welshman, Norman and Scandinavian in his See. If Rhys captured Penfro, it was far from certain that he would let matters continue as they were. Wilfred might even have to move back to Tyddewi. His reverie was interrupted by his servant's urgent knock at the door.

'My Lord Bishop, my Lord Bishop, I have found a letter.'

'What letter, Hywel, who has brought it, where is it man?' asked Wilfred in surprise.

Hywel bustled excitedly into the room bearing a mud-stained, but important looking, missive, heavily embossed with red seals.

'I found it in the lane, just opposite the front door when I was going for milk from the farm, my Lord.'

Although the letter was very dirty, Wilfred could see that it was addressed to Arnulf de Montgomery, whom he knew was Gerald de Windsor's Liege Lord.

'You have done well, Hywel, very well. Now leave me to examine the letter, and see that I am not disturbed.'

---

* *The use of names in West Wales is complicated. Most places have two names, a Welsh one and an English one. Usually when a Welsh speaking person is talking I have used the Welsh name.*

The letter, written in French, was brief and to the point.

'My Lord, do not trouble yourself about my situation here at Pembroke. I have ample supplies, adequate for four months siege. In the meantime I am tying down Rhys' army here in the West, the better for you to strike at his heartland in the East.'

'How very fortunate that this letter has fallen into the hands of one of the very few men of my race, who could read it,' thought Wilfred. 'I must pass it at once to King Rhys ap Tewdwr.'

His servant helped him to dress quickly, but not before he had found time to finish his cakes and ale! He called for his horse, and trotted off down the Pembroke road accompanied by his syce and two retainers. He had found that it did not do to be too informal. People high and low, Norman and Gael, all expected a Bishop to have a certain gravitas. He was after all God's representative in Dewisland, and therefore not as other men.

As he rode, he discouraged conversation with his servants. He wanted to think things out. A rather devious man himself, he looked for deviousness in others. The more he thought about it, the more the discovery of the letter seemed more than co-incidental. How strange that it happened to have been dropped at the door of the only Welshman in the area who could read it. Why would any messenger from Gerald to Arnulf choose to go past his door anyway? Surely any man in his senses carrying a message from a besieged castle would skirt all villages, to avoid any possible contact with their inhabitants - that is unless someone in his own household was in the pay of the French! In either case he was meant to read the letter. Why?

If, in fact, the letter had been dropped on purpose, then whoever had done so would expect Wilfred, as a good Welshman, to take the letter to King Rhys ap Tewdwr. Wilfred grimaced. He was doing just that.

What effect would the letter have on Rhys? Wilfred knew that Rhys' men were tired of the siege. The letter was likely to convince them to abandon it and to go after easier pickings. The more Wilfred thought about it, the more he thought this would be a good idea! He thought that God's work, and his own comfort, would both progress much more happily if Rhys' army went away and peace returned to the area.

As he approached the Castle, he found that Rhys' camp was not well guarded, and he was able to ride right up to the King of Deheubarth's entourage before he was challenged.

The King greeted him with something rather less than enthusiasm. 'What brings you here today, my Lord Bishop? I would have appreciated your blessing yesterday before the last assault. I find myself asking where the loyalties lie of a Welsh Bishop with a Saxon name, who is apparently cosy with the Normans.'

'I hope I am a good Welshman, who knows his duty both to God and to the land of his birth,' replied Wilfred smoothly. 'I am here, your Royal Highness, because my servant, only this morning, has found a letter sent by Gerald de Windsor to Arnulf de Montgomery. I have brought it here at once for your inspection.'

Rhys examined the letter gingerly while his Chieftains gathered around impatiently. Wilfred could tell at once by their behaviour, that none of them could read it, be it written in Welsh, French, Latin or any other language!

'I do not have my Clerk with me, My Lord Bishop, and my eyes are not what they were. I see that the letter must be an important one due to its heavy seals. However, I cannot discern its content.'

The Bishop, with an inward smile, read out the letter, translating it into Welsh as he went, while the King and his Chieftains listened with mounting anger. He had hardly finished before all of them wished to shout their views at once.

'We have been tricked,' roared Meredydd ap Merfyn, speaking for them all. 'At this very moment, while we cool our heels here entertaining this smooth, vile, pig-dealing, Norman Castellan and his jeering men, Arnulf de Montgomery will be pillaging our lands and carrying off our wives and cattle.'

Rhys was not convinced. 'But this letter may be yet another trick to achieve our departure. Think men, think! This Norman is crafty. What say you, my Lord Bishop?'

Wilfred paused for only a moment as he decided whether he was now truly Bishop Gruffudd, the Welshman - or Bishop Wilfred, whose best interests lay in making peace with what would probably be the winning side - the Norman Red King and the reconstructed Church of Archbishop Anselm. He tried to think that, perhaps, even his flock might be better off under the Normans. He squirmed mentally as he heard the weasel words coming out of his mouth, the words of a traitor to his King and the Land of his Birth.

'Your Royal Highness, these Frenchmen have conquered the Land of Lloegr (England), because they are cunning in war. You have been persuaded, by false counsel, to journey with all your army, far from your heartland of Dinefwr, to attack this well provisioned fortress, while the cunning Arnulf strikes deep at your vital interests. Unless you move quickly all Deheubarth will soon be under the Norman heel. It is a miracle that this letter has come into our hands. God is Good!'

As all Rhys' chieftains shouted their approval of his words, words the Bishop's intelligence and education knew to be false, Wilfred suddenly had a vision of his real Master standing before him, staring sadly into his eyes. The entire scene of soldiers, castles, Princes and battles seemed to fade, and he heard his true Lord, the Lord he had sworn to serve, say, 'Wilfred, Wilfred, what have you done?' He felt his knees buckle under him and he knew no more.

'Give my Lord Bishop a cup of water. The strain of the gallop here has been too much for him,' ordered Rhys. 'I think he has advised us well, and we are in his debt. In the meantime, let us break camp and march quickly to Brycheiniog to outwit the Norman plans. Release the Norman knight. The man Cadell shall remain with us: he may be useful.'

chapter four

Nest hoped that she was going to die. She could not bear to live any longer after the horrors that she had witnessed during the last two hours.

The battle still swirled around the hillock where her father, King Rhys ap Tewdwr, had made his last stand, but he no longer stood defiant amongst his chieftains. She had somehow believed her old father to be immortal, but a few moments ago she had glimpsed the flash of the Norman sword as it cleaved his head from his shoulders. A moment later she had seen her eldest brother Goronwy speared and fall dying. She could not believe such terrible things could happen to those she loved.

Now the Normans, scenting victory, were cleaving their way towards the Tewdwr (Tudor) standard, which was still flying proudly. The last of her father's Men at Arms were defending the Dragon Flag - and her.

Her brothers, Gruffudd and Cynan, were in the thick of the battle, still felling all before them, but she knew now that there was no longer any hope. She felt herself praying that death would not hurt too much when it came.

As the fighting came nearer Bethan, her maid, picked up two bloody spears lying nearby. She placed one of them in her hands.

'Sell your life dear, my Lady. Do not let them take you alive. It is worse if they capture a woman.'

Seizing the spear, Nest made ready to thrust it at the first Norman who appeared before her. Suddenly, she found that Gruffudd was beside her, astride a horse, and Cynan on another.

'Quick, jump up behind me, and Bethan, you ride behind Cynan. We will try to break through their lines. We are not finished yet. The French shall not prevail while we live.'

Both girls were used to horses and climbed astride, despite their long dresses, with the help of nearby soldiers. They then clung on for very life itself, as the young men dug in their heels to force their mounts through the Normans, who were nearly upon them.

Nest had a vision of surprised faces and ill-aimed blows. Suddenly they were through the French soldiery, and away across open grassland at full gallop. Turning her head, Nest could see Cynan close behind. They had escaped! A second glance, however, brought her heart to her mouth. Several other horsemen were in close pursuit and seemed to be gaining on the heavily laden Welsh horses.

'Gruffudd must live,' she thought, 'he is the only one who can carry on the fight for us now. He must live. He is the only hope for Deheubarth. I cannot let him be taken. I must lighten his horse.'

Without further thought she shouted to her brother that he must get away to raise another army, and then she rolled herself off the horse and fell heavily in the path of the pursuers.

Two Normans pulled up beside her as she sat up dizzily. She was pleased to see that her action had caused the remaining horsemen to hesitate briefly before continuing the pursuit. Those few yards might make all the difference.

As a Norman knight pulled her roughly to her feet, she spat in his face. 'My brothers live, and they will return to avenge us. And to drive you from our land!' she shouted, hitting out at him. The knight, infuriated by her attack, felled her to the ground with his mailed fist, and then raised his sword to despatch her.

'Stop, stop, Sir Guy!' shouted a newcomer. 'This young wild cat is the daughter of their Prince, and must be taken unharmed to Westminster, on the express instructions of the King. I would not like to be in your shoes should the King be disobeyed.'

Her left eye almost closed and her nose dripping blood, Nest was hauled to her feet again, to find herself under the amused inspection of a handsome, but rather cruel looking man, who removed his helmet to have a better look at her. The slim, blonde girl standing unsteadily before him still created a strong impression. The strength in the green eyes and the defiant air were unusual in one so young. He had been told that she was only twelve, but she had the presence of someone much older.

'Robert Fitzhammon, Lord of Gloucester, my Lady,' he said mockingly.

'You must be the Princess Nesta, that Jestyn tells me of. He told me that you were beautiful, but it seems that Sir Guy has marred your looks a little. I hope your features will recover so that I can confirm Jestyn's opinion.'

'Prince Jestyn is a traitor to all the land of Cymru. Without his treachery, and that of the base men of Morganwg, you would never have beaten us. My brothers will return to kill him,' she shouted defiantly.

Her eye and her nose hurt badly now, and she wanted to cry for the pain of it, and for her Father and Goronwy, but she would not let herself break down in front of these foul Normans.

'I can see that it must be very galling for you, that so many of your race, seem happy to help us. However, I must now make arrangements for you. I see that your maid approaches, also sadly abandoned by your brothers.'

'They would never abandon us! We jumped off so that they could get away.'

'Very gallant!' sneered Fitzhammon. 'I will leave your maid to tend you, while I make arrangements for you to be taken to Gloucester. Anyway, have no fear. I have given orders that no one should harm you, or your maid. My servant shall bring water so that your face can be bathed. We must make sure that the King has a good view of his prize.'

Remounting, Robert Fitzhammon and the other knights rode off, leaving Nest and Bethan guarded by several men at arms. Nest was delighted to have Bethan with her again, but she was anxious about her brothers.

'When I saw you roll off Prince Gruffudd's horse, I decided to join you because you might need me, and also to lighten Cynan's horse. The Normans were very close behind.'

'You did well Bethan, and I am glad you are with me. I only pray that my brothers are safe and far from here. I do not care what happens to me, so long as Gruffudd reaches Ireland to raise another army. My father and Goronwy must not have died in vain.'

She sat on a wooden shield, whose owner had no use for it - his body lay close by. All about her lay the full horror of war. Some of the dead, mostly Welshmen, lay in heaps. Others were lying in ghastly close embrace with their enemies, frozen in their final acts of violence. Why must men fight, she agonised? What a waste of the love and care of the mothers that bore them. But, even as she mused about the folly of war, she knew that if she were a man she would fight, and maybe die, to protect her family and her country.

As Bethan bathed her face, her guards became bored with taunting her about what the King would do to her body, and started to search the dead soldiers for valuables. They still kept one eye on the girls, however, so there was no chance of escape.

As the soldiers turned over the fallen, Nest became aware of a new factor - some of the fallen were still alive! Faint groans and sighs started to come from all round them.

'Let us see if we can help some of these poor soldiers. They are our countrymen,' whispered Nest, now sick at heart. The sheer enormity of the carnage was beginning to take its toll of her courage.

The first Welshman they found alive was partly overlain by a dead horse. It took the combined strength of both girls to free him. He had lost much blood from a deep sword cut in his arm, so, tearing the hems of their dresses, they tried to bind his wound. The man began to regain full consciousness as Bethan held his head to give him a sip of water.

Fitzhammon's Men at Arms came over to see what the girls were doing. 'That's our business, leave that to us,' said one, as the girls were dragged from their attempt at mercy. 'The master is coming back. He will beat us if he finds you tending the wounded.'

'Are you monsters?' shouted Nest. 'Many of those men are still alive and need help.'

'Look yonder, Welsh Princess. There are others appointed to clear the battlefield.'

Raising her eyes from the immediate area, Nest realised that the fighting had stopped, and that the Dragon Flag no longer flew in the breeze. All round the battlefield the Normans and their Welsh allies were examining the bodies. The obviously dead were being piled onto carts and the unwounded prisoners were being rounded up and marched away to serfdom. She saw that the Norman wounded were sitting in a group being tended by monks from the nearby Priory - and, to her horror, Nest realised that the Welsh wounded were being speared to death, to avoid the trouble of tending them!

As Fitzhammon rode up, he was amused to see that the fiery little Princess had just seized a spear from one of his men and was standing guard ferociously over a badly wounded Welsh soldier.

'To kill him you must first kill me,' she shouted. 'You are all savages, and God will punish you.'

Just in time, Fitzhammon restrained the furious reaction of his humiliated men.

'Leave the girl unharmed. I see she has more guts than any six of you. Now, my Lady, enough of this defiance! The battle is over, so come to the wagon that I have brought to convey you to Gloucester. You shall be well housed and fed, and on the morrow you shall start your journey to Westminster, where you will be kept as hostage for the good behaviour of your people.'

'I shall not leave here until you promise, on your honour as a Knight, that this man at least, shall be allowed to live and be cared for.'

Fitzhammon laughed. 'If you care for the base serf so much, you shall tend him yourself. He shall go on your wagon with you. It will be one less grave for my men to dig.'

When the Welshman's wounds had been dressed to Nest's satisfaction by the reluctant Men at Arms, she supervised him being placed in the rear of the covered wagon, which Fitzhammon had provided for their transport.

The journey, which followed, seemed interminable. Although Gloucester was only about forty miles from Brecon, it had been dark for many hours when the wagon eventually arrived at the West Gate of the city. Nest was roused from her bumpy, uncomfortable, exhausted slumber, by the sound of Fitzhammon shouting to arouse the sleeping gatekeeper and his sentinels.

'By the breath of Our Lady, you shall pay on the morrow for your lack of care,' he shouted, when the gate was finally opened and the frightened man was cringing before him. 'With Welsh soldiers less than a day's march from the city, you choose to sleep while you are on watch. I will see that you, your so-called sentinels and your Captain, will have such a beating, that you will be reminded of your duty for many weeks to come.'

Nest did not regret saving her soldier, but he had needed constant nursing on the journey. In many ways it had helped to make the very uncomfortable ride go more quickly. He rewarded their efforts by surviving the night. In any event, Nest was completely exhausted by the time they reached Gloucester. The death of her father and two of her brothers, the terrifying carnage, and the end of the life she was used to, had been a tremendous

34

strain on a twelve year old, however brave. The result was that, when she was shown to her room in Fitzhammon's house, she passed into a very deep sleep, and knew nothing of the very kind arrangements that were made for her accommodation by the Lady of the House.

The soldier, Gelert, was also taken into her care, and his wounds bathed and dressed.

The sun was streaming into the window of her room when Nest awoke, and Bethan was standing by her bed, accompanied by a tall blonde haired lady.

'I am Lady Aelgifu, the mistress of this house.' She smiled kindly at her young and traumatised guest. 'I trust that you slept well after your long journey. I shall do my best to make you comfortable while you are in my care. Bethan has brought a warm drink to give you a good start, and she will bring hot water so that you may wash and feel like a woman again.'

Nest found herself responding to this obviously caring lady. 'You are very kind my Lady.'

'While we are alone, please call me Aelgifu. I would be honoured if you would call me by my first name. You are, after all, a Princess. When you have bathed and dressed, Bethan shall bring you to me, and we shall eat breakfast together and talk about our lives.'

When the Lady Aelgifu had left them, Nest plied Bethan with questions.

'Who is the Lady Aelgifu? She is very kind and she does not look like a Norman. And where is Robert Fitzhammon? I hope he has gone away?'

Bethan was glad that her young mistress was feeling recovered enough to display normal female curiosity.

'It seems that the Norman Lord rode off early this morning because of some urgent matter to do with yesterday's battle, my Lady. I know not what the matter is. As for Lady Aelgifu, I am told by her servants, that she is Saxon, and that her father was forced to marry her to Lord Fitzhammon, to avoid the Norman King seizing his estates. Many of the servants here are also Saxon, and they seem to hate the Normans just as we do.'

'Things are stranger in our world than I thought. My father said that the Saxons were our oppressors in former years, and we know sadly what the Normans do with us in our own times. Now it seems that the Saxons are oppressed by the Normans.'

There was a tap on the door, and Bethan admitted a smiling Saxon servant girl carrying a neatly pressed pile of clothes. She curtsied and said, in French, that the Lady Aelgifu had found some clothes that she hoped would fit the Princess. They had belonged to her daughter, who had now outgrown them. She hoped that they would be of service to Princess Nest until she had the opportunity to rebuild her wardrobe.

'Please, tell Lady Aelgifu that she is truly kind. I have no dress other than the one I wore to come here, and it is dirty and a little torn. I have no other things at all.'

'My Lady says please try the clothes on, and says that she can find others if these are not suitable. Unfortunately, there has not been time to wash and repair your own dress.'

When the maid had gone, Nest stripped and washed away the dried blood and dirt of the previous day, and delightedly tried on Aelgifu's gifts, parading before Bethan for her approval.

'See, my Lady, she has also sent a braiding for your hair like the Norman ladies wear, and bangles and beads. She does not want you to look like a beggar girl when you reach the King's Court. With these clothes you look like a young Norman woman, but I think that may help you if you are to live among them.'

When she was ready, and Bethan had brushed and braided her hair in the Norman style, she went into the Solar followed by Bethan. She saw the Saxon servants staring curiously at her, so she tried to stretch herself taller and enter regally, as a Welsh princess should. She imagined that her father was watching from Heaven to see how she comported herself amongst the enemy.

The Lady Aelgifu rose from her chair and advanced, smiling, to greet her. 'Come and sit with me at table Princess Nesta. My servants shall wait on you. Bethan can go to the kitchen where she will be well fed.'

Nest soon found that she could talk very easily to this warm woman who so obviously wanted to be kind. She soon told her about the terrible battle yesterday, and the death of her father and brother. As she told Aelgifu what had happened then, and after, she was suddenly wracked with a terrible grief and sobbed piteously, quite forgetting her resolution to be regal and brave.

Aelgifu motioned for the servants to leave, and she drew Nest close to her bosom to comfort her. When the young girl was once more in control of her tears, Aelgifu decided to advise her.

'When you are alone with me, you are with a friend and can talk as you please. I too have suffered at the hands of the Norman oppressors. I was forced by my family to marry the Norman Lord, who brought you here, Robert Fitzhammon. He is a hard, sometimes cruel, man, who looks upon me as his property, and treats me little better than his dog. I should not tell you this, but I see that the mark of his fist is on your face, as it has often been on mine. Most Normans are like that. It is the only way a few thousand of them can keep control over perhaps two million of we Saxons. They think if they show any kindness or compassion, it will be judged as weakness, and my people will rise against them. They know there are few of them and many of us.'

'If I had such a husband, he would have to fear that I would stab him to death while he slept. Can you not do something to get yourself rid of him my Lady,' said Nest fiercely.

37

Aelgifu laughed. 'My husband says that you are a little Welsh spitfire who needs beating. It seems you have impressed him.' Then her face clouded over and she said sadly, 'I fear that I am not as brave as you. Perhaps you are right, and one night we Saxon women should rise up and kill the stern Normans who lie in our beds. However you have much to learn about the World, Nesta. Not many women are as resolute as you, and perhaps that is as it should be. Life has to go on, babies have to be reared and loved, and homes made safe and calm for them to grow up in. Food has to be found and prepared. We have to hope that the gentle world that we women make around us will, generation by generation, make our men kinder and more loving. In the meantime it is sometimes very hard.'

'I will never marry a Norman. I would rather go into a nunnery than marry such monsters as the cruel men I saw kill my father yesterday, along with my brother, and hundreds of my people, and then kill other Welshmen who lay wounded.'

Lady Aelgifu took her hand speaking earnestly,

'This is a terrible, terrible time for you, and my heart grieves that you should have to face it, above all being so young and on your own. Always remember that you will be in my thoughts and prayers. It may be, that one day we will meet again, in better times.

'However, I fear time is short and I must advise you while I can. My husband will soon be back, together with several of his knights. After that it is unlikely that we shall be able to talk freely. You must remember that, no matter how provocative their words may be, you must keep your own counsel. Also, when talking to a Norman, never mind how kind some of them may seem. Know that they cannot be trusted and your words may be repeated to another of their number with a sterner heart. I learned this lesson the hard way when I spoke too freely to Norman ladies who seemed to befriend me. However, I think I hear my husband and his men returning. I must go to him. I advise you to return to your room. It may be that my husband intends to set off to London this very day with you. He has not told me his plans. I hope that we will meet again at a happier time for you.' With this Aelgifu embraced her, and went from the room to meet her husband, and to check that food was ready in the Great Hall for their meal.

Nest decided to take her advice and returned to her room. Bethan was brushing and combing her hair, when much noise and commotion in the courtyard drew Nest to the window. A number of Normans on horseback had newly arrived, and were milling around a cart, which seemed to contain the prone body of a man. He was weakly trying to lift his head. 'Dearest God, it is my brother Cynan, they have taken him! Oh Bethan,' she screamed, 'what have they done to him? Look at the blood.'

Without more ado she rushed from the room and down into the courtyard and straight to comfort her brother. The Normans were taken by surprise, and for a moment did not react.

Cynan's agony stricken face cleared for a second at the sight of his sister, and he tried to smile as she seized his hand.

'Gruffudd got away. He will be in Ireland by now.'

'Thank God! But what have they done to you, dear brother?'

A stinging pain crossed her back, and she turned to see a mounted Lord Fitzhammon raising his whip to lash her a second time.

'Get back to your room, you little Welsh slut, or I'll be tempted to give you what you obviously need, a thorough Norman rogering, to bring you under control. Your brother here at least, will give us no more trouble. We have cut off his balls. That should calm him down at little.'

Ignoring the whip, Nest threw herself at the horseman, beating puny blows at his legs. The horse, panicking, reared up, nearly unseating Fitzhammon. He was enraged to be shown up by a woman in front of his men and charged at the young girl, knocking her to the ground.

Shielding her face with one arm from the cruel whip, Nest screamed defiance at him.

'I swear you shall die, cruel, savage Knight. Your men have killed my father and my brother, now you have maimed my dear Cynan. I shall kill you. One way or another you shall die horribly for these deeds. I am no soft Saxon. I am a Welsh princess and I swear I will take a terrible revenge for your cruelty, no matter how long I have to wait for my chance.'

Looking down into those piercing, angry eyes, Fitzhammon felt a surprising chill in his marrow. It was as if someone had walked over his grave.

The journey from Gloucester to Westminster seemed interminable. It took a week of miserable bumping over a terrible road to reach the Norman new seat of government.

Robert Fitzhammon, whom Nest now hated with a deep ferocity, because of his appalling cruelty to her brother, seemed to be under instructions from the King to escort her personally. She could not imagine why someone of so high a rank should have to accompany a mere twelve-year old girl. Certainly, carrying out so boring a task had put him in a very bad temper. She heard him say to his Squire, that he had intended to go by sea from Bristol, but that the King's instructions specifically forbade it.

Each night the wagon and its escort stopped at an inn and Fitzhammon went through the pretence of making sure that the young Princess and her maid were accommodated comfortably. He treated the traumatised young girl with a patronising mock courtesy, which Nest found particularly hard to bear. This night was no exception.

'Are you sure your Highness will find this room suitable to her needs. I am sure it does not match up to your Highness' expectations?'

'It is a better bed than my father now lies in, Sir Knight. If my brother Gruffudd were here, he would thrust your mocking words down your throat. I may be a weak girl, whom it pleases you to torment, but do not deceive yourself that I would not use a knife to avenge the cruel things you did to Cynan. You call yourselves cultured men, but you are naught but savages in fine clothes.'

Stung by her words, Fitzhammon slapped her face hard. Forcing back the tears, she screamed back at him, 'now you prove my words by your actions. How very brave and gallant! Is this how you treat your lovely wife, in the privacy of your chamber?' She regretted the words as soon as they were out of her mouth. No doubt this brute would punish his gentle Saxon wife on his return.

On this and similar occasions, Fitzhammon would storm out of the room, cursing himself for allowing her to get the advantage and swearing inwardly that he would succeed in bringing her to heel, before they arrived in Westminster. However he knew full well that his cruel and unpredictable master, William Rufus, was very quick to find reasons to bring his Lords to task, and this spitfire of a girl was quite likely to denounce him on their arrival.

Despite the rigors of the journey, Gelert continued to gain in strength, and his wounds started to heal, free from infection, helped by the girls' careful nursing. As each day passed and he continued to improve, both girls started to relax and to take notice of the places they were passing through. Having been brought up knowing only the largely timber structures of Deheubarth, Nest was impressed by the new stone castles and churches being built in towns and villages on their route. The earlier wooden stockades, which the invaders had erected to control each conquered area, were now being rebuilt in stone. Everywhere it seemed, the industrious Normans were organising teams of the local Saxon peasants to erect scaffolding, to press on with the work.

When they reached Oxford, Robert d'Oilly, Lord of Oxford, received Fitzhammon, in his new stone castle. Fitzhammon was embarrassed to find that old d'Oilly's Saxon wife, Aethelfleda, unlike his own, was far from submissive. She insisted that Nest and Bethan were properly accommodated and treated with respect, and made a point of showing Nest the new cathedral, despite Fitzhammon's protests that she was a hostage under escort. Nest was awe-stricken by the soaring columns and magical stained glass windows. She had never seen anything so beautiful in her life.

While she was alone with Aethelfleda in the Cathedral, Nest told her what had happened to her brother Cynan, and begged her to try to find out where he was now, and what would be his fate. Later, at meat, Aethelfleda embarrassed Fitzhammon in front of everyone, by asking him directly.

'Robert, our young guest is very worried what is now to happen to her brother Cynan. Perhaps you can reassure her?'

'He is a rebel against the King and fortunate not to have been put to death. However, he is not likely to be any more trouble after what has been done to him and will probably be freed eventually, if he survives,' he added with a smirk.

'Leave Fitzhammon alone Aethelfleda. He is our guest. Let us talk of other matters,' put in old man d'Oilly.

Nest flashed Aethelfleda a grateful smile. At least Cynan was obviously still alive, and would likely be freed, but what did Fitzhammon mean by 'if he survives.' She longed to be there to look after him.

Next day, before resuming their journey, Fitzhammon was persuaded to attend mass at the cathedral with Robert d'Oilly's family. Robert's wife assumed, as a matter of course, that Nest would sit with her, to Fitzhammon's chagrin and Nest's delight. Nest was deeply impressed by the ceremony. The Bishop and his clergy processed in their rich vestments, chanting hymns and accompanied by the amazing sound of the new organ. It was all very beautiful.

That night, as she lay awake in yet another inn on their seemingly endless journey, she wondered how she could reconcile in her mind these two very different images that she now had of the Normans. On the one hand they were stern, and extremely cruel, as she knew only too well. On the other these 'savages in fine clothes', as she had called them, were capable of creating a beautiful cathedral and raising fine praise to God.

When they finally arrived at the outskirts of London, Nest could see the tall, nearly completed, White Tower of William Rufus' fortress gleaming in the distance, while close at hand was the amazingly large, also nearly completed, Westminster Hall, next to Edward the Confessor's old palace. Nest knew what the buildings were, because Fitzhammon's friendly squire made it his business to give a running commentary whenever he thought his master was out of earshot.

The long journey was now at an end, and suddenly Nest found that the cruel, obnoxious Fitzhammon had handed her over without ceremony to the King's Steward. She and Bethan were given a room in the Old Palace, at the end of a long corridor.

She felt completely exhausted after the journey, and she hardly took in the details of her new quarters. Instead she lay down on her new bed and slept, with Bethan on a chair beside her. The new manservant, Gelert, his wounds now starting to heal, lay across the doorway, taking up the role of guard, servant and fellow Welshman that he was destined to fill for many years.

chapter seven

Nesta (she had become used to the Norman version of her name now) had almost begun to feel comfortable at the Norman court after three years. She had a large room of her own, with a view of the river. She had to share it with Bethan of course, and Gelert slept in the corridor just outside her door. She loved to watch the constant movement of shipping and the ebb and flow of the tide. There was just one bed for the two girls, but that was better than back home in Dinefwr, where three or even four in a bed was not uncommon. After all, most people slept on the floor.

However, she never forgot that she was a Welsh Princess, and that the courtly ladies and gentlemen, that she now knew so well, were of that same foreign race who had killed her father and one brother, and cruelly maimed another. However, there was nothing she could do about it at the moment, so, after a long period of adjustment, she had decided to make the best of her situation, whilst not forgetting who she was.

She was now sixteen, and her mirror told her that she had become an attractive young woman. This assessment was regularly confirmed by her maid, Bethan, and, much more so, by the increasing attentions of the men at the Court. She had long blonde hair, usually braided, and she had taken to wearing a 'couvre chef' or veil, in the Norman style, arranged to fall to one side of her face, and held in place by a light silver coronet which marked her as a noble woman. With her piercing green eyes and now shapely but slim figure she had become very beautiful.

When she had first arrived at Westminster, she had only coped with her desperate grief and homesickness through the ceaseless love of Bethan, and Gelert, the wounded soldier, whom she had saved from death at Brecon. He had soon recovered from his wounds, and had made it his job to protect and support his brave young mistress. His very presence, standing behind her chair, hand carelessly on the hilt of the sword she had insisted that he be allowed to bear, had deterred many a young blood seeking to press his unwelcome attentions on the inexperienced girl.

No, she was not alone in her captivity, as she was constantly attended and supported by two of her own race.

After a while at the Court, one or two of the younger Norman ladies had found that Nest was interesting and amusing to talk to, and now frequently joined her little group in the Great Hall after the main meal of the day. This was eaten mid-morning, and Nest had originally found this strange, as, at her father's court, the main meal was in the evening.

Besides becoming fluent in French, she had also picked up the necessary graces in table manners, courtly conversation and behaviour. Rather surprisingly, the Norman ladies found they had much to learn from her, particularly in the arts of embroidery and stitching, acquired at her mother's knee, and in which the Welsh were apparently more advanced than the Normans.

Her servants, Bethan and Gelert, had also become fluent in French. Because of this, one of the ladies had discovered one day that Gelert claimed to be able to recite from the Mabinogion, a collection of myths and legends. The lady had heard recited excerpts from the Mabinogion while she had been in Wales with her husband the previous year, and had been deeply impressed. She therefore asked Nest if Gelert could recite for her, and Gelert had been happy to oblige with a few stanzas about the doings of Pwll and Rhiannon, and their courtship in the magical Arberth Forest. The lady had then brought her husband over to the group, and asked to hear some of it again.

The Welsh, Saxons and Vikings had one thing in common. They had a tradition of dramatic recitation of the ballads and sagas of the heroes of long ago, along with tales of the lives of their gods and goddesses. These were often accompanied by the strains of the harp or lyre, to which they listened in their great halls, or round the fireside in their camps. The Normans, however, Vikings though they originally were, in their rush to ape the ways of their neighbours, the French, had embraced Christianity, and renounced their old gods and the sagas that portrayed them. They had therefore lost most of their folk culture in their determination to be civilised and Christian.

Gelert had a strong, melodic voice and, as he sang the ballads of Pwll and Rhiannon, the haunting strains awakened something in the hearts of the Normans, and they would gather round him and the young Princess, and yearn for that which was lost.

Each morning, after the meal and the short Matins in the chapel, a group of younger Norman lords and ladies would gather around Nest, and would ask her to tell Gelert to sing for them. She usually agreed, but not every time, because she found that she liked the little bit of power that refusal put in her hands.

One day, as Gelert sang, Nest became aware that the King's brother, Prince Henry, had arrived silently at her side, and was listening intently. She had seen him often in the Court, usually accompanied by other great men and women, but he had never previously taken any notice of her. She knew from others that he was thirty-two years old, but she thought he looked younger. He was of medium height with short brown hair, and dressed simply. He was called Henry 'Beauclerc' because he was well educated. He was not married but greatly admired by the ladies. Nest thought him by far the most interesting man in the Court.

When Gelert had completed the last haunting note, Henry led the

44

applause for his skill. When the clapping died down, he turned to Nest and said,

'Your servant sings well, Princess Nesta, and his skill gives us much pleasure. Your nation is fortunate to have such a rich tradition of music and song.'

Rising from her chair, Nest offered him her hand with her newly acquired courtly skills, and Henry kissed it, lingering rather longer over the matter than convention required. He was not truly handsome she decided, but he had beautiful, deep grey eyes, which seemed to enter into her very soul. Despite herself, she felt herself attracted to him, in a way that she had not felt for any other man. It is just because he is a Prince, and older and more experienced in life than I am, she reasoned.

'It seems you have brought the music and songs of your native land to entertain our Court. It evokes real feeling in we Normans, because we have put away the sagas of our own past, and the music reminds us of how much we have lost.'

'You are very kind to speak so, Sir,' said Nest retrieving her hand. 'To bring out the full beauty of our music, I fear Gelert would need the services of a Welsh harp and harpist, but I doubt that such things exist outside Wales.'

'I will send to my brother's vassal, the Lord of Morgannug, asking him to send you what you require, and we shall have music which will delight the whole Court.'

'You will not expect the name of the Lord of Morgannug to give me any pleasure, sir. He is a traitor and a base knave. However, if he sends me a harp and harpist, I shall not be too proud to use them,' she added more gently.

'It seems you have not forgotten who you are, and I admire you for that. We see too many fawning, deceitful people here in Westminster, people who hate us in their hearts but smile at us with their faces.' After a moment he added, 'perhaps you would be good enough to accompany me as I progress through the Court. I think it is time for you to meet my brother, the King, whose order brought you here, and who may very well have forgotten that you exist.'

As she moved through the press of people on Henry's arm, Nest found that she liked to be the focus of so much attention. She had arrived here as a despised young girl of a subject race: now she was being treated as a woman desirable enough to attract a Prince. It would be rather fine to be a Norman Princess she thought. The Welsh, although respectful of their Princes, were far more matter of fact in their dealings with them. There had been little formality in her father's hall.

Henry was murmuring quietly to her as they strolled. 'You may find my brother, the King, somewhat coarse in his speech. He also has a violent temper, so it would be wise to keep your spirited views to yourself. Only last month he, personally, pushed a man who had displeased him to his death from the battlements. I do not say this to frighten you, but rather to stress the need for caution.'

'Thank you, Sir, for your concern. I will be careful in my speech with his Majesty,' she whispered back, 'but surely he is not violent with women?'

'Do not count on your womanly looks to weigh with him in your favour. He is not attracted to women and is, therefore, set against your sex in principal.'

'Oh!' said Nest, dismayed, 'How, then, must I speak to him?'

Amused, Henry said, 'just be respectful, but not cowed. Answer his questions but do not provoke him with your answers.'

'Good advice Henry,' said a sudden, rough voice behind them. 'What other gems of wisdom have you provided her with?'

Nest was shocked to find that the King had somehow come up behind them, unobserved. Even the suave Henry seemed a little off balance. Intrigued Lords and Ladies waited to hear the rest of this interesting exchange. Nest had previously seen this stout, red haired man only once and that in the distance, as he was usually away in Normandy controlling that fractious Dukedom. Close to, she found him quite frightening.

'My brother, I was merely advising this inexperienced girl to be cautious in speaking to a King.'

'She looks a lively enough strumpet, Henry. Have you got her into bed yet? Just your type I should think.' With this offensive greeting, the King offered Nest his hand.

Flushing angrily, Nest found it hard to control her response, despite Henry's advice.

'Your Majesty does my Nation, of which I am a Princess, and myself, great dishonour by speaking so. Sire, you do no credit to your own honour by taunting a young maiden in this way.'

'Silence, you Welsh slut!' the King roared. 'Your charms might work with Henry but not with me. Any more retorts like that and I will be pleased to see you whipped. I remind you, Princess,' he sneered, 'that you are here as hostage for the good behaviour of your people. I hope that you know what that means? I will explain. If your cur of a brother, the one that got away to Ireland, chooses to return and lead a rebellion against me, then I assure you that you will pay for his temerity with your life.' With these encouraging words the King nodded to his brother and abruptly marched off through a side door.

'Oh dear,' said Nest, 'I did not do very well did I?'

'You must learn to control that temper. You were lucky to get away so lightly. However, no harm appears to have been done. He has met you now. He knows you are not a wilting violet and will not forget about you.

Yes, on balance, no harm has been done at all.'

They walked back through the Court together, her arm on his. It seemed very natural to her. Everyone was looking now. They had heard the exchange with the King, and realised they would have to take her more seriously. When they reached the spot where she had been sitting she turned to him and said, 'shall I return to my place now?'

'There is another matter I would speak to you about. Please join me in my room for a more relaxed discussion, away from prying ears and eyes.'

'I think I would like that, sir, but I must bring my maid with me. I cannot let the King taunt me with lack of modesty.'

Henry smiled. 'By all means little Princess, but please leave Gelert behind. He makes me nervous.'

Nest was having a little reverie. Bethan had brushed and braided her hair ready for the day. She had also helped her to put on a new gown. It was apple green, but its main interest to Nest was that it incorporated some of the excessively long sleeves that were all the fashion now. They had to be at least two feet longer than normal, with their ends tied in loose knots and left to dangle. Both women thought they looked quite ridiculous, but that did not stop Nest wanting to try them.

'What do you think, Bethan, do I not look really silly?' she asked, as she twirled in front of the mirror.

'I cannot deny that people in Brecheiniog would laugh if they could see you now, but, here in Court, you will be considered to be in the height of fashion. In truth, you do not look half as silly as the young blades who have taken to growing their hair as long as a girl, and cultivating little, curly beards.'

'Prince Henry says that his father must be turning in his grave at such un-Norman behaviour. He says that his brother, the present King, has encouraged it, as he loves to shock all the older people. I think it is fun to try new clothes. It helps to pass idle hours.'

'I confess, my Lady, that I think your interest in the new fashions might have some other cause than just amusement,' said Bethan rather primly.

'I cannot think what you might mean, Bethan.'

'I think that today's French lesson with Prince Henry might be more of a motive?' replied Bethan, and then regretted it. She had noted lately, that Nest was no longer a child, and that she would be wise to be a little more diplomatic with her advice.

Nest's eyes flashed. 'I think you do exceed yourself, Bethan. I am quite capable of defending my honour against Prince Henry, and you are impertinent to suggest otherwise.'

'Forgive me, my Lady, I meant no criticism. It is just that he has loved many women and several have borne him children. I think...

'Please keep your views to yourself, Bethan.' Nest spoke sharply. 'I find the lessons helpful. I have to improve my French conversation if I am to be taken seriously in Court. Today, I believe he is to help me both write and read in French. In any event, I shall want you to accompany me, so my precious virtue will stay secure whatever Prince Henry's intentions might be.'

Bethan had then, rather huffily, asked permission to withdraw, since when Nest had been lying on her bed staring into space and daydreaming.

She knew that Henry had a bad reputation. It was apparently true, that several women had had children by him. However, no doubt, they had thrown themselves at him, throwing caution to the winds. He is very handsome, she thought. What harm would there be in flirting a little? There was very little else to do in this stifling, boring, Norman Court. Far from the first time, she wished that she could be back in her father's hall, which would be echoing with laughter and song, and there would be boys of her own people to dance and flirt with. But, she was not in Welsh Deheubarth now, but Norman Westminster, and it was fun to put the proud Norman ladies' noses out of joint a little. It was obvious that they were jealous of Henry's recent interest in her, and they were now being forced to take her more seriously. She was no longer a frightened little Welsh girl, newly brought down from the hills to a strange foreign court, apprehensive as to what might happen next. She was a woman, with womanly powers, whom a Prince appeared to desire. It was all quite exciting.

Last time, when he had taken his leave, he had again held her hand a little longer than custom required, and, as he did so, those grey eyes seemed to penetrate her. To her surprise, her legs seemed quite weak, and she felt her face flush. Bethan had noticed, of course. Hence her concern. She remembered her mother warning her that Tewdwr girls were very warm blooded, and that she was to take care not to meet men without a chaperone. So this was what she had meant. How very disturbing and exciting it was.

Bethan was back again. 'Prince Henry sends word that he attends you in his room, and asks if you are ready for your lesson,' she announced rather stiffly.

Prince Henry's room was quite small: there was just about room for a table and two chairs, apart from his bed and two clothes chests. Henry had arranged the two chairs closely, side by side, so that when they sat down his legs were nearly touching hers.

'I see you have brought Bethan with you. How very modest! She will have to sit on one of the chests, and twiddle her thumbs while we work,' he said, smiling.

Nest found his nearness disturbing and wondered how she would feel if his leg accidentally touched her own. She tried to concentrate on what he was saying.

'You told me that you learned to read and write Welsh in your father's hall, so that is an excellent start. You have also learned to speak French fairly well, here at Westminster. What I hope to do is to teach you to read and write in French also.'

'My Lord, my father thought that education was very important, and insisted that all his children could read and write. Some of us also had instruction from the monks in speaking French and Latin. Forgive me sir, but I do not understand why you are being so kind as to spend time in teaching me in this way. I do appreciate it, but you are the King's brother and must be very busy.'

'You are of royal blood, and worthy of honour and consideration for that reason. You have been required by the King to stay in our Court far from your home. It is fitting that you should be able to continue your studies, and there are not many in this Court who are educated enough to help you. Unfortunately, Norman society despises learning, and considers it fit only for monks and clerics. Holding that view, it discourages its womenfolk also. This, I am sure, is wrong, and a severe weakness in our culture. Alone amongst my brothers, I am fond of books, and am teased by them for my studies. I am keen to spread the learning of reading and writing in the Court, so that when I find a bright young girl who is keen to learn, I feel I must help. Now let me write a few sentences and we will work out their meaning.'

chapter nine   *Prince Henry's Hunting Lodge, Epping Forest*
September, AD 1096

It was just after dawn. Nest could see the chinks of light coming in through the skins on the window openings. She felt warm, lazy and loved. Henry was still asleep at her side. He stirred as if reliving in his dreams what had happened the night before. She stroked his hair and cuddled up to him. Perhaps he would wake soon and need her again.

She idly remembered the events leading up to her seduction. She was not sure if Henry had planned for it to happen. Perhaps he had. If things had continued as they had been in the Palace, he would have been unlikely to make much progress, since Bethan and Gelert were always nearby. She stretched herself sensuously. So that is what it was like to be a woman loved by a man. She resolved not to blame him, whatever he had done. She had not been forced to go hunting with him in Epping Forest, and in her heart of hearts she was tired of her maidenhood. Henry was obviously a very experienced lover, and had been very gentle. At the thought of their lovemaking she felt very warm again. She felt her body stirring. Perhaps she would wake him soon, accidentally of course!

When he had proposed the trip, he had said that since it would be only a very small hunting party, consisting of himself and two or three close friends, it would be possible to break convention and for her to go to the hunt with him. Also, since it was a very small lodge, there would not be room there for servants, other than one cook, two syces, and one ladies' maid, so she would have to manage without Bethan and Gelert. However, there would be another woman in the party, so her reputation would be safeguarded.

'Who is the other lady? Do I know her?'

'She is Lady d'Etaples. It is possible that you have not yet met her, as she is not often in Court. She is an interesting lady: you will like her. Her maid can look after the both of you.'

Nest had been thrilled and excited by the prospect of such an adventure. She had often gone riding at her father's court and loved horses. To Henry's surprise, she had readily agreed to his suggestion, asking him only if there would be gossip.

'They always gossip about anything at all,' he had replied. 'I should not care much if I were you, Nesta. It means that you are worthy of interest. You are young, beautiful and, above all, alive. They will not gossip much about you when you are dead'*

Bethan had made a big fuss, and told her that Henry was only taking her to the hunting lodge so that he could get her into bed more easily. She had even managed to stir up the stolid, loyal Gelert, who begged her to

51

reconsider. Nest was so happy and excited about the trip that she decided not to be high and mighty but to reason with them.

'I know that you both love and care for me, and I am very lucky to have two such loyal people to look after me in this foreign court, so far from home. However, I am grown up now, and must make my own decisions. I do listen to your advice but, in this matter, I shall follow my heart. Prince Henry is a powerful man in this land and may even one day become King. I am lucky to have the interest of such a man and I find much in him to admire. You should also remember that, if I do gain favour with him, he might find a way for us all to return safely to Dinefwr. Do not forget that I am my father's daughter, and shall always know where my true loyalties lie.'

Bethan, surprisingly, had gone quiet after that. She was becoming very fond of Gelert and she realised that Nest's escapade would allow her to spend time with him, alone. But, she also felt a little guilty and thought she ought to try harder to stop Nest going.

The hunting party had left very early one morning. Bethan had not made any further protest, only saying that she wished she had been allowed to come. Nest and Lady d'Etaples rode in a small carriage with Elise, Lady d'Etaples' maid. Accompanying them on horseback were, besides Henry, Henry's cousin Lord Stokesay, three young men whom Nest had not met before, and three servants.

'You must call me Adela. Can I call you Nesta?' Lady d'Etaples gushed. 'I may as well tell you about myself. My husband is away in Normandy visiting his estates. In fact, he is rarely here, so I feel very neglected. Lord Stokesay is my lover and Prince Henry sometimes invites us to his hunting parties so that we can meet without scandal. I hope you are not shocked. You are very young.'

Nest was not sure how she felt. She knew that in the hot house of the royal court such liaisons were not uncommon and provided raw material for lively gossip. Until recently she would have been uncomfortable with such a confession, but now, knowing her own developing feelings for Henry, she was beginning to understand how other women might want to behave.

'I have not had enough experience of the world, Adela, to make judgements. I simply know that I will only marry a man whom I love and that I will try to be faithful to him.'

'That is what we all want when we marry, but, alas, husbands often stray. What is a warm woman like me to do but take a lover. I cannot, however, expect you to understand these things, Nesta. I hope, when you marry, you will be happy, and lucky enough to have a husband whose eyes are only for you. However, you have not told me anything about yourself. I know only that you are a Welsh Princess and that you are not allowed to

---

* In this he was wrong of course, people are still gossiping about Nest in her native Wales after 900 years!

52

return to your native land. Anyway, I presume you are not here just for the hunting,' she added with a smile. 'Lord Stokesay tells me that you are a friend of the Prince.'

Nest found herself in some difficulty, in explaining to this worldly-wise woman, why she was there.

'It is true that Prince Henry takes some interest in me. He has been teaching me to read and write in French. However, we are not lovers. I know his reputation and have taken care to guard my honour. He thinks I am bored, so far from home, and suggested this hunting party to amuse me. He said I might get a chance to ride.

Adela laughed rather coarsely. 'I fear, young Princess, that the one to be ridden will be you. You are very naïve. I have no doubt that you have been invited here to make it easier for Henry to have his way with you. I suggest you become used to the idea and make the most of it. Not many of us have a chance to be bedded by the most powerful man in the country - save the King, of course - and he is no good in that department.' Adela laughed again, crudely.

Nest coloured hotly. 'You misjudge me, madame. I am no kitchen maid to be taken at whim. I do not find your conversation agreeable. I leave you to think of your forthcoming coupling with Lord Stokesay and I will concentrate on enjoying the sights of the journey.' She felt very angry at Adela's crudity. However, to her surprise, she felt a warm glow at the thought of Henry's possible designs on her.

Early Autumn in Epping Forest was very beautiful, and, as the carriage rolled through the ancient trees, Nest was spellbound by the glorious spectacle of the sun shining through the brown, yellow and green leaves. She had never seen such trees. Of course there were trees in Dinefwr, but nothing like those displayed before her. She quite forgot her annoyance with Adela.

Soon they arrived at the Hunting Lodge, and Henry himself handed her down from the carriage and walked with the three women to the door of their room, with Lord Stokesay at his side.

'There are yet three hours until dark, and it is still sunny and warm. I suggest that you ladies might like to get changed after your journey, and then, perhaps, you might like to take a walk in the forest with Lord Stokesay and myself. As you can see, it is very beautiful here and we should appreciate it while we can, in case it is raining tomorrow.'

Half an hour later Nest, Adela, Henry and Richard Stokesay strolled happily into the forest, Elise having been sent to help in the kitchen, to her great annoyance. The sun was still shining, and the syces had tied the horses to trees near the simple lodge and were rubbing them down.

The path led down through a grove of oak trees to a wooden bridge over a little stream. Nest was thrilled to see trout darting into shadows under the bridge. She seized Henry's arm and led him to see.

'There are trout like these in Dinefwr, Henry, and my brothers often tried to teach me to catch them. You have to be very patient and lie on the bank, your hand resting lightly in the water. If you are lucky, a fish will drift nearby and you can tickle its tummy. They seem to like that and, when they relax, you can seize them with your hand. Here - I'll show you!'

'You really are a rustic little peasant, Nesta,' said Adela, with a superior smile.

'I must confess that I can think of a more pleasant tummy to tickle,' laughed Robert. 'May Adela and I have your permission, Henry, to walk on ahead, while you two do your fishing?'

'I hate Adela,' fumed Nest, when Adela and Robert were out of earshot, 'I think she is a crude, stuck-up, bitchy woman. She tries to make me feel like a country bumpkin, but what is wrong with loving beautiful places like this and remembering catching trout with my brothers. You understand, do you not, Henry?'

'Of course I do,' said Henry, strangely moved by the enthusiasms of the beautiful girl at his side. 'We can lie on my cloak by the water and try to catch the trout. Come! Show me how to do it. I am glad that Adela and Robert have gone ahead. I also do not care for Adela's company She is a very shallow person and not much fun.'

Henry spread his cloak on the bank close to the stream and Nest threw herself down and turned to see if Henry was joining her.

'Come down here beside me, Henry, and I will try to remember how to catch them.'

After a moment of regal hesitation, Henry decided to forget his great rank and to indulge Nest's memories of her childhood. Nest told him to roll back his sleeve, and then showed him how to extend his hand slowly, ever so lazily, towards a small school of trout.

'You must turn your hand gently upwards, with your fingers slightly curled,' she instructed.

The fish initially backed away a little, but, as the pair waited very patiently with the cool fresh water flowing gently over their arms, Henry could see that the trout were becoming used to the arms being there and were tending to drift a little nearer.

Suddenly, they both jumped with surprise, when one of the fish hurled itself upwards and out of the water to snatch a damselfly, which had unwisely come within range.

'They have forgotten that we are here,' whispered Nest. 'Wait until one comes even nearer and I will show you what to do.'

The trout drifted closer, until one was only a foot or so above Nest's hand. Slowly, slowly, her hand drifted up under the fish until her fingers brushed its scales. The fish did not move. She brushed her fingers very gently along the fish's body and, again, it did not move. She started to gently move her fingers lightly from front to tail under the fish, and Henry, hardly daring to breathe, could see that her fingers were each time moving more towards the tail. Suddenly, there was a tremendous commotion as she seized the fish and yanked it out of the water.

'I've got it, I've got it!' she yelled with delight as the fish threshed wildly, trying to slip out of her hand. 'Help me, Henry. I cannot hold it.'

The fish was now on the bank, near the edge, with Nest kneeling, trying with both hands to stop it from jumping back into the water. Henry, still prone, rolled over to help her. Somehow the fish escaped, and both Nest and Henry fell in the river. Henry staggered to his feet and helped Nest up. They were standing knee deep in the water, soaked to the skin and covered in mud.

As Nest tried to stand, her clothes heavy with water, she staggered and nearly lost her footing. At once Henry came to her aid and she found herself in his arms. He did not let her go, and she savoured the delicious feeling of his body pressing against hers. She did not resist.

'Dear Nesta, you make me very happy. I have never tickled trout before. I think I could get to like it.'

'And now you are tickling me,' she said and offered up her mouth for him to kiss, surprising herself by her boldness. The sensuousness of his kiss spread like waves through her body, and the strength of it was overpowering. Her legs were like water and she clung to him again for support.

'You are the most beautiful woman I have ever met,' he said, which was no less than the truth, for she was one of the most beautiful women of all time. 'You are a joy to be with, and I think I have never been so happy as at this moment.'

In return she seized him fiercely round the neck and smothered him with kisses on any part of his face that she could reach. She was born to love and now she knew it.

Surprised and delighted at this sudden onslaught he, too, lost his footing, and clutching at each other and shrieking with laughter, they both fell back into the water, with Nest on top. She took full advantage. She had had no practice in the art of love but with very little instruction she found that it was natural to her.

It was at this moment that Stokesay and Adela appeared on the bank, looking very surprised and aloofly amused at what they saw.

'I knew at once, Henry, that the Welsh hussy would bring you low,' tittered Adela.

'Is this how they play the game of love in Dinefwr, Nesta?' laughed Stokesay, with a superior look on his face.

Henry found that he did not give a damn about the loss of his dignity and immediately took the initiative.

'Come Nesta, my love, let us make sure that these proud Norman courtiers in their fine clothes do not miss out on the fun,' he said, and started to scramble up the bank, pulling a grinning Nest behind him. She knew at once what he intended to do. Nest seized the astonished Adela by the waist, while Henry held her legs, and, accompanied by her yells of outraged horror, they managed to throw her into the stream. Once there, she somehow tottered to her feet soaked to the skin, howling with shocked surprise, her ruined hair clinging wetly to her face.

'Now it is your turn Stokesay,' said Henry.

'My Lord, I do beg you to desist. It is no doubt very amusing to play these rustic Welsh games, but I fear I have a weak chest and...

'Get in the water, and do so speedily,' roared Henry, giving Stokesay such a shove that he too slipped on the muddy bank and fell into the stream.

The sight of them soaked and standing dripping, thigh deep in the brook, was so lugubrious, that Henry and Nest clung to each other yelling with glee.

'I have not had so much fun since I was a child,' gasped Henry.

'Let us go into the water with them to try to cheer them a little,' suggested Nest.

'Come on you two! Forget about your Norman dignity and let us have some fun,' laughed Henry.

'Yes, let your hair down,' shrieked Nest, at the sight of Adela's ruined hairstyle.

Nest remembered a game she used to play as a child and, tying her scarf into knots to make an improvised ball, she threw it to Stokesay, who caught it despite himself.

'Is not this the best hunting party ever?' cried Henry. 'Come on, Adela, join in the fun. Relax a little'.

Slowly Adela and Stokesay tried to see the funny side of the situation, and anyway deemed it politic to pretend to enjoy the game. Adela eventually forgot to be a lady, and decided to tackle Nest to retrieve the ball. Both girls rolled in the water quite happily until Nest cheated by untying Adela's gown, leaving her half-naked.

'I think it is time to go back to the lodge,' said Henry wisely, while Stokesay helped the infuriated Adela to recover her modesty. The men helped the sodden girls out of the stream and they started to walk back to the Lodge.

'We can meet in the Hall later when we are in dry clothes and have had time to recover our dignity. There will be a fine fire there and I am sure we will appreciate it.'

Walking back into the Lodge past the eyes of the amazed servants had been a little difficult, but once back in Henry's room they could not restrain their glee.

'Did you see Adela's face when we threw her in? She could not believe it was happening,' laughed Nest.

'Stokesay will never forgive me,' gasped Henry.

It was a little while before Elise tapped on the door to offer to help Nest dress. By that time it was a little late since Henry had already eased off Nest's sodden clothes and wrapped her in a large towel.

'It will not be necessary, Elise. Go and help Lady Adela. I am sure she needs you more than I,' said Nest, trying not to laugh again.

Soon they were both naked, save the all-enveloping towels, and they sat on the end of Henry's bed supping the mulled wine that Henry's manservant had just brought them.

'I am still a little cold,' Nest said provocatively, once more surprised at her forwardness.

'Then I must warm you,' smiled Henry, as he pulled her gently into his bed.

'You know that I am still a maid,' breathed Nest, as he took her into his very experienced arms. 'Please, be very gentle.'

She need not have worried. Henry endlessly kissed and stroked every extremity of her beautiful body so that she was almost crying with desire and frustration before he even started to explore her more secret places. The pain, when it came, was almost a relief: she wanted to feel him inside her; to receive him into the empty, yearning void that needed him so much.

Bethan had said, that the first time for a girl was often very disappointing, even possibly a non-event. She could not expect the loss of her maidenhood to be more than an essential step on the way to more responsiveness, which would hopefully come later with practice. She was, therefore, very surprised when Henry's skills conjured up the most amazingly powerful, explosive feeling that she had ever known. At the same time she heard Henry groan and gasp as he fell down beside her.

'My love, my love,' she whispered, and taking his head to her breast, she stroked and kissed his soft, close-cropped hair. 'My love, I have never known such bliss.'

She had slept in his arms, snuggling up to him, savouring the wonder of it.

Later he had woken and insisted that they dress and attend dinner, as the other guests would be waiting for them. She had clung to him, sleepily protesting that he should remain with her there a little longer.

Dinner itself had seemed interminable. The three other men whom Nest had not yet met, had now returned from their hawking, and they had somehow heard about the events in the stream and boringly wanted to know every detail, while Stokesay and Adela sat with frozen smiles. The food was of a high standard, but Nest found it rather filling, and she just hoped that the meal would soon be over so that she and Henry could be alone together again.

However, Henry had called for the entertainment, which he had arranged. This took the form of jongleurs, acrobats and clowns, who had apparently reached the Lodge from Westminster quite late in the afternoon after a very dusty journey, from which they had hardly recovered. Still, they did their best, and Nest tried to be interested and to applaud them when they did well, but she really wished that the rigours of the journey had been even greater so that they had not managed to arrive at all!

Once back in his room, Nest was pleased to see that Henry's servant had lit a log fire which was radiating wonderful warmth. Instead of taking her to bed as she expected, Henry slowly stripped off her clothes and drew her down beside him onto a fine bearskin rug in front of the fire.

'I feel shy, Henry. You may think it strange after this afternoon, but no man has seen me naked before. Besides, your attentive servant may return.'

He laughed, 'I have warned him not to, on pain of death, but, to make sure...' Henry drew his sword from its scabbard and stuck the blade in the floor jamming the hilt under the latch.

'Do you feel safer now?' he asked, joining her on the rug.

'What must I do to please you?' whispered Nest. 'I know nothing of the games of love.'

'Just do whatever you feel you want to. That will please me best.'

For a while they lay quietly on the rug, just savouring the nearness of their bodies and the warmth of the flickering fire on their bare skin.

'It is wonderful to be alive and young. I want this moment to last forever. Do you, Henry?' she said, turning to look into his face, wondering if he felt the same. 'I wonder if other people are as happy as we are when they make love?'

58

'Sadly many are not,' he said, as he started to kiss her breasts. 'Most men do not know or care how to please women in that way and just take what they want, leaving their women frustrated.'

'Then I am lucky to have you for my lover,' she said, kissing his neck and chest.

Henry kept himself still and encouraged Nest to continue her exploration. She found herself aroused by the contact and started to crawl over his body kissing him ever more adventurously.

'Can a woman take a man Henry? It seems strange, but that is what I want to do. Is that normal? Is there something wrong with me?'

'My love, you are a delight. Just follow your instincts. I shall love every moment.'

chapter eleven

Strange happenings in the New Forest,
August 2nd, AD 1100

The King was having a bad day. He had woken early at his hunting lodge expecting an energetic day's sport with his brother, Prince Henry, but when he had sent his servant to see if he was up and ready, Henry had come back to William's room, still in his night gown, to explain why he wasn't coming. Although they were alone, his manner was strangely formal.

'Sire, I beg you to give me leave not to accompany you today. I am a little strained from our hunt of yesterday, and I hear that my horse is lame. By your Majesty's leave, I will content myself with resting this morning, and I will take a gentle ride this afternoon.'

'Please yourself,' replied Rufus testily. 'I did not take you for a milk sop, brother. It is perhaps as well that I am King and not you. A weakling stay-a-bed could not govern this country for long.' Not being able to resist a dig at his brother's literary skills, he added, 'you have wasted too many hours learning to read and write with spineless monks. Such things are not manly. They have weakened you, brother. You must spend more time in the saddle as a good Norman should.'

Henry decided that it would be counterproductive to expand his excuses and took leave from his brother as quickly as possible. He was in a hurry, his mind filled with dreadful thoughts, unworthy of a brother. As planned, he took one of the spare horses in the stables, which had been ready saddled, and rode out alone into the forest.

He usually loved the forest with its huge beeches and oaks and the glorious rides, but today the forest seemed dark, even sinister, and Henry shivered. It was sinister! He shivered again. He knew it to be sinister, and dangerous, and that was because of what he, Henry, might decide to do, in the next few hours.

It had started a few months ago, with certain Lords hinting that they wished that Henry had inherited the throne, not William Rufus or, Heaven forbid, Robert. He had then started to realise that many of William's nobles were not happy with him as King. When he did not object fiercely to these views, as a loyal brother should, the hints became formulated into stronger ideas. As he rode slowly through the forest, his mind listed the themes which many of the great Lords had touched on: William was unmarried and had no children; he was a homosexual and was therefore unlikely to provide the firm succession on his death that the country needed for stability, and there was also the unsolved problem arising from Normandy and England now being two separate countries. Most Norman Lords had estates in both England and Normandy, leading to dangerous divided loyalties should their leaders come to blows. It was obvious that men like these wanted a strong

King, like the Conqueror, who would reunite the Norman lands.

The Norman nobility still saw themselves in the role of holding down a highly-populated and rebellious Saxon kingdom, whose inhabitants still hated their conquerors thirty-four years after the Conquest. Any dispute between the Norman elite about the succession, worse still any armed strife between them, would give the oppressed Saxons their chance to regain control of their Kingdom. No, the succession must be secure. Better to have Henry as King, who was already begetting children far and wide, and who was planning to marry well and wisely. Even Holy Church, in the form of several bishops (but not, of course, the saintly Archbishop Anselm) had told him that William was a wicked man who did not fear God and who kept the income from vacant sees in his own hands for years, by delaying the appointment of replacements. No! Holy Church would shed few tears over William Rufus.

Perhaps there is something wrong with me, he mused. I should love my brothers. The truth of it was in his heart he did not love either of them, and resented the fact that he had not been given either England or Normandy by his father. He knew that his father had had the power to make him King of either country, even though he was the youngest. In those uncertain times the principal of primogeniture, that the eldest son inherits the throne, was not yet firmly established, and The Conqueror had indeed passed over Robert, the eldest, for the throne of England as he had deemed him too easy going and weak.

When Henry had failed to react to these latest treasonable ideas from the Magnates and Bishops, he had been approached openly by Count Robert of Meulan, who, after a little verbal sparring, came straight out with a plan. There was no need for Henry to do anything actively against his brother: others would plan and carry out the assassination. All he had to do was to agree not to pursue William's killers when he became King, and to give the final go ahead for a particular day, when Henry had managed to persuade William to go hunting on his own.

Henry had thanked Count Robert for his advice and said he would give his answer in three days. He had said this so coldly that Count Robert had not slept well that night, thinking that Henry might denounce him to his brother.

However, the more that Henry thought about being King, the more the idea attracted him. His loyalty to William Rufus had been severely strained some years ago, when he had found that William had agreed a secret treaty with his brother Robert to prevent Henry ever becoming King. They had plotted between them, that if either died without leaving a legitimate son and heir, then the other would succeed to both England and Normandy. Henry had never told either of his brothers that he had found out, but it had festered in his bosom ever since. He would make a much better King than either of them. He was sure of that. In contrast to their near illiteracy, Henry had been well-educated. He would make England solvent, make peace with the Church by allowing back the saintly Archbishop Anselm, who was presently sheltering in France, and make peace with his France, and with Scotland. He alone could do all this. However, he knew that he had to act soon, as brother Robert was on his way back from the Holy Land. Robert and his crusaders had fought their way to Jerusalem, and he was returning, full of glory, together with a beautiful new wife. No, Henry's chance was now! He must act very soon. Once Robert had returned, his chance would be gone. *

Henry rode up to a grand old oak that he and Count Robert of Meulan had fixed for their meeting. Count Robert was there, waiting for him. With him was a third man, whom Henry recognised as Walter Tyrell, a French knight, who often accompanied Rufus when he went hunting.

'All will agree that it was an accident,' said Count Robert. 'It has been arranged that two stags will be driven towards Rufus and Walter Tyrell. Tyrell here, will take care to be a little distance apart from. the King when the hunt reaches the chosen place. One stag, and then the second, will dash between the King and Tyrell. Tyrell will then shoot the King as if by accident.

'You, your Highness, will be riding, with your retainers, at East Leam which, as you know, is a good two miles from this spot. You will take care to have with you not only a goodly number of Knights whom you can trust, but at least two or three Knights who are friendly with the King.'

'For what purpose will my party be composed in this way?' murmured Henry, who had already guessed the answer.

'William's men will later bear witness that you had nothing to do with the sad accident that will befall the King. If, unfortunately, your brother survives Tyrell's arrows and suspects foul play, then it will be difficult for him to prove you had any part in it.'

'What happens when William falls dead?'

'I will ride to East Leam to advise you of his death, and I, and others, will kneel before you as our King.'

'I suppose I will then have the unsavoury task of visiting the scene of the accident and shedding false tears?'

'Far from it, your Highness. There are many in high positions who have sworn to make your brother Robert King, in the event of William's death. You must act very quickly to avoid these people seizing the throne on his behalf. As soon as I ride over to advise you of the accident and to kneel

* *William the Conqueror, on his deathbed, had given England to William Rufus and Normandy to Robert, splitting his inheritance, and also the loyalties of the great Lords who had lands on either side of the Channel. Henry was not given any land but did receive a considerable sum of money. For this reason he was sometimes called 'Henry Lackland'.*

before you as our new King, you must make all speed, together with men you can trust, to Winchester to seize the treasury. Having gained it, you must then ride rapidly to Westminster Abbey Church and have yourself crowned. Any delay, and all will be lost. Robert could himself arrive at Westminster within two or three weeks, together with a large and warlike following. If, in the meantime, his friends have had time to organise themselves, your own cause would be forlorn indeed, probably lost.'

'The plan seems well crafted,' mused Henry. 'Like all desperate plans, it could fail in the details. It would take me many days to reach Westminster, having to seize Winchester on the way. In the meantime, a party of William's men could ride directly to Westminster and proclaim Robert King before my arrival.'

'That is true Henry, which is why all speed is essential. No brotherly weeping over William's body! No enquiry into the accident! No conveying his body ceremoniously to lie in a church! Just ride as if the Devil himself were behind you, to seize the Kingdom. You can say masses for William's evil soul when you are safely King. I have taken the liberty to arrange teams of fresh horses at suitable inns on your route. With this planning in advance, you can be crowned King within three days.'

'So be it, Count Robert. I see that you have risked much for my cause already, and your position here may be difficult after my departure. You too, Tyrell, will risk your life for me. What will you do to avoid instant death at the hands of William's men?'

'It is all planned, your Highness,' answered Tyrell. 'When William falls, I shall run to his side and weep copiously over his body, blaming the stumbling of my horse for my bad aim. Count Robert will then arrest me and ride off with me during the confusion. Whatever the outcome, I shall then flee to France, to my estates, and there await news.'

'Sir Knight, please forgive me for my questions. I understand the position of Count Robert. He is my close friend. When I am King his star will rise high in the firmament, that is natural. Also, he believes that I will make a good King, and will take firmer Norman control over this turbulent realm, and eventually reunite England with Normandy. That I understand. It is your position, Sir Knight, that I do not follow. Why will you take this grave risk? You are not a Norman. You are French. You do not have estates here. Why should you help me so directly?'

'My Lord, you are right to question my motives, and my answer will be starkly plain. When your father, who was then Duke of Normandy, asked my father to join his great expedition to defeat Harold and conquer England, along with many great Lords from Normandy, France, Flanders and elsewhere in Christendom, his courage failed him, and he stayed on his estates in France. He cursed himself for a coward and for lack of ambition when you Normans seized this rich realm and were rewarded with great estates and noble titles.'

'Ah!' said Henry, comprehending. 'Do not doubt, Sir Walter, that I will give to you what was not given to your father. There will, of course, have to be a suitable interval, not to make it too obvious.'

Turning to Count Robert he asked, 'How many days will be needed before this deed takes place?'

'It must be today. Everything is ready. You have his leave to ride separately. He has invited Sir Walter to join him in your place. He has also been promised a shot at the legendary Great White Stag, of which Tyrrel here claims to know the whereabouts.'

Henry was a cautious man who, however, knew when he had to be decisive. This was his chance - perhaps, his only chance. Any delay and the King might come to hear about the plot. It seemed that many hands had necessarily been involved in the planning. Someone might try to sell their knowledge to Rufus.

'So be it! I will return to the Lodge and collect a small hunting party and ride to East Leam and there await events. I am greatly in your debt Sir Walter, for the risks that you are taking for me. As for you, Count Meulan, I look to see you shortly to tell me that I am King. We must tarry no longer here. We may be seen. God speed you both.'

The hunt was at full gallop, with the King and Sir Walter Tyrrel in the lead. 'This is good sport, Tyrell,' shouted the King, 'but where is the Great White Stag you promised me so convincingly?'

Before Tyrell could reply, all could see that progress was halted by a thick belt of trees, and the sweltering, steaming horses were forced to draw up, some rearing and plunging. William was furious.

'May God burn in Hell, Tyrell,' he roared. 'I will flay your French hide for this. You have brought me on a wild goose chase and I swear by Christ's bones that you shall regret your empty promises.' Many around the King winced, not for the first time, at the King's blasphemies, and feared for Tyrell's fate at the hands of their violent master.

'The Forest here is thick and tracks are few, your Majesty. That is why the Great White Stag is seen so little. He is cautious and cunning and has chosen his home well. However I saw him here only yesterday, and I know his ways. I cannot promise for sure to deliver him into your hands today, or even that you will see him at all. However I believe him to be near, and have sent men to drive him towards us.'

Before Rufus could decide on his response, a huntsman rode up to the party from a narrow track through the trees on the left. Approaching the King, he said, 'Your Majesty, my men have the White Stag confined to a copse a few hundred paces ahead. He is with his favourite hind.'

'This is better, much better. A gold coin for you if I have a fair shot at him,' exclaimed the King. 'You had best tell me the best place to be when he might come.'

'Sire, I would respectfully suggest that you and Sir Walter move forward very quietly to where a patch of birch trees flank the road. The White Stag is cunning, and if he hears the noise of many horses, he will break away in a different direction.'

'Yes, yes!' exclaimed the King, standing up in his stirrups so all could hear him. 'I will ride ahead with Tyrrel, and you, Huntsman, will ride a little behind us, as we may need your advice. Everybody else will keep two hundred paces behind. I mean to have that stag, and if any one of you spoils it for me, then by the blood of The Martyr, I will see you rot in the Tower.'

'My men will give one blast on the horn when they start to drive the stag. That may be at any moment Sire, so let us move forward now.'

Grumbling quietly to each other, the main party hung back, while the King and Sir Walter walked their horses carefully down the track, with the huntsman, Garth, a few paces behind.

'The stag will break from the left, your Majesty,' said Tyrell. 'I beg leave to suggest that to give you the best shot, you should be on the right of the track, a little ahead of me. That way you will get one clear shot and maybe a second.'

'Good, Tyrell! However I must have that stag. You are the best archer in the Court, so you must also shoot, just after me. And shoot straight and true if you know what is good for you. The others are too far behind to see whose arrow brings down the stag, and you will keep quiet later if you value my esteem.'

At that moment a horn sounded in the distance, and almost at once a hind broke through the trees on the left, just ahead of them. William, in his excitement, mistook her for the stag, and released his arrow, hitting her in the rump.

'God's teeth, it is only the hind,' he bawled. He was fumbling to draw another arrow, when the Great White Stag himself burst out of the trees, paused for an instant at the sight of his stricken mate, and then hurled himself across the track. 'Get him Tyrell,' the frustrated King shouted, getting an ill-aimed arrow off at last.

Even before the King's words reached him, Tyrell's first arrow pierced the stag's heart and lungs. Then turning in his saddle, he deliberately and carefully loosed his second arrow at almost point blank rage at the exuberant King, who toppled slowly from his horse, his last look being of amazed surprise.

As Tyrell jumped down from his horse to run to the King, the huntsman Garth, who had seen the whole incident, hurriedly dismounted to join him. The rest of the Court, who had just come into view, realised that something was wrong and broke into a canter to catch up.

'Is he dead, Tyrell? You will be dead too when the Court gets here.'

'You know what we agreed Garth. Keep your nerve and we will carry this off.'

As he lifted the King's head, Tyrell was horrified to find that he was trying to speak.

'Why you, Tyrell,' he breathed.

The huntsman panicked. 'I cannot support you now, Tyrell.'

The leading riders of the Court had now arrived and were gathering round in shocked surprise.

'It was an accident,' shouted Tyrell. 'The King ordered me to shoot and then came across between while I was taking aim. It was not my fault.'

'The King still breathes. Let us bind his wound and get him back to the Lodge in case the Physician can save him,' shouted Sir Godfrey de Lacy. 'Seize those men,' he added, pointing at Tyrell and Garth, 'and bring them back to the Lodge so that we can get to the truth of what took place.'

The King's wound was bound and he was placed on a stretcher. A relay of men carried him at a run towards the lodge, but all knew that he was breathing his last.

Count Robert decided that it was time for him to assert his rank. 'You accompany the King to the lodge, Sir Godfrey, though I fear he is already with his Maker. I will send word to Prince Henry, and will take these men under guard to Winchester.

The main mass of William's hunting party started to move away towards the lodge, urgently discussing the situation. Events had unfolded so quickly that most of the Lords present could not imagine what would happen next. Rufus had been such a violent, ruthless figure that his sudden removal from the scene was hard to take in. There was much to discuss. As a Norman King, many had found in him much to admire; he was strong and decisive, he was a good soldier, rebellions were soon put down and England had powerful leadership. Many others were appalled at his apparent contempt for God himself and at the way he trampled over the Church, driving the saintly Archbishop Anselm into exile and keeping the vacant Bishoprics unfilled for years while keeping the income from them for his own use. Most Lords had lands on both sides of the Channel and many had taken care to keep in the good favour of Duke Robert for that reason.

Many now argued, as they rode, that a Council would have to be called to decide on a successor. It was widely known that King William had agreed with Duke Robert that he would be King if William predeceased him. What then, would the wily Prince Henry's attitude be? If there were to be a conflict between Robert and Henry, it would be important to be on the winning side. Life had seemed good this morning, as they rode joyously to the Hunt. Everything, now, had been changed by just one arrow. The future suddenly seemed very uncertain, and even dangerous.

In the meantime, Count Robert of Meulan had taken care to keep only men he could trust behind with him in the forest. As soon as the King's party was out of sight, he sprang into action.

'You, Tyrell, take Garth with you, and ride straight to Southampton. I want you out of England by nightfall. Talk to no one, and explain nothing. Your lives and many others depend on it. Take ship to France and go to your estates. Stay there, and lie low until you hear from me. I want you out of reach of the Court until things settle down. Meanwhile, I have my own urgent tasks to perform.'

chapter thirteen

Nest was feeding baby Henry. She did not have to; Henry had sent her a wet nurse as soon as the baby was born, five months ago. It seemed that all the high born Norman ladies had wet nurses for their babies, but Nest immediately made it clear that no one but she would be feeding her baby. He was going to grow straight and strong, with nothing but good Tewdwr milk She was glad of the help of the young Welsh girl, Carys, whom Bethan had found to look after the baby when she was busy. It was a matter of compromise. Nest intended to spend as much time as possible with baby Henry, but she also had no intention of neglecting his father.

She had returned to her own quarters when the baby was born, but Henry had remained very attentive, staying with her for several hours on most days. He was delighted with his little son and had insisted that he be named Henry. Nest knew that he already had several bastard daughters by other women, but this was his only son, and Nest had started to believe that Henry would now marry her. Surely he would not have chosen the name Henry if that were not so. Certainly, many of the Norman ladies in her circle had encouraged her to believe it. She hoped it was true. She loved Henry. True, he could be cold and distant sometimes, but he always made up for it later.

Gelert and Bethan said it would be good for Wales if she married him. Bethan, who could be a little bawdy in her speech, said, that Nest so beguiled Henry in bed, that she would regain there the battle lost by her father at Brecon. Nest had pretended to be cross, but in her heart she was glad.

Henry had returned to her bed only four weeks after the baby was born. He had come into her room in the middle of the night and had nearly been cut down by Gelert, who still slept outside the door, sword at his side. Both Bethan and the nursemaid, Carys, slept in the room and both had to sleepily withdraw on Henry's arrival. It had been quite an occasion. The baby had been woken up by all the noise, and Henry had had to lie patiently by her side until his greedy little son had had his fill. Finally, she had put him back in his cot and had crept back into bed with Henry, whom she was delighted to discover, was equally greedy.

After that he came back most nights, and was very patient when the baby woke. They were quite a little family, and Nest was blissful.

Two weeks ago he had told her that he had to go hunting in the New Forest with the rest of the Court and had invited her to go too. She had refused, saying that she would be in the way and that the facilities at the hunting lodge might not be suitable for a baby. He had reluctantly agreed, smothered her with kisses and promised to bring her a beautiful deerskin for baby Henry to lie on. After two weeks, she was missing him and was uneasily wondering if she had made the right choice.

The sun was streaming into the room through the window. It was going to be another hot day. Suddenly there was a blast on a horn outside and the clatter signalling the arrival of many horsemen. She rushed to the window. Henry had returned, apparently in a great hurry. He was already swinging off his horse, not waiting for any assistance. She must go to him at once.

She thrust the baby into the arms of her surprised nursemaid, gathered up her skirts and ran off at full speed down the corridor, not caring a jot for decorum.

When she reached the Great Hall, Henry was already striding in at the main door with many great Lords puffing to keep up with him. She rushed to embrace him and he greeted her warmly but briefly. Then, still with his arm around her, he turned to address the crowd, which was still assembling from all over the building.

'Let messengers be sent to all Lords in London not already present and in particular to his Grace, the Bishop of London. Let it be known that I call an emergency council for noon, to be held in the new Westminster Hall. In the meantime, steward, bring meat and drink to my chamber, and hot water, that I may refresh myself after my journey.

Come, Princess Nesta, join me in my rooms and ask that my son be brought to his father.'

Once they were alone, his kisses were as passionate as ever. Nest was as hungry as he, but she must know what was afoot.

'Why the sudden unannounced return, my love? What has happened? Is there some peril? Where is the King and the main body of the Court?'

Sitting himself on a couch, Henry drew her down beside him. 'You are to me not only a very beautiful and desirable mistress, but also my closest friend and counsellor. I have known many women in my life...

'And still do,' grinned Nest wryly.

'But you are the only one that I can trust with secrets of state, and I need your support and counsel now,' he continued.

At this point servants arrived with food, wine, and hot water, and Carys brought the baby. Behind them, Count Robert and other Lords sought audience.

Taking baby Henry in his arms he kissed and hugged him.

'What I shall do in the next few days will affect your life, my son, and I must think deeply. I need rest. Please leave me to relax, my Lords. We all meet at noon. You, Count Robert, I will see one hour before. I need your council. In the meantime, dear friends, please leave me.'

Everyone left the room and, gnawing at chicken leg in one hand and drawing Nest close with the other, Henry decided to trust her completely.

'You should know that the King is dead and his death is no accident, though it will seem that way.'

Nest gasped, but somehow she was not totally surprised. William was a violent man. She would have questioned Henry but, raising his hand, he bade her wait.

'You are a Princess, and you must know by now that Kings and Princes are not as other men. They cannot be. The affairs of state put pressures and strains on them that force them to act in a way that would be unnatural in other men.

My brother was very wicked, and cared not for God, man, or the law. Even worse than that, in a King, he lay with men rather than women, so that he has no children to succeed him, leading to stresses and tensions round the throne.'

'I suppose that Duke Robert will now return from the Holy Land to succeed him,' said Nest, her mind racing ahead. 'But you have not told me how William died or what suspicions you have about his death?'

Henry turned to look at her, and his terrible expression made her heart grow cold.

'You - you killed him!' She voiced the unbelievable suspicion that had sprung unbidden to her mind.

Henry became matter of fact. He knew Nest to be stronger than any ordinary woman and, being of royal blood, would understand the hard choices that someone like him had to make.

'I did not kill him Nesta, nor did I have him killed. But, I was made aware of what others planned to do, so I was ready to ride here to seize the throne. I intend to be crowned at Westminster this very afternoon, thus giving my brother Robert no chance to forestall me.'

Nest took control of her voice and her emotions. She must make certain of the facts before her feelings took over. She stood facing him, clasping their baby tightly to her bosom.

'They told you that they planned to kill your brother and you did nothing to save him?'

Henry was suddenly aware that he had been unwise to trust her.

'England needs a strong, just King and a secure succession. I can provide that security. I will be a good King and I will reunite England with Normandy.

'So, you have killed one brother and plan to kill another,' she screeched in his face. Henry drew back from her as if bitten.

'How dare you scream at me like that!' he said coldly. 'I was obviously mistaken to confide in you. You will please remember to keep anything I have told you to yourself.'

'Or what? Would you threaten me now? Is that all I mean to you? See here the baby we made together in that very bed and who bears your name. What sort of man are you who can calmly admit to murdering his brother? I love my brothers. Nothing would induce me to harm a single hair on their heads. How could I be so mistaken in a man? A man who could kill his own brother is a monster and not fit for my bed or to be a King of any country.'

Losing his composure for a moment, Henry slapped her face. The baby started to cry. 'You have gone too far. Today I shall be crowned King of England. No one, not even the mother of my child, speaks to me like that.'

Henry swept from the room. On this, the most important day of his life, he must keep cool and purposeful. Damn, damn, damn the woman, that she had the power to unsettle him! He had seriously considered making her his Queen, although he had known there would be opposition from the Church. He had thought she would have been ideal - beautiful, intelligent, a foil for all his projects. He had been wrong. She would oppose his plans, be difficult and tempestuous, and, worst of all, unsettle and weaken him when he knew he had to be ruthless. No, she would have to go from the Court. He would make a diplomatic marriage that would strengthen his power. He would think of some arrangement for her.

In the meantime he had a Kingdom to seize, plans to be made, men to organise and control. This was no time for worrying about emotional women. He must see Count Robert and then the Bishop. There was much to be done.

Nest clutched her baby to her and threw herself on her bed. She cried and cried as if her heart would break, and baby Henry cried with her. She cried for the love that was lost. She cried because she had been a fool to think Henry was noble and good. She even cried for the foul William shot down in the forest.

As she lay there sobbing and alternately trying to soothe her baby, she cried for other things that were lost. She might have been Queen. She might have had the power to help her poor native land, Wales, now being overrun and possessed by the greedy Norman lords. She might have had the power to save her own fugitive brother Gruffudd, now hiding in Ireland. How stupid she had been to let fly at Henry like that. She had lost everything by her loss of control. She might even lose her baby!

At that thought she became icy cold. What had she done?

In the meantime, Henry threw himself into consolidating his seizure of power. After consulting Count Robert, he addressed the Great Council at noon, telling them that William had died in an accident and that he intended to have himself crowned that very afternoon to prevent anarchy, and to ensure strong, effective government. He said that he intended to restore a good relationship with the Holy Church by inviting back Archbishop Anselm and making a new concordat with him about the role of Church and State.

Once they had got over the shock of the news of William Rufus' death, the nobles decided to throw themselves behind Henry, who had obviously already seized the levers of power.

His coronation was a model of pomp, piety and rectitude, in contrast to that of his father, when buildings nearby had been set on fire, and William had hurriedly put the crown on his head himself, to make sure it happened.

In his coronation speech, Henry promised to rule wisely and fairly for the benefit of all his subjects. By the time Duke Robert's supporters arrived from the New Forest later that afternoon it was all over. Henry was King of England.

chapter fourteen

Henry had virtually ignored her since that fateful day of the coronation, the day he had admitted complicity in the death of his brother. She was no longer invited to sit beside him at meat. Now she sat with a group of young, unmarried women, further down the table.

She felt an aching void in her life. Only a few weeks ago she had been Henry's acknowledged mistress, believing that he might marry her. She was the only one of his mistresses to have borne him a son. Surely this was important? Now, he no longer came to her bed and she felt a desperate longing for him. She could not believe that his feelings for her could change so drastically and so soon.

He still sent for little Henry most days. A servant would arrive saying that Henry wished to see his son, and she would put the baby in Carys' arms, and watch wistfully as she took him away. Sometimes they would be away for an hour or two, and Nest would begin to worry. When they did get back Nest would question the girl closely about what had taken place. It seemed that Henry would initially hold the child and carry him about, and then Carys would be told to settle him in the cot, which had appeared in one of the King's rooms. Henry would often show the baby to his noble visitors, and they would converse in low voices so that Carys could not hear what they were saying.

One day she awoke full of purpose: she knew what she must do. Henry had definitely finished with her; she must accept that. For reasons unknown to her, he did not want her anymore. She must ask him if she could go back to Wales. Henry was probably feeling guilty about her, and she must take advantage of that to persuade him to let her go back to her own people in Dinefwr. William was dead, and she could see no reason why Henry would want to keep her at Westminster. She posed no threat to the Norman Kingdom. Her people were quiet and her brother Gruffudd, still believed to be in Ireland, had not been heard of for two or three years. She resolved to write Henry a note asking him to let her go. He might be reluctant to part with his son but she was quite willing to come to London from time to time so that he could spend time with him.

She dashed off a brief, but well argued, note at once, and sent it by Bethan. Bethan came back with the answer almost at once; the King wanted to see Nest in his rooms now. She was to bring Bethan, Carys, and the baby. Nest felt a gripping chill in her heart.

'What was he like, Bethan? What was his mood when he read my letter? Why does he want you and Carys, and the baby, to go with me?'

'My Lady, he was cold, calm, and purposeful. It was as though he had already decided on some action and your letter had prompted him to go ahead.'

When they reached the King's rooms, they found a little group of curious hangers-on loitering nearby. A Courtier said that Henry would see Nest alone: the others were to remain outside.

It was strange and yet not strange being alone with him again. He stood there cold and aloof, but she still felt an overwhelming impulse to rush into his arms, even though she was almost sure he would reject her. She just wanted him to hold her again for the last time. Casting caution to the winds, she ran forward and threw herself at his feet, kissing his legs and thighs. To her surprise and joy, he drew her to her feet, wrapped his arms around her and smothered her with kisses.

'My love, my love,' he whispered, and drew her to a couch.

This was madness. Nothing had been resolved. There was nothing but the overwhelming power of her need for him one more time. For him it was the same: he loved this girl, this woman, more than any other before. They said he was a cold fish, but with her it was different. She had got under his skin. He needed her, wanted her. For a few moments he made himself believe that it would be all right; that he could make her his Queen and forget a diplomatic marriage to the King of Scotland's sister. He was King now. He could make it all come right.

As they made love, with an urgency that they had never felt before, they forgot the courtiers, the high men of state, and the servants who waited just the other side of the unlocked door. Even the baby in his cot had the wit not to cry at the moment of his parents' need for each other.

When the violence of their passion was suddenly spent, it was she who recalled him to his duty, she who made certain that when those waiting outside were called in, that they saw only their King sitting in a chair and his former mistress cuddling her baby. Only Bethan, deferentially waiting in the rear, was not fooled. She saw her Lady's heightened colour and her kerchief cast carelessly on the King's couch.

73

The morning after they had made love on Henry's sofa, with half the Court waiting outside, Nest had received a rather cold note from Count Robert de Meulan, asking her to visit him that very day at noon, since he had matters of high import to communicate to her.

Nest knew that Count Robert was a close friend of the King, but she could not imagine why he would want to see her. Bethan said that she could only suppose that he was going to tell Nest something that Henry did not want to tell her himself. Nest again felt that terrible fear that had gone away for a while after they had made love. She could not bear the uncertainty and decided she must visit Henry at once to make sure of him. When she had arrived at the door of his suite, the soldier on duty fetched a page. She was informed that Henry was away for the day. So she had returned to her room none the wiser.

At noon, she took both Bethan and Gelert with her to visit Count Robert. Gelert was told to wait outside, but Nest was glad to have Bethan with her when she was ushered into the presence of a grim and formal Count Robert, who was flanked by several other great Lords and their retainers.

'Please sit down, my Lady.' When she was seated he continued, 'I am empowered by His Majesty, the King, to bring certain matters to your attention -

'But, why cannot Henry tell me himself? Why all this formality? I am sure if I -

'Please be so good as to not interrupt, Princess. This is a matter of state.'

'A matter of state, Count Robert? What nonsense is this?'

Count Robert stood up, and shouted down at her. 'You will please listen with respect to the information that His Majesty has instructed me to pass to you. I remind you that you came here as a hostage, and that you are still a hostage. Please hold your tongue and listen carefully.'

Nest felt like crying but was determined not to do so.

Sitting down again, Count Robert continued in a kinder voice.

'His Majesty the King wishes to communicate his continued love and affection for you, and for his dear son. However, he wishes you to be aware that Kings cannot live their lives as other men. For reasons of state, and for the security of the Realm, it is necessary that he marry the King of Scotland's sister Edith, or Matilda, as she will be known in England.'

'But how has all this been arranged? Why did not Henry, I mean the King, tell me all this before?'

Count Robert looked a little embarrassed. 'I am sure I am not going further than my instructions when I tell you that, at first, the King was reluctant to accept the advice of myself and other advisors that this marriage is necessary. It is painful to him to send you away.'

'Send me away?' gasped Nest.

'Such is his affection for you, and such has been the central part in his life that you have recently played, that he has been persuaded that he would not be able to enter into this marriage with you still present in Court. Therefore you are to be sent back to Wales.'

While Nest tried to steady herself, to absorb the full significance of what she was being told, Bethan whispered advice in her ear. Pulling herself together, Nest said.

'What then is to be the fate of our son? Is he to accompany me to Wales? Also, what thinks the King will be the opinion of my people when I am returned to them, the rejected strumpet of the Norman King?'

'These issues are sensitive and complex, and have concerned the King and his advisors greatly. Firstly, on the subject of your status and reputation, the King is greatly concerned about this. He has, therefore, decided to give your hand in marriage to Gerald de Windsor, the Castellan of Pembroke, who, under Arnulf the Earl of Pembroke, administers the King's lands in Pembrokeshire. He is a noble, brave, but kindly, man, who sits high in the King's regard. Marriage to such a man would greatly support your reputation both here and in Wales. Also, the King will give you in dowry the lands and appurtenances in the district of Carew, which, you may know, is near Pembroke Castle.'

Nest could not believe what she was hearing: that Henry had arranged so much without any part of it being discussed with her.

'It seems the King has given deep thought to many matters. It is a pity he did not think it necessary to tell me of them himself. But what of my son?'

'It is with the deepest regret, that His Majesty has to inform you that it will not be possible for his son to accompany you to Wales.'

'His son - I am to be separated from my baby? I cannot believe that he would do this to me. I will not part with my baby.' Nest started to sob uncontrollably.

Bethan ignored the great Lords and took Nest in her arms.

Count Robert struggled to complete this difficult interview.

'Princess Nest, please calm yourself. It would not be safe for baby Henry to be taken to Wales. As the King's only son, he would be at serious risk of abduction, or worse, by any rebel leader who wished to put pressure on the King's Government. In addition, the boy is very dear to the King and he wishes to advance him in power and position.'

Nest now became completely distraught, and was led from the room, comforted as best they could by Bethan and ladies of the court.

chapter sixteen

On board the Raven
October, AD 1100

The ship rolled and plunged to the westward and Nest was going back to Wales. She knew she ought to be happy; after seven long years away from her homeland she would soon be back in the land of her birth. In spite of this she felt desperately sad. She felt very seasick and - she had lost her baby.

Henry had been as considerate as he knew how to be. He had arranged for her to marry a Norman Lord, who was said to be kind; he had given her a considerable store of jewellery and gold, and he had let her keep her fine clothes. He had sent Bethan and Gelert to look after her, and he had personally escorted her to her carriage when she left for Bristol.

'The road is passing fair to Bristol, he told her, 'and I have arranged for my own ship, the 'Raven', to take you on to Pembroke, so that you do not have to bump over those terrible Welsh tracks. I have also given you land at Carew, near Pembroke, where you and Gerald can build a house of your own, which is independent of Gerald's position as Castellan of Pembroke Castle.'

It all seemed very reasonable, and Bethan said she was lucky to have so much from the King. When she had arrived at Westminster she had been a hostage, with hardly more than the clothes on her back, and with her life always in danger should her kinsmen choose to rise in rebellion. Now, she was a Lady, an acknowledged Princess, and she was to be married to Gerald, the Lord of Pembroke, who would not dare to treat her badly, she, the former mistress of the King. It was true, but, as she retched with seasickness, her breasts cried out for her baby who had been taken from her. Her darling little child was now being cared for by wet nurses: they surely could not love him as she loved him. It was all so hard to bear.

Henry had said that little Henry was his only son and would become a great Lord, and would have a fine life. He had to stay in London as he had royal blood and might even one day inherit the throne. In any case, as Henry had pointed out, the baby would not be safe in Wales, where, as the King's son, he was at risk from kidnap or worse.

Perhaps it was true, but why was Henry sending her away? Why could she not stay at Westminster? What did it matter that Henry had to make a dynastic marriage to some ugly Saxon matron: she and Henry loved one another. Why could they not carry on as before? Many a King had a mistress. Edith could sit next to him on the throne, but surely she, Nest, could remain in his bed. But, it was no good going over all that again: she must pull herself together.

'My Lady, the land of Penfro is in sight. I can see an island and breaking seas, and behind it the cliffs of the mainland.'

Helped by Gelert, Nest emerged from the little cubby-hole that the

76

Captain had lent her, his own cabin, and steadying herself on the starboard gunwale, she saw her new home. The ship still rolled in the following wind, and a wild sky promised a change in the weather, but there it was, the land of Penfro.

Near at hand, the cliffs of a high rocky island enclosed a beach, where powerful rollers crashed onto the shore. Beyond the waters of a swirling Sound, was the mainland with more cliffs and bays, forests stretching into the distance, and far away, beyond that, misty mountains. Despite herself, Nest was interested. Never before had she seen such a beautiful place.

Soon the ship was approaching a headland, where a proud flag strained in the strengthening wind. The sea was wild and confused now, and the Raven rolled and plunged, the girls having to cling to the rail to avoid being thrown overboard. Nest found that the Captain had appeared at her side.

'Saving your presence, my Lady, is it not a fine sight to see the King's flag set in so remote a place? Your future husband is said to be a good soldier and skilful governor, to be able to control such a land so far from civilisation.'

'Good Captain, you obviously mean well, but I should remind you that my people were civilised and Christian while the Normans were still pagan barbarians in the northern mists.'

'Forgive me, my Lady, I am a Saxon myself and, sadly, have grown to accept that our Norman masters are at the peak of all things civilised.'

'I confess that we have all learned to guard our tongues, Saxon and Welshman, but tell me Captain, what manner of man is this Gerald that I am to marry on the King's orders? I would be glad of some advance information,' said Nest wryly. 'Please speak freely, as an honest view is important to me.'

'I have met him several times, my Lady. The Raven has occasionally been sent with supplies when Gerald's own ship has been out of action. I would say that he is a stern, yet fair, man. It is said that he ordered the hanging of fifteen Norman knights when they would have betrayed him to your father, King Rhys ap Tewdwr. Yet he wept when he saw it done. He is a man of learning and has many books. He seldom smiles, yet he is kind to his men.'

'When he is not hanging them,' added Nest grimly.

'You put me in some difficulty, my Lady. I try only to help you as you asked me to be frank. Either Gerald or his Overlord, Arnulf de Montgomery, would put me in Pembroke Dungeon if you breathed a word against me. I would be wise to keep my own counsel.'

'Fear not, good Captain, your words are very helpful to me, and I swear they will go no further. Now, on a more delicate matter, tell me are there any ladies in his life, this stern, yet caring Gerald? Has he ever been married?'

'Some say he loved a lady once, and he would have married her, but his father, the Royal Constable of Windsor, objected to the match and persuaded the King to send him down here to prevent him from wooing the lady.'

'Poor Gerald,' said Nest. 'Is he a living the life of a monk then? The King told me that he is now thirty-three.' The Captain looked uncomfortable.

'Speak freely,' urged Nest. 'I see there is something that I should know.'

'They say that he has a woman, a concubine, who has borne him two children.'

'Oh!' exclaimed Nest, aghast. 'Will this woman be there when I arrive?'

'I know not, my Lady. She does not appear with him in public.'

Nest and Bethan exchanged glances, wondering what Nest's new life would be like. Perhaps Gerald might not want to send this woman away, especially if she had borne him children.

Further speculation was postponed, by Gelert pointing out to her that the Raven was entering a wide estuary. Nest could see that the entrance to the estuary was about two miles wide and running inland in a west to east direction with two craggy islands close to the southern shore. The northern shore seemed to be wild and rocky. The wind was now more or less directly ahead so the captain called the crew on deck to take down the sail and to start rowing.

The tide was making strongly up the estuary and Nest could see that the ship was speeding past the land despite the slackening headwind. As the estuary narrowed, they passed men fishing from anchored boats, surrounded by swooping gulls. The fishermen waved to the sailors on the 'Raven', glad to see a King's ship maintaining a rare connection with the settled Norman lands further east.

'Are those my own people in the boats?' asked Nest.

'It is not likely my Lady. This land of Penfro is not like the rest of Wales. Most native Welsh people were driven out after your father's last attempt to regain this area from the Normans. For centuries the Vikings used this waterway as a winter resting place, and many of their people settled here, mingling and intermarrying with Irish and Welsh people. When Robert de Montgomery arrived and built Pembroke Castle seven years ago many Saxons and Normans arrived with him. The population of the area is very mixed. It can no longer be said to be truly Welsh. However, your people are still not far away, across the hills, perhaps waiting their chance to regain their lands.'

'Who is Robert de Montgomery? I thought Arnulf to be Gerald's Overlord?'

'Indeed,' replied the Captain, 'Robert built the fort and then handed over to his younger brother, Arnulf. However, there is not much difference. I have heard it said that the Montgomerys are a savage breed; five wicked sons born of a wicked mother. It is whispered in the taverns that our Lord the King should watch the doings of the Montgomerys very carefully.'

'You have been informative to the point of rashness,' said Nest, rather surprised at such dangerous views so freely expressed.

'My Lady, do you think I would venture such opinions to you if someone very powerful, and who cares for you, had not asked me to. That someone also cares for your new husband and wishes you to guide him in the right direction when he is put to the test.'

'Could you tell me who this powerful person is?' breathed Nest.

'That I cannot do,' said the Captain, 'but, be assured, he has your best interest, and that of Gerald, very much at heart.'

Nest was now feeling very confused. Not only was she about to meet a man she had been ordered to marry, but she now had learned that that man might be in danger if he followed too slavishly the orders of his Overlord. This was all in addition to the uncomfortable fact that her new husband held sway over lands seized from her father, and her own Welsh people were waiting in the hills to regain it, now that she no longer remained in Westminster as hostage for their good behaviour. Henry had put her into an almost impossible situation.

'The Raven' was now turning to enter a much smaller tributary leading inland to the right. Many trees lined the muddy banks. The steersman was having difficulty in following the twisting channel, marked by withies, and was guided by a sailor standing in the bows. The Captain started to shout at the crew, ordering them to prepare mooring ropes and fenders for their imminent arrival at Pembroke.

Nest began to feel nervous. How could she possibly marry a man she had never met? The very thought of it made her stomach churn. What would happen to her if she refused to go through with it? She still loved Henry, that Henry who was forcing her to marry another man.

The quay had come in sight together with a stout wooden fort set on a cliff overlooking the landing place. A small crowd was waiting. As the quay came nearer, Nest could see a tall, impressive-looking man, obviously a noble, waiting with his Knights and several Ladies.

'My Lady,' whispered Bethan, 'that must be him, Gerald, your future husband.'

BOOK TWO

NEST AND GERALD

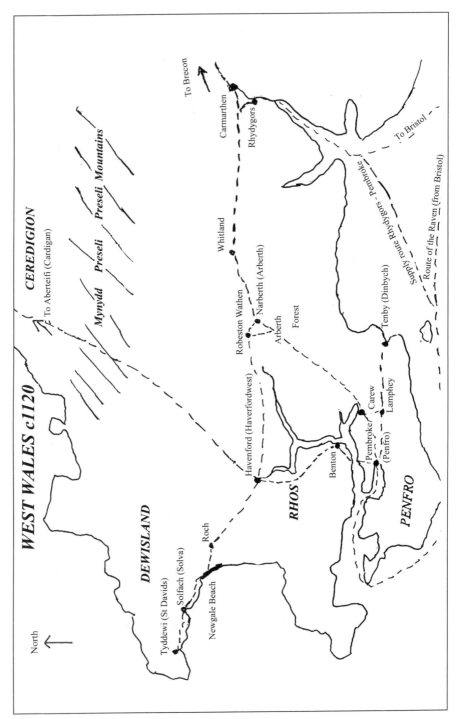

chapter seventeen

Nest meets Gerald,
October, AD 1100

The next few minutes seemed to Nest to be one confused whirl. One minute she was quietly waiting for the ship to be properly secured alongside the quay, the people ashore still a mass of unknown faces, and the next she found herself being swept up the gangplank to the man on the shore.

For a second, before he was close enough to greet her, she had time for a quick glance. In that brief moment she saw that he was of medium build and broad-shouldered and had short, mousy hair, cut in the Norman style. She found that she shared the same impression as the Captain, that he was serious and rather grave. Above all, he was a man in authority, a leader of men. How shall I ever be able to relate to him she thought? Her heart sank. Now he was holding out his hand to her, the other still resting on the hilt of his sword.

'Welcome to Pembroke. I hope you travelled well.' His grave grey eyes assessed her calmly, much as she supposed he would receive a new knight joining his garrison. Turning to the ship's captain, who had walked up beside her, he said, 'welcome to you too, Captain. I trust you had no trouble from Irish pirates on this voyage?'

Nest thought she had better speak up promptly or Gerald and the Captain would start up a cosy conversation about ships and the sea, cutting her out completely.

'Thank you for your greeting sir. I confess that I have not travelled by ship before, so it was a very unusual experience for me. However, I was well looked after by my two servants, and our good Captain, whom I believe you already know, was kindness itself, giving me his own cabin. Where he had to sleep, I fear to think.'

'Good, good! Let me introduce my senior knight, Sir Gilbert de Hoda, and his Lady.'

Nest was aware of a tall, very handsome young man in his late twenties, taking her hand and giving her a broad smile. She felt that she had always known him. His stocky wife curtsied to her but did not smile.

Nest was aware that the other people on the quay were now crowding round, male and female, all curious to meet the woman who was to marry their Lord on the morrow, and who might become very important in their lives. Afterwards, she could not remember all the new men and women whom she had met, and hoped she would get a second chance to learn their names.

Once all the confusing introductions had been made, Gerald offered her his arm, and led the whole party up a steep ramp, through a portcullis and into the fort. On the way he kept up a continuous commentary on the progress of the construction work, rather as if she were a visiting dignitary from another area.

'There was only a wooden stockade at first. It did the trick during the first siege by King Rhys ap Tewdwr.'

'My father, Sir!'

'Yes, yes, had to be done, had to be done, but a close thing! After that, everything was strengthened and the area within the walls extended, so as to provide more space for accommodation and for keeping animals. Now, this is the new portcullis, which I am quite pleased with.'

Nest found her attention drifting a little. Was this the man who would be sharing a bed with her tomorrow night - and, for the rest of her life? It all seemed so unreal.

The party had now reached a small house near the centre of the compound.

'This building is the living quarters of my liege Lord, Arnulf de Montgomery, when he makes his occasional visits here. He is not here at present so it is available for you and your servants tonight.' Waving away the rest of the party, he said, 'I will see you all at supper. In the meantime, I will have a private word about the arrangements with Princess Nesta.'

He showed her into what he described as the solar.* It was a fairly basic room compared to the wonders she had experienced at Westminster. Skins covered the two windows, as glass had not yet reached Pembroke. There was a large good bed and two chairs, and a rug on the floor.

'What a lovely room,' said Nest, anxious to bring some warmth into their discussion. 'Are you going to sit down and tell me about everything? Bethan and Gelert can go and make themselves at home.'

When the servants had gone, Gerald perched himself on a chair, and began to attack the problem of their marriage in the same resolute way he would tackle a rather difficult defensive position held by an enemy.

'Regarding our marriage, I fear that I must make clear that the match has been forced on me by my father, and ultimately by the King. It was not of my choosing any more than, I presume, it was of yours. I understand that you have had a close relationship with the King, and that has now cooled.'

'I am sorry, Sir, that the marriage is distasteful to you. It is no more welcome to me, and Henry has retained our child in London. I do not know how we are to proceed now, if you are set against it.'

'We will have to get married. It is not possible to oppose the direct instructions of the King. If you refuse, he will have you locked up in a nunnery. If I refused, I would be stripped of my position at the very least. If we were an ordinary pair, without previous relationships, we might find that

---

* *Solar the room occupied by the Lord and his family, usually providing much better accommodation than any other room in the Castle. Pembroke Castle at this date was mostly of wooden construction so the 'solar' would have been fairly basic.*

such an arranged marriage would be a happy one. Parents are often good judges of who will please their sons and daughters. You, however, no doubt still have deep feelings about your broken relationship with the King, while I ...

'Yes, Gerald, what is your situation? I presume I may call you Gerald, if we are after all to be married?' Nest interrupted.

'I have a concubine, a relationship of many years. We have two children whom I love deeply. I am not willing to put her away so as to tidy matters up for His Majesty's marriage to the sister of the King of Scotland.'

'What, then, are we to do? I will not tolerate a concubine trailed publicly before my nose. I would complain to Henry that I was not being treated with respect.'

'I suggest we have an arrangement. Tomorrow we will marry, as we must, but the marriage will be in name only. You will share my quarters as my wife, but not my bed. I will spend my nights with the mother of my children. You will be treated with respect as my wife, and my concubine will not be seen with me in public. It will be made clear to all that you are in full charge of my domestic arrangements, and I will be glad to consult you about any matters which concern you. It may be that at some time in the future, if the King so allows, we will be able to seek an annulment of the marriage and each marry whom we then choose.'

'I see you have thought long about the matter,' said Nest bitterly. 'I confess it was not what I hoped for when I came to Pembroke. I even hoped that one day we might grow to love one another, when I had put Henry behind me.'

'You are an intelligent and most beautiful woman, and I am sorry that fate has treated you so ill but I cannot ...

'You cannot accept another man's leftovers,' finished Nest sadly. 'I cannot truly blame you for that. Well, I have another solution. Please let me return to my own people, and then you will be free of me. You can tell the King that I refused the match when I arrived here, and that you had no wish to force me.'

'I fear, Nesta, that that cannot be. I have also received a letter from Count Robert de Meulan, setting out your situation.'

'My situation?'

'It seems the King wishes to free you from your position as hostage for the good behaviour of your people, but that is only made possible by a suitable marriage. I cannot let you return to Dinefwr. Your people might use you as a focus for another rising against Norman authority. Your brother, Gruffudd, still remains at liberty in Ireland and might at any time raise another army there to try to regain Deheubarth.'

'So nothing has changed. I am still a hostage in all but the name.'

'It is very difficult for both of us. However, I will do my best to ensure you are happy. My people here in Pembroke are in a great state of excitement about our wedding tomorrow, and we must not disappoint them. They have all heard of your beauty and, to them, it is a fairy tale romance, linking Norman with Welsh, which union they hope will bring permanent peace to this troubled land.'

'How very sad! I wish it could all be true. I will try to play my part to please them,' said Nest, 'but how am I to do so without a wedding gown, or my family?'

'Oh, yes,' said Gerald casually, 'I have invited a lady to help you get ready. She may be waiting outside.' Moving over to the door, he called someone in.

Nest could not believe what was happening. The woman who was moving towards her, her eyes streaming with joy, was her dear mother, whom she had not seen for seven years, and whom she had believed to be dead.

Nuptials at Pembroke
October 31st, AD 1100

The joy of being reunited with her mother was overwhelming. She had not realised what a huge hole in her life had been made when she was taken to London. Everyone else of her age had father, mother, brothers and sisters. For seven years she had believed she had lost everyone, except, far away, Gruffudd, exiled in Ireland, and poor, broken Cynan, whom she had not heard of since Gloucester. Now, while Gerald quietly withdrew, her mother took her in her arms, and she wept again for her slain father and brothers, for all the lonely years without her family and for the happiness of finding her mother again.

Gwladus was too happy to weep. 'For months after the battle I believed you dead, together with your dear father and your brothers. I stayed with our kinfolk in Dinefwr and grieved for our slaughtered family. Then one day, cariad, your old Uncle Trahaearn appeared at my door with delight all over his silly face. 'I have someone to see you,' he said and he stood aside to reveal a tall, heavily cloaked young stranger with an untrimmed beard. It was your brother, Gruffudd. He told me that he had fled to Ireland after the battle, and had been trying to raise an army to recover our lands. In the meantime he had smuggled himself into the country to find out for himself the state of things here. He told me that you had been captured by the Normans, together with Cynan and your maid. He later returned to Ireland, and I have had letters from him since. I did not know your fate at their hands until a Saxon trader, months later, told me that you were well established in the Norman Court in London.'

'It grieves my heart to tell you, Mother, that poor Cynan was cruelly mutilated by Robert Fitzhammon soon after the battle, and I do not know his fate since. I asked Prince Henry for news of him and he claimed to have made enquiries, but said that he had disappeared.'

'The poor boy has been safe with me these many years. The monks sheltered him until his shameful wounds were healed, and then he walked back here taking many weeks on the journey. He is at home now in Dinefwr. He will meet no one and occupies himself tending sheep on the mountainside. He tells me that he composes sad songs and sings them to the sheep. It is a poor life for him, but at least he is alive.'

'But mother, how did you come to be here? I still cannot believe that it is really true. It is so wonderful to have you with me for my wedding, even if it is not the wedding that I wanted. The King has ordered me to marry this grim, cold Gerald, even though he says he still loves me. He has kept our dear child with him in London and is now to marry the King of Scotland's sister.' Nest unburdened herself to her mother of the sad wreck that was now her life, and wept again for her baby son whom her mother might never see. When she was calmer, Gwladus tried to cheer her up, and to advise her.

'At least you are here, back near your own people in Cwmru, after all those lonely years among strangers. As for your love for the King, it seems to me that you are well rid of him if, as you say, he allowed his own brother to be murdered. Such a man cannot be natural. I grieve with you for my little grandson who has been taken from us. That is very hard to bear. There is always hope, however, that you will be allowed to visit him, and it is certain, when he is older, that he will insist on knowing his mother. I also realise that the King took advantage of your youth and vulnerability, but surely you would not have been content to remain the King's mistress? That is not a suitable role for you as a Princess of the proud Tewdwr family.'

'I loved him, mother, and believed that he would marry me.'

'So say many men when they want to get a maid between the sheets.'

'But what must I do now mother? I do not love this Gerald, and he does not love me. He has a concubine and two children already, and he tells me that he loves them and will marry me in name only, because the King has so ordered. I cannot bear it. It is all too much for me.'

Putting her arm around her daughter again Gwladus said, 'take heart, all is not yet lost. Have you never looked in the mirror, Nest? If you did you would surely see a remarkably beautiful woman. What man could resist you for long? I wager your marriage will be a real one before many days are past. We women know the ways of men, and to one such as you, Gerald will be putty in your hands.'

'But he is so stern and cold, and cares only for battles and power. I shall have no appeal to him.'

'I have had more time to study this man than you have, my daughter. It was he who sought me out as soon as he knew you were being sent here. He took the trouble to ride to Dinefwr to see me, and took some risk in doing so. He said his new wife would need her mother and showed concern for you. I think there is good in him, Norman though he is. To feel constancy to his woman is a sign of steadfast character. If we can make him fall in love with you, then to you he will be equally constant.'

Nest smiled, despite her sorrows. 'Then tell me, mother, how do 'we' propose to seduce this cold fish.'

'I will speak to a Wise Woman and she will give me something to help you.'

'I do not believe in such witchcraft, and anyway, I would like a man to love me truly for myself, not because he was bewitched.'

It was Gwladus' turn to smile. 'Oh Nest, how you do deceive yourself. We women create illusions all the time to make us more attractive. Do we not wear our best dress, adorn our hair and scent out bodies when we most wish to appeal? Do we not study ourselves in the mirror to see which of our profiles is the most attractive? The last thing we wish our desired man to see is the unadorned, real woman. Now enough of this idle gossip. You are to be married tomorrow. Let us see what I have brought with me to dress you for the wedding.'

The next few hours were spent very happily with mother and daughter rediscovering one another as they prepared for the wedding. It was wonderful for Nest to have the support of her mother. She realised how alone she had been for the last seven years, apart from Bethan, and she rejoiced in being part of a family again.

*Wedding Day, Pembroke,
November 1st, AD 1100*

It had been dark for many hours, and Nest, not being able to sleep, had decided to take a walk on the battlements with Bethan. It was a cold, clear night and the stars were burning in the heavens just as they had long ago when she was still a young girl at her father's hall.

The wedding had been beautiful. At noon the trumpets had been sounded from these same battlements, and Nest, adorned in all her bridal finery by her mother and Bethan, had walked on the arm of Sir Gilbert, who had agreed to give her away. They walked in procession out of the main gate of the castle and along the main street of the little town of Pembroke to the new church of St Nicholas, where Gerald was waiting for his new bride. The sun was shining, and the people cheered and shouted in greeting all along the route. Bethan and Gwladus held her train, and Sir Gilbert whispered that she was the most beautiful bride in the whole of Wales. It should have been perfect, but Nest knew that it was a mockery. As she stood with Gerald in front of the Bishop, ready to make her vows, Nest grieved that Henry was not standing there, making her his Queen, instead of Gerald, who did not want her.

After the ceremony, they had all processed back to the great hall of the castle, where the cooks had prepared an enormous feast to which everyone had been invited, high and low. The minstrels had sung of her beauty, and of the power and wisdom of her new husband. The food had been wonderful, and skilfully cooked. The knights and their ladies had crowded round Gerald and Nest to wish them 'every happiness', although Nest suspected that they all knew that the marriage would be in name only.

After the feast, Gerald had taken her back to his quarters, dismissed the servants and offered her a glass of wine. He plainly did not know what to say or do next. He looked so woebegone that suddenly Nest felt sorry for him.

She took the proffered cup of wine and perched on a stool. Gerald suddenly realised she looked breathtaking. He had never seen such a beautiful woman. When she had joined him in front of the Bishop and they had knelt together, the scent of her hair had captivated him, and when she made her responses to the Bishop her voice was lovely. Her smile, as she turned to look at him, was so penetrating, that he wished that it could have all been otherwise. Now, he was surprised to see that Nest was smiling at him.

'Poor Gerald,' she said teasingly. 'What a desperate situation for a man to be in; here in front of you is your new bride all ready to be bedded, and nearby, no doubt, your lady-love, also desperate to get you into her bed to be sure of you. What is a man to do? Being the upright person you are, you will have no doubt discussed your dilemma with the Bishop. He will have told you that you will have to bed me at least once or else the marriage will not be legal.'

'I see that you can already read me like a book. I have always dreamed of possessing a beautiful wife such as you, and now that I have one, my principles will not let me break my word to Myfanwy. I wish I had defied my father and married her long since, even though she is not of my class and station. I would not then be in this impossible situation.'

Nest rose from her chair and walked over to him, kissing him lightly on his cheek. Again, her nearness affected him powerfully. He had a strong urge to take her in his arms. No woman had ever unsettled him so much before.

'Dear Gerald,' she said softly. 'I do not hate you for your predicament. My mother tells me that the stars foretell that we will be lovers, one day. I am content to wait for that day to come. In the meantime, I shall not put pressure on you. I know you to be an honourable man who will find the right thing to do in your own way.'

When she had said this, she had felt brave. She was being the woman she wanted to be. She wanted Gerald to choose her of his own free will. Later in the dark, in her lonely room, she did not feel so brave. Perhaps she had made it too easy for Gerald. She had left his room without further ado. Perhaps her mother was right and she should use any method known to the wiles of woman to get her man.

Now, on the star-lit battlements, she wanted so much to be with a man who loved her, whom she could cherish knowing that he wanted only her. He would also have to be a soul mate with whom she could share her deepest thoughts. She longed to feel his arm around her and to share the magic of the night. She wanted to talk about the stars and whether they had any meaning for mankind. She sighed knowing how much she needed and how far she was from finding the answer to her dreams. Bethan did her best but was a poor substitute.

'My Lady, there is someone in the shadows following us. It cannot be the sentry because I saw him marching well ahead.' Both women turned to see who it was.

'It is a woman, Bethan. She is approaching as if to speak to us.'

'Forgive me Lady Nest, I do not mean to startle you, but I can bear to wait no longer, I am so sick at heart.' In the dim light of the stars Nest could see that the speaker was not of the Knightly class, nor yet meanly dressed. She was speaking in Welsh.

'Who are you, and what is it that distresses you so?'

To Nest's surprise it was Bethan who answered.

'My Lady, I see that it is my cousin Myfanwy, whom I have not seen for seven years.' Bethan made no move to embrace her cousin.

'Lady Nest, I do not wish to upset or disturb you in any way, and I do hope that you will forgive me for approaching you. I confess that I am that

Myfanwy who has borne two children by Gerald de Windsor. I am truly sorry to approach you, but I do not know what else to do.'

Bethan replied angrily to her cousin, 'you should leave my lady in peace, if you know what's good for you. She has much to bear without you thrusting yourself in her path. Go away and leave her be on her lonely wedding night.'

'Please, withdraw a little, Bethan. I will speak with your cousin since she wishes it, although I confess I had hoped that such a meeting could have been avoided.'

'Do not trust her, my Lady. She is a desperate woman, and although of my own kin, I would not see her alone with you.'

The woman Myfanwy now threw herself at Nest's feet, mouthing words almost incoherently.

'Please, go back to London, to your fine Norman friends. You are so beautiful you could have any man. You do not need to steal my Gerald whom I have loved and cared for these many years. Please sail away in your ship and leave me alone with my man and my children. I beg of you, please do not steal all I have. Please take pity lovely lady, you who could take your pick of London.' With this, Myfanwy burst into wild sobbing and wrapped her arms around Nest's knees.

Nest was becoming concerned how this distressing situation might be resolved.

'Please, calm yourself, Myfanwy. Please let me help you up so that we can talk peacefully together.'

Bethan could hear the sentry approaching, attracted by the commotion, and down below in the courtyard, Gerald had appeared at the door of his quarters, looking up to see what was going on.

Bethan took Myfanwy's arm, to try pull her away from her mistress, but the distraught woman leapt to her feet, snatched something from her belt and aimed it at Nest, narrowly missing her. Bethan seized Myfanwy round her waist from behind and tried to pull her away from Nest.

'My Lady, she has a knife. She means to kill you. Guard, guard, come quickly, this woman has gone crazy and will kill someone.'

'Leave me be, false cousin,' screamed Myfanwy, slashing wildly behind her trying to free herself.

'Run, my Lady, run for your life. She has gashed my arms and I can hold her no longer.'

Nest, at last realising her danger, tried to grab the knife, but Myfanwy, now free of Bethan, who had sunk to the ground clutching her arm, pushed Nest against the parapet wall and raised the knife for another attempt to thrust it into her rival. The sentry, who had now arrived, could see that the Princess was about to be stabbed by someone he assumed to be a marauder and, without hesitation, cut Myfanwy down with one sweep of his long sword.

'Stop! Stop!' shouted Gerald. 'What is this madness? Stop before more harm is done.

'Guard! Guard!'

chapter twenty

Baby Llinos was crying in the next room and Nest could hear her four-year old brother John trying to console her. Nest lay listening to the little boy and desperately wanted to go to them. A new girl, Bronwen, had been taken on as Nanny after the children's mother had died, but she did not seem to relate to the children very well. Because Nest had in effect lost her own son she was doubly sensitive to the needs of Gerald's children.

Where was Bronwen? Was she still asleep, or had she left the children's bedroom for some reason? Nest decided that, if the girl did not return soon, she would have to go to them, even if Gerald disapproved.

Nest could hardly bear to think of the events of that terrible night, a month ago, when the sentry had killed Myfanwy. She had been lucky to survive such an unexpected attack by a deranged woman. If the sentry had not been so close it would have been she, Nest, who would have been buried next day. Gerald had run to Myfanwy, in the desperate hope that she could be saved, but she had died in his arms almost at once.

'My poor love, it is my fault. I should not have let you be so tested. It was all too much to ask of you,' he had sobbed.

Nest was distraught to be the catalyst of such a tragedy.

'I am so very sorry. I should not have talked to her. I should have withdrawn at once when she tried to approach me. I must go to Bethan, who I believe is bleeding badly.'

Gerald ordered two of the numerous soldiers who had now arrived to carry Bethan to the guardroom so that her wounds could be dressed.

'Brave Bethan, you did very well to guard your mistress thus.'

Gerald had then ordered the guards to carry Myfanwy's body to the chapel and sent word that Wise Women be fetched to lay out the body.

'See that she is cleansed of her wound and dressed in her finest things and laid in the chapel.'

Turning to the terrified sentry, who had been disarmed and was now held at sword point by the Captain of the Guard, he said, 'you have taken the life of the mother of my children. What have you to say in your defence?'

'My Lord, as I patrolled the battlements, I heard a violent argument and as I approached to investigate, my taper lit up the face of the Princess. At the same time, I saw a hooded figure and the glint of the knife that the figure aimed at her. I did not know it was a woman. I had only a second to decide what to do. I acted to save the Princess. I beg you to forgive me, my Lord. I did not know it was Myfanwy.'

'Soldier, remember that it takes but a moment to take a life, but we can never give it back. Go to the chapel and spend the night praying for the soul of my poor Myfanwy whose mind was tormented. Pray also for my two little children, and for me, that I am able to answer them when they ask for their mother.'

Turning to Nest he said, 'I shall also go to pray now. Do not blame yourself, Nest. I saw and heard the whole terrible incident. You could not know how fragile was the state of her mind. After giving birth to Llinos, her brain seemed affected. She did not want to hold her baby and spent hours weeping instead of being joyful. She was strange with me and with our son, John. At one time I nearly decided to prevent her going near the children. I had to find a wet nurse for Llinos as her mother could not bear to feed her.

'It took her many weeks for her to become anything like normal. I was told by the physician that he has seen cases like that before, and that it was, in his view, an illness which can only be cured by care and understanding. Some said that she was possessed by an evil spirit and that she should be sent away, but I knew her to be a good woman who had much love in her.'

After that things had been very difficult between Gerald and Nest, in some ways worse than before, because Nest now felt that there was now another barrier between them.

Baby Llinos continued to cry. Obviously, Bronwen was not there. Nest suspected that she may have slipped away to talk to one of the soldiers of the guard, so she wrapped herself warmly in her cloak and went into the children's room. Llinos was sitting up in her cot, crying piteously, while four-year old John was trying his best to comfort her.

Nest gathered up Llinos in her arms and rocked her on her knee.

'Get back into bed, John, you have been a very good boy. Your father will be pleased with you when I tell him how grown up you are, looking after your baby sister.'

'She is crying for Mummy. She has gone away. Llinos needs Mummy. Daddy said she has gone to Heaven. Will she come back soon Nest?'

Nest was overcome with compassion for the motherless children. She sat on the little boy's bed with the baby on her knee. Unknown to her, Gerald had slipped into the room and was hidden in the shadows.

'Your mummy loves you with all her heart, and one day she will be with you in Heaven.'

'But, why has she gone away if she loves us Nest?'

'Your poor mummy was tired, and very sick, and the Lord Jesus has taken her to his home in Heaven to make her better. I am going to ask your Daddy if I can be your mummy, because I love you and want to look after you. I can never be as good as your real mother but I will do my very best.' Tears pouring down her face, Nest hugged the poor orphans that she felt she had unwittingly deprived of their mother.

Llinos had now drifted off to sleep, and Nest gently put her back in her cot and tucked her in. Going back to John, she kissed him and said, 'sleep well little man. One day when you are grown up, you will be the best sort of man who is gentle to women and children, and who makes the world a better place for us all to live in.'

With one last glance, to make sure all was in order, Nest went back into her own room, and knelt to pray. She had many things to pray for, so she prayed aloud to make sure she did not forget anything.

'Lord God, please love and protect these dear helpless children who have lost their mother because of me. If it is your will, let Gerald take me as his true wife so that I may care for them and for him - he who is so stern and cold. Let him want me to love him and let me bring warmth, joy and love into his life so that he will want to make this harsh castle a better place. And, dear Lord God, please help my own baby, who has been taken from me and who is now in the care of others. Let them care for him and love him, and, if it is your will, one day let him be restored to me.'

Nest had intended to go on to pray for Henry the King and for her dead father and brothers, but she broke down and crept into bed sobbing, smothering her anguish with the covers so as not to wake the sleeping children. As she tried to calm down and compose herself for sleep, her bed creaked. Someone was getting in beside her. She thought it was John, but it was not. Strong arms wrapped themselves round her and were pulling her close.

'You sweet girl, you shall not suffer more. I am so lucky that you have come into my life. Please let us be married properly. I know I will be a better man because of you. You are right. I know how to be brave, stern and just, but I long to be compassionate, loving and an inspiration to those who serve me. My children love you and need a mother. Please, let us put all the problems and sorrows of the past behind us. I promise to try to be the loving, caring husband that you so richly deserve.'

Nest turned to give herself to him. 'My love, I need you so much. I am glad you want me. God has answered my prayers.'

96

chapter twenty-one

Nest was happier than she had ever been. Once Myfanwy's funeral was over, Gerald had seemed to relax and had become almost a different person. And now, for the first time, a man was making her the centre of his life, and taking every opportunity to find what made her happy.

Of course, his public role was the same. As Constable of Pembroke he wielded life or death powers over thousands of people. However, Nest began to discern that increasingly he seemed to use persuasion more than force, inspiration more than compulsion. He often consulted her about difficult decisions, especially those concerning her own people the Cwmry, who still lived over the hills to the North and East. In these more peaceful times, some came each week to the market at Pembroke and to markets at the new towns of Arberth and Havenford. This latter was a new settlement growing at the lowest crossing point of the great estuary of the Daugleddau, whose many tributaries included the Pembroke River, on whose banks was Pembroke itself.

Gerald and Nest soon became fast friends as well as lovers, and took great trouble with each other, seeking to find out exactly how each felt about every aspect of life. To the amazement of his Knights, Gerald often now asked them to deputise for him in roles that he had previously guarded jealously for himself, while he took long walks with Nest along the river bank, or went browsing with her among the stalls at the Wednesday market. Their obvious, deep interest in each other was a source of much comment both in the Castle and the town.

'She is making a rod for her own back,' said one old wife to another. 'She will learn that it does not do to tell them more than they need to know.'

'That is true,' said the other. 'Did I not rue the day I let slip to my man that sometimes I had a little nap after I had seen him off to the fields. He's never let me forget it, and always makes sure I have twice as much to do now while he is away. Tell them nothing they do not need to know, I say.'

Within the Castle comments took a different track.

'It will look very ill if Arnulf de Montgomery rolls up for a surprise visit while the loving pair are off strolling by the river,' said one concerned Knight.

'Yes, and I wager he has gone so soft on her, that if the Welsh Army arrives at the gates, he will dreamily invite them all in for a flagon of ale,' replied his wife, a little miffed that no man had ever gone dreamy about her.

Nest had immediately taken to John and Llinos, and she found that it did not seem to matter to her that they were not her own flesh and blood: having had her own son taken from her she had a deep need to satisfy. They too, responded to her quite easily. Of course they missed their real mother, but because of her mental condition she had often been either withdrawn or else over-critical with them. Nest, on the other hand was consistently loving and supportive.

Gerald was of necessity often away visiting his domains. He sometimes took Nest and the children, but of course that was not always wise or desirable, so Nest had plenty of time to spend with them. The children's nanny, Bronwen, had been replaced by Bethan, and she soon became so completely besotted, that they found they could twist her round their little fingers - in the nicest possible way!

One of the happiest times for Nest was when the children were tucked up in bed, and Gerald took her out onto the battlements to look at the stars. Gerald's father, Gerald Fitzother, now Constable of Windsor, was a well educated man, and had made sure that his son had a wide ranging education and a deep curiosity about both the Earth and the Heavens. Nest too, had learned much from Henry, who had had many theories about the stars and the planets. On a cold, starry night, Nest would cuddle up to Gerald on the walkway and he would wrap her to him with his thick cloak. Then they would happily try to work out the meaning of the orbs of light in the firmament.

'When I was a child, I thought that the sky was a great black curtain concealing the bright light of Heaven, and that God had left hundreds of little holes in the curtain so that we could guess at the wonder of life with Him.'

'I did not get much chance to invent my own ideas,' said Gerald, stroking her hair, as my father took a keen interest in the Heavens and told me the names of the stars and planets. He said they were different sized discs set in the firmament and, like mirrors, they reflected the light of the Sun. He showed me Sothis, the North Star, which guided his ancestors, the Vikings, on their great voyages.'

'I know that you do not like me to talk of my life with Henry, and I promise I will not dwell on the subject. However, he did tell me that the fixed stars were all set in place on a great spherical firmament, and that they all revolved together round our Earth, and that the planets like Venus and Mars moved somehow on different spheres.'*

'You are right,' said Gerald, lightly smacking her bottom. 'I want to forget about when you were with Henry. I dread he will one day come here on a visit, and claim you again for a few nights. I also worry that he was a better lover than I am?'

Nest turned to look up at him, and put her arms round his neck. 'I am yours Gerald, and perfectly content. I would never, never agree to go to him again, whatever pressure he put on me.'

Gerald pulled her to him and kissed her gently. 'Let us go to bed now. It is cold here and I need to warm you.' He wanted her to confirm that she was truly his now and that her past with Henry had little relevance.

After they had made love, Nest snuggled up to him and began to talk about the arrangements for Christmas.

'My love, I hope you think that I am learning some of my wifely duties satisfactorily. For example, you have made no complaint of my behaviour in bed.'

'Nor shall I, you can be sure of that!'

'And I try to be a good companion.'

'No complaints in that direction either.' He nibbled her ear. 'But, where is all this leading?' Gerald sat up in bed.

'I have not the least idea how to run the domestic side of a castle and, what is really scaring me, I cannot begin to imagine how I am to organise the Christmas feast.'

Especially now that Arnulf de Montgomery will be joining us!' Gerald added teasingly.

Nest started to tickle him and rain him with mock blows. 'You beast, how can you be so cruel, even if you jest. You are jesting are you not, you monster?'

Gerald became serious. 'I fear not. The messenger, who arrived yesterday, not only brought general news, but also said that our Liege Lord will be with us for Christmas. I did not like to break the spell that I feel exists between us.'

'Whatever shall I do?' she wailed. 'I have never been so afraid in my life. The arrangements will be a disaster and it will reflect on you, my darling.'

Gerald was amused. 'Can it be, that the little spitfire who spat in the face of Robert Fitzhammon and who dared publicly to correct William Rufus, can take fright at arranging some food? Look, it is not so difficult! How do you think matters have been arranged until now? The meals arrive on time, and I

* *The Ancient Greeks had far more accurate ideas about astronomy than had the people of Gerald and Nest's time. The Arabs developed these theories further, in their great Observatories at Damascus and Baghdad. But that knowledge, such as the Sun being the centre of our Solar System with the planets including the Earth orbiting round (the Earth being a sphere), was lost to the West until the Sixteenth Century. People in Western Europe thought that the Earth was the centre of the Universe, and in any case the World was flat. They thought that a great ocean surrounded the continental land mass and if you sailed too far you would soon encounter monstrous sea monsters and eventually fall over the edge of the world to your death. There was little interest in the heavens except for the study of Astrology. Even the great supernova which became the brightest light in the night sky for a few weeks in the mid-eleventh century, was completely overlooked in the West, while the Chinese and Arab astronomers took careful note of it. However, the astrologers viewed the arrival of Halley's Comet in the night sky as a bad omen for Harold, before the Battle of Hastings.*

think you will grant they are well cooked? I have a servant, Rollo, and he acts as my major domo. I just tell him my general ideas and then largely leave it to him.'

'Oh,' said Nest, relaxing a trifle, 'but, do you think he will take kindly to a woman giving him orders?'

'It is just a matter of diplomacy. Surely a young woman with your looks should be able to get on with an ugly, middle-aged servant. Anyway, do not worry about it. You shall meet Rollo tomorrow. As for Arnulf, I confess that I am not very keen on him myself. He gave me my position here as Constable and of course I owe him my gratitude for that. However, he is not the type of Norman that I admire and I fear that eventually I shall come into conflict with him over some matter of principle.'

'I know that Arnulf's brother, Robert, is Earl of Shrewsbury, but I do not know much more than that.'

Gerald's voice became more serious, and he spoke very quietly so that there was no fear of being overheard.

'There are actually five brothers, and I think I do not exaggerate when I say that they are all extremely violent, ruthless and cruel. In fact they are proud of it, and were brought up to it by their appalling mother.

Fortunately, Arnulf has mostly given me a free hand here in Pembroke, so he and I are not often together and we have fewer chances of disagreeing. However, I have witnessed dreadful cruelties at his hands against your own people, the Cymry. I have often tried to improve matters after his departure, but my conscience has been very troubled, and I am seeking a way to leave his service.'

'But this is dreadful, Gerald. Are you saying that when he comes, he may commit some cruel act against my people and I am supposed to keep quiet?' Nest saw suddenly that the wonderful start to their marriage might soon be turning into a nightmare.

'My darling, I believe in justice and compassion and will do my best to rule here fairly. We are together in that. Just try not to oppose him. Leave it to me. His visit will be short; let us hope that all the feasting and merrymaking will divert his attention from other matters.'

chapter twenty-two

Arnulf arrives at Pembroke
Christmas, AD 1100

The sound of distant trumpets alerted Nest, and everyone else, to the imminent arrival of Arnulf. He had not been expected until the morrow. She felt a moment of panic. Supposing he were critical of the feast, or spoke roughly to her. Before she was married to Gerald she would not have cared: she would have remembered who she was, and defended herself vigorously. Now that she had a husband to think about, she had to be concerned that her actions or words might have an adverse effect on him.

He seemed to read her mind. 'Do not worry my love, just come with me to meet him. You have met much greater men before, this one should be easy after William Rufus. After we have received his party, just go as soon as you can to Rollo to make sure everything is ready for a meal. Arnulf is always hungry after a journey. I am sure all will go well.'

The gates were thrown open, the Earl of Shrewsbury's standard was raised on the flag pole on top of the tower, a line of trumpeters on the ramparts prepared a fanfare and everyone, except the soldiers on guard, rushed to receive Arnulf's party just inside the gate.

As Gerald and Nest waited, surrounded by the Knights and their Ladies, Nest could not help remembering what it was like when she herself arrived only a few weeks ago, and saw Gerald waiting, as now, surrounded by his entourage. It seemed so long ago. How vulnerable and alone she had felt. She took his arm and squeezed it. He turned and gave her a friendly smile: she was not alone now.

'He certainly has style,' Gerald whispered, as Arnulf's party, led by a standard bearer, broke into a gallop for the final approach to the Castle. The net effect was of violence and confusion as rearing horses were pulled up in the narrow confines of the castle yard with some of the crowd having to retreat for their lives amongst the dust and plunging steeds.

'I would call it reckless showing off,' Nest whispered back very softly.

One of Gerald's syces managed to seize the halter of Arnulf's horse, and he immediately swung himself down squarely in front of Gerald.

'Didn't expect me today, did you Gerald? 'Always keep people on their toes', that was my noble father's advice.'

'Greetings, my Lord, welcome to Pembroke. I hope you would always find the Castle ready, either to repulse the Welsh, or to provide hospitality to yourself. I trust you had a good journey.'

'Indeed I did, Gerald, and I have brought some interesting human booty with me. However, I hear you have got married. Congratulations! Perhaps you will introduce me to your wife?'

Nest now felt Arnulf's gaze upon her. As he took her hand she found

101

herself looking at someone who was just as Gerald had described him: hard, violent, and cruel. She felt she could add to that - proud, arrogant, and highly sexed. She took her hand away as soon as possible. The man made her flesh creep.

'Very attractive, Gerald, you have done well for yourself. Charmed to meet you, my dear! Pity you are Welsh though. You might have some adjustment to do here, on a frontier station. We sometimes have to ride your people hard, very hard. Cope with that, can you?'

'I know how to support my husband, Lord Arnulf,' replied Nest diplomatically, repressing her longing to lash back at him. Why did he remind her so much of Robert Fitzhammon?

'Better watch this one, eh, Gerald! With those looks half your knights will be wishing to cuckold you.'

Nest responded to this crudity by hugging Gerald and striving to keep her temper.

'I love my husband, Lord Arnulf, and I have no desire to look elsewhere. I am sure he will know how to protect me against unwanted attentions.'

The main body of Arnulf's force had now arrived. Nest thought she glimpsed two or more prisoners tied to their horses. She thought they had halters round their necks. She also thought that they were probably Welsh. 'Please God let Gerald and I have time to love in peace. Please let this nightmare go away,' she prayed silently.

'Well Princess, I hope you have provided some meat and good cheer after our journey. I would like to swill some of the dust from my hands and then go straight to the hall to eat.'

'I am told that your food is ready, Lord Arnulf. You can eat at once, if that is what you want.'

'I can provide some sport for you and your Knights after dinner, Gerald. Yesterday we caught two Cwmry behaving very suspiciously in the area of Brecheiniog. We shall have to toast their feet in the fire in the Great Hall, to see if they know anything about a certain Welsh Prince, who might be back in the area from Ireland to stir up trouble for us.'

'Are you referring to my brother, Prince Gruffudd?' asked Nest very quietly.

'Yes, Princess. Difficult is it not, now you are married to one of us. We will all have to hope that our little sport after dinner leaves your family in the clear.'

'My Lord, I really must protest that this is very distressing to my wife.'

'I am surprised you are so concerned. This will be an opportunity for her to show where her true loyalties lie. We Normans, need strong, loyal wives who know how to back us to the hilt. I am sure Princess Nesta will be able to give that level of commitment if needed. Now, let us all go in to meat.'

The feast, for that is what it developed into, soon became drunken and noisy. Nest noticed that Gerald became very free with his wine, making particularly sure that Arnulf was well supplied, being seated next to him. While Arnulf's attention was elsewhere, Gerald whispered to Nest that he hoped to divert him from torturing his Welsh prisoners, by getting him drunk. Nest smiled her thanks. He seemed to know that she was anxious and worried. It seemed that her new, wonderful relationship with Gerald was going to be put under test too much, too soon.

Rollo had certainly seen to it that there was plenty to eat and drink. Nest was just beginning to relax about Arnulf's threat to torture the prisoners, when he suddenly lurched drunkenly to his feet shouting for one of his Knights.

'Sir Guy, Sir Guy! Where in God's name are you? Get yourself here if you know what is good for you!'

The unfortunate Knight, prodded by his neighbours, staggered from his bench, avoided with difficulty some prone men nearby, and rolled over to his Lord.

'Bring in the prisoners, Sir Guy, and get some branding irons sent in so that we can entertain ourselves a little.'

Nest got to her feet. She knew she could not stand by, seeing her own people tortured. Yet, nor could she humiliate Gerald. For the first time in her life she took the easy option.

'Madam, I gave you no leave to part from us. The evening is yet young and I am looking forward to a little sport, and part of it will be seeing your reaction to it.'

Gerald now tried to save the situation. 'My Lord, as you know, I have young children, and they do not settle at night until my wife tells them some story of chivalry and valour followed by hearing their prayers. I would be grateful if you would give my wife leave to go about her duties.'

'Gerald, I will not be gainsaid. Sit down Princess, and observe our entertainment. I am sure that, for this once, the children's nurse can care for them?'

At this delicate point, Sir Guy hurried into the hall, followed by several guards.

'My Lord, the prisoners have escaped from their cell. I took the liberty of calling out the Guard, but I fear the prisoners will get away unless we take stronger action.'

When eventually the drunken hue and cry to recapture the escaped Welshmen had failed to find them, Arnulf had flown into a wild rage. He had seized the unfortunate Sir Guy by the throat and, using his immense strength, lifted him off the ground, and held him there.

'Someone in this castle knows how they escaped, Sir Guy, and when I find that man or woman, I shall find a very nasty way for them to die.'

Gerald had tried to defuse the situation before the stricken Knight choked to death or his neck was broken.

'I have despatched three mounted search parties, My Lord, and I do not think the men will have got far on foot. I would vouch personally for Sir Guy's loyalty. I beg you to release him.'

The released Knight had slumped onto a bench while Arnulf had bellowed in frustrated anger.

'Watch that shapely Welsh wife of yours. Make sure she knows where her loyalties lie. She was with us at table or I would be asking her some questions.' Arnulf had punctuated each furious accusation with a deep swig from a flagon. The effect had soon taken its toll, and he had tottered off to bed, supported by a manservant.

Later in the privacy of their bed, Nest and Gerald went over the events since Arnulf's arrival.

'You have been amazing today, my love, dealing with Arnulf. I was sure you would have not been able to stop yourself telling him some truths.'

'He is a cruel, foul man, Gerald. You did not exaggerate the base depths of his character. I do not know what I would have done if he had started to torture my people. I could not have sat there and let him do it, and what trouble that would have caused for you! How fortunate that they escaped.'

'You have now seen the true nature of the man who is my Liege Lord. As I said, I would dearly love to leave his service, but it is not so easy in such a remote place where we are continually in danger of attack. Some time ago I sent a private letter to my father, who is the Constable of Windsor, asking him to use his influence with the King to find me another position. I hope the letter did not fall into the wrong hands.'

'But how did those men escape, Gerald? I feel that there is something I do not know. You seem very relaxed about it?'

'There is an astute brain in that very pretty head of yours, my love. Poor Sir Guy allowed himself to take the blame for the escape, and nearly got his neck broken.'

'Arnulf must draw his strength from the Devil himself to lift a fully grown man in that manner.'

'Indeed, he is cruelty and strength combined. I long ago realised that at all costs I must prevent Arnulf provoking your people to a revolt by mindless cruelty. You are not only the most wonderful, lovely friend and wife a man could hope for, but in addition I see now, that our marriage, Norman to Cymro, is a way that, with firm and just government, all the people of this area may eventually meld together in peaceful prosperity. In fact, my love, I was very clever to marry you.'

'Beast!' she whispered, as she gently bit his ear. 'Anyway, Beast, you will now have to pay a price for all your cleverness. In fact,' she continued, as she climbed on top of him and started to kiss his neck and shoulders, 'I shall so rouse and torment you that goodness knows what beastliness I shall conjure out of you. However,' she demanded, as her kisses progressed further down his body, 'how did you prevent Arnulf playing with his nasty toys?'

'I asked Sir Gilbert to withdraw the guard from the area of the cell, and the nearby battlements, and I sent Gelert with the key and a rope. Now enough of this talk. I feel my beastliness welling up strongly and it must be given its head.'

Nest allowed herself to be rolled onto her back, and Gerald was just starting to caress and kiss her when there was a loud knock at the door.

'My Lord, come quickly! Lord Arnulf is up again and demanding that you attend him.'

'May Lord Arnulf fall in the moat,' answered Gerald under his breath.

'Speak louder, my love. I did not hear you clearly,' giggled Nest.

'Lord Gerald, come quickly, I beg you,' shouted Sir Gilbert.

Arnulf, when Gerald at last reached him, was in a very drunken but less violent mood after his short sleep.

'Sorry to drag you from the honey pot, Gerald,' he smirked. 'I tried it myself with one of the maids but she pulled a knife on me and ran off. You are lucky to have found a friendly one here. I never have any trouble with the Saxon wenches, but these Welsh women are quite unpredictable.

'Anyway sit with me by the fire. I have matters of grave import to discuss with you. That nonsense with the Welsh captives quite took my mind away from my main purpose in coming here. Hey you, Rollo, fetch a flagon each here and be sharp about it, and then clear everyone out of the hall. Let them sleep elsewhere. I care not where, but make certain the Constable and I have complete privacy.'

Rollo called his kitchen servants and between them they woke the now comatose revellers and helped them out of the hall, only to deposit them in any available floor space in stairwell or corridor. Some unfortunates finished up on the chilly battlements. When the hall was finally empty, Arnulf took a further swig from his flagon and fixed Gerald with a calculating eye.

'Let me see if I have weighed you up aright, Gerald. It was we Montgomerys who advanced you and gave you the chance to prove your worth. You have done well here, I grant you. You fought the Welsh off when they besieged you, and you have established firm Norman control. I think well of you: you should go far in the service of my family.'

'I have sworn fealty to you, my Lord Arnulf, and I am grateful for my promotion. But I feel there must be some purpose in sending for me when everyone else is sleeping?'

'Indeed there is, but I must be sure of you. What I am about to say, is dangerous stuff, and must be kept very quiet. I will be plain with you; what would be your position if we Montgomerys were in dispute with the King?'

Gerald felt a chill grip his heart. This was indeed dangerous stuff. If, after the last question, Arnulf had any doubts about him, then for certain his life would be in danger. If however, he supported Arnulf and his family, then he would be deemed tarred with the same brush, after any rebellion which subsequently failed.

'What then of your Welsh wife, Gerald? You would have been wise to consult me before marrying her.'

'It is nought but the truth that I have grown to love her dearly. However, the King himself arranged the marriage, with my father. I had little say in it. But you know that already, my Lord, from my letters.'

'No one can force a man to marry, Gerald, not even the King. I am surprised you were so pliable.'

Normally a very straightforward man, Gerald had learned to use a modicum of guile in dealing with the Welsh, and this came to his rescue now, also, with Arnulf.

'You need have no fears for my wife, regarding the King. She hates him with a fury she finds hard to hide. She sees herself as a discarded mistress, and to crown all, Henry has deprived her of her child. But, if I may be so bold, my Lord, it would not be wise to torture or ill treat Welsh people within her knowledge, as that would stretch her loyalties. I know we have to be very firm with them on occasion, but our overall policy indicates that we should not test her too hard. I married her for her beauty, and because I knew that the people of Deheubarth would be more easily governed with her presence at my side.'

'Blah, blah! You married her because Henry wanted rid of her and told you to. However, she is here now, and could be useful. I will explain how in a minute. Very reluctantly, I take your point that I should not provoke her too much, although it grieves me to be too soft with the Welsh. Now listen well Gerald, and know very surely, that if a word of what I am about to say gets to the King, then you will be praying for death long before you die. Is that plain enough?' With his cruel mouth, angry eyes and exuding unstoppable force, Arnulf was pretty frightening.

'There is no need to threaten me, my Lord, I know where my loyalty lies.'

'Good, good! Now, listen well. My family, the Montgomerys, has never

106

accepted Henry Beauclerc's seizure of the throne. We regard him as a usurper, whose role in his brother Rufus's death must be more than a little suspect. The rightful King is now Robert who has been forcibly deprived of his succession to the throne of England. More than that, not to mince words, we Montgomerys have lands on both sides of the Channel. If Robert can be put on the throne then all our lands will be in the same kingdom. It is very hard to please two masters, as is the case at present. We propose to put matters to rights.'

'I realise that many Lords are in the same position as you, with estates in two countries, and many are not happy with the situation. Henry knows this of course, but he is now firmly on the throne. Surely, nothing can be done Lord Arnulf?'

'Clear your head of such compliance. Something must be done and will be done. We Montgomerys have powerful castles at Arundel, Shrewsbury, Bridgnorth, Tickhill and here at Pembroke. My brother Robert de Belesme, as Earl of Shrewsbury and head of our family, intends to arrange secret talks with the Welsh Princes and King Muirchertach of Munster. He has already gained the support of King Magnus of Norway, who keeps a powerful fleet in the Isle of Man. Duke Robert of Normandy is, of course, fully behind us.'

Gerald was shaken by the extent of the conspiracy, but managed not to show it.

'I am impressed by the advanced nature of your preparations, Lord Arnulf. You have managed to keep it very close. I had not any idea of it. However, how do you see my role in this enterprise?'

'I see you as my roving ambassador and negotiator. With the help of Princess Nesta, you can bribe the Welsh Princes to our side, promising the earth in land and treasure. Their role will be to harry the King's supporters in the North of England, aided by the King of Norway and his fleet. In addition, I shall send you to Ireland to enlist King Muirchertach. The way to his heart is to ask for his daughter's hand in marriage, for me. He would believe, then, that I would support him against the other Irish chiefs and warlords.'

'I assume then that your family's plan is to set up a Norman /Celtic/ Norse alliance against Henry's Norman/ Saxon Kingdom?'

'You have a good overall view, Gerald. I see that I have chosen my ambassador well. Your first task will be to return to your 'love-Nest'.' He laughed loudly at his own joke. 'Make sure of her support, because your second task will be to go, with her, to negotiate terms with the Welsh Princes, Cadwgan, Gruffudd, Iorworth and Meredydd.'

'I see the point of enlisting the support of the Welsh Princes but, knowing that, I cannot see the point earlier of wanting to toast your prisoners toes to get information about Gruffudd?'

'Just my jest, Gerald, to test your new wife a little. I actually wanted to find who had attacked our party yesterday. Just brigands I presume. I like a little sport over dinner, and it teaches a subject race their place. I hope you are not a yellow liver, Gerald. I need a man with a strong stomach for my enterprises.'

Thoroughly disturbed by this potentially mortal turn of events, Gerald returned to his room. A rather sleepy Nest seemed ready to resume the game of love where it had been interrupted two hours before. She soon found that Gerald had other things on his mind. As he explained the new and dangerous turn of events, Nest's very astute brain began to add missing pieces to the overall picture.

'I am not really surprised about all this, my love. When I took ship here, Captain Thomas warned me that Arnulf was already being talked about in the taverns as plotting against the King. He also counselled me to try and guide you in the loyal path. I asked him who had asked him to speak to me in this way, and he said only that it was someone very powerful, who cared for us both. It seems to me that we would be very unwise to side with Arnulf; Henry is very astute and cunning He must already know about the Montgomerys, and is ready to crush their rebellion. In any case, the whole family is loathsome and cruel. Henry, on the other hand, although he has rejected me, is a good King, who has brought order and stability. To act against him would be morally wrong.'

'I think we must be very careful. I, like you, loathe the Montgomerys, but he is my Liege Lord, and I am sworn to his service. I think you have overlooked that Arnulf has asked me to contact the Welsh Princes, including your brother Gruffudd, to form an alliance. They will be given land and power. Arnulf claims that he is on your people's side.'

'Who can trust such a one as Arnulf? He can promise anything and deny it all later when he wins. My love, you can see his real attitude to my people, when he proposed to torture innocent men who happened to be in his path.'

'My instincts tell me that you are right. Henry has the cunning to outwit such as louts as Arnulf. He will probably win any future conflict. However, we are here, in his service. It would be madness to oppose him openly. I suggest we appear to go along with his plans, but somehow send a message to Henry - perhaps via Captain Thomas - he is due here shortly on 'The Raven' - warning him of the imminence of the rebellion, and pledging our support for him.'

Having decided what they were going to do, they tried to resume the game of love. It was not a success and Nest tried not to remember what a very skilful lover Henry had been.

She told herself that she loved Gerald and what really mattered was that she was secure in his love and that this love was legitimised through marriage. She would find ways to teach Gerald very subtly how to please her more in bed. In the meantime there was a more pressing concern on her mind, the lunar cycle of her body. Fourteen moons had waned now since she had last fed baby Henry, her rhythms should have returned to normal by now. Could it be that she was pregnant again? Was this the moment to tell Gerald? Would the news be welcome?

chapter twenty-four

Pembroke Market
December, AD 1100

Nest was idly drifting round the stalls in the Saturday market with Bethan and Gelert. She had no specific purchases in mind, but she needed to escape from the Castle for a while. She found that the atmosphere there had changed completely since Arnulf's arrival. Normally it was a cheerful, busy place, everyone knowing what they had to do and happily getting on with it. Gerald did not tolerate idleness or inefficiency, but he was just and appreciative. Arnulf, on the other hand, was known to be violent, cruel and unpredictable, so everyone kept out of his way if they could, or kept their eyes down if they could not.

Only this morning, a nervous kitchen maid had dropped a pile of platters in the Great Hall when Arnulf had merely glanced at her, entirely due to nervousness, in Nest's opinion, and Arnulf had ordered her to be whipped. Perhaps she was the one who had managed to escape his drunken advances last night and Arnulf was getting even.

'Forgive me, my Lady,' ventured Bethan, 'but you do not seem yourself this morning. Are you well?'

'Do not pry, Bethan,' smiled Nest, 'you know me better than that. Let us ask the silent Gelert what is his opinion about my lack of conversation this morning?'

'I think that my Lady wishes that Lord Arnulf would go away.'

Nest looked around to make sure they were not being overheard.

'You both understand perfectly well that I do not find Lord Arnulf very congenial. I had hoped that he and his entourage would be departing soon, but I fear I am to be disappointed. In fact, it is we who will be departing.'

Both servants looked very surprised.

'We will be accompanying my husband on various visits shortly. I would have told you tonight but you may as well know now.'

'Where are we going, my Lady? This is quite a surprise?'

'I am afraid I cannot tell you. The matter is very secret and must not be talked about to the other servants. I do not know the details myself yet. You are to prepare for a journey of over two weeks, and we will be travelling on horseback. Both Lord Gerald and I will need some of our finer items of clothing as well as those suitable for travelling. A number of matters have suddenly arisen and they are causing me concern. That is why I am preoccupied.'

Bethan would have tried to elicit further clues, but at that moment Gelert spotted a man apparently staring at them from behind a fish stall. He did not look like a stallholder, and there was something unusual about him.

110

'I see him, my Lady,' said Bethan. Do you think that he is a spy, sent to follow us by Lord Arnulf?'

'Let us ignore him and move to the cake stall at the end of the row. I would like to buy something sweet to put Lord Arnulf in a better mood. We will then see whether the man is really following us. I have a strong feeling that I know him, despite his hood.'

As the two women were examining some rather unappealing dough cakes, they found that the man had moved up close behind them.

'Move back, give more room to the Princess,' cried Gelert, roughly pushing him away.

'Do you not know me Nest, and you too Bethan,' he said softly.

Both the young women gasped in surprise.

'It is you, Gruffudd,' whispered Nest amazed. 'It is wonderful to see you, brother, after so long, but surely you are in danger here? Take care not to attract attention to yourself. Why are you here? You can speak freely. Bethan you will remember from the old days, and Gelert has my complete trust.'

'It seems a lifetime since that young girl so bravely rolled off my horse to save me from the Normans, sister. Let us walk on slowly not to attract attention. Now, listen carefully, as I must not stay near you long. I am here because I am ready to bring an army from Ireland to recover our homeland, and I do not want you or yours hurt in the process. I want you to tell your husband that I am ready to spare his domains if he does not try too hard to oppose me from taking the rest of Deheubarth. I hear that he is a good man, Norman though he is, and after all he is your husband.'

'It is a strange coincidence that you have come to Pembroke now, brother, since I know that Arnulf de Montgomery has just instructed Gerald to try to make contact with you. He wishes to parley with you, but it must be in secret. Some of his knights might think it strange to see a Norman Lord in close discussion with a Welsh rebel Prince.'

'Can I trust him Nest? Are you sure it is not a trick to take me?'

'You can trust Gerald, brother. He is straight and true. However, Arnulf de Montgomery is at the castle at present, and he is a cat of a different colour. Do not take any risks with him. We must think of something quickly. I suggest that Gerald and I could come by boat to meet you, tonight, say one mile from the Castle. There are some fish traps near the riverbank. That would be a good place to meet.'

'That sounds a good plan. I will come with just one servant. Let us make it midnight. How many of you would there be in the boat?'

'Just Gelert here, Gerald and myself. You must believe that I will not allow anything to happen which might put you in danger, Gruffudd. I think we should part now. People are starting to notice our discussion. We'll see you at midnight. I am sure Gerald will accept the plan. He has some offer to put to you.'

Reluctantly, brother and sister separated. 'Perhaps we shall have a chance to catch up on each others news tonight, sister?'

Thrilled to have seen her brother after so many years, yet concerned for his safety, Nest returned to the Castle to tell Gerald the latest developments. She felt terribly confused about the different pressures on her loyalties and tried to work out her concerns in her mind. She knew that her first concern now must be for Gerald and the baby in her womb. Instinctively she felt that Gerald's best interest lay in loyalty to the King. Although Henry had sent her away from Court and kept her baby, Nest believed that Henry had wanted to marry her and had been dissuaded only by pressures of state. She thought he was a good King and she wanted to support him.

Her immediate reaction to Arnulf's planned treachery had been to advise Gerald to warn Henry of his plans. However, her dear brother was now confusing things. He wanted to regain his rightful inheritance in Deheubarth, and here was Arnulf offering him just that, in return for support in his rebellion against Henry. If she denounced Arnulf she might be putting Gruffudd at risk. She tried to think what was really right and what was wrong.

Suddenly she came to a decision. She stopped Bethan and Gelert in their tracks and sat them down on a wall a few minutes walk from the castle. In a few words she told them her dilemma and asked their advice. Perhaps their less sophisticated but honest minds would find the problem easier to solve.

Bethan was surprised, but pleased to be asked for advice. Of recent years Nest had rarely consulted her.

'I know nothing of concerns of state or the schemes of great Lords, my Lady, but I know that Lord Arnulf is a wicked man and anything that he wants to do is likely to be wicked too. Your husband is a good man, and it seems unfortunate for us all that he has to follow the orders of such as Lord Arnulf. I think your brother Prince Gruffudd would be wise not to trust too much in what Lord Arnulf may promise. Forgive me my Lady, I hope I have not spoken too freely.'

'Thank you, Bethan, you have spoken from the heart and I trust your judgement, as always. What do you think Gelert? Do you agree with Bethan?'

Gelert scratched his head. 'You know me, my Lady. I am but a simple man. Bethan is a lot sharper than I, so I would go along with what she says. One thing though! Prince Gruffudd has waited a long time to find an army. He says he has one now and I think he will want to come with it soon to claim his inheritance whatever other people may propose.'

Strangely strengthened by the words of her servants, Nest sought out Gerald and told him of the events of the afternoon, including discussion of her doubts with Bethan and Gelert.

'You have done well, my love. How amazing your brother has turned up just when I have to contact him. I shall not tell Arnulf about the meeting tonight until Gruffudd is safely away. Fortunately, Gilbert de Hoda is guard commander tonight with some of our own men. There should be no problem in leaving the castle without Arnulf's men being aware of it.'

At midnight it proved easy to leave Wogan's cavern by boat. Gilbert made sure there was no one from Arnulf's party still about, and soon Gerald and Nest were gliding silently out onto the river, rowed very gently by Gelert with muffled oars. Nest shivered and pulled her cloak more tightly round her. She thought it a great adventure but wished it could have been August instead of December. There was only a light wind, and the current was slack, as it was close to high tide. Gelert was able to make good progress rowing along the riverbank towards the fish traps. The moon had started to rise giving a ghostly look to the scene. Gerald too found it cold. Noting that the light wind was from the south east, he knew that it could mean snow at this time of the year. Despite the clouds there was just enough moonlight to pick out two figures near the traps.

'Gruffudd,' called out Nest, 'is that you?'

Reassured, the two men ran down to the water's edge to guide the boat in and to help the crew ashore. Brother and sister embraced, and Gerald shook hands warmly with his brother-in-law for the first time. Nest was overjoyed to be with him after so long, and wanted to pinch herself to make sure she was not dreaming.

Gruffudd was accompanied by Dafydd, a Man at Arms. He seemed content to stand a few feet away, on watch in case Arnulf tried to play foul.

Gruffudd came to the point first. 'I think you should know, before we discuss whatever Lord Arnulf is proposing, that in any attempt I make to recover my father's lands, I would make no attempt to capture Pembroke. This is because you are married to my dear sister - provided, that is, that you made no serious attempt to frustrate me in my plans.'

Nest thanked her brother warmly.

Then Gerald said, 'you know that at present I serve Arnulf de Montgomery and I must obey his orders. You have my word that I will do my best to avoid attacking your lands, should you recover them. However, the message I bring to you from Arnulf does not conflict with what you say. He has asked me to approach you and the other three Welsh Princes, Cadwgan, Iorwerth and Meredydd, with a proposition. Can I speak in the strictest confidence?'

'You also have my word, brother in law.'

'Then I must tell you, that Arnulf's brother, Robert de Beleme, now Earl of Shrewsbury, does not accept the right of Henry Beauclerc to sit on the throne of England, and is asking your support in a rebellion to unseat him.'

Gruffudd whistled through his teeth. 'You are trusting in my silence about a major conspiracy, Gerald. What does the Earl of Shrewsbury offer me in return?'

'He offers you your lands back, with the exception of Pembroke, Arberth, and Havenford and the areas which surround them.'

'What must I do to show my support?'

'He asks you to come over with your army and harry Henry's lands in the English Midlands, so as to split his forces. King Muirchertach of Munster is also being asked to bring an army to attack Chester.'

'That old rogue! And, what inducement will be used with him?'

Gerald laughed. 'Arnulf has offered to marry his daughter. He has heard that she is very comely and that there is a large dowry.

'Beautiful she may be, but over the other side of the water everyone knows she is a nymphomaniac, who is working her way through the whole of King Muirchertach's court. He wants to be rid of her to save further embarrassment.'

Nest laughed. 'It sounds to me as if she and Arnulf deserve one another.'

'What will Arnulf offer the other Welsh Princes, since they are firmly in possession of their lands already?'

'That is still for discussion, Gruffudd, but it will involve treasure and horses.'

'Tell me frankly, sister, what you think of these proposals?'

'I have thought long and hard about them, and I have discussed my fears with Gerald. We are both a little uneasy, both on our own account and on yours.'

'Tell me why, little sister.'

As he spoke Nest thought how strong and brave her brother looked in the moonlight. 'He has matured into a fine man,' she mused.

Gerald spoke now for both of them. Many times in his life he had had to make vital judgements about a man's character and although he had only just met Gruffudd, he knew he liked him. He felt certain that he would do nothing to put Nest, or those she loved, in danger.

'We are glad that Arnulf is offering to ease the recovery of your lands, but you should not trust Arnulf too much. He could easily renege on his offers after he has overthrown Henry. Certainly, never put yourself personally into his power. We must now trust you with a further slant to this story; Nest and I have no love for Arnulf and are now debating whether to reveal the plot to Henry.'

Gruffudd whistled again. 'This is truly a complex situation. Why would either of you be tempted to do such a thing?'

'For myself,' said Nest, 'I am very torn between the joy of the thought of my brother being restored to our family lands and my horror at the prospect of Arnulf and his wicked family seizing power in England. Such a purpose must be both wicked and vile, such is the nature of the Montgomerys.'

'Then, what do you propose that I do? I now have an Irish army ready to come over here, and Arnulf will apparently not oppose me. Yet you, my sister, wish to undermine everything by revealing all to Henry.'

'I think you must think long and hard about this, Gruffudd.' cautioned Gerald. 'You must protect your own interests. One solution would for me to reveal the plot to Henry and say you will support him against the rebels in return for your lands.'

'That prospect is too vague, too uncertain. I am ready to strike now.

'When are you going to Ireland, Gerald? I could meet you at the Court of King Muirchertach in say three weeks time, if that fits in with your plans. I will have been able to consider everything by then.'

After further discussion, Gelert warned them that the tide was now dropping and they should return to the castle at once. Gerald and Gruffudd hurriedly finalised their plans to meet in Ireland. Then they all embraced and parted.

Cuddling up to Gerald in the boat, Nest prayed that the dangerous times in which they lived did not destroy any of those she loved. How simple it had been at Westminster when she was growing up. All she had to worry about then was whether the Norman ladies were despising her for being a country bumpkin!

Nest was riding behind Gerald, and the party was descending the valley towards Aberteifi (Cardigan). It was a glorious day and the sun was warm on their backs. The fields on the other side of the valley were dappled in light and shade as the lazy wind pushed small puffy clouds across the sky. It was unusual for this time of the year.

To be away from Pembroke and to be off on a journey with Gerald was sheer bliss. It had been a long, tiring ride however, and Nest tried not to think about any risk to her baby. She had not told Gerald about her pregnancy yet because he would not have taken her. She had probably been foolish, but she wanted to see more of her own land after her absence in London, and she definitely did not want to be left in the company of the obnoxious Arnulf. Besides, Gerald needed her for his mission. She would be useful, maybe vital, in his dealings with her Uncle Cadwgan, Prince of Powys. Anyway, she had not spent any quality time with Gerald since the arrival of Arnulf, and these were still early days in their marriage and they needed to build on their relationship.

What if she lost her baby because of the long ride? At the last stop Bethan, riding behind Gelert and seeing that Nest was tired, had started to nag her about the risks she was taking. Nest decided to ask Gerald if they could stop for a while. She was also worrying about her role in persuading her brother, and now her Uncle Cadwgan, to rise against Henry when she was having serious doubts about the matter.

Gerald halted the party on a bluff overlooking the river, within sight of Cadwgan's Llys or Court, which was about a mile away. The twenty or so Knights and Men at Arms dismounted and sat talking and refreshing themselves with ale, bread and cheese, while Gerald lifted Nest down, and they strolled to sit on a rock above the river.

'You look a little tired my love. Has the journey been too much for you?'

This was obviously the moment to tell him why. Or was it, in view of the imminence of their arrival?

'My darling, I know this is not the right moment, but I can conceal my news from you no longer. There is good reason why I am tired and ...

Gerald was at once full of concern.

'Are you ill my love? Your Uncle must be asked to send for a physician when we arrive?'

'No, I am not ill, but I was perhaps unwise to come with you on this long ride. I so wanted us to have more time together, away from Arnulf. I am with child, darling. We are going to have a baby.'

Gerald was at once a mixture of delight and concern. He did not know whether to admonish her for her foolhardiness in coming on the journey, or to be overjoyed at her news. He decided to be practical. He gave her a big hug despite so many of his men being near.

'You should not have come, but you know that. I am so very happy my sweet, so very happy, but worried what we should do now. You obviously must rest when we reach your uncle's hall.'

'I promise I will. Do not worry. I will be all right.' Her eyes were full of love. They were a family now. But even as she shared her secret with him, she resolved to herself that she would still find love for his other children, who might feel left out when the new baby came. With all the talk of revolts and rebellions, and the strife, which seemed to be the lot of men, she would make a little haven of peace for their family where everyone would be happy. She also now knew what she would say to Uncle Cadwgan.

The rest period had given time for the arrival of the party to be spotted by Cadwgan, and a small troop of his Teilu* rode out to meet them. Their leader, the Penteilu, said that the Prince sent Gerald greetings and that he would receive them at his Hall, and that there would be a great feast of welcome. Sadly, Cadwgan's son Owain was away in Arduddwy so would not be able to see meet his cousin Nest, whom he had not seen since childhood.

As they approached their destination, it all came flooding back to Nest about what her father's Llys** at Dinefwr had been like all those years ago. Cadwgan's court was very similar. It consisted of a large wooden enclosure around a considerable number of buildings, and in the centre she could make out a much bigger structure, which would be his Neuadd.

The Prince of Powys, Cadwgan ap Bleddyn, to give her uncle his proper name, was waiting at the entrance to his Llys, when they arrived, and greeted his niece and her husband with every appearance of great pleasure. 'Croeso, croeso, Gerald de Windsor, and croeso, croeso niece. I trust you travelled well. Please join me at my fireside. This is the first time a Norman Lord has graced my Neuadd and you do me great honour. We can discuss the purpose of your visit tomorrow, but in the meantime we shall carouse the night away. My bard shall sing of the days long ago when the Lord Pwll, King of Dyfed, hunted in the Forest of Arberth, and the Lady Rhiannon became his love. I am sorry my son, Owain, cannot be with us for he would have been pleased to meet his cousin after all these years.'

'I am delighted to be received at your Court, your Royal Highness, and particularly pleased to be able to bring your niece, my wife, to see you. She insisted on coming with me, although she is with child and now tired from the journey. I hope I do not presume on your hospitality when I beg you to allow her to go somewhere to rest while we celebrate.'

'Warmest congratulations and - please, forgive me, I am forgetting my

---

* *Military retinue* ** *Court*

117

manners. My Steward shall take you both to your room so that you can refresh yourselves after the journey. My niece can then remain there, if she wishes, while we feast. My Steward can also show your Knights to their quarters and the Captain of the Guard, my Penteulu, shall find room in my barracks for your Men at Arms.'

When they were at last alone in the privacy of their room, Nest lay gratefully on the straw palliasse which had been provided for their bed, and they discussed their first impressions. Gerald got his view in first.

'I know he is your Uncle, but my initial impression is that he is a devious, wily, old bird, a survivor, who will finish smelling of roses come what may.'

'Very astute, my darling! I had reports of him from time to time when I was in Court. He has survived many a rebellion and ambush and still lives to be Prince of Powys.'

'I gather that he has a number of women who share his bed from time to time, and that he has children by all of them. So, altogether, we find him to be a randy rascal, a wily old goat - even if he is your Uncle.'

Nest laughed, and then frowned unhappily at the thought of why they were there.

'I had time to think on the long journey here, and I am now sure about the way we should approach Uncle Cadwgan. He is a cunning old rogue and well able to take care of himself; however we have our own consciences to live with, and must do what we truly think right for ourselves and best for our native lands. You have sworn fealty to Arnulf, and while still in his service, you must carry out the instructions, which he has given you. That is why you are here about to confer with Cadwgan. We both know Arnulf and his brothers to be wicked, and a victory for them in their rebellion would be bad for England and probably for Wales. Most probably, even Gruffudd and Cadwgan might find that Arnulf would renege on his lavish promises.'

'We have discussed all this many times but not really solved our dilemma.'

'I think there is no doubt that you have to carry out your instructions from Arnulf and negotiate with the Welsh Princes as he has ordered. If you agree, I suggest that I, as a Welsh Princess and Cadwgan's niece, should speak to them privately and urge great prudence. By all means let them accept gifts and promises from Arnulf, but, I will tell them that the plot is known to the King and that they should be ready to accept approaches from him also. I will tell them confidentially that the plot is likely to fail so that they should not completely burn their bridges with Henry.'

'You really are a most devious little creature. Who would have thought that such a loyal, honest and loving wife could plan such cunning diplomacy,' said Gerald, with shocked admiration.

'We, too, have to survive in these troubled waters my love. We must make sure in the last resort that the fragile barque, which is our little family, will live through the turbulence that will soon be on us. If we can, at the same time, do what is plainly good for our people, then that would be right too.'

'I must go to the Great Hall to attend your uncle's feast. I will ask his Steward to make sure that some food is brought for you here, as you will be resting.'

Gerald went to give his wife a friendly kiss on his departure and discovered that she was looking very alluring as she lay on their bed. In fact, the way she was lying and the expression on her face, were sending out very strong signals. Not for the first time he discovered that when she needed him she projected such desire though every part of her being that it was almost impossible to resist her, whatever the unsuitableness of the moment.

'I - I really have to go. Your Uncle is waiting, and you are here to rest. You know it is impossible.'

She reached out her arms. 'Just because I am pregnant does not mean we have to give up lovemaking. Come here, you reluctant lover. Come and lie with me a moment. The baby is fine, and his mother needs you more urgently than Cadwgan.'

Gerald had never been involved in impromptu lovemaking before he had met Nest, and he had had to learn fast. In their short marriage she had already persuaded him to make love on the riverbank at Pembroke, in broad daylight, which had been a severe shock to him. Not many nights later they had made love on the hard stone of the battlements, while the guard was temporarily absent. Since then she had discussed with him the practicality of making love on a spiral staircase or on a table! She was also interested in trying different positions and had sought his guidance.

Up to now, he had avoided having to confess his lack of experience in these, to him, bizarre practices. He had an excuse now because he could say they might be bad for the baby. He must clear away from his mind many preconceived ideas, which associated such behaviour with quick fumbles with serving wenches, or whores. When he had hinted at his thoughts, she had laughed and said, 'why should whores have all the fun?' He found that he actually liked most of her ideas, but had difficulty in relaxing if there was a chance of being caught out.

'But, Bethan is sure to arrive in a minute.'

'Bethan has been my servant, friend, and companion since I was a young girl. She knows when not to intrude. Now come here and prove you still desire me, now I am with child.'

Gerald smiled knowingly. 'You must have plotted this with Bethan, you sexy little minx.' He gave in. Anyway, what man could resist her for long? She was the most beautiful woman in Wales.

When he eventually tore himself from his wife's bed, and dressed himself, he found Cadwgan, in person, at the door, waiting to escort him to the feast. He had had the forethought to borrow Gelert to act as interpreter.

119

Gerald had always been curious about what actually went on in a Welsh Court. He had picked up various bits of information from Nest talking about her childhood, but this was the first time he had visited one socially. When he entered the Neuadd at the side of the Prince, he found it was already full of people awaiting their arrival. Cadwgan sat at the head of the long table with Gerald on his right side. Apart from Gerald's Knights, most of those seated were dignitaries of the Commote of Aberteifi, as there had not been time to summon others from the rest of Ceredigion.* Also seated, were several of Cadwgan's sons, sons-in-law, nephews and cousins, together with the Penteulu (Head of the Military Retinue). There were no women seated at the table and Gerald wondered if there would have been if Nest had attended.

After everyone had quaffed a flagon of beer, the Chamberlain called on the Court Poet to declaim his hurriedly constructed poem for the occasion of Gerald's visit. This he did in dramatic style. Gelert, standing behind Gerald's chair was supposed to translate quietly into his ear, but soon proved unequal to the task, booming a few words from time to time tending to drown out the poet. It might have run like this:

'We Sons of Aberteifi, how proud we are this day,
The Norman Lord is with us, feasting on his way.
Nest, his lovely Mistress, graces our shabby hall,
Our Lord, the Prince of Powys, charms us with ...

Interrupted by Gelert booming his inadequate version:
'Everyone round here is very pleased to see you and we think Princess Nest is pretty good to look at ...

Smiling, Cadwgan raised his hand to interrupt the poetic flow. Speaking through his own interpreter he came to Gelert's rescue.

'Lord Gerald, I do not think your otherwise admirable man is quite giving full value to the words of my poet. Might I suggest my nephew, Geraint, could help you in this matter.'

Things progressed better after that. When the Court Poet started up again, Gerald learned in very flowery language how very proud the Prince of Powys, and indeed every last soul in the land of Ceredigion, was, to receive so great a Lord as Gerald in the Llys of Aberteifi.

Geraint also proved to be a good source of information about the staffing of Cadwgan's Court. He learned that for his domestic arrangements, apart from a butler and a steward, Cadwgan also had a priest, a physician, a cook, a head brewer, a candlemaker and a laundress. As well as a poet, he also had a bard, who was soon much in evidence. As far as other activities were concerned, apart from his Teilu, or military retinue, he had a chief huntsman, a chief groom, and even a court judge.

* *Cardiganshire*

There seemed to be so many servants, retainers and hangers on, that Gerald, who knew a great deal about feeding and keeping stores for the garrison of a castle, asked how so many people could be fed in so small an area, as well as the normal population.

'Perhaps I should not be saying this to a Norman Lord, but you have realised immediately the weakness of the system. To sustain this great body of people and to enforce his power in every part of his lands, a Welsh Prince has to travel regularly on circuit from one district Llys to another. In this way, the Prince's Court is sustained: by all his people, throughout his lands. And, at the same time, the Prince is able to exercise justice and dispense any largesse at his disposal.'

Gerald would have liked to learn more from the very informative Geraint, but the feast soon became too uproarious for this to happen, as one flagon of beer followed another.

The feast continued until late into the night, and despite his best efforts to stay sober, when Gerald eventually staggered to his room, he was far from steady on his feet. He was quite relieved to find Nest deeply asleep, as his powers would have proved inadequate to another session in showing that he still found her attractive.

The rich green hills of Munster were shrouded in uniquely Irish rain which, seemed to melt out of the skeins of ragged clouds as they drifted up the valley. There were gaps in the clouds and rays of sunshine illuminated the farmsteads and the cattle with a strange bright light.

Gerald thought that the whole blend of light, rain, sunshine and shadow was part of the Irish condition - as was the state of having one's cloak permanently half wet.

He had arrived at King Muirchertach's Court yesterday accompanied by two Knights, several Men at Arms, and the requisite servants. They had been received very warmly, and in the evening the King had arranged a great feast, which lasted well into the night.

'Forgive my curiosity, but are you here for some deep purpose or do you need a roof over your head for a while - like your brother in law?'

It was obvious that he knew Gerald had arranged to meet Gruffudd there.

'You should know, Norman Lord, that word travels fast in Ireland.'

'I am here, for two reasons, O King. The first you know: the second is deep and secret, and may be of great interest to you.' Gerald had taken advice on how to approach Irish Chieftains and thought he was doing fairly well.

'Then we will meet again privately in the morning, here in my Court, when our heads have cleared of the mead, and I have decided whether Norman visitors are best listened to, killed, or sold for profit.'

Gerald thought that perhaps he was not doing so well after all. He hoped the King was jesting.

Now, next morning, watching the rain tumble from the sky, he was wondering why the King had not appeared. Gerald presumed that the King's head had taken longer to clear than he expected. There was no sign of his entourage either. Gerald's own Knights, Bernard and Saer, had reported for duty earlier, but he had allowed them to return to their quarters as he wished to meet the King unaccompanied. Now, kicking his heels for half the morning, he was beginning to regret that decision. The rain seemed heavier and the shafts of sunshine were disappearing, so the prospect of a thoughtful walk up the valley was less appealing. In any case, the King might appear at any time and take exception to his absence.

A serving girl, bringing him a platter of porridge and a flagon of ale, showed that life was beginning to stir. He decided to take as long as possible over consuming the strange meal, while watching the King's servants belatedly start to clear up after last night's feast. It seemed that they too must have consumed a fair quantity of mead.

A hand touched his arm from behind. He turned to see a slim, very beautiful girl, with long copper coloured hair. Her eyes were green and saucy, and she was smiling in a very friendly way.

'You must be Gerald de Windsor,' she said in passable French. 'I am sorry I was not able to meet you at the feast last night. My father said that I had to attend to my sick mother.' She touched his arm again. 'Forgive me. I should introduce myself. I am Siobhan, the King's daughter. Things are pretty dull round here. I am hoping that a visit from a Norman Lord will enliven matters?'

Gerald had never been particularly susceptible to the allures of strange women, but he could not help himself stirring in the presence of Siobhan. He was surprised to find that, like a callow youth, he did not know what to say. Siobhan laughed. Obviously she was used to having a powerful effect on men.

'We have heard of you, back in Wales, Princess Siobhan,' he started.

'How very gallant, and how formal!' She laughed again. 'You must tell me all about Wales, shy Gerald. Perhaps, given encouragement, you can be coaxed to being a little braver. Perhaps, ...

To Gerald's relief, further discussion was ended by the arrival of a rather dishevelled King Muirchertach and his equally hung over retainers.

'Leave the Norman alone,' growled the Chieftain, then put his hand to his head because speaking made it hurt. 'Go attend to your mother. I have private matters to discuss.'

'So have I, but they can wait,' purred Siobhan and glided away.

'Daughters, daughters! That one will be the death of me. Come sit by the fire and tell me the secret reason you are here, so far from home.'

'The matter is very deep and confidential, O King, and I can only discuss it in private.'

The King waved away his retainers and their hangers on, who moved off a few paces, looking disappointed. Gerald began to apply himself to his task. He started to sense that there was something indefinable about Muirchertach, which was convincing him he must take the Irish King a little more seriously.

'Your Majesty, by some means you have become aware that I have arranged to meet my exiled brother in law at your court.'

'He has already sought my permission for the meeting.'

'Your Majesty, I hope you do not mind me making such an arrangement? It will be entirely in your own interest, as I mean to explain to you.'

'I hope so, Norman Lord, for your sake.'

'He is at present banned from Wales, to the distress of his sister, my wife, Princess Nest. Your Court seemed a good place to talk to him in safety about something of interest to him and, I hope, to you.'

'Yes, yes! Now, delay no longer. Tell me of the matters, which brought you here.'

'My Liege Lord, Arnulf de Montgomery, of whom you know, has sent me on this delicate mission. He wishes to enlist your support for a great enterprise. I tell you this in strictest confidence. He supports the claim of Duke Robert of Normandy to the throne of England, and he is raising a mighty rebellion against the usurper Henry.'

'What does he want of me?'

'He desires you to send a fleet, with the pride of your soldiery, to support the attack of the Welsh Princes on Henry's forces in the English Midlands, while Arnulf's brother, the Earl of Shrewsbury, attacks Henry's main power in the south. When I speak to you of these things, I take a great risk, for Henry is a vengeful man.'

'Have no fear of that, Sir. Your mission has some interest for me. My young men are bored, and this would occupy them and stop them plotting against me. It would also give the bards something to sing about me.'

Gerald knew that the struggles and intrigues among the Irish Kings were nearly as bloody and ferocious as among the Welsh Princes.

'I have heard it told, O King, that you might have hopes and plans that one day you will be crowned High King of all Ireland at Tara.'

The King's face then became dark and threatening, and Gerald feared that he might have been unwise to mention the matter. However, after a moment, Muirchertach's face cleared again, as if on reflection he had decided that, if Gerald had heard about it, then it meant that so many people in Ireland were expecting him to become High King that it had become known in Wales. Yet again, Gerald was reminded that the King was violent and unpredictable, and that Arnulf had sent him on a dangerous mission.

'Forgetting the matter of Tara, what rewards and inducements does Arnulf de Montgomery offer me to send my men to aid him. Half of Wales? A thousand war-horses?'

'I know that you jest, O King. My Lord Arnulf will offer you horses, indeed, and gold.'

The King thought deeply. 'You have met my daughter. I speak frankly when I tell you that she is my biggest problem. She is insatiable and has bedded half the men in Munster, and will work her way round the rest, given time. To be responsible for such a daughter is to be laughed at all over Ireland. She has ruined any chance of a good marriage here, and not helped me in my ambition to become High King.'

Gerald tried to make vague, sympathetic noises.

The King went on, 'your Lord, he is not married I am told?' Gerald shook his head.

'Tell your Lord that he can have the support of a great Irish fleet packed with warriors if he becomes betrothed to my daughter, Siobhan. My greatest wish is that she should be safely married to a great Lord - and out of Ireland.'

Gerald was quite taken aback. He had been prepared to bargain in gold, horses and even land, but had been unsure how to approach the subject of Arnulf's offer of marriage. Now, he felt it prudent not to mention the offer,

124

as Muirchertach might think of more things to demand.

'I will take your offer of Princess Siobhan's hand in marriage to Lord Arnulf,' said Gerald formally. 'No doubt, he will consider it carefully. I will also have to ask your leave to return to Pembroke soon, as Lord Arnulf will be impatient to know what help he might have from the King of Munster.'

'I have planned another feast for tonight, which you might find interesting. In any case, I have learned that your brother in law has been delayed and will not reach us until tomorrow.'

Gerald spent the rest of the day fly-fishing for trout with the King himself and two of his chieftains. Along with many of his countrymen, Muirchertach was fanatically devoted to fishing and needed little excuse, taking Gerald's presence as good reason for another half day standing in the nearest river.

Gerald was no expert, despite some training from Nest, and had to endure considerable taunting from the King for his lack of technique. His only consolation was that Bernard and Saer had no idea at all, and spent most of the afternoon falling in the river or bloodily removing their fish hooks from their arms and legs.

'Alas Norman Lord,' the King roared with malicious laughter, 'there will be no fish left in all Ireland if you stay a few days more.' This quip was much appreciated by his chieftains who fell about laughing until tears ran down their faces.

That night the Normans groaned at having to attend yet another, interminable feast. It was the usual formula of vast quantities of unpalatable food and increasing drunkenness,* accompanied by Irish harps producing haunting laments. Gerald had never admitted it to Nest, but he had no ear for Celtic music, being tone deaf.

Matters were enlivened considerably when Muirchertach Ua Brian, now maddened by mead, announced a spear-throwing competition. The Royal Hall was quite large, but crowded as it was with very inebriated people, there was very little room for wild and reckless spear throwing.

Gerald, Saer and Bernard were standing close to the King, but even there, the odd spear came uncomfortably close. Saer murmured to Gerald that it would be wise to withdraw if diplomatically possible, as he had seen mead fuelled competitions like this go disastrously wrong in the past.

The King seemed to have overheard.

'So, it is all a bit too exciting for you proud, sober Normans. Let us make it a little more so for you. You must have an Irish story to take back to Wales. Have a turn yourself stiff Gerald. Show us Irish the warlike skills, which have gained you so many victories.' He handed the reluctant Gerald three

---

* *Mead drinking in excess often resulted in drink crazed violence. Soldiers often went into battle in this condition, as they became oblivious to danger. The Irish probably learned to drink mead from the Vikings who are believed to have drunk themselves 'berserk' before battle.*

spears and told him to hurl them at a crude effigy of a man fastened to one of the hall's main wooden pillars. People were now crowding round so closely that Gerald was concerned that he might injure someone.

'Go on, go on,' shouted the drink crazed King.

Like all Norman Lords and Knights, Gerald had spent much of his early years training in such skills as this, and had no difficulty in hurling all three of the spears into the effigy at twenty paces.

'Very good, very good, Norman Lord, but see what an Irish King can do.' To Gerald's horror, Muirchertach seized a spear from a retainer and hurled it straight at a man leaning drunkenly against another pillar, near the effigy. There was a sickening groan and the man fell, transfixed by the spear.

The King now lurched around brandishing another spear. Everyone drew back, not knowing what target he might choose next.

The three Normans rose to their feet, protesting that they must go to their beds. They were appalled by this senseless murder.

'Yellow livered Normans, so proud and full of contempt. You will not get away with such graces here. You will not withdraw until you have pitted your skills against three of my warriors. No effigy this time, the three of you at twenty paces from my three men! Three spears each!'

Gerald protested vigorously that this was a breach of hospitality and no way to treat emissaries of a Norman Lord, but, surrounded by armed men, they had no choice but to obey. He contemplated for a minute shouting for his eight Men at Arms who were seated at the far end of the hall, but realised that with so few men the matter could only end in useless slaughter. It was obvious that mead had driven any sense of hospitality or treaty advantage out of the King's head.

The three Normans allowed themselves to be lined up to face three wild warriors, who had already stuck two of their three spears in the ground in front of them, and were balancing the remaining spear in their right hands, while bragging to all and sundry about their skills.

Gerald murmured to the others that he could see no way out of the situation but to hope that drink would make their aim inaccurate, and that their own chain mail would stop the worst injuries.

At this moment a shrill voice rang out, berating the King. The hall fell silent, and Gerald could see that Muirchertach's frail wife had risen from her sickbed and was at his side, striking him weakly with a stave.

'You drunken oaf, do you want to bring a Norman army to these shores? What madness is this? Do you want to be High King or no? Sit peaceably with your visitors and keep our laws of hospitality. I am ashamed of you.'

To Gerald's astonishment the King was instantly subdued and, despite being humiliated in front of his whole court, he clutched his head and said, 'you are right, wife. Come, Lords, return to your seats. I fear the mead has fuddled my brain.'

Later, when the feast had finally run its course, and Gerald was at long last in his bed, he mentally congratulated himself on surviving such a day. He would have much to tell Nest on his return. Blowing out the lamp he settled down to sleep. Gruffudd was due tomorrow and he must have a clear head.

Suddenly, there was a faint rustling and someone very warm and friendly slipped into his bed. Was there to be no end to his problems that day?

'Well, Gerald,' murmured Siobhan, wrapping herself round him. 'Are you not grateful? Who do you think summoned my mother?'

chapter twenty-seven

The 'Dragon' was just passing the Isle of Grassholm, and the tide was beginning to turn, about to start its overwhelming sweep up the Severn Sea. It was fortunate that the Ship's Master knew these waters so well, since he had chosen to steer to the south of the isolated rock, and from there directly to the mouth of the Haven. If he had passed Grassholm on the north side, the great strength of the tide would already be pushing the ship towards the string of underwater rocks, which stretched in a line nearly to the coast.

As the 'Dragon' passed close to the tall, strange, rocky isle, the thousands of gannets which were nesting there, suddenly panicked at the approach of the vessel, and surged into the air at once, circling the ship in a vast white cloud.

'You will not be popular with our fishermen, Master John, alarming the birds. They say that the birds smash thousands of eggs when they panic.'

'These waters are dangerous enough without worrying too much about birds' eggs my Lord. I have seen the bones of many a ship on these rocks. We have to keep close in, so that the reef protects us from the force of the current that would sweep us away far up the Severn Sea. The wind is light and there is a risk that we will not be able to enter Penfro Haven.'

Gerald knew enough about the sea to be aware that there was enough wind today for the Dragon to make the estuary, and if the wind dropped they could always row; the Master was trying to impress him with the perils of his trade. He had encountered perils indeed, and would again, but not today.

Both Saer and Bernard had been strangely quiet on the voyage back from Ireland, and Gerald had had plenty to think about. From the overall view the visit could be said to have reached its objectives. He had seen Gruffudd and he had confirmed that he would be launching an attack to try to regain his lands in Deheubarth. They had agreed that he would not attack the area around Pembroke out of consideration for Nest and Gerald. He also had accepted that both of them were in a very difficult situation and that neither of them wanted to see Henry deposed. Gruffudd had no interest in the throne of England; his sole concern was regain his lands. The forthcoming rebellion would weaken the Normans and Gruffudd saw it as a great opportunity.

Gerald had found his dealings with Muirchertach Ua Brian very distasteful. He had been dragged in by Arnulf to conduct the negotiations and he had no stomach for it. The Irish King was violent and barbaric, and he knew the Montgomerys to be an evil family, even by the standards of the times, and he knew Henry to be good for England. Nest agreed with him, and they both wanted to extricate themselves from the situation if they possibly could; however Gerald had sworn fealty to Arnulf so it was hard to see a way out.

There was also the matter of Princess Siobhan and the betrothal he had been asked to arrange. He felt that his position as emissary had been dangerously compromised when she had climbed into his bed. He squirmed as he remembered what had happened.

'This is not seemly Princess. I am a guest of your father. This is a breach of his hospitality. I think ...

His speech was interrupted. Siobhan climbed on top of him and planted her lips very firmly on his. She also seemed, simultaneously, to be doing something very personal to him with one of her hands. He felt he was in the grip of an octopus of fable and legend. Despite himself he found he was becoming aroused. He now knew how it must be like for a woman to try to fend off the unwelcome attentions of a man.

Pulling himself together, he pushed Siobhan firmly off him, climbed out of the bed, and tried to pull her out too.

'Go back to your room Siobhan. This is unseemly and dangerous. One of my Knights is in the next room. We could be discovered at any moment.'

Siobhan got out with him and attempted to embrace him again.

'Silly Gerald, am I not comely? I promise you I know all the tricks of love. Do not worry about my father, he knows I have to have men, every night if possible. Why do you think my Father wants to marry me off so desperately? He cannot marry me to an Irish Lord because most of them have bedded me already.'

Gerald found he was quite shocked. He knew some women of the lower classes to be very wanton, but for a Princess to frankly admit that she had bedded half Ireland was very disturbing. How was he going to recommend her to Arnulf now that he officially knew?

However, his immediate concern was to get her out of his room. He knew that rejected women could become very nasty. She could denounce him to her father who might decide to use him for spear practice! The whole situation filled him with revulsion. He had been an upright man all his life but he now found himself using a base stratagem to try to save the situation.

'I confess Siobhan that I find you dangerously attractive, and I long to spend the night with you. However, when I was in a tavern recently, I unwisely went with a harlot in a weak moment and contracted a loathsome flux of my private parts. I am being treated by a physician, but I do not detect any improvement as yet.'

'How vile,' said Siobhan, 'and to think I was so close to catching it myself. Ugh!' Without more ado, she had glided out of the room leaving him disgusted with himself that he had got into such a situation.

Now on the 'Dragon', he shivered at the memory, and wondered what, if anything, he was going to say to Nest about the matter. Bernard and Saer had

129

been conversing up in the bow of the ship, and now they made their way back to his side.

'What did you think of Princess Siobhan, my Lord?' said Saer, glancing at Bernard. Gerald was embarrassed but tried to conceal it.

'Very comely, but perhaps a little forward to recommend to Lord Arnulf,' he responded cautiously.

Saer laughed. 'Forward indeed, my Lord. She got into my bed last night and was so noisy as I pleasured her, that I feared she might wake Bernard in the next room.'

'He need not have worried,' laughed Bernard. 'She appeared in my room later in the night and I found her to be insatiable. Saer and I were wondering whether we should keep our own counsel about the matter when we get back to Pembroke. It seems to us a pity if Lord Arnulf were deterred from the match. If the marriage were to go ahead perhaps such a lively bird might distract my Lord from his too frequent visits to our castle.'

Very relieved that the adventures with Siobhan would not be reaching Nest's ears, Gerald readily agreed with the others, causing more mirth. Unknown to Gerald, Siobhan had complained to them that she had rejected his bed, as he was rife with the pox! Fortunately for Gerald's 'amour propre', they had no intention mentioning it.

chapter twenty-eight

Henry was in his private quarters and he had dismissed all his servants and guards. He did not want anyone to overhear his discussion with the Captain of the 'Raven'. He was holding Nest's letter.

'Dear Henry,

I presume I may call the father of my child that. I hope you are not now so regal that you cannot appreciate a well-intentioned letter from someone who still holds you very dear.

What I am going to say may be dangerous in the extreme to Gerald and me, if you do not believe what I say, or if the letter falls into the wrong hands. If I cared more about my own safety than yours, I would keep quiet and not take this risk. I hope for all our sakes that you can accept this.

Now, for the dangerous part! Gerald and I find ourselves to have a Liege Lord, who is a traitor. Arnulf and his family, are actively planning an armed rebellion, to cast you from the throne and to crown your brother Robert in your place. We both have a deeper loyalty to you, my Lord King. Gerald has just returned from a visit to Munster, ordered by Arnulf, to enlist King Muirchertach's help in this. He has also been ordered to enlist the help of the Welsh Princes. He can do no other than obey these orders. To show any opposition to Lord Arnulf's plans would be to put both our lives immediately in danger.

I urge you to strike speedily against the Montgomerys, before their preparations are complete. If I were still at your side, I would employ my Welsh guile, and urge you to invite as many as possible of the brothers to London, with the pretext of granting them some lands or new favours, and then arrest them and try them for treason.

I had to wait for the arrival of Captain Thomas on the 'Raven', because I knew him to be loyal and true, and that this letter would be safe with him. I am sorry for the delay.

Please take this letter very seriously. You were my first love, and I care for you. I want you to rule wisely and well. England needs you. Robert would be weak and feckless.

When you win this struggle, do not forget those who warned you of your danger, and in particular show mercy to Gerald, who is a good man, and cannot but carry out the instructions of his treacherous Lord.

Please give a big kiss to our son, and tell him that his mother loves him.

My thoughts are with you both, always. Life must be sometimes hard for you now. I will never forget our happy days - and nights.

Nest'

As Henry read the letter, his thoughts tumbled over in his mind. His first, overwhelming thought was that he believed every word she said. He must act quickly to save the situation. The letter confirmed strands of evidence that he had already received. He knew his brother Robert had returned to Normandy from his Crusade to the Holy Land some months previously with his new and beautiful wife. He had also had reports that Robert was trying to enlist support from great Norman magnates who had lands in both England and Normandy, persuading them that their situation would be much easier if they only had to serve one master - himself, Robert. This would be achieved if Robert became both King of England and Duke of Normandy with their support.

His second thought was that he missed Nest. He knew that he still loved her, despite his new Queen and his many mistresses. Margaret was already known as 'Good Queen Maud' by the native English, reflecting her pious nature. Unfortunately, she was also pious in bed, with lengthy prayers before turning in, and more prayers, kneeling at her bedside, if she awoke in the night. Sex, she seemed to find a little distasteful, an unfortunate duty for the begetting of children and to meet the needs of the baser side of her husband.

Life had been fun with Nest. He had been able to cope with the stresses of running the country, and the intrigues of the great Lords, much more easily when she had been there to discuss it with, or to see the funny side of things. She was also unusually wise for one so young. She could often see straight to the heart of a matter with uncanny clarity when he had been deceived by the details. He found himself wishing that she were with him now. He remembered her naked on the bearskin rug at the hunting lodge with love in her eyes, and afterwards laughing at the events in the stream. He suddenly felt very lonely. If she were there beside him he would be much happier and feel a lot safer on his throne.

He resolved to take her advice, and immediately called in Count Robert and other trusted advisors to discuss what action should be taken. He did not tell them of Nest's letter. He told them that he had received warning of the treachery of the Montgomery family from a trusted agent.

Count Robert said that he, too, was becoming worried about the situation and had been on the point of discussing his fears with the King. He also had disquieting news; the wily Bishop Ranulph Flambard, former chief advisor to William Rufus, whom Henry had put in the Tower of London on his accession, had escaped, by means of a rope, which had been smuggled to him in a barrel. It was believed that he had fled to Normandy to put his services at the disposal of Duke Robert.

The King and his counsellors now agreed upon the text of a letter to the Earl of Shrewsbury, inviting him to come to London, with his brother Arnulf de Montgomery, to discuss 'the future of some church lands which would become available shortly, and other matters of interest'. On their arrival in London they would be arrested and closely questioned. If the Montgomery threat could be nipped in the bud, then Duke Robert might be more readily persuaded to avoid an armed contest with his brother.

The next day Henry called Captain Idwal Thomas back for another private audience. The King dismissed his attendants and greeted his old friend very warmly.

'As always I hold your friendship and your loyalty in very high esteem Captain. You will also know that the matters we are dealing in are very delicate and dangerous, touching both the safety of the realm and the depths of my heart. So deep and so dangerous are these matters that I cannot reply to Princess Nest in writing. I am relying on you, good Captain, to convey my reply to her secretly and accurately.'

'Your Majesty, I am proud that you feel able to trust me, a lowly sea captain, with such high matters, and prouder still that you, a King, call me friend. You can rely on me to truly be your friend and to serve you as best I may until the end of my days.' Thomas now choked with Welsh emotion.

Henry threw his arm round Thomas's shoulders.

'Go back to Nest, Idwal, and give her my reply very privately, well away from Gerald, Bethan or anyone else. Tell her that I love her and need her here, back at my side. I need her love, I need her friendship and I need her counsel. I will act on her warning: she has probably saved my throne. Tell her that I made a mistake in marrying Margaret and that I openly admit it. If she is willing to come to me I will forswear all other women (Idwal Thomas smiled inwardly knowing his King very well) and that I will take advice about putting Queen Margaret aside. She will know that I have recalled Archbishop Anselm from the exile to which he was driven by my brother William Rufus, and I am certain he will find some way to make her my Queen - and our wonderful son legitimate.

The more Henry thought about matters after the departure of Captain Thomas to join his ship at Deptford, the more he thought he had done the right thing. He was a man who usually considered matters long and hard before making a decision. 'A cold, calculating man', his brother Robert called him, and he had certainly surprised himself by his own spontaneous decision to try to recall Nest to his side, with the many likely consequences of that action. He had as good as offered her marriage, and that would need the support of the saintly Archbishop Anselm in obtaining divorces from their respective spouses. Certainly, the Church had looked very favourably on his seizure of the throne on the death of the foul Rufus, but would Anselm go as far as to agree to the divorces? He might, reasoned Henry, as a marriage between Henry and Nest would bring a large slice of Wales under direct English rule, consolidating the Church's control over the See of St David's and probably, also, that of Llandaff (Cardiff).

Henry smiled ruefully at the thought that these reasonings now came after his decision to bring her back to his side, rather than before. This was not the way his crafty mind usually worked. What other consequences would there be? Certainly the King of Scotland would not like his sister being put aside, and many Saxons might be alienated as Margaret was a direct descendent of their great King Alfred. However, he only had to think for a few moments of Nest's beauty, warmth, wisdom and love, for such concerns to pale considerably.

The next few weeks were so busy with dealing with the danger to the throne that Henry did not have time to think much about what Nest's reply was likely to be. In fact the 'Raven' had fair winds on both her voyage out to Pembroke and for her return to Deptford, a most unusual occurrence, so Nest's reply arrived the day before the one from the Earl of Shrewsbury.

'My dearest Henry,

I am shocked but flattered by your offer to try to make me your Queen. The truth is that we should never have parted. We belonged together, and our marriage would have been good for both our countries. I confess that I cannot stop myself from loving you. Gerald is a very good man, and an honourable one. However love does not work like that.

You have it in your power to order me to your side, and part of me would be thrilled if you did. However, I must reluctantly urge you not to do so - for many reasons. There are, first of all, my womanly reasons. I bore Gerald a beautiful son - whom we have called William - last year, and we love him dearly. I have also made myself mother to Gerald's two delightful children by his concubine, who died very tragically, and they all need me. I think too, that Gerald needs me.

He has a difficult life in this remote outpost and I am fairly certain that I can help him in the many difficult decisions that he has to make. To be truthful, I have come to love him and would not like to betray him. I swore to love him and be faithful to him when we married, and I should keep my promises. I cannot deny that the thought of being with you excites me, but I must not allow myself to feel like that.

My other reasons for urging you not to send for me are ones that your own head must be telling you. If you attempt to marry me, you will make an enemy of the King of Scotland, adding him to the list who may invade England. If you put aside Maud, the Saxons will think you have insulted the memory of their beloved King Alfred.

I can think of other reasons. Do not do it, my beloved, even if it grieves us both. I will keep a place for you always in my heart.

Yours always, Nest'

As she had lain awake beside Gerald in bed the night after sending the letter, Nest had examined her actions and her feelings. How could she send such a missive? Until she had received Henry's reply to her warning, she had convinced herself that she now loved Gerald, that she was happy with him. Henry's offer to try to make her his Queen had thrown her feelings into chaos. She had always thought she was a good person at heart, but now she was asking herself if she was really a strumpet. How could her feelings betray her so? She should have been very cold and firm in her reply, but instead she had sent Henry a mixed message, perhaps hoping in her heart that he would order her to join him.

When Henry read her letter he hated the thought that she had born Gerald a child. Somehow it brought home to him that her desirable body was now the property of another man - and he did not like to think of it. In particular he did not like to think of her bearing Gerald a precious son. He resolved to defer thinking what he should do about her for a while.

However, by next day matters had moved on apace. Henry was awakened to hear that the messenger that he had sent to the Montgomerys had returned, badly beaten, together with a message of defiance from them. The Earl had declared for Duke Robert and had already moved to besiege the King's castle at Ludlow. Later in the day, news arrived that Duke Robert had evaded Henry's ships in the Channel, and through the treachery of a local magnate, had been able to sail directly into Portsmouth Harbour, and had already landed there with a considerable force.

The next few weeks tested Henry's mettle as a King to the full. As the full extent of the threat to his throne became apparent it would have been very easy to lose heart.

The Montgomerys' power was based on castles, the main ones in England being at Shrewsbury, Bridgnorth, Tickhill and Arundel. The one at Arundel initially concerned Henry the most, since it provided a power base in the south of England, not far from the capital, and in a position to assist Duke Robert's likely assault on London. Overall, Robert de Belesme, Earl of Shrewsbury, and his brothers controlled the second most powerful force in England, after the King's own.

After Duke Robert's dramatic and unopposed arrival in Portsmouth, Henry's spies reported that his brother seemed initially content to remain there with his forces, while those Barons favouring him, and there were many, rallied to his side.

Meanwhile reports were coming in of Muirchertach's wild Irish troops landing at Deeside, and of the Welsh Princes Cadwgan and Gruffudd rising in rebellion. Cadwgan was moving against the King's castle at Rhydygroes (Carmarthen), and Nest's brother, Gruffudd, had landed a force at St Davids in Pembrokeshire, from Ireland. It was not yet clear what the two remaining Princes, Iorwerth and Meredydd, intended to do. Henry was not a man easily panicked, but the situation was becoming blacker by the hour.

Henry decided to call a conference of his advisors, at noon, in Westminster Hall, headed by Count Robert de Meulan and Henry's new Justiciar, Robert, Bishop of Salisbury. When it assembled Henry was shaken to note how many of his magnates were missing.

'They have made various excuses not to attend, but I am certain that they have already joined Duke Robert, or are waiting to decide which side to back, your Majesty,' whispered a very grave *Robert de Meulan, with an equally gloomy Justiciar at his side.

Having outlined the latest situation to the magnates, Henry sought their counsel.

'Well my Lords, a difficult position! But how do you advise me to tackle matters?'

Robert de Meulan spoke first. 'It is very apparent, your Majesty, that Duke Robert poses the most immediate threat. Not only is he within an easy march of London, but should he reach the capital while you were away dealing with the Montgomerys, he would have himself proclaimed King and declare you, your Majesty, to be a usurper. He will have to be tackled first.

* *Robert was unfortunately a very common Norman name*

Cut off the head and the body must fall.'

Someone at the back was heard to say clearly, 'yes but whose head?'

'What say you Earl Hugh?' asked the King, refusing to be rattled.

'Frankly, your Majesty, I consider your present situation impossible, and advise you to consider treating with one or more of the forces against you so as to even up the odds. If that proves impossible, then I would advise you to offer the throne to Duke Robert while your forces are still intact. He is said to be a generous man and may very well spare your life.'

'Your advice is frank indeed!' retorted the King. 'Heaven help me if I am forced to take it.'

At this point the Constable of Windsor entered the room.

'Many apologies for being late, your Majesty.'

'I am glad to see you Lord Walter, late or no. Perhaps you will have a more optimistic view of my situation. If so, I look forward to hearing it.'

'Your Majesty, I would urge you to reconvene this meeting later in the afternoon. I have received another embassy from Wales, which I urge you to hear before coming to any firm decisions on how to proceed. I have the envoy waiting in another room close by.'

Henry was glad of the chance of a break from the meeting in view of the pessimism being expressed, but he could not imagine what embassy from Wales could bear anything to his advantage. However, he told the assembled magnates that the meeting would reconvene in two hours and urged the members to use their collective wisdom to come up with a more positive plan of campaign.

Once out of the room, Lord Walter, whom Henry recollected was the father of Gerald de Windsor, Nest's husband, took his arm to explain what had happened.

'What is going on Lord Walter? What is so urgent from Wales that I must break off from deciding what action to take to save my throne?'

'Your Majesty, you know me to be an old friend and deeply loyal to you. Forgive me, but I see you being forced into decisions, which may very well cost you your throne, and, quite honestly, threaten the lives, or liberty, of those closest to you. I urge you to meet this Welsh envoy, as I have been convinced after long discussions this afternoon, that the proposals suggested may be the only hope now for our cause.'

Lord Walter now led the King into an adjoining room saying, 'it will perhaps be better if I beg permission to leave you here in privacy,' and closed the door, leaving the King in what appeared at first to be an empty room. Fearing some trick or attempt on his life, Henry made to draw his sword and to shout for his Men at Arms.

'That will not be necessary Henry,' said a familiar voice behind him. Next moment, Nest ran forward and threw her arms about him.

'This is a very welcome meeting, my love, but hardly what I was expecting or, sadly, likely to save my throne, as Lord Walter seems to believe.'

'My love, please sit down with me a moment and listen to what I propose. Forget our exchange of messages. I am not here hoping to be your Queen: matters have gone far beyond that. I am here, with the agreement of my husband, to put to you proposals, which we have discussed together, that seem obvious from afar, but perhaps not so obvious when you are close to those problems.

'We left secretly from Pembroke on the 'Dragon', and when Gerald and I arrived at Deptford, we went to his father, Lord Walter, at Windsor. I find him to be a dear and very wise man. He was at first unwilling to even discuss matters of state with me, a mere woman, but on Geralds's urging he began to take notice of what I was proposing.'

'I will listen to advice from any quarter, such is my situation, and advice from you always went to the heart of any matter. However, I cannot see how any advice can alter the facts, or the threat to my throne?'

Squeezing him gently, Nest turned to look into his eyes. Despite the urgency and gravity of his situation, Henry felt himself relax. In this lovely woman's eyes he saw the wisdom of another culture, and the balance of an intelligent, female viewpoint. A viewpoint that he could trust because he knew now that she still loved him!

'Stand back from the picture, Henry. This matter does not have to be resolved by the movements and intrigues of a few thousand Normans, foreigners who have invaded and oppressed the proud and ancient peoples of England and Wales. Use the power of the native people, Henry, the people who long to regain their pride again, the pride which has been taken from them by arrogant Normans.'

'But, I am a Norman, Nest.'

'You have made yourself more than a Norman, Henry: you have learned the English language and you have brought back the saintly English Archbishop Anselm. Also, I must force myself to say it, you have married the Saxon Queen Maud - may God bless her holy fanny - she who is descended from King Alfred. The English want to love you, Henry. Make yourself their leader. Call out the Saxon fyrd. Send messengers to every county. Tell the local leaders that England is in peril, and that thousands of men are needed to drive the proud Normans from their over-mighty privileges. Train them yourself to tackle the Norman cavalry, then go to meet Duke Robert with such power, that he will see the game is not worth the candle and go away.

'Give him gold if you must. You can always decide not to pay again next year. Once Duke Robert has withdrawn, turn to deal with the Montgomerys. Without Duke Robert, they will not last long. When they are beaten, offer them their lives so long as they go into exile.'

'This is all music to my ears, my darling. But, if I spare them, what is to prevent the Montgomerys plotting abroad, to return with new forces?'

'You have not yet really understood, my sweet. You are now an Englishman. You will give power back to the English. Once they have regained some of their ancient power they will never again listen to the arrogant blandishments of their former oppressors.'

'But what of your own people? What of your brother who is now in St. Davids with a new army, seeking to regain his lands while I am otherwise engaged?'

'Again, my sweet, approach the problem in another way. Do you think that I want my brother in rebellion? Do you not remember that I tried to escape from the battle on the back of my brother's horse to raise another army? I am Welsh and I want what is right for my people, Henry. Treat Gruffudd in a different way. Offer him his lands back but insist that he holds the lands from you and that he must give you homage. He will accept that and be your ally in Wales. The other rebels will soon collapse after that. But show them mercy and make them your allies too.'

Strength visibly poured into Henry and he immediately seemed to grow in stature. He opened the door to find a smiling Lord Walter a few paces away.

'Go straight to Lord Robert, Walter, and ask him to reassemble the Council immediately. I will announce my plans, as I am now fully resolved on a course of action.'

Closing the door again he said, 'I will never stop loving you as long as I live. I do not know, now, what to do or say to you. You have convinced me that I can save my throne.'

Nest snuggled up to him. 'Tomorrow is another day. Tonight, after your meeting, please let us be together, but, I think it will have to be the last time.'

139

Nest was lying with Henry in a comfortable bed in a room in the White Tower. Henry had told her that it was the very same room, from which Ranulph Flambard had recently escaped, so it was, fortuitously, furnished and available.

It was just getting light. She turned to snuggle up to the sleeping Henry savouring each minute with him. As the light from the window increased, Nest could see the effect of the unusual shape of the room. Because the room was in a large tower, the outer wall was curved, whereas the other three walls were of equal size and straight. The room was richly furnished with tapestries, rugs, a table, chairs, and a fine settle: not one's idea of a prison cell! Nest supposed that Flambard had generously bribed the Governor to provide these comforts for his captivity.

The daylight was coming into the room from a large window, and she tried to imagine the scene a few days ago when a barrel of 'wine' had been delivered to the Tower from Flambard's friends and the Governor had allowed it to be taken to Flambard's room. The barrel had contained a long length of rope, which he had used to climb down the eighty-foot drop to the foot of the Tower. Nest could not but admire his courage and resource. He was now believed to be in Normandy, safe from retribution for the time being.

She mused about her own situation. She could not believe she had been so wanton. She had thrown caution to the winds and had been with Henry openly for a few days - and nights - now. After giving him her life-saving advice, she should have gone back to Gerald and his father at Windsor, and no harm would have been done to their marriage. She might even have got away with one secret, stolen night with Henry by sending a message to Gerald that she had had to stay over in London because of the lateness of the hour. She had done neither of those things.

She had told herself that Henry needed her for the next few crucial days, while the fate of England, and Wales, was in the balance. That was probably true. But, equally true, was that she desperately needed a few blissful hours with him. She was like a sunflower which needed the sun, or a field of barley which needed the rain. She was a creature born to love. She wanted to soak up enough love and joy to last her for the rest of her life. She was terribly sorry about Gerald, who would know by now where she was spending her nights. She could not help herself: this was how it had to be.

Her thoughts were interrupted by the increasing noise of many people outside the Tower. She slid from Henry's sleeping arms and ran to the window. On the open space below large numbers of armed men were assembling, some carrying the Royal Standard.

'Wake up Henry, the Fyrd (Saxon Militia) is arriving. You must dress and go down to greet them. With their help you can defeat Duke Robert.'

By the time Count Robert and a number of the King's Council had arrived at the door, Henry had sluiced himself with cold water and hurriedly dressed. Nest was amused to see that even Kings were perfectly capable of getting ready without the help of servants, when they had to!

Henry had other things on his mind.

'Come, my love, this is your moment too. You must join me while I address the Fyrd. I shall be the stronger for knowing that you are with me.'

Smiling at Count Robert, Nest said, 'I shall stand with Count Robert, your Majesty. I shall not confuse the loyalties of those worthy men. I pray you, do not forget that you are King of a largely Saxon nation with a Saxon Queen.'

There was a huge roar of greeting from the Fyrd when the King and his advisors emerged from the main gate.

'Long live the King, long live the King!' they shouted beating their shields with their swords with deafening clatter. Before Henry had time to react, a group of them rushed forward and lifted a rather nervous King onto a wagon.

'England, England, England!' they roared, stamping their feet and waving swords and spears.

'This is the moment. This is make or break time,' Henry told himself raising his arms to speak. He knew he was no orator, and certainly no leader of the masses, but he had to rise to the occasion. His throne depended on it.

'Quiet, men!' a Captain shouted. 'Silence for his Majesty the King.'

Nest, standing with the Counsellors, prayed that he would know what to say. She need not have worried.

'Long live England,' the King shouted. 'Death to her enemies.' There was another loud roar of approval from the soldiers.

'Our beautiful, proud and noble land is threatened by many foes. I need your help.'

'Long live the King, long live England!' they shouted.

'My traitor brother, Duke Robert, has landed at Portsmouth with a host of greedy Norman Lords, and, even as we speak, is preparing to march on London. The wicked and cruel Earl of Shrewsbury has risen against me and will march to join Duke Robert. I need an army of Englishmen to defeat their grasping plots.'

'Death, death to all traitors!' they shouted.

'My aim is to build a united nation where Saxon, Norman and Dane can live together in peace and prosperity. Saxon Lords must be restored to their lands. We are all English. The shame of the Conquest must be wiped out forever. An army of Englishmen will decide the future. Normandy will see the march of English feet and shall belong to England, not England to Normandy.

'Loyal Normans, who love England and will swear to serve her, can remain. The rest shall be driven from our shores. Saxon and Danish lands and rights shall be restored. I will govern England for the benefit of all her people, not just for a few greedy Normans.'

'The King, the King!' resounded on all sides and, rushing forward men seized the King and bore him in triumph round the assembled troops, who yelled with delight once more clashing their swords on their shields.

There was repeated acclamation as the Fyrd and its leaders realised that they had the power to reverse the shame of Hastings and end the Norman oppression of their once proud land. Here was a King, Norman or not, who would give them back their pride.

'My God,' murmured Count Robert to the startled shivering Counsellors. 'I hope he can control the hurricane that he has raised or we are all done for.'

chapter thirty-one

Leaving Henry with his men, Nest returned to their love nest in the
Tower. Suddenly everything was different; the room was just a room,
and the events of the last few days were just a dream. Somehow she must
pull herself together and decide what she really wanted. If Henry, on her
advice, had raised the whirlwind with the Saxon soldiery, then so had she,
with the future of all she really loved.

It remained true that she had been passionately reminded how much her
body could respond to a man who knew how to thrill her. It had been
wonderful and very satisfying physically, yet at the end it had not been
enough. The price she would have to pay would be the probable destruction
of her marriage. She knew that she loved Gerald in a very deep and fulfilling
way. His lovemaking was as bread and butter to Henry's cake, and he did not
know how to raise her to ecstasy. It was sadly true though, that one could not
forever live on cake.

She felt safe and happy with Gerald. He was her friend as well as her
husband, and she could talk to him about anything. She loved her little
family and she wanted to have some more babies with him. Now, by her wild
and reckless behaviour she had probably ruined everything that was really
important to her.

When Henry came back from addressing the troops, he came back to a
different woman, one who had already decided to try to escape from the
situation into which she had put herself. Henry gave her an opportunity by
raising the matter with her as soon as he bustled into the room, full of new
found purpose.

'Today, before marching with the troops to confront Robert I will see the
Archbishop. I will tell him that the security of the realm demands that I
divorce Margaret, that you divorce Gerald and that we marry and make our
son legitimate. Thanks to your council my enemies will be defeated, I am
sure of that now, and the succession to the throne will be made safe. You, my
darling, have given me the key to solving all my problems.'

Nest went up to him, and taking his arm led him to a couch.

'I am so glad, Henry, that we have had this time together, and so happy
for any small help that I may have been to you in saving your throne. But,
Henry, very, very sadly, I cannot marry you.'

Henry bristled at once. 'I remind you that I am the King and can marry
whom I choose.'

'Henry, please listen. It would all cause too much trouble, and even you
would come to blame me eventually. I have a family now with Gerald, and I
know he needs me too. My actions over the last two days will have hurt him
dreadfully. He may, quite reasonably, not forgive me, but I must make the

attempt to save my marriage. As for you my darling, now that the Fyrd has arrived, your problems are well on the way to being solved. Your Kingdom will be safe.'

Henry stood up and glared angrily at her.

'Princess or not, you are too high and mighty in your speech with me. You cannot treat Kings like this, blowing hot and cold. If I so order matters, you will have no option but to marry me. I am the King and will not be gainsaid. I remind you that I can put both you and Gerald in the Tower if I so decide.'

'Henry, what love is this that would threaten me with the Tower? Two hours ago you told me that I was your only true love. What constancy is this? I, too, love you desperately: that is why I came to help save you and your throne. Please remember my children. Please Henry, try not to get angry with me, and understand.'

'This hardly can be tolerated. Once again I have a Kingdom to save, and once again you try to put my mind in turmoil when it is vital that I stay calm. I do not want an unwilling Queen. However, do not imagine that you and Gerald can escape the consequences of your actions completely unscathed. It is true that you belatedly warned me of the Montgomery Conspiracy, but it was weeks after you learned of it yourselves. You helped Gerald to enlist the support of Cadwgan and King Muirchertach to attack me. You met and conspired with your rebel brother. The list is endless. I will spare Gerald's life, because he is your husband, but he cannot remain Castellan of Pembroke. I cannot let him remain in such a key position after his active part in the conspiracy.'

'He had no choice Henry. Arnulf is his Liege Lord. He had to carry out his orders or be killed. Surely you would not have taken action against him if I had agreed to marry you?'

'Again you presume to argue with your King, Nesta. Not a wise action in any subject, however well born. Gerald was no humble soldier on the battlements. He was a man in high authority with much power. He should have refused to conspire against me, and informed me immediately.'

'He would have died, Henry.'

'Well, these are dangerous times Nesta and those in authority live dangerously. In the meantime you cannot return to Pembroke. Both you and your husband must remain under my protection. You will both accompany my army, and Gerald will join my staff. I shall make a decision about your future once I have time to do so after this rebellion is defeated.'

Nest was standing with Gerald on the fringes of the King's party. They were not at ease with each other. Duke Robert had just entered the tent with his great Lords. All were in full armour. Henry and his Barons were grouped together at the far end of the tent. The two armies were facing one another nearby. It was a serious moment. King Henry of England and Robert Duke of Normandy were parleying to decide whether they could avoid a battle to decide who was to reign.

Outside, the men of the Saxon Fyrd were shouting, 'England! England!' in their thousands at the top of their voices. Henry was reluctant to send word to silence them, as he noted that the sheer volume of their clamour seemed to be rattling Duke Robert and his Lords.

Despite the magnitude of the occasion, Gerald and Nest were still locked in the events of their recent past. It had been a very distressing time for both of them when she had returned to Windsor after her nights with Henry.

When she had first gone into his room she had said as he stood there grim faced.

'I have betrayed you Gerald, and for that I am so sorry. I could not help myself. Henry was my first love, and he is also the King. He needed me. I hate myself. You are a wonderful husband. You are also my friend. I am very happy with you. I cannot explain my behaviour even to myself.'

As he still stood there still silent she said, 'I understand if you want to put me away, lock me up or simply kill me. It would be your right, I deserve it all.'

Instead of striking her, or cutting her down with his sword, as many a cuckolded Norman husband would have done, Gerald still said nothing. Nest felt even worse.

Finally he said, 'I hurt inside more than I ever thought I could. I had come to believe that you were now truly mine, and that your attachment to the King was finished. I could kill you I know, and it might momentarily soothe my wounded pride.'

'Then do it Gerald, I deserve no better.'

'I suppose he wants to marry you now and put Holy Maud aside. I believe that he is considering doing that, to make your son Henry his heir.'

'Your dear father would have told you that I suppose.'

'So you will soon be Queen of England, when he has squared things with the Archbishop?'

'I have refused him Gerald. I told him I wanted to stay with you if you could ever bring yourself to forgive me. I told him he must keep Maud and thus maintain the support of the Saxons.'

Going up to him she knelt at his feet.

'Henry may have been my first love, but you are my soul mate and my partner through life. I have been truly happy with you. We have our little family, we talk and laugh together, we walk on the battlements and talk about the stars. If you will still have me I shall feel safe on the long journey through life. I am truly sorry I have treated you so. Please forgive me. I promise from now onwards that I will be a true and faithful wife, so long as I live.'

Gerald lifted her to her feet and wrapped his arms around her.

'I cannot bear the thought of life without you. You are the most wonderful thing that has ever happened to me. I suppose I am lucky, in that the King does not insist on keeping you at his side permanently. Let us be reconciled and put all this horror behind us. However you must promise never to humiliate me like this again.'

She had loved him even more for that, and when they had made love that night, she felt more than she had ever had before.

Henry, of course, being a King, had not made things easy for Nest. When the Royal Army had marched to confront Duke Robert, Henry had sent word that he expected Gerald and Nest to accompany him, together with Gerald's father, Lord Walter.

The message had said; 'It will not be safe for you to return to Pembroke now that Arnulf is aware of your having informed on him. I will consider whether you can return there when the Montgomery rebellion has been suppressed.'

Gerald had been very unhappy with the situation and Nest had pledged that she would refuse any further intimate requests from the King.

'Refusing a King can be difficult, even dangerous, Nest.'

Somehow the last few days had been coped with, and an uneasy Gerald and a worried Nest were in the royal tent at Alton to see if a battle could be avoided between the English and Norman armies.

Duke Robert and his mailed Lords had cautiously entered the tent and now stood a few feet apart from King Henry and his party. There had been no brotherly embrace on meeting one another.

'Greetings brother,' started Henry smoothly. 'I hope you travelled well from your most worthy crusade. I also must congratulate you on your recent marriage. I am told that your wife is most comely and gracious. However, I find myself surprised that you have seen fit to bring a small army with you, now that you have come to congratulate me on becoming King of England.'

'You mistake me, Henry, and make mock of me, which will cost you dear. I am not here to congratulate you. I am here to see if you are willing to peacefully renounce the throne in my favour, that which is legitimately mine. I should also tell you that my army is made up of full-blooded Norman Knights and Men at Arms. It will be more than a match for your rowdy Saxon rabble. You have usurped my inheritance brother, and you will return

146

it to me. The only decision to be made here is what I shall do with you. Shall you die, as you richly deserve, or shall you be locked up for the rest of your life.'

Henry laughed. 'I am afraid you have made a serious mistake Robert. To come here to congratulate me, and perhaps to offer to reunite Normandy and England is one thing, but to come over the English Channel to challenge me for the throne of England, is quite another. Your army is small, far from home, and clearly no match for the massed ranks of England. The thousands outside, Robert, are merely the advance guard. The Fyrd of Hereford, Oxford, Warwick and Northampton will be with me today, and the full strength of the rest of the country is marching to join me. I am the King of a powerful land, Robert. I am also truly King of Saxons and Normans, Welshman and Danes. The country is united behind me and determined never to be under the Norman heel again. You have no prospect of success in your rash mission, only defeat and ruin.'

The Norman magnates with Duke Robert now drew him to one side, and Nest and Gerald could clearly hear them urging him to attack Henry's army before the reinforcements arrived. Nest heard one Magnate reminding Robert that his father, the Conqueror, had won at Hastings only because he started the battle before powerful reinforcements had had time to reach Harold. Robert himself seemed unsure and hesitant.

Henry moved forward to address his brother again. As he did so further shouting outside was followed by the arrival in the tent of two beefy Saxon Lords who were at once brought forward to speak to the King.

'Your Majesty, we have brought the Fyrd of Wiltshire and Gloucester to join your power. We also know that a further, large body of men is approaching from the north. We saw them from the last hill.'

Their arrival could not have been more opportune. Henry greeted them warmly.

'You have done well my Lords and your loyalty shall be rewarded.'

Henry's attitude now seemed to change. Certain now, of overwhelming power, and aware of Duke Robert's uncertainty, he took his brother's arm and led him away from the mass of his blustering nobles.

'Come my brother, I am sure there is a way to arrange matters so that honour is satisfied and no blood spilt. We Normans should never spill another Norman's blood. There are too few of us for that.'

'Your sentiments are desirable Henry, but not achievable. My proud Norman Magnates are expecting many good things from my assumption of the throne of England. Nothing less will satisfy them now.'

However, despite this, Robert eventually agreed that negotiations could be entered into. A table and two chairs were set up at one end of the tent, and the two brothers took wine while the opposing parties of noblemen glowered and strutted in the background, hands resting belligerently on the pommels of their swords.

Henry was smiling encouragingly. Nest knew that smile; Robert would be unwise to trust it.

'Let us face the facts, as they are, my brother. You have brought an army to England expecting to push me off my throne. Your nobles are expecting land, titles and wealth. However, here at Alton you have discovered that the inexhaustible massed ranks of the Saxon Fyrd are here to support me. They have accepted me as their King and are not prepared to allow a further influx of Norman lords. You cannot win Robert, and if in the very unlikely event that you did, your victory would be a Pyrrhic one. The Saxons would soon overcome you.'

'Nevertheless, Henry, that is what I have to do. My Lords are here to fight and fight they will.'

'Robert you know you cannot win. I am already firmly seated on the throne of England, and the Church and the Saxons have given me their blessing. The task you have recklessly undertaken is an impossible one. However, I recognise your disappointment, and to put it bluntly, I am prepared to make it worthwhile for you to march back to your ships and return to Normandy. Let us say, that I will pay you three thousand gold marks a year to help soothe your wounded feelings, and to help you keep your nobles in contentment.'

'You try to bribe me brother?'

'Not a bribe Robert. Look at it as consolation money for disappointed expectations. I can afford it: England is a rich country. You will be able to share some of it with your leading nobles. I am sure that despite their bluster, many of them are beginning to wonder if they will survive the day. The prospect of going home richer men, without risking their lives, might be very attractive to them.'

Duke Robert now rose from his chair and moved back to his nobles for a muttered discussion. From where Gerald and Nest stood, it was hard to hear anything said, but some of them seemed to be angrily resisting whatever he was proposing. Others were nodding grimly.

'I do believe that Robert will back down,' whispered Gerald. 'I wonder what Henry has proposed to achieve that.' Nest contented herself with a knowing grin and kept her own counsel. She did not want Gerald reminded yet again of her days and nights with the King.

At this moment Duke Robert went back to the King, and after a few words they moved forward together to address both groups of nobles.

Henry motioned to Robert that he should speak first. Adopting a rather forced smile, Duke Robert attempted to square the circle, make palatable the unacceptable.

'I am sure you will all be happy to learn that my brother and I have reached an accommodation. It is not right, and against nature, that brother should fight against brother, that Norman should fight against Norman. We have resolved to avoid that. It is also not right that my nobles, so loyal in their support, should see their cousins in England waxing rich while we in Normandy see no fruits from my father's conquest.'

This latter statement went very ill with the English contingent, which started to murmur and rattle their swords. The men from Normandy however received it very well.

Robert continued, 'in recognition of what we in Normandy have lost, my brother is to pay me a bounty of a substantial sum in gold each year. This I will use to make the lot of myself, and my nobles, more comfortable. In return I agree to recognise him as King of England, and he confirms his recognition of me, Duke Robert, as rightful Duke of Normandy. No one needs to die today and we shall all sail away richer men.'

The relief on the faces of most of his Lords was very obvious, and few now remained truculent.

'Well spoken my Lord of Normandy,' said Henry smoothly. 'Blood will not be spilt today and all will be the richer.'

Gerald whispered to Nest under his breath. 'It seems that Henry has found the secret of the Alchemist's gold: he can give it to all, but still remain with more in his hand!'

The two parties of nobles now started to mingle and to greet one another with rather strained bonhomie, while servants placed trestle tables in long lines for a feast. Henry and Robert sat at the head of the top table, while the leading nobles of each army sat facing one another with forced banter. They were still uneasy lest some drunken exchange bring back the threat of war. Many on Duke Robert's side were wondering if Henry were plotting to suddenly have them murdered, once they were relaxed in their cups. Considerable numbers of armed guards started to appear behind their seated masters on both sides of the long lines of tables.

Despite this strained start, everyone started to relax a little. Wine was drunk copiously and vast quantities of meat consumed by one and all.

Nest was surprised to find that the King was inviting her to join him at his side at table and, perhaps reluctantly, inviting Gerald to sit next to his wife.

'He is being clever,' murmured Nest. 'A few women joining the company will lower the tension.'

So it proved at first. A number of the King's nobles had brought their ladies with the rear party, and these were now sent for, and this served to leaven the martial company with laughter and flirtation. Gerald had to suffer not only the extravagant attentions of the King to his wife, but also the bawdy remarks of the Norman contingent.

' I would have carried on the war if I had known that such a tasty lady would have been amongst the spoils,' said an already drunken Count of the Vexin.

'I heard your lovely lady was already captured as spoils, Gerald, but that Henry the King wants her back from time to time,' said the Count of Falaise.

This latter was too much for Gerald who rose from his bench white with fury, sword half drawn.

The King had also heard this last remark.

'My brother, our new accord will be soon be at an end if our ladies are to be impugned, and my honour, and that of my Magnates, besmirched.'

Duke Robert rose from his seat, and turned to address the Count of Falaise. 'Enough! Enough, Falaise! Your drunken, oaf-like behaviour is a disgrace to our company. You will apologise or answer to me in the lists and forfeit your lands. Princess Nesta, please accept my own, sincere apologies. I am sure in Normandy we have nothing but the highest regard for your reputation. Get on with it man!' - this latter to the offending Count.

A shaken Falaise rose to his feet and tried his drunken best to make amends.

'I am but jealous of your beauty, my Lady. I freely confess that, and apologise to you, to King Henry and to you, proud Gerald, for my unseemly remarks.' He then rather spoilt it by adding 'If you had seen my hag of a wife you would understand how a man might be envious of Lord Gerald.' He sat down heavily and resolved to drink himself insensible by the end of the feast, but silently.

So it was, that very much later a relieved King Henry and his army saluted the army of Duke Robert as it commenced its march back to Portsmouth and thence to Normandy.

'Well, my Lords,' said the King, 'we will leave the Hampshire Fyrd to keep an eye on things here, to make sure that my brother really does sail away as he has promised. The rest of us, in mighty strength, will march to invest the Earl of Shrewsbury's castle at Arundel. It will not hold out long without the support of Duke Robert. When Arundel falls, then we will march to take the rest of his castles at Tickhill, Bridgnorth and Shrewsbury itself.'

Smiling in the direction of Nest, he said, 'I would congratulate those close to me on their advice. It has proved invaluable so far.'

'What does he mean,' demanded Gerald suspiciously.

'He means that I advised him to call out the Saxon Fyrd, and that swung the balance in scaring Duke Robert away.'

'Let him take his advice from someone else in future,' Gerald growled, grasping her arm. Although he felt enormous relief that he had escaped further punishment, he still could not bear the idea that Henry might yet make some claim on his wife in the future.

She turned to smile at him. 'He does not need me anymore Gerald. It is all over.'

And so it proved. With the massive support of Saxon England, and very half hearted help from his remaining Norman Magnates, a Norman King, now calling himself English, smashed the power of the Earl of Shrewsbury's revolt. He besieged the castles and captured them: he bought off the Welsh Princes, and drove away King Muirchertach. The Earl of Shrewsbury, and his 'wicked brothers,' including Arnulf de Montgomery, were driven into exile, and played no further part in the history of the Nation.

Arnulf's bride, Princess Siobhan, indeed sailed to marry him, but by a strange stroke of fate, the Danish King of the Isle of Man intercepted her ship and kept her for himself. By an even stranger twist of fortune, she was eventually handed over to Arnulf in Normandy, but he died the next day, possibly from exhaustion!

Gerald and Nest remained at Windsor, while the rebellion was squashed, their own future hanging in the balance. Nest could not help worrying about the children. She had left them in the capable hands of Bethan, but she had now been away from them far too long, and longed to go back to Carew.

Finally the day came when the King ordered Gerald and Nest to appear before him at Westminster. He was accompanied by several of his advisors, but Nest noticed that Gerald's father was not with them, perhaps he was in trouble too, by association? The King's manner was cold and businesslike. Nest could hardly believe that this was the same man who was her first love and mother of her eldest child, and who recently wanted to make her his Queen. Nest was motioned to a side seat while Gerald stood alone before the King.

'I have considered long and hard, Lord Gerald, what I should do about you and your position at Pembroke after the exiling of your former Liege Lord, Arnulf de Montgomery. You are formally absolved from your oath to this traitor. Your own role in the rebellion was a mixed one. On his orders you took a major role in the enlistment of the Welsh Princes and King Muirchertach in support of the rising. On the other hand, on the advice of your wife, you belatedly recalled where your true duty lay and came to London to make me aware of the conspiracy. I already knew that serious matters were afoot, but to have the detail was useful in preparing my plans.

'After consideration of all these matters, and also in recognition of the esteem in which I hold Princess Nesta, I have decided to impose no formal punishment on you, nor will you be sent into exile with Arnulf. However it would not be appropriate for you to resume your post at Pembroke for the time being. In the meantime, Saer will be Lord of Pembroke, and you will be required to retire to your wife's lands at Carew, until I am certain that I have seen the last of the rebellion.'

Nest fumed on her chair but managed to keep silent. Afterwards, as they walked away, she took Gerald's arm.

'What a harsh man! Whatever did I see in him? I am really looking forward to making a home at Carew. I think it will be fun. I am really tired of battles and conspiracies. We have survived, Gerald, and in that we are very fortunate. Let us go and make a safe, lovely home, both for us and for our children.' Turning to give him a very friendly smile she added, 'and, let us make some more babies.'

Nest and Gerald were walking round the new fish pool with the children. It was a nice day, sunny and warm, and Nest was glad to find that the path to the pool from the recently completed fort had largely dried from the effects of the heavy rain of the last week.

'I can see a fish,' shouted five year old John excitedly. 'Look, there it is.'

'Shush John,' said his father. 'We must be quiet or all the fish will be frightened away and we shall not see them.'

'I can see one too,' shouted Llinos, who was nearly three, not to be outdone by her brother. 'There it is, near me.'

Nest and Gerald smiled at one another resignedly.

'We shall just have to come back later, without the children, to check if the lake has been properly stocked,' said Nest. 'I just do not trust that man from Arberth. I am sure he has not introduced the amount of young fish that you ordered and paid for. Anyway it is obvious that the children are going to be happy here, even if the accommodation is still basic. It is good to own a real place of our own. Pembroke Castle was hardly a good place for family life. I know you feel terrible about losing your position there, and you are out of favour with Henry, but at least you have your freedom and a new home to make your own. I have you all to myself and I am very happy for that.'

'Bethan was carrying Baby William, who was babbling contentedly. 'I am not happy at all with that pool, my Lady, not happy at all,' complained Bethan. 'It is not safe for the children. They are just at the age to drown themselves in it.'

'We will just have to keep an eye on them Bethan.'

Nest was aware that the wooden fort, which was now their home, was still little more than a large building plot. Although Gerald had started work on it soon after the King had given it to Nest as a dowry, it had only made slow progress while they were living in the castle. Hence, they found it to be only barely habitable when finally they had returned there three weeks ago from their exile in Windsor. The first phase had been the construction of a small wooden fort with a palisade outer wall, surrounded by a moat, which had been completed last year.

Nest had seen to it that stage two, had been for a higher order of accommodation for themselves than would have been normal in a purely military structure. That, however, was not yet finished, so they had to make do.

Gerald, with time on his hands, had been thinking on other lines. He led the family to a fallen tree beside a lower, marshy area.

'Let us all sit down. You also, Bethan. Your ideas are valuable. I want you all to help me with a plan.'

'What is a plan Mummy? Where is it?'

'I think Daddy has some ideas about how we are going to make a nice new garden and he wants us to think about what we would like in it.'

'Good,' said John. 'Will there be lots of things to do?'

'There will be big lawns to play on and plenty of apple trees for children to climb. Anyway, what I want you all to do now, is to pretend we can make magic, and imagine all our ideas can come true straight away. Look at this horrid, muddy marsh. We cannot make a garden there since the sea often covers it when the tide is high. However, we have already put a bank round part of it to make this pool to grow our fish. We had to keep the nasty salt water out from the sea, and then fill it with fresh water from the stream, so that useful fish like carp could be happy in it.'*

'But what will you do with the rest, Lord Gerald,' asked Bethan interested enough to address him directly. 'The salty mud does not look useful for any purpose.'

'Now then everyone - Hey Presto! Just imagine a new bank across the entrance to the big river. What would happen then?'

'I suppose you would be making another large pool because the stream would fill it up too, my Lord.'

'Yes, it will be a medium sized lake when completed. There will then be several advantages. Firstly, we will lose all the unsightly mud. It will also act as a sort of moat on one side of the castle to protect us from enemies. Then we will eventually be able to stock it with ducks and swans, which will look pretty and provide us with extra meat. However, most important of all, I am planning to experiment with the idea of a tidal mill.'

'Sorry my love, I do not know what you mean. Please explain this latest flight of imagination to us dimwits.' Nest's tone was teasing, but she was impressed that Gerald had managed to work out this complex plan without asking for any input from her until now.

'Well if we had a water gate in our lake wall, we could open the gate to let the sea in when the tide was high, and then shut the gate so that we had a big mass of water in the new lake. When the tide had gone right out in the main river, we could use the flow from the lake to drive the wheel of a water mill, which would grind our corn.'

Nest and Bethan were tremendously impressed with this plan since the advantages were immediately obvious. There was no windmill in the area as yet, and ground corn was at present brought by sea from Carmarthen at high cost.

'How can you be sure that this would work, my love? I have never heard of such a thing. The stream itself is quite small and could not turn a mill on

* *Medieval fishponds were a valuable source of food. Freshwater fish such as carp were fed on kitchen waste to provide a useful supplement to the diet.*

154

its own so you would be reliant on the water from the sea to make up the difference. Also, where would you get the machinery for it?'

'As usual, my clever wife can see the weak point. However, Saer assures me, that such mills do exist in Normandy. My father is due to visit Normandy soon so I have written to him asking him to find out more for me. I assume that the machinery will be very similar to that of a windmill, so I should be able to get someone from Carmarthen to actually make that.'

He walked over the ground with his family and showed where a leat* would be dug to carry the water to the watermill. Even John could understand the gist of the idea now.

'The lake will come right up to the fort and we will probably be able to make a moat round the other sides too.'

'This is all very grand Lord Gerald,' said Bethan rather primly, ' but where will Gelert and I be able to grow the vegetables. I was hoping we could grow our own so that they do not have to be fetched from Pembroke Market.'

'Very important, Bethan. I think that flat plot over there near the track from Pembroke will probably make a good garden, and as you say we should not then be dependent on the market.'

'Can we have some bees, my love? My father had bees kept when I was a child, and he taught me how to take care of them and the method of getting their honey.'

'That would be an excellent idea,' said Gerald happily. 'I think we are all going to have a lot of fun and satisfaction creating a whole new estate.'

'Some things have happened already,' said John pointing to the new rickety fences containing their two milking cows and a small flock of sheep.

'By your leave, my Lady, I think I should take the children back to the fort now. William needs changing and John and Llinos will be hungry.'

'Please do so Bethan,' said Gerald, taking his wife's arm. 'I think we will walk a little longer and really put this plan together.'

As they set off, Nest kissed him lightly on the cheek and said, 'how does the idea of being a landscape gardener and watermill engineer compare with your former glory, my Lord? 'Do you not think you will soon become bored?'

'Not at all, my love. It is wonderful not to have the responsibility for a time. I can really enjoy being a husband and a father.'

Nest smiled and was very happy. She had Gerald to herself now and could try her best to compensate him for all the pain she had caused recently. It was a role she convinced herself that she could sustain indefinitely.

---

* *A channel from a lake or river bringing a constant flow of water to drive a waterwheel.*

chapter thirty-four

It is Nest's twenty-third birthday and at Carew the rain is pouring down outside. Inside, in the main hall, it is cosy and warm by the roaring log fire. The children are excited. John, and Llinos, are old hands at birthdays. Their enthusiasm has infected sixteen month old baby William, who knows something good is afoot, and is rushing precariously around on unsteady legs, yelling with glee, with Bethan and Gelert trying to save him from falling in the fire. Nest is very happy. She is safe with Gerald and the children, and they have a real home of their own at last. Taking his hand, she leads him a few feet away from the family and hugs him to her.

'I am so happy my love. I wish things could always be thus. Am I the first woman to long for time to cease so that we could always be together, just as we are now? Is there somewhere a magician or sorcerer, who could wave a wand so that we never get a day older.

'We are still young. Our personal problems are behind us. John and Llinos regard me as their mother, and you have given me a sweet little boy of my own. Now we are building our own home. Best of all, I have you all to myself, here at Carew, now that you have no great castle to command, lands to rule, or hosts of rebellious knights to control. Am I being selfish?'

Holding her at arms' length and smiling into her eyes, Gerald knew that all the pain and jealousy that the King had caused between them was now washed away.

'I too am very happy. I love you my darling. We are so lucky that the wild breaking sea of recent events has spared our lives, and thrown us up safely at Carew, like happy castaways on some welcoming island. No man could have so beautiful and loving a wife, or such a wonderful family.'

Nest laughed and put a finger on his mouth to silence him.

'Stop my Lord, you will swell my head with such compliments. They tell me that it is not wise to over-flatter a wife.'

Llinos pulling at her skirts interrupted such idle thoughts.

'Come and play with us mummy. Bethan says it will soon be time for dinner and John and I want to play Blind Man's Buff.'

Gerald kissed his wife lightly and said, 'sadly, time did stop for a precious moment, but now it seems it is moving on again.' He clapped his hands and called everyone to come near.

'Let us all play Blind Man's Buff. We have a little time before dinner. John and Llinos, you are both experts at this game, so you do not need any advice from me - except not to run round too wildly. We must remember to watch that the Blind Man does not hurt himself, as well as keeping ourselves out of his clutches.'

'What about William, Daddy? Is he going to play too? Is he too young?' asked caring Llinos.

'You are right, Llinos. He is a little too young to be blindfolded, so perhaps he can help Bethan.'

The game was in full swing when the doorkeeper bustled in importantly.

'My Lord, my Lord. There is a King's Messenger at the gate seeking audience with you.'

Nest and Gerald looked at one another; their little moment of happiness really was over. What could the arrival of such a messenger mean? There had been no prior warning. They had been left severely alone since arriving back at Carew last year. Since taking control of Pembroke, Saer had remained awkwardly friendly with his old master on the few occasions when the two men had met. However, Gerald had kept away from Pembroke as much as was possible, and felt out of touch with what was going on politically.

Gerald said, 'the poor man must be wet and cold after travelling in such weather. Do not keep him waiting outside, but bring him in here by the fire. He can give me his message as he gets warm and dry.'

Nest said, 'Bethan take the children to the solar. Sadly it seems our game is over for the present. You had better feed them there, as the messenger will have to join Lord Gerald and myself for dinner in here.'

The gatekeeper had not yet left them.

'My Lord, the King's Messenger is accompanied by two servants and, apart from their horses, there is a syce leading a fine grey mare.'

'Just bring in the King's Messenger, man. Take the servants to the kitchen and tell the ostler to look after the horses. Do I have to remind you of all the details of your duties?' Gerald's feeling of warmth and wellbeing had already gone, and he had started to feel strained.

The King's Messenger was indeed very wet and glad of a warm by the fire, but not before he had presented his letter to Gerald. It was signed by Lord Robert de Meulan, but, as he read it aloud for Nest's benefit, Gerald detected the real author of the letter.

'To Gerald de Windsor, Lord of Carew.

I am commanded by his Majesty the King to inform you of various changes that are to be made in West Wales. The Castellan of the royal castle at Rhyd y Gors (Carmarthen), Richard de Serle, having recently sadly died in the King's service, his Majesty has ordered me to appoint the present Castellan of Pembroke Castle, John de Saer, to replace him with immediate effect.

His Majesty the King has a high opinion of your military skills and general ability as a governor. He also holds your wife, Princess Nesta, in particularly high esteem. For both these

157

reasons he is minded to overlook any previous transgressions against the throne and to reappoint you to your previous position as Lord of Pembroke, with immediate effect.

His Majesty also recalls from happy times long ago, that this letter is likely to be delivered on or about the date of Princess Nesta's birthday. In token of his continued high esteem, his Majesty hopes Princess Nesta will accept as a birthday present, the fine grey mare, which will accompany his messenger.

Signed, Robert de Meulan'

Grey with anger, Gerald threw the letter down.

'This is intolerable,' he shouted.

Nest, concerned that Gerald's reaction would likely get back to the King, drew him to one side in an attempt to placate him.

'My love, I beg you to take a care what you say in front of the messenger. It will likely be reported back to Henry. Indeed, it may be that he intends to provoke you, to give him an excuse to take further action against us.

'It seems he is still angry at my rejection of his proposal of marriage and is giving the knife just one more twist in the hope of stirring you to react against him publicly.'

Gerald was still fuming, but kept his voice low.

'I cannot bear that he makes it plain he considers you still his mistress. He makes it obvious that he is reinstating me for that reason, and expects me to accept you receiving expensive presents from him.'

'Do not let pride destroy us both, my darling. We have our love and our family: we must not let Henry spoil it for us. He has reminded us that we live in dangerous times and he is right. He is our greatest danger. We must use guile to survive. We must hope that his fancy will soon turn to another, easier, conquest. I detect that he is torn on the one hand, between jealousy at the strength of our relationship, together with the need to have a healthy male heir, and on the other his very real need of a strong governor in this difficult outpost.

'It does not sound to me that he is very confident in your old friend de Saer. After all, with you and I gone from Pembroke, the pact that we had with my brother is broken, and there is no reason why he would spare Pembroke next time he brings over an army to regain his inheritance.'

'As always you are right, my sweet. I either have to accept Henry's offerings with good grace and a ready smile, or risk everything we have. I can see it is not an option to turn down my reinstatement, or the horse. He would react violently against us. No, I must convince the messenger that I am overjoyed at his letter, much though it grieves me.'

'On reflection, I think your initial reaction will be reported, together with your later happy acceptance. I think no harm will be done. It will give Henry some evil satisfaction that we were forced to eat humble pie.'

Gerald now returned to the messenger with the broadest smile that he could muster, and sent for the priest to scribe his letter of acceptance, couched in gratitude and loyalty.

Both Gerald and Nest insisted, despite the weather, in visiting the grey mare in the stables, to admire her. Nest then wrote a short letter herself for the Messenger to take to Henry. It was carefully worded.

'Dear Henry,

I am delighted with my birthday present, and so happy that you remembered it in the midst of your many duties. She is a beautiful creature and I look forward to riding her.

I hope you will not think me presumptuous in saying that I am sure you have done the right thing in reinstating Gerald. He will be an excellent Lord of Pembroke and a firm and wise Governor. You will also be well aware that my rebel brother will never attack Pembroke while I am there.

I do not have any suitable gift to send you in reply, but I am asking the Messenger to take some combs of honey from our hives here at Carew, that I hope will please you?'

There was more in the same vein.

Within a few days Gerald took over control of Pembroke Castle from Saer, and Nest moved in with him and the children.

chapter thirty-five *The aftermath of the Great Storm*
March, AD 1107

G erald and Gilbert de Beauvais, with a company of Men at Arms and a party of workmen, were on the way to St.Davids. They had crossed the Western Cleddau at Havenford,* using the new wooden bridge, which had only been completed the previous week. This was part of the big public works programme started by Gerald, to mark his reinstatement by the King, as Lord of Pembroke. It was a big improvement on the ford, which was normally shallow, but which could be unpleasantly deep after heavy rain in the Preseli Mountains. So much water was pouring down the river as a result of the recent storm, swelling it to overflowing, that it was obvious that, without the new bridge, the river would have now been impassable at this point.

This appalling storm, which had struck the area two days previously, had devastated farms and house for miles around, and Gerald had received numerous requests for help: however the message sent by the Bishop of St.Davids seemed to be of a different order. The letter spoke of the roof of the great Cathedral being totally ripped off, and many ecclesiastical treasures ruined. The settlement itself had been badly damaged, and the little harbour at nearby Porthclais had been hit by a huge tidal wave, which had drowned scores of sailors, fishermen and their families. The messenger, whom Gerald had personally interviewed, seemed exhausted and dazed, claiming that the road beyond Roche** had been swamped by deep mud, and that the coastline itself had been changed by the great storm.

On reaching the little fort at Roche, Gerald found that the Knight in charge of this post on the border of the Welshry, Serlo de Guise, was supervising repairs to the roofs of several outhouses.

'Please come up the tower with me my Lord. You should have a view of what the storm has done.'

There was a clear view from the tower of the way towards St.Davids. However, despite this, Gerald did not realise at first the full extent of what had happened. True, the sea was still wild and dangerous, but that was to be expected, after near hurricane winds. Then he realised: a huge bank of stones and shingle, perhaps two miles long, had been thrown up by the sea. It completely blocked off what had previously been the little estuary of the Brandy Brook, the border between the Englishry and the Welshry***. A

* *Havenford is now Haverfordwest, the County town of Pembrokeshire.*
** *Roch was originally spelt Roche, meaning a rock in French, because the fort was built on a high rock.*
*** *The area north of the Brandy Brook is still known as the Welshry.*

whole new beach of glistening sand had already built up against the shingle and was now revealed in its entirety by it being low tide. He could also see that the road onwards towards St Davids seemed to disappear under a sea of mud where the old fort used to be.

'That way is now impassable,' said Serlo. 'I have been too busy repairing damage here, to have found time to work out a new route to St David's, but I suggest you try riding down the track to the coast. Then, you could either try picking your way along the sands or else lead the horses along the top of the stone bank. It will not be easy going, but better by far than struggling through the deep mud round the site of the old ford.'

Gerald decided to take Serlo's advice, and pressed on down to the new beach. The huge, new bank of stones and shingle, perhaps twenty-five feet high, and stretching a considerable distance in either direction, proved difficult, but not impossible, for the horses. When Gerald's horse 'Windsor', struggled and staggered to the top of the ridge, Gerald promised himself, that he must bring Nest and the children to see this magnificent beach, by far the longest that he had ever seen, before the sea took it away again in the next big storm.*

Although the tide was right out, there were still large waves in the bay, and in the far distance Gerald could see high white plumes, a hundred feet high, as even bigger waves smashed into Skomer Island. Nearer to, the glistening sand of the new beach was covered with driftwood, some of it obviously wreckage from the numerous fishing boats which had been overwhelmed by the storm.

The party soon found that it was far easier for the horses to move along the new beach than along the top of the stone bank, but Gerald realised that this would not be an option at high tide.

As they entered St David's, Gerald and Gilbert were appalled at the devastation. The roofs of many of the houses had been blown off, and the still dazed inhabitants were beginning to try to repair them. The walls of the great cathedral stood gaunt against the morning light, with its roof stripped off and the nave blocked by fallen timbers and broken tiles. Bishop Wilfred and several other clergy came to meet Gerald's party, bewailing the disaster that had befallen them. Gerald had never liked the Bishop, regarding him as scheming and worldly. The shock of the devastation had not improved him.

'Lord Gerald, Lord Gerald, our beautiful cathedral is wrecked and ruined! Our holy treasures lie unprotected against the rain. You must at once send workmen from Pembroke to save God's house.'

'My Lord Bishop, I am appalled at the loss of life here, and the damage to the town. My first concern must be for people who have now no shelter from the weather. The workmen I have brought with me will concentrate on

* He need not have worried. The beach at Newgale is still there after nine hundred years, but it is now believed to be in danger because of global warming.

helping them. I will, of course, send what further help I can from Pembroke to start to repair the Cathedral, and I will try to get new tiles for the cathedral roof from Rhryd y Gors. However, my main concern is to help the people of

this town to restore their homes before the weather deteriorates again. That must be my first priority.'

This statement of intent did not satisfy Wilfred one bit, and he resolved to try to countermand Lord Gerald's instructions after his departure.

chapter thirty-six

The coming of the Flemings
AD 1107

It might have been a little out of date in design, thought Gerald, but there had been some advantages to having a wooden castle: life had been a whole lot quieter! Pembroke Castle was in the process of being rebuilt in stone. He was watching two year old David, as he clattered noisily across the stone floor of the new dining room, pursued by four year old Maurice and six year old William. As was often the case, the children's nurse Bronwen was nowhere to be seen. I should have sacked her years ago, he muttered. He should not have to be involved in the control of his children when he was here on duty, as Castellan of the castle and Lord of Pembroke.

'We are huntsmen and David is the bear. We are going to cook him and eat him when we catch him,' said William.

David started to cry. 'It's not fair, Daddy. They are being horrid to me. I want to be the huntsman now.'

Gerald loved his growing family, but keeping up the authority and dignity of Lord of Pembroke was very difficult, when up to five of his children were running amok in the castle. He decided to discuss the problem again with his heavily pregnant wife. Later, in the Solar, he broached the subject, having first made sure that Bronwen was occupying the children elsewhere.

Nest was resting on a couch. The baby was due soon and she was finding the recent, unusually hot, weather very tiring.

'I am so sorry you had to get involved in controlling them darling. Bronwen is getting very lazy and Bethan is usually busy with other duties. I know it is very unsatisfactory.'

Gerald realised that he had to put his foot down, but in doing so managed to sound rather pompous.

'I like having the family here, but I cannot keep up the necessary gravitas for my position. I have to impress my Knights and others with my status. They are supposed to be aware that I hold powers of life and death over them, but it is a bit difficult when the likes of David run to hide under my gown.'

Nest tried not to smile: she really would have to do something about that wretched girl Bronwen. She had got away with too much just because she was a distant kinswoman from Dinefwr.

However, Gerald had not finished. 'I really have no choice but to ask you all to go to live at Carew. The building work is coming on well and it would make a good family home for us all. When I am on duty I shall be here at Pembroke. Otherwise I will leave Gilbert in charge and live with you at Carew.'

Nest sighed. 'I have been thinking the same thing myself but kept hoping it would all work out. Soon, another child will be here, and I fear it will not be long before we will have more children running around than you have Knights. Carew is only four miles away so you will mostly sleep with me, have your breakfast with us all, and then ride to work at Pembroke. I can still come over myself to see you most days - without the children. It will be all right.'

Gerald relaxed and smiled. Nest had worked it all out.

'It is the sleeping with you part which is causing the trouble. Soon we will have a small army of children.'

Nest got up and took his arm. 'But they are all lovely, are they not? And the getting of them is so much fun.'

Gerald got more serious again for a moment. 'I shall have to make sure that my spies keep me posted on any threats of raids from the Welshry. A fine fool I would look, if we were all captured by raiders, leaving Pembroke leaderless.'

At that moment a trumpet sounded from the top of the new stone keep and, almost immediately, a soldier ran to the door of the Solar.

'My Lord, a King's Messenger is approaching on horseback from the east.'

Nest and Gerald exchanged glances: they were not expecting anyone. The routine supply ship had arrived from Rhyd a Gors only a few days ago, and there had been no information about future visitors. King's Messengers were rare beasts, so by the time he arrived at the castle gate, most off-duty occupants were there to meet him headed by the Castellan and his wife.

The King's messenger leaped off his horse very vigorously for one who must have spent many hours in the saddle. Nest could not help wondering if he had had a sleep just down the road so that he would arrive at his destination lively and fresh. He lost no time in presenting his missive to Gerald with a flourish.

Having hurriedly perused the contents, Gerald decided to ask Gilbert to read it out.*

'To Gerald, Lord of Pembroke, from Henry, by Grace of God King of England, Duke of Normandy and Count of Flanders.' Gerald noted how

---

* Henry had followed Nest's advice concerning his brother Duke Robert only too well. He simply paid Robert the 'annual' subsidy just once, and when Robert tried to retaliate, eventually manoeuvred him into the Battle of Tinchebrai in Normandy. There, using a mostly Saxon army, he trounced Robert's Norman army. Robert was captured and spent the rest of his life locked up in Gloucester Castle. The battle was fought exactly forty years to the day after the Battle of Hastings, thus restoring English self-esteem.
Henry then assumed the role of Duke of Normandy as well as King of England. These interesting developments were outside Nest's life at the time and therefore outside the scope of this book. A list of further reading is included as an appendix.

quickly Henry was glorying in his victory over brother, Robert, at Tinchebrai last year, when he had reunited the two countries. However, he had not heard previously that Henry had somehow become Count of Flanders.

'Be it known to you and your staff that, under treaty, the King of England is also Count of Flanders. In this capacity we have received an urgent appeal from the people of that country, concerning a recent serious inundation by the sea, causing many leagues of heavily populated land to be permanently lost. As their Count, we have considered how we may help them and also if England may somehow benefit from this calamity.

'We are informed that many of these people are worthy citizens, with useful skills such as masons, carpenters, farriers, farmers, smiths, boat builders, soldiers, sailors, wheelwrights, potters, and jewellers. It has come to our mind that, with the establishment of a Norman settlement in South West Wales, most of the previous Welsh inhabitants have been driven out, but still wait on the fringes of our land seeking some weakness in our power which would allow them to regain their farms. There is, therefore, fertile, uncultivated land in Penfro, which should be settled with these useful Flemings in such numbers as to prevent any future invasion by the dispossessed Welsh. The skills of these people would also be very useful in an undeveloped frontier region.

Be it also known, that we have arranged shipping and the first of these people will arrive in Pembroke shortly. Up to ten thousand persons are likely to reach you, over four or five months, and you should plan to house and feed these now destitute, but potentially very valuable, people on their arrival. Land abandoned by the Welsh a few years ago should be allocated to them according to their rank, taking account of the fact that they will come with their own burgesses and minor Lords. All, however, will be under your authority, and must be required to swear oaths of fealty to the King and to you, as Lord of Pembroke, on their arrival.'

When the contents of this letter had been absorbed, everyone started to talk at once. So large an influx of foreigners was completely unexpected and was going to change the whole character of the area. They obviously would not be able to speak Norman French, or English - or Welsh. Gerald, for one, knew that the present population of the Englishry, as the Norman enclave was curiously called, did not total as much as ten thousand, even if you included all the citizens of the new settlements of Havenford, Arberth and Pembroke. The present mix was of a few hundred Normans, perhaps two or three thousand Scandinavians, a similar number of Saxon settlers, an interesting make weight of Irish and a few Welsh. St. Davids was Welsh still, of course, but being holy ground, was a special case. Many of the Normans had taken Welsh or Saxon wives and the other communities were beginning to mix by marriage too. The new influx was going to swamp the existing situation.

165

Gerald made arrangements for the care of the King's Messenger and he and Nest withdrew into the Solar to discuss the implications of the imminent arrival of the Flemings.

'I feel so sad,' said Nest. 'I love you dearly and would not dream of any harm coming to you, but I am still Welsh and this is Welsh land. Somewhere inside myself I thought that somehow, some way, my people would be able to come back to their land one day. When the Flemings come, there will be so many that this area will cease to be Welsh from that time forth.' She wondered what her brother would think when he heard the news, his plans for restoring Welsh rule to Deheubarth were bound to be affected in some way by this influx to Penfro.

'I fear you are right, my love. I too, Norman though I am, hoped that one day such peace would reign that your people could be resettled here. That is obviously not going to happen now.'

166

The mead was flowing, the men were laughing and Prince Owain was back in his father's hall. Cadwgan, Prince of Powys, felt that he could relax.

'It is good to have you here, Owain, with your uncle and your brothers, to feast with me at Christmas. Your campaign in North Wales has brought you fame and respect, and I, with all my family, am pleased to share in your achievements.'

Owain glowed with satisfaction: to bask in the admiration of his father and his uncle was for him to drink from the horn of pleasure. Of course, he thought his father was a genial nonentity, far too cosy with the Normans, but to have him loading him with public praise was very acceptable. Only one thing was missing: he needed a beautiful but compliant wife. It was time he settled down and had children.

He had always taken his fill of serving girls and countrywomen whenever he felt the need, and being the man he was, he took them whether they objected or not. However, recently, he had begun to feel that this was not enough and that he needed a suitable woman to wife, one that would worship the ground that he walked on, not object to his sexual adventures, and provide him with sons to carry on the family line. He was now thirty, after all.

The mead was beginning to go to his head causing him to start to complain loudly about the entertainment. His father groaned inwardly. Having his son back home was not an unmixed blessing.

'Let us have something more lively than harps, father. Use your imagination a bit. What we really want are some of those scantily clad dancing girls that I have heard Moorish traders can provide. That would stir up our boring Welsh Halls.'

'Such talk does not please me my son, nor does it your good mother. Here in Wales we do not need lewdness in our Courts. However, I can see you are restless, and should take my often stated advice that you should get yourself a good Welsh girl to wife.'

Owain's Uncle Meredydd now put in his contribution. 'I agree with your father, nephew. It is time for you to take a wife, someone like your Cousin Nest. It is a pity she married that bloody Frenchman, Gerald.'

'I last saw Cousin Nest when she was eight. She was a bit over-mighty then, so I assume she has not improved,' laughed Owain.

Meredydd turned to Cadwgan. 'My brother, bring on the bard to sing about what Owain has missed, so that he will have some idea of what a good Welsh girl can be like.'

The Prince nodded and called to the Chief Bard.

'Come, sing of Nest's beauty. My son does not seem to know what she has become.'

The bard sprang to his task with enthusiasm and soon had Owain entranced. The Welsh language lends itself very readily to beautiful, flowery description, particularly of women. However, the following, although in mere English, contains the gist of it.

> 'Such an exquisite creature has rarely walked the earth, famed Troy's Helen does hardly compare.
>
> Her long blonde hair, lustrous green eyes, and such regal bearing, makes mere mortal men stand in awe.
>
> To possess such a woman, and to have her love, makes us other men gasp, with envy and desire. Only the greatest, most noble and handsome of our heroes could hold a candle to such as she.'

'Enough,' shouted Owain, silencing the bard. 'Is it true, any of you? How come you all know of this beauty but not a word has reached me until now?'

'You have been much away in the North, Owain,' said his brother, 'and in any case she is that Nest captured in battle by the Normans in Brycheiniog when only twelve years old. She was then taken to London, and after beguiling the King of England, returned to Wales to marry Gerald, Lord of Pembroke. She came visiting here in Aberteifi, with Gerald, some years ago, but you were away whoring in Gwynedd as usual. Gerald normally keeps her very close, which is wise of him with such as you about, brother.'

'I must see this Nest,' shouted Owain, inflamed by the drink. 'I will ride to Pembroke tomorrow to claim kinship with her. Her foul Norman husband does not deter me. What right have they to take our women? We do not go to Normandy to take theirs.'

'Enough, my son,' counselled Cadwgan, beginning to be alert to an unnecessary problem developing under his very nose. 'I will not allow you to provoke the Norman Lord in this way. We have managed to live in peace with the French for many years, and that is how I want matters to remain. You shall not go to Penfro without my authority.'

Meredydd, always willing to undermine his brother, murmured in his nephew's ear, 'I counsel you to agree to your father's order, and leave your visit until after Christmas. If you would see your cousin, make it easy for yourself by calling at her home at Carew after New Year, when I believe the Norman Lord will be visiting Rhyd y Gors.'

The befuddled Owain stared at his uncle blankly, but in the morning when he had slept off the effects of the mead, he remembered his uncle's words.

168

He decided to say no more to his father about Nest, and to slip off to Carew after New Year, as part of a tour of the southern part of his father's domains. In the meantime he could not put Nest out of his mind. Such charms must be viewed.

chapter thirty-eight

Owain's journey through the outer Norman domains had been surprisingly easy. The area had been at peace for many years. The lands to the north and east of the Norman Enclave were ruled over by his father, Prince Cadwgan. Gerald regarded him as a friend.

He had ridden up to the Norman checkpoint at Robeston Wathen with only four men: the other twelve were already in Penfro with orders to occupy themselves with selling some ponies. He had told them there might be some interesting work for them later on, and he would send word to them if they were needed. As the Captain of the Guard asked him his business in the Norman Domain, Owain had sat straighter on his horse and taken off his hat.

'Perhaps you do not recognise me Sergeant. I am Owain, Prince of Powys, on his way to visit his cousin, Princess Nest.' He had been waved through the checkpoint with gruff apologies from the Sergeant.

Now two miles down the road, Owain was asking himself what strange compulsion had brought him with sixteen armed men and extra horses, to see a cousin that he had not met for twenty years. What madness was gripping him? Why was he doing this? Ever since the Bard's colourful praise of Nest and the enthusiasm of his brothers for her beauty, he had felt a burning and unreasonable lust for her. He told himself that this was some insane fever brought on by the lack of a wife, but whatever it was, he could not fight it, and the feeling had not diminished since that fateful Christmas feast.

He tried to reason with himself, telling himself that his boiling desire was just a mix of envy and hatred for the Normans, and Gerald in particular, mixed with lustful desire for a dream; the image of a beautiful Princess, which no real woman could possibly equal. He would laugh aloud, a bitter laugh, he was sure, when he eventually managed to see the reality of Nest, the wife and nursing mother. He was sure his passion would evaporate then. In the meantime he had to know.

Hearing his laugh, his companions, Madog and Ithel, comrades of many a battle and many a whorehouse, looked at him strangely. Their boss was acting oddly, and had done so for a while. Whatever it was that was ailing him, they had decided between themselves that it was not healthy and boded ill for them. They knew that one day he would be Prince of Powys and out of their league, but in the meantime there was plenty of life in Cadwgan and therefore many more years of fighting, drinking and whoring in the company of Owain.

It was time to get to the bottom of what was ailing him. Ithel decided to break the ice, ignoring the something about Owain that warned him not to.

'What the hell is wrong with you Owain? You are like a boar with a sore head these last two weeks. And, what in heaven are we doing here amongst these bloody Normans. Put one foot wrong and Gerald will hang you in Wogan's Cavern. He is good at that.'

Owain's reply was cold as ice, full of the other world, princely blood that they knew he had, but had long forgotten in their day to day companionship.

He pulled up his horse, drew his sword and jabbed it menacingly towards Ithel.

'Watch your tongue, Ithel, or see the future Prince of Powys cut it out. What I do, what I plan, what I order you to do, is for my consideration only. You will keep your views to yourself and do exactly what I say, or see your guts spill on the ground.'

Ithel, seeing the way the wind was blowing, wisely kept his counsel, but Madog, not believing that Owain was capable of truly turning on his comrades, leapt to Ithel's defence.

'It's that woman Nest, ain't it? You are planning some folly concerning her. For God's sake, Owain, let us turn our horses round and tumble some Welsh girls in the hay, before any real harm is done. Ithel is right: messing with Normans is just stupid.'

His face distorted with rage, Owain slapped Madog across the chest with the flat of his sword.

'You heard what I said to Ithel. No more playing games! One more remark such as that, and you are a dead man. You will do exactly what I say. Remember who I am, and show me proper respect or I will kill you. Do you understand?'

After that, the rest of the journey had been a very quiet one. It was obvious their master had taken leave of his senses, and intended to do some foolish act, concerning the Norman Lord's woman. All they could do now was to go with him and hope to save him from the worst consequences of his actions.

After riding for an hour or so, Owain led the party off the Pembroke road up a well-worn track, to the new Castle of Carew. When it came into view round a bend in the road, Owain could see that Gerald had built a small wooden fort close to a largish lake, separated from an arm of the Cleddau River by a tidal dam. Owain felt a rising tide of resentment against the Normans: only a few years ago this was Welsh land and Owain intended to do all he could to make it so again when he became Prince of Powys. In the meantime he hated how they were making the area their own.

The Castle gate was closed when they reached it, so Ithel was instructed to shout for the gatekeeper, giving Owain a chance to examine the gate closely. It was well-constructed and very stout.

When the man belatedly arrived on the palisade above the gate to ask their business, Owain could see from his blond hair and stocky build, that he must be one of the new Flemish settlers with whom the English King was said to be flooding the area around Penfro.

'I am Owain son of the Prince of Powys, cousin of the Princess Nest, and I seek an audience with her to claim kinship. I do not like to be kept waiting and demand that you hurry to open the gate.'

'Lord Gerald is in Pembroke and will not be back until evening, and the Princess Nest is busy with her children and does not usually receive visitors in her Lord's absence.'

Owain controlled himself with difficulty. 'Will you please inform the Princess that her cousin Owain is at the gate and is claiming kinship with her. Be quick about it.'

After a further interval, while Owain fumed, the Fleming returned and this time unbolted the massive gate and bid them enter the courtyard within. Waiting there, was a Welsh servant who greeted them in their own language.

'I am Gelert. My mistress bids me welcome you, and to escort you to the Great Hall where she will receive you. Your servants are to go to the kitchen where they will be given refreshment. Your horses can be tethered here and I will see to it that they are fed and watered.'

The 'Great Hall' proved to be a very modest room when Gelert showed Owain into it. He noted that there was a cheery fire and that a very beautiful woman, accompanied by a maidservant, was rising smiling to greet him. He was surprised to find that, try as he might, he could not say a word. He found her whole presence so overwhelming, that he just stood there, tongue-tied like a lovelorn youth. Nest was not unused to having this effect on men. She tried to make matters easier for him.

Holding out her hand she said, 'greetings, Cousin. This is a big surprise. It must be many years since we met. Please sit down by the fire. Bethan will take your cloak. I am pleased to see you. However it would have been better to have warned us of your visit so that my husband could have been here too.'

Owain tried to pull himself together. Truly the bard had lied: words could not describe the beauty of the woman before him. She was the most stunning creature who had ever walked the earth. Her penetrating green eyes were smiling into his now, seeing deep into his mind, reading his thoughts. It was useless to try to make small talk. She knew.

'I - I had heard the bard sing of your beauty, and I had to come and see for myself. That is why I am here. I know now that it is all true.'

Nest laughed. This was all a little too serious, flattering though it was to have so unsettled the son of the Prince of Powys.

'Come Cousin, enough of this nonsense. I had too much of that in the Norman Court. We are cousins, and I would like to hear news of my Uncle

Cadwgan who was so kind to me when Gerald and I visited him some years ago. Also, tell me of your life since I last met you, when we were but children.'

Owain was not to be diverted. Moving forward he held her hand.

'Nest, I know from my dreams that we were born to be together. You cannot love this Norman whom you were forced to marry. Come with me and we will make a new life together in Ireland. You were destined to belong to me. Surely you know that too, seeing me here. I am willing to risk all for you.'

Horrified by how events were unfolding, and scared what Owain might do next, Nest tried to snatch her hand back from his. Failing to do so, she struck him hard across the face with her left hand.

'How dare you force your attentions on me, you oaf. You have abused my hospitality. You will leave at once or I will ensure my husband knows how you have behaved. Bethan, call Gelert, and see my 'cousin' out of the gate. It seems he does not know how to behave.'

Owain went white with rage. No woman had ever rejected him so scornfully. Who did she think she was? He had dreamed for weeks that she belonged to him: she could not treat him so. She was his and would have to learn. His face still stinging from the slap, he made as if to seize her, to make her realise her mistake.

At this point Gelert and two retainers ran into the Hall armed with axes, and Owain spun round to face them, hand on the hilt of his sword. Belatedly, the already tipsy Madog and Ithel appeared in the doorway, attracted by the commotion and still wiping food and drink from their faces.

Nest found Bethan at her side, dagger drawn, and decided that matters were getting out of hand. Drawing herself up regally she decided to bring Owain to his senses.

'It seems cousin, that some mad dream has possessed you and caused you to embark on a folly that I know you will wish undone in the morning. I urge you, Owain, to leave my castle quietly, and with proper respect, and I for my part will try to forget that your visit went so badly wrong. If you do as I say there will be no need for my husband, Lord Gerald, to be troubled, or complaint made to your esteemed father. Now, please be gone.'

Still boiling with rage and frustration. Owain swung on his heel, and strode out of the Hall accompanied by his bemused companions. When he was out of the main gate and safely out of earshot he spat, 'You Ithel, get yourself to Penfro and bring my men under cover of darkness to join me, one mile back towards Robeston Wathen. I shall make that haughty wench sing another tune once I have had her on her back later on tonight.'

chapter thirty-nine

It seemed like déjà vu: once again Nest was holding on to a horseman's back as he galloped furiously away from his enemies. But this time, it was not her beloved brother's horse, it was that of her loathed Cousin Owain, and he had just raped her and was carrying her away from all she loved, for his pleasure.

She felt degraded, battered and devastated. Events had moved fast after Owain had raped her. He had half dragged her and half carried her out of the blazing castle. He had told her brusquely that she could either ride normally behind him, or, if she wanted to be difficult, he would tie her across a horse and she would bounce like a sack of turnips for the rest of the night. She had chosen to ride behind him. She hardly cared what happened to her. She had managed to stay strong until she had made sure Gerald and her children were safe, but after Owain had violated her, she had collapsed. All her thoughts of remaining separate from her feelings were gone. She felt dirty and worthless. How could Gerald want her now?

It was perhaps her fault. When Gerald had returned she should have told him how Owain had behaved and how out of control he had been.

Knowing that, Gerald would have doubled the guard or even taken her to the security of Pembroke for the night. However, like many a woman before and since, she had made light of Owain's behaviour to Gerald, as she did not want any more trouble.

As the horsemen galloped away from the last Norman outpost, and she was forced to cling to her violator, Nest longed to throw herself in the path of the horses behind and hope for a quick death. But she did not do it. Even in the midst of her misery some little part of her hoped that she could somehow get through this and escape back to Gerald. But would he want her if she did?

The horses continued to rush through the night, and Nest tried to take her mind off her grief by attempting to think of things other than her ravaged body, such as where they were going, or how Owain could possibly think he could get away with it. But her body was torn, she thought, not only violated, actually torn. She kept back going over the horrors of the last few hours. She knew now why women said that rape was worse than death; this vile Owain had forced his way into her and her body had resisted and been torn in the process. She had been made dirty, in mind as well as body.

She felt too diminished as yet to plan vengeance, but that would surely come one day, when either she herself would regain the strength and means to kill Owain, or Gerald would do it for her. The thought was only a faint thing, but it was something, and she felt a little better for it.

In the meantime, she just had to get through this: to survive, to endure. First she must cope with this endless dash across the moonlit hills, her wrung out body being thrown up and down by the horse. Then she would have to endure Owain's further violations of her that she knew would come for perhaps weeks on end. His first attack had been primitive, crude and very quick, but she knew herself to be a sensuous woman and she already had a growing fear that Owain would somehow learn how to make her body respond and that it would betray her. She had heard of at least one woman who had been raped, who had come to love her attacker. She hoped and believed that she would be able to lie dormant and unmoved under him and to keep her innermost self safe for Gerald.

She found herself wondering how whores coped with endless men without being aroused by them. Perhaps women like that were good at their trade because they were not passionate by nature. Perhaps they had been put off feeling anything by the nature of the men who used them. Whatever the truth about these things, she knew that she must lull Owain into a false sense of security and take the first chance to escape.

They had been riding for some hours now, and Nest had not seen any people or human dwellings since they had skirted the last Norman outpost at Robeston Wathen. Owain had said nothing to her since they had started, other than ordering her to put on a man's rough sheepskin jerkin when she had started to shiver in the cold January air. She had obeyed him, thinking that if she decided to kill herself, there were more suitable ways to do it than by freezing to death. Suddenly Owain raised his arm and the whole troop of horsemen pulled up.

It was not really dark because of the patchy moonlight, and Nest recognised Ithel and Madog amongst the other riders. Owain's voice was strong and harsh.

'Well done lads. You have done well tonight and will be rewarded. Gerald and his knights may only be a couple of hours behind us, so I do not intend to delay. We have to be in a place of safety by daybreak, or some peasant may earn himself a groat or two by selling news of our route.'

'Are we heading for your father's court at Aberteifi?' shouted one man from the darkness.

'No! That will be the first place that Gerald looks and anyway, I do not wish to hide behind my father. No, I have other plans, which I will reveal later.'

This was Nest's chance. That former Nest, the brave young princess who spat in Fitzhammon's eyes at Brecon, would have known what to say. Nest longed to use her vantage point to shout at Owain's men, to tell them that Owain had gone mad, and that the only way to save themselves from Gerald's vengeance was to turn on him and take her back to Carew. It might have done some good, because surely his men would know that Owain was

175

out on a dangerous limb now, and even his own father was unlikely to support him. But Nest was aware that she felt debased and diminished, and no words would come. Instead of her brave words, she heard some of his men, telling Owain that he had carried off 'a lively lass', and no doubt he was hoping for some good sport when they reached sanctuary. It was galling to her, but she kept quiet, and sat sullenly on Owain's horse, appalled by what had happened to her and what was going to continue to happen to her.

Soon they were on the way again, and Nest saw that they were skirting the first Welsh settlement at Gelli. Owain was leaving the main track to Aberteifi and commencing to work his way north-west, and then west around the area under Norman control. Nest's brain started to work properly for the first time since the ghastly trip began. Where was Owain taking her? Probably soon to some remote bothy, or cottage, for the night - and then where? The north-westerly route led to St David's. Surely the Bishop would not give sanctuary to Owain? The western track led soon to the sea - perhaps that was Owain's plan.

After more endless miles, Owain again pulled the party up and sent Madog forward to reconnoitre. When he returned, Owain led the troop up to a group of low buildings which proved to be a ramshackle barn containing hay and other smaller structures, which Nest thought might provide shelter for sheep in severe weather.

Owain now lifted Nest down from the horse and spoke to her for the first time since they started.

'We shall stay here for the rest of the night and the daylight hours of tomorrow. You have no maid now: you will have to get used to that. Take my horse's blanket and find a quiet place for us to sleep at the back of the barn. I will settle my men and the horses and Ithel will organise some food. It will hardly compare with your dinner at Carew. If you wish to relieve yourself, Madog will keep watch while you go behind the barn. I will be sharing the horse blanket with you later, so you can look forward to that.'

When it grew colder, she covered herself with the pungent blanket and fell into an exhausted sleep. She hardly cared when she realised that Owain had joined her and was using her body. It scarcely seemed to matter and afterwards she soon fell asleep again.

When she slept she had a wild dream, that Owain was King of England, and that Gerald was playing the lyre and she had to sing to his court of his great victories. They knew if they stopped that Owain would pop another of her children in the great stew-pot boiling in the centre of the building. Angharad was already in the pot and kept calling for William to come to play with her, with the water boiling round her. Bethan seemed to be able to fly and cawed like a crow from the rafters, calling out that it was Nest's fault, for being too beautiful.

When she awoke it was broad daylight and Owain was with his men interrogating the farmer, who had unfortunately come to check his barn and was now in deep trouble. Madog was saying that the man knew too much and would have to be killed. Clutching the blanket around her she moved over to the men and pleaded for his life.

'Let him come with us, Owain. No doubt he will be useful for whatever plan you have in mind. Whether you kill him or not, he will still be missed, and if you take him with you he will be one more sword to save you from the wrath of Gerald.'

Owain turned to look at her calculatingly. He did not trust her, and had been thinking during last night's ride that when she recovered from her ordeal he would have to make sure she took no knife to their bed. He realised that this intercession on behalf of the farmer meant that she was feeling much more herself today.

However, she was known as a passionate woman, and he had taken her again last night. Perhaps she had liked it. He decided to go along with her wishes, whatever her motivation.

'You, Geraint, ride down to the farmhouse and give these coins to this man's wife. Tell her that he has joined his Prince for a week or two and, if she is sensible, he will return safe and sound. In the meantime, she is to give no information to the Normans when they call, or she will never see her man again.'

Before nightfall they all had a meagre meal of rough bread and a portion of cheese washed down with water from a stream. There had been a sudden alarm when Ithel had spotted a party of Normans approaching the farmhouse below. Owain had hidden his men and horses amongst large boulders behind the barn. He took Nest there too, and held a knife to her throat, warning her to keep quiet.

The Normans stayed only briefly at the farmhouse and then moved off back towards the east. This time Owain went himself to see the farmer's wife to question her as to what had been said. He learned that she had told the Normans that her husband had seen Prince Owain riding along the Aberteifi track earlier that morning, and that he and his party appeared to be drunk. The Normans had believed her and made off in pursuit. Owain again warned her of the danger to her husband should she talk, and gave her some more money.

Owain kept his men under cover during the rest of the day in case they were spotted. When it got dark, the party set off again towards the west. Again Nest was ordered to ride behind Owain. It seemed he was not going to give her the chance of slipping away from him under cover of darkness.

They rode hard for several hours. Owain often lost the way and was forced to consult the farmer. Nest was glad she had saved his life but rather ruefully wondered if, in doing so, she had aided Owain more than she had intended.

About the middle of the night the troop started to pick its way down a rocky valley, and soon Nest was aware that they were approaching the Welsh fishing settlement at Solfach*. It seemed that they were expected, because a group of men greeted Owain. However, instead of leading then down to the quay where Owain obviously believed he had a vessel waiting to take his party to Ireland, it seemed that there was a problem.

'The Norman Lord's men arrived here today and have been searching the ships in the harbour for his runaway wife. We have been told to look out for you, your Highness. There is a reward for you, dead or alive - five pieces of gold!' he added hopefully.

Owain started to swear, but not too loudly. The nearest Normans were only a few hundred yards ahead down the track. He drew Ithel and Madog to one side to confer.

'We will have to lie low for a while. Bloody Gerald has already secured the ports. I had hoped to be one step ahead of him. We will go by a back way to Aberteifi and ...

At this point Nest saw a small chance of escape. She started to shout for help at the top of her voice, at the same time rolling off the horse. She managed to land on her feet and quickly stabbed the horse's flank with the pin end of a brooch that she had torn from her dress. The horse reared and bolted, with Owain desperately trying to keep control. Nest gathered up her dress and started to run away into the darkness towards the harbour.

'Catch her,' shouted Ithel, 'or the bitch will get us all hung.'

It was a brave attempt, but a forlorn one. Hampered as she was by her dress, she was rapidly outrun, and was dragged back screaming to a very angry Owain, who smacked her hard across the face to keep her quiet. While Ithel and Madog held her, Owain forced a small cloth into her mouth and secured it with a scarf round her head. She was then tied like a sack of corn across the back of a packhorse and Owain made ready to lead her off. However, the leader of the Solva men stood in the way holding out his hand.

'Sorry, Prince Owain, but I must have five pieces of gold to keep my men quiet. You would not get far if they went unrewarded. We live in hard times.'

Cursing, Owain handed over some gold, and headed his party back into the hills. For the next two nights he aimed roughly north-east, across the Preseli Hills, skirting the few isolated farmhouses. The days were spent lying low. Eventually they reached a remote part of the coast, ten miles from his father's Llys at Aberteifi. The men led the horses down a steep defile towards the sea and then along the low-water beach for about a mile until they reached a large sea cave. Nest's legs were untied from the packhorse, and Owain set her on the ground.

* *Solfach, the settlement called Solva in English, has had a long history of seafaring. It is now a popular holiday resort and yachts ride at anchor in the pretty, sheltered harbour.*

'This is likely to be your new home for a few weeks, Cousin dear. I will send word to my father but I doubt he will be brave enough to offer me sanctuary. We will stay here until the hue and cry dies down, and then double back to Solfach to take ship to Ireland. You are the only woman with us, so make yourself useful and prepare a meal.'

Owain called his men to gather round him. 'Ithel and Madog will remain with me and will accompany me to Ireland, when it is safe to do so. The rest of you, return to your homes until I need you again. I have gold here for each man. Thank you for your loyalty.'

The one named Geraint blurted out a query. 'When your father learns of our return, what account are we to give him?'

'You will all stick to the same story. No mention of us laying up here in the cave must be made. You will tell the old man, Norman lover that he is, that you overheard me talking to Ithel and that we planned to make our way to Ynys Mon (Anglesey) with a view to escaping to the northern part of Ireland.'

After the bulk of the men had gone, life in the cave soon settled down to a routine. Each morning Madog and Ithel would set off to find what they could to eat, and Owain would bring wood from the beach for Nest to light in the cave mouth, in the embers of last night's blaze. There was a freshwater spring near the cave, which she had had to clear and deepen, so that she could fill the cooking pot, free of sand or seaweed. While she was there she would do her best to wash herself while the men were away. She had realised the very first morning that her chance of escape was almost nil, as the cliffs were not climbable, and that Ithel and Madog had gone one way along the beach and Owain the other, thus cutting off escape in both directions.

Most days the men would return with a rabbit or hare from the snares they had set overnight, but that was not always the case and they then had to find something else less appetising such as clams or edible seaweed. There was usually a supply of turnips, stolen from distant farms, so Nest could prepare some sort of a meal, however primitive. If Owain lowered himself to go foraging, he often brought back more useful extra items such as chickens, eggs or sacks of grain because he was more daring.

One night he was badly bitten by a farm dog, and Nest bound up the wound with a strip torn off her underskirt, having first washed the injury with seawater, as she had learned from her father's Moorish physician. She had long since come to the conclusion that, escape being impossible, she must appear to acquiesce, focussing on her survival for the sake of her husband and children. For the first time, Owain seemed touched by her care.

When they lay down for the night, he tried much harder to please her. Despite herself, she found that her traitor body was responding. She forced herself to shout as if in pain and sprang up away from him. It was a bad moment, but Owain made it easier for her, by calling her a cold bitch and slapping her face. Ithel and Madog grinned at each other in the firelight but took care that their master saw nothing.

As days turned into weeks, Nest decided to ask Owain if she could try to catch some fish to vary their diet. He was deeply suspicious of her motives and set Madog to watch her, in case she had some plan to escape. She employed Madog to shape a hook from her dress into a fishhook. One end was opened up to take the meat from a clam, the other was bent round into a small circle to which she attached a length of twine from Madog's saddle repair kit.

Watched afar off by her water-shy guard, she pulled her dress up to her knees and waded out to the nearest rock, where she sat casting her line until she caught something. For the first time since her abduction she started to enjoy herself: it was like being back with Henry catching trout, except that her first conquest was a large crab! However, this was large enough to be edible.

Her second catch half an hour later was a plump mullet, whose soft mouth slipped off the hook when he was hardly out of the water. Not willing to lose him, she threw herself onto him before he managed to struggle back into the sea. She had had the forethought to steal Owain's travel sack to imprison any possible catch, and this was soggy with her catch when the rising tide forced her to struggle ashore.

The men were delighted that evening with the improvement in the diet, but Owain was enraged at the condition of his bag. However, he did let her go fishing again, from time to time, as long as she took some other container for her spoils.

Nest was not allowed to walk far from the cave, but on warmer days she often sat by a rock pool, lost in thought. She still hoped that Gerald would somehow find her, but it did not seem likely unless someone betrayed Owain. They had seen no one since they arrived, except the occasional boat passing far out to sea.

As week followed week, Nest began to believe that she would have to live like a savage forever. Worse than that, she wondered if Gerald might give up on her and abandon her to Owain, now that he had had her in his bed for so long. If only she could send some message to Gerald, anything. Her efforts to bribe Madog to take a message to a farmer, who would be bribed in turn to take it to the nearest Norman outpost, ended at once when Madog betrayed her to Owain. The only result was another beating.

She wondered why Owain continued to keep her captive: he appeared to be getting little benefit. She assumed that his overweening pride would not accept that she would not eventually be won over by him. For her part, Nest had early on decided to be purely practical: there was no point in sullen non co-operation. Life would be more comfortable for her if she cooked the food and lit the fire. There was always the hope that Owain might relax his guard, and she would be able to seize some chance to run away. However no such opportunity ever occurred.

It was not until the spring flowers were blooming on the little patches of grassland near the cave, that Owain announced that it was time to make another attempt to travel to Ireland. The horses had gone when the rest of Owain's men had returned home in January, it having been decided that it would have been impossible to keep their presence secret had they remained. Ithel was therefore despatched on foot to make the arrangements, and was gone nearly a week. When he returned he was leading a small pony that Owain announced that Nest would ride, 'so that she did not slow down their progress'. She was glad of that, since she knew that the men would travel over twenty miles each night.

The journey back to Solfach took two nights, but was uneventful. They did not pass through any villages, and met no one on the way. They arrived at the outskirts of Solfach in the middle of the night. Their arrival was expected, and they were taken at once down to the harbour. A tense Owain pulled Nest quite roughly off her pony to gag her for the last mile of the journey. She was hustled on board a ship lying alongside the quay and the crew cast off at once. Within twenty minutes the ship had been towed past the rocks guarding the narrow entrance, the mainsail had been raised the wind being fair, and the ship had set off for Ireland.

T he Irish girl, the one called Niambh*, was brushing Nest's hair too energetically for her to concentrate on her attempts to think properly. She wanted to think about her children back in Wales. She tried to imagine what they might be doing, and whether they were all right. She was sure Bethan would be looking after them well, and Gerald would do what he could when he was there, but surely her children were missing her.

The bigger ones, John thirteen, Llinos ten, William eight, and even Maurice five and David four, were old enough understand when Bethan told them that Mummy still loved them, and that one day Daddy would find her and bring her back. However, poor little Angharad, who would not be two until September, would not understand at all, and must be quite devastated. Then another thought struck Nest. Perhaps, after several months, they were not thinking all that much about her, and had even got used to her absence!

Nest felt that she had now been in Ireland forever, although she knew it was only a few days. Owain's ship had crossed a very rough sea to Munster, and it had been wet and cold. Nest had wondered if there would ever be an end to her sufferings at Owain's hands. There was one benefit of the stormy trip however: she had recovered her will to live.

Several times the ship had been hit by huge waves which had partly swamped her, and despite desperate attempts to bail her out, it had been touch and go whether she would be buoyant enough to rise to the next great sea. Nest had started to care very much about her survival. She found herself fervently begging God to let the ship reach port safely, and promising Him, equally fervently, that that if it did she would somehow escape from Owain's clutches, return to Gerald, and become a model wife and mother. She also promised herself quietly, hoping that the Almighty would not hear, that she would make sure Owain paid a very serious price for what he had done to her and hers.

One morning she had woken from an exhausted sleep to find the ship was alongside the quay at Waterford and Owain was hassling her to get ashore. He had then hired horses to take them to the court of King Muirchertach. On the way her spirits had started to rise, because she knew that Gerald had visited the court some years ago and believed that he had been well received. Surely she could appeal to the King to save her, and possibly even turn the tables on Owain. However, once there, reality had been rather different.

The whole party had been ushered into King Muirchertach's presence, and Owain had knelt in front of the King and asked for sanctuary.

'Noble King, I am Owain, eldest son of Cadwgan, Prince of Powys. I

* *Niambh is pronounced Neeve*

have had to flee my native land because of the cruel Normans whose power is now everywhere. My father knows you to be a hospitable and mighty King who has often succoured my family in the past. I beg you to give me sanctuary, so that I may lick my wounds before going back to fight the cursed French, to recover what is rightfully mine.'

Muirchertach had risen from his throne and was about embrace Owain when Nest ran forward and threw herself at the King's feet.

'Noble King, I am Princess Nest, daughter of King Rhys ap Tewdwr, late King of Deheubarth, wife of the mighty Gerald, Lord of Penfro. This vile Owain, who has the temerity to call me Cousin, has broken into my Lord's castle, violated me, carried me off, woefully misused me and deprived me of my husband and children. You will know that my husband, the mighty Lord Gerald, has visited your court in former years and that you received him with great hospitality and friendship. I beg you, great King, to free me from this cruel abduction and return me to my Lord Gerald in Penfro. I also entreat justice, and I ask you put these criminals in chains, and to send them to their just deserts at the hands of Lord Gerald. I have no doubt that my Lord is even now ranging the Irish Sea with a powerful fleet, seeking me, and great will be his wrath against anyone who gives sanctuary to his wife's abductor.'

Owain was still kneeling. He stared, astonished at Nest's dangerous plea. He had been certain that she was far too cowed to speak up for herself, and he had deceived himself into believing that his frequent possession of her had made her appreciate that she now had a real man between her legs. It seemed that he had been far too complacent and this unpredictable and violent King might be persuaded by her words.

To everyone's astonishment the King began to laugh. Tears ran down his face and he clutched his sides with mirth.

'This is the most amusing thing that has happened this year. So you have had the temerity, Owain, to run off with the Norman Lord's woman, none other than the proud and passionate Nest. Oh dear, oh dear! You really like to live dangerously do you not? What a state he will be in, his Knights riding everywhere, seeking to recover his wife and to slaughter you. Every night that passes he will be in such a fret thinking of what you are doing to her. Have you not thought, you reckless Welsh Prince, that the Norman King himself will be seeking your blood, because she was his mistress first, was she not?

'Ha, ha, I do like to find a man after my own heart, a man who does not give a toss. Well, you came to the right place for help young man.'

Owain was very relieved.

'Thank you your majesty. I knew that I could rely on you for help. Please let me know how I can serve you while I am here. But first, let me drag away the Norman's hellcat so that I can give her a good beating. She shall learn to be respectful.'

'Oh no, no, my impetuous friend. Matters will be arranged on my terms. You and your men are given sanctuary, and I will certainly expect you to aid my soldiers in their skirmishes with the King of Connaught. In the meantime you will leave this Nest with me. She looks very lively: I will borrow her from you for a while and try her out. I must have some reward for my trouble.'

Both Nest and Owain were shaken in their own different ways by the King's decision, but Nest was the first to act. Rising to her feet, she rushed up to the throne shouting her defiance. Two of his courtiers came to his side in case she tried to injure him.

'What manner of King are you? Have you no respect for a Princess of the Royal House of Dinefwr? Am I to be treated like some trull from the stews to be passed from man to man for sport? Have you no thought for the consequences of your barbaric treatment of me? Can you not see that this will bring the English King's army to your shores to punish you for your treatment of the mother of his eldest son?'

'Ha, ha, Owain, you have a gem of a girl here. She must have some Irish blood. Are you sure you can manage such a firebrand? I look forward to taming her for you. I have had plenty of practice.'

'My Lord King, I must protest. I did not bring the Norman's woman here to have her taken from me.'

'Do not worry my lad. You can have her back soon, when my wife gets tired of seeing her around. She allows me my diversions but does not like any of my women to settle in too comfortably.

'Now young Prince, go off and install your men in my barracks, and I will find some military task to keep you happy. In the meantime, the Princess shall be taken to my quarters.'

Despite protests from both Owain and Nest, she had then been taken to a room in the King's private part of the palace, and the door had been barred from the outside. Nest threw herself on the truckle bed and could not help herself weeping. Her situation was now even worse than before. She now had not one, but two, loathsome men who intended to use her body in any way they willed. She could not imagine how she was going to escape now, nor how she could cope with her situation.

Nest continued to be anxious about Muirchertach's intentions towards her after what he had said when she arrived, but there was no sign of him as yet, so perhaps she was worrying needlessly. After all, he had a wife who might take some interest in his activities!

In fact Niambh was her only visitor so far. She seemed a friendly girl, if rather rustic compared to Bethan. Nest had felt that things were beginning to improve, even though she did not yet know what ideas the King had in mind for her. She decided to try to gain some information by subtle questioning while she had the chance.

Niambh told her that various members of Muirchertach's family had rooms nearby, and Nest was rather unnerved to learn that the King himself had the room next door, which, however, he usually shared with the Queen. Niambh was quite happy to tell her that the Queen was a fierce, little, old lady, who could reduce the King to a nervous jelly, if she so decided. Another room nearby belonged to Princess Siobhan, the King's daughter.

'You are helpful Niambh, and I am truly grateful. One thing, however, puzzles me. I thought when my husband, Lord Gerald de Windsor, visited Waterford some years ago, he arranged for Princess Siobhan to marry Lord Arnulph. Did the marriage not go ahead?'

Niambh, relieved to find that the Welsh Princess was more open to normal female gossip than she appeared, confided in a low voice that Princess Siobhan had indeed been betrothed to Lord Arnulph. A ship had set sail, taking her to meet him. Niambh's voice now became even quieter and more conspiratorial.

'However, my Lady, the Princess's ship was intercepted by Magnus, the Viking King of the Isle of Man, and he carried her off, so that Lord Arnulph never enjoyed the charms of his betrothed.'

'I thought you said that Princess Siobhan is now living in a room nearby?'

Niambh looked a little uncomfortable and seemed unwilling to say any more, but Nest gave her a sweet smile.

'It is a big help to know what has happened, and I will never tell anyone about our conversation.'

'I should not be saying this, my Lady, but you will no doubt hear this elsewhere. The Princess is very warm blooded, and it is said that not many men can cope with her demands for more than a night or two. The outcome of the abduction was that King Magnus soon sent her back to Ireland, with a bag of gold coins to ease her father's pain.'

Despite her concern about her future, Nest could not avoid grinning at this outcome of Arnulph's would be nuptials.

After Niambh had departed, Nest began to wonder when the King would be coming to enjoy his prize, what she could do to foil his intentions, and whether she could have any hope of the Queen having any influence over his actions. Thus, when Nest heard the bar being withdrawn again, she was very apprehensive as to what would happen next. The door opened and a very beautiful auburn-haired woman came in.

'I am Princess Siobhan. I thought you might like a little company. I have brought you a glass of mead for your refreshment.'

Nest had never liked mead, but thought it unwise to offend the King's daughter, so she accepted the gift with a smile. She is truly beautiful, she thought, but there is something just a little chilling about her. She could not help feeling that Siobhan was looking at her in a rather predatory way, but could not imagine why. She felt very uneasy, but tried not to show it.

'I am very pleased to see you, Siobhan, another woman of high station. As you probably know, my loathsome cousin Prince Owain has abducted me, and your father, the King, has kindly sent Owain away, thus freeing me from his attentions. I am now hoping against hope, that your father will decide to ship me back safely to my husband in Wales. I am sure he would want to reward anyone who is kind enough to help me.'

'Oh yes, the noble Gerald! I remember him well. Rather a cold creature I thought. There he was, far from home, lonely in his little bed, and rest assured, all I wanted to do was to show him a little Irish hospitality. However, he shot out of the bed like a scalded cat. Now then, why would he do that? Surely I am not so unattractive?'

Nest tried not to flare up at the implications of that statement; she thought that Siobhan might be her only hope of escape from her situation so she tried to avoid reacting. As for what had gone on with Siobhan during Gerald's visit, she was not too concerned. She knew that many Knights sought out women when travelling, and there would be little point in a wife making too much fuss about it. Anyway she had never worried about Gerald in that regard, and she was just a little amused to find that this alluring woman had apparently been rebuffed by her husband.

However it seemed that her amusement was unwisely showing on her face and Siobhan's voice took on a crueller tone.

'It is a pity that you find me amusing Princess Nest. I had toyed for a moment with the idea of helping you, but you have changed my mind for me. Other ideas are more promising. Strange pains in various parts of his body have lately affected my father's powers with women. It would be a task stimulating for me if I helped him bed you. I think I really like that idea, it makes me feel warm in a very special way. Also a tumble with you is just what the dear old man needs to revive his jaded appetite.'

Despite being shocked by Siobhan's apparent depravity, Nest tried to reason with her. She thought Siobhan was just trying to frighten her and would not, when it came to it, stand by and do nothing to prevent her being violated.

'Siobhan, I beg you, please help me. You are my only hope in this foreign land. I am desperate to get back home. Gerald told me you were a kind, intelligent, sensitive woman: I am sure you do not really want me to be forced against my will. Dear Siobhan, please help me to get away from here. I am sure you have the power if you so choose.'

As she said that, she began to feel strange and remote, as if she were not really present. Her legs felt like jelly and she was forced to sit down on the bed. She could not imagine why she had been arguing with Siobhan, it did not seem important now. Nothing did.

Siobhan's face took on a look of malicious triumph.

'Come in dear Father. I think your bird is ready for plucking,' she called. As she said this, her face seemed to Nest to swell and then contract rhythmically. Nest felt she was now out of her body and looking down at the scene.

She noticed without any surprise that all the colours in the room had changed. Siobhan's previously auburn hair was now bright green, her cream linen sheets were now blood red, and the previously ruddy face of the King, who had just entered the room, was now bright yellow. She felt a burning feeling in her groin, but it did not matter, because she was not in her body so the King could have it if he wished. It was all very strange: beautiful in a way, but truly she no longer cared what he did.

'I have given her the draught, Father. The proud Welsh bitch will be happy to have you now. Please let me stay. I want to see you with her.'

The King, not for the first time, found his daughter's needs repugnant. He had realised long ago that Siobhan was not just avid to go to bed with any capable man in Ireland, but that she also was attracted physically to him, her father, and she was trying to satisfy this incestuous need by seeing him have sex with Nest. Violent and full of lust though he was, he showed his distaste by propelling his daughter vigorously out of the door.

'Now, my dear,' he said, joining Nest on the bed, 'let us get to know one another a little better.'

Nest felt remote, as if it was all happening to someone else. As the King pulled her unresisting body to him, the pains and the choking feelings that he had experienced intermittently over the last few weeks, came back violently behind his eyes, and in his throat, nose, and ears. He reared back above Nest, clutching his face and neck, retching and gurgling. As he did so, the head of a huge maw worm forced itself through his mouth and seemed to peer curiously around at the outside world. Nest, who had been partly stupefied by Siobhan's potion, was dragged back into full consciousness by the King's choking yells, only to find the he had been trying to violate her. She made to scratch at his face, and then screamed with terror as she saw the unbelievable horror of a huge worm pushing its way through his mouth, and another worm coming out of his nose.

The King fell over on his back clutching at his face and choking, just as the old Queen, Siobhan, and half the Court of Munster rushed into the room attracted by the commotion. They all stared horror stricken as the giant worms writhed out of the King's face.

The old Queen did not take long to pull herself together.

'My poor love, this woman is a sorceress. She has bewitched you. Come you cowards, help me to pull him away from her and then you must cut off her head. That is the only way to destroy her powers. She is an evil witch.'

The King's retainers hung back fearfully, but encouraged by the Queen, the Captain of the Guard and several chieftains, pulled the choking King away from the bed while others seized Nest. The Queen, changing her ideas as events unfolded, seized a knife and held it to her breast.

'You do not frighten me foul witch. Take your wicked spell off my husband the King or I will kill you,' she screeched.

Nest was trying hard to pull herself together and to clear her head. She knew that her life depended on it. She remembered that she had seen such a phenomenon before, as a child in her father's court in Dinefwr. Her father's physician had been from Spain, and had studied in the Moorish City of Grenada. He did not believe in sorcery and looked always for a physical explanation for the body's afflictions. He had befriended the young Princess, and allowed her to witness how he ministered to some of his patients.

After a skirmish, a wounded soldier, suffering from complicated fractures of the leg, had been brought to the Physician to have them set. The operation was going to be long and painful so the Physician had given the soldier a strong analgesic known only to the Moors. Unfortunately, before the operation could start, the man began to choke to death and the quick-witted doctor forced open the man's mouth, to reveal the head of a large and loathsome worm, which was obstructing his throat. The doctor had poured a strong saline solution into the man's mouth, which caused the worm to come free. Unfortunately the man had died while the treatment was being administered.

Afterwards the physician had explained the sequence of events to the young Princess, in the hope that she would not complain to her father about being exposed to such horrors. He had told her that such worms were not uncommon in the stomach, and could occasionally migrate to other parts of the body, such as the liver, lungs, or throat. They could even appear through the nose or the mouth, and even, very distressingly, poke round the side of an eyeball.

Meanwhile the Queen's knife had been pressed more tightly to Nest's breast.

'Your last chance, Sorceress. Free my husband the King from your spells, or you will die.' Thinking that perhaps a captured witch might need more positive motivation, she had added, 'free him and I will send you back to Wales with a bag of gold - but do it fast.'

'Take your knife away, my Lady Queen. I can do nothing until I am on my feet. Also, give me back my cloak, so that I am decent before the Court.'

Nest was helped upright while she wracked her brains for a way out of her situation. She knew that they would hack off her head unless she outwitted them. Meanwhile, the Queen and Siobhan were trying to comfort the worm-afflicted King. It was obvious to Nest that none of them had ever seen a giant maw worm, so she decided to use this situation, taking full advantage of their fears.

She stood as tall as possible, and pulled her cloak tightly around her. She pointed fixedly at the stricken Monarch, and then turned to address his still shaken family and chieftains in a loud, and she hoped, threatening voice.

'King Muichertach has offended against all laws of hospitality by trying to violate me, a Welsh Princess, who has sought sanctuary at his Court. Unfortunately for him, he has unwisely chosen for a victim, no ordinary woman, but one who has inherited great powers from her ancestors. I do not like to use these powers because they are dangerous, but today I had no option. The spell I have used is a very strong one. It grows more powerful each moment that passes, so, if I am to try to remove it, I must act very quickly.

'However, before I do so you, your Majesty, you must swear to ship me safely back to my home in Wales when I have removed the spell.'

'I so swear, I so swear,' came the choking voice of the terrified King.

'Only rid me of these foul worms and I will return you to Gerald and with gold besides.'

'You must swear on the bones of your forefathers, that you will return me safely to Penfro, or face the return of the worms to torture you until you die of them.'

The King began to choke again as the worms filled his mouth and throat.

'Yes, yes! I swear to return you on the bones of my forefathers, but stop my torment quickly,' he gasped.

Nest tried desperately to remember what cures her father's physician had recommended all those years ago, or indeed if there was any cure. Anything she used would have to sound like sorcery to gain the right effect.

'Bring me the blackest cat in Munster. It must be very soft and with green eyes to match mine. Then bring me some ground salt. Finally, bring me a lighted candle of the best quality. But bring them quickly, or the worms will choke the King before I can free him of the spell.'

In remarkably quick time the requisites were produced and even the frightened black cat, dragged from the kitchen, seemed soothed by Nest, and happy to be held by her for a while.

Clutching the cat to her shoulder with one hand, and pointing straight at the King's head with the other, she started her incantation. It was actually a cookery recipe, in Welsh, given to her by her mother for the making of broth of pig, but it sounded convincing to the awe stricken Court. She hoped that the Welsh language was remote enough from Irish, to prevent anyone recognising her mother's ingredients. She now settled the cat on a cushion and took a handful of the ground salt.

'The King must be held down firmly, as the cure for his affliction will be painful,' she ordered.

When she was sure he was held down so tightly that he could not move, she hovered by his head, endlessly repeating her incantation, while really waiting for one of the worms to reappear. Suddenly, there was a gasp of horror from the onlookers as a worm pushed its head out of one of the King's nostrils. As more of the worm came out, its head circled round Muirchertach's face, as if examining it. This was Nest's chance, and conquering her revulsion, she seized the loathsome creature tightly just below its head with her fingers. Pulling at it firmly, to expose more of its body, she quickly applied salt lavishly with her other hand. The extra pressure caused the King to faint with pain.

The worm now started to writhe powerfully, and Nest had difficulty in keeping her grip. Finally, the giant maw worm went limp, and she was able to pull the whole repulsive nematode slowly but slowly out of the King's nostril, finally dragging the complete eighteen inches of it free of his face. She then reversed her grip on the maw worm and applied the lighted candle to the creature's head, repeating her incantation until most of its body was shrivelled up. The blackened remains she then threw contemptuously to the Captain of the Guard, who backed away in horror.

She then repeated the process with the other worm.

When she was satisfied that both the worms had been dealt with she pronounced that the King must be given a sleeping potion and should rest in bed for three days and three nights, and he would then recover completely.

'In the meantime let arrangements be made for a ship to take me to Penfro in the morning. Be warned that if any attempt is made to cheat me then the King will again be smitten, this time fatally.'

Nest was still wondering if they would really let her go, when the old Queen began to chuckle, and then to laugh out loud, holding her sides as if she might burst.

'Thank you, thank you, young Welsh sorceress. I think you may have taught the old rogue a lesson. He will be a little slower in bedding a reluctant maid in future. You have done me a favour. You shall be delayed no longer. The sea is quiet and a ship shall sail this very night to carry you back to Lord

Gerald. You shall take gold and silver to the Norman Lord as recompense for any failings in Irish hospitality. Give your husband a kiss from me, and tell him I would have kept him for myself, had I been younger when he came to see us.'

chapter forty-two

*Trying to get back to
normal at Carew
May, AD 1109*

It was mid afternoon. Gerald had gone off on a mysterious 'patrol,' and Nest had decided to rest on their bed in the solar. What was the good of being a Princess and Lord Gerald's wife and having a house full of servants, if you could not go and lie down, when you wanted to, she reasoned? Quite unexpectedly, she found she had burst into tears. Once started, she could not stop.

Bethan, who was nearby and could hear Nest's sobs, came bustling in and was instant concern, going at once to the bed and putting her arms round her. 'There, there, my Lady, whatever ails thee?'

Being Nest's maid is not always straightforward, she said to herself. Sometimes she is very much in control and very regal, and Heaven help me if I pry on those occasions. I have often been slapped down when I misjudge her mood. At other times, like this one, she needs a friend, an equal, who can understand her nature and her situation, and can give her advice without fear or favour. She is very complex and it is hard to always get it right. I am only a servant and cannot always understand, but she knows I love her like a sister.

The sobs continued, and Bethan judged that it was best to just be there with her until she was ready to talk. It was only a month since she had escaped from Ireland after being raped and abducted, and goodness knows what was going through her mind. It was still very early days after her ordeal. Finally the sobs started to subside.

'My mind is in such a confusion, dear Bethan, and strange thoughts come pouring in unbidden, making it difficult for me, for example when I must play my role of wife or mother. At night, I sometimes wake from a terrible nightmare where perhaps a terrifying monster is chasing me through dark woods. Lord Gerald is often woken by my phantoms. He tries his best, but he is a man and cannot know what it is like for a woman to be forced against her will. Sometimes it is even worse. I find in my dream that this woman, who must be me, is searching for her violator as if she wants him. At other times, the dream is as it really happened, and Muirchertach's Queen has ordered my head to be cut off. I can see the axe coming down and know I will never see my children, or my Lord Gerald, or you, true friend, again.'

Bethan hugged her even tighter.

'It may be many moons before you can put this terrible experience behind you my Lady. It is sadly not uncommon, in the rough times in which we live, for a woman to be violated. I have known various women to whom this has happened, and it has always gone very hard for them, never mind if they be timid and meek, or else lively and bold. Some women can not bear any man near them afterwards, even if he be her husband. Others, who were formerly very active in their marriage beds, afterwards just had no feelings left. They had to pretend things were well for their husbands' sake.'

'Thank you Bethan. It helps me to know how other women have fared. I should not be talking to you about how it is between Lord Gerald and I. It is not seemly. But, I must talk to someone, and we have been together since we were girls. I know I can trust you.'

'Please, tell me anything you wish. You know that your secrets are always safe with me. It is much better if you are able to talk about what happened to you, and that may be the only way that your troubled mind can be healed my Lady.'

All the feelings that Nest had suppressed over the last few weeks suddenly started to pour out of her. It was like opening a floodgate.

'Lord Gerald loves me and I him and he was overjoyed that I was able to come back to him. However, he has been open with me, and tells me of his unworthy suspicions that I had somehow encouraged Owain to do what he did, and even if that were not true, that I had come to enjoy the experience. I cannot blame him, because in the darkness of the night I lie at Gerald's side unsleeping, and look for some guilt in myself. I wonder why I did not tell him just how outrageous Owain was when he came to Carew that afternoon. I feel so guilty even though my mind tells me that I did nothing to encourage him, and I know I feel absolutely nothing for Owain save loathing, and I tried my very best to escape from him.

'Despite Lord Gerald's love for me I feel sullied in his eyes, just like a beloved painting that has been accidentally scratched. It is still loved, but not so prized as before. Because I know he feels like this, I cannot give myself fully when we are in bed. He knows this too and perhaps worries that I am thinking of Owain. That is why he goes off without a word each morning. I believe he is hunting for Owain. Lord Gerald thinks he may be back here in Wales hiding in the forest. He believes that I will not truly be his again until he has killed Owain with his own hands. Only then will we be free of him.'

'Prince Owain will be caught and killed one day, my Lady, you can be sure of that. Lord Gerald told me after you were taken away, that the King himself was outraged when he heard of it, and ordered a hue and cry throughout Wales to recover you and to bring Owain to justice.'

'Even that will not truly have pleased Lord Gerald. He will have suspected that the real reason for the King's concern was that he still regards me as his personal property, and that my abduction was lèse-majesté. I do so wish that we all could go back in time to those happy days when we first came to Carew.'

'If I can be bold to say what you should do, my Lady, then I would suggest that you should cling to the thought that time will cure all your ills.

You must live each day, one at a time, knowing that this bad time will eventually pass. Lord Gerald is a good man and I can see that he loves you and all will be well eventually.'

Nest went quiet, and Bethan thought that her words had helped her. She was concerned, therefore, when Nest began to sob again.

'You do not know the worst of it. I believe I may be pregnant and Prince Owain is likely to be the father. What shall I do Bethan?'

chapter forty-three

Nest flees to Dinefwr
May, AD 1109

●

Yet again Nest was on the back of her horse. She was riding hard to try to bypass the guard post at Robeston Wathen before Gerald came after her. Gelert and Bethan accompanied her, both very reluctant and concerned. She had hardly slept at all the previous night worrying about what was best for her to do.

She was pregnant, she was sure now, and the baby must be Owain's. Her mind churned with conflicting thoughts. Gerald would never accept the baby as his own and would reject her too, if she insisted on rearing it. However, her maternal instincts told her that the unborn child was innocent of the wrongdoing of its father and she must love it and protect it from the world.

However, she had other duties. She had four children of her own who needed her, and she had accepted Myfanwy's John and Llinos when she died, so she already had six children who loved and needed her. Then there was Gerald, whom she loved dearly, who was trying to come to terms with her recent abduction, and for whom she wanted so much to make everything right again. How could she deal with her new situation when she knew that she was not her normal self? Even without her pregnancy she would have needed months to recover from what had happened to her with Owain.

Bethan, desperate about what Nest might be driven to, had offered to bring a wise woman to abort the baby, while warning of the serious risk to Nest's health from such a course of action. She had begun to think the unthinkable, that Nest's mind would crack, and that she would throw herself from the battlements. She had even thought of breaking her word to Nest and telling Gerald how things were with her mistress. However, events had moved on quickly before she had had time to do anything.

Early this morning Nest had decided what she must do. She could bear no longer the stresses of her situation. She waited until a stern looking Gerald had ridden off for the day to Pembroke hardly finding a glimpse of a smile for her when he left. She then called Gelert and Bethan and told them she had resolved to return to Dinefwr, and that they were to prepare to depart secretly. They were to load just the very minimum for the journey. She told Gerald's Steward that she had decided to spend a few days at Pembroke. She called Bronwen, the children's nurse, and told her she would be in full charge of the children for the time being. Everyone was surprised at her sudden departure, as Gerald had not mentioned it, but no one dared to question her decision, especially as the grim-faced Bethan and Gelert kept silent.

Once they were clear of the Norman enclave, Bethan decided on one more appeal.

'My Lady, please forgive me, but I think that what we are doing is unwise. If we go back now perhaps no harm will have been done. We can go to Pembroke just as you told everyone. Lord Gerald will be surprised to see you but will think it just a woman's impulsive action.'

'I need my mother, Bethan. She will tell me what I must do. I can bear no longer to twist in my bed at night struggling with my demons and then wake to the real world and have no relief for my tormented mind. If my mother cannot help me then I am truly lost and do not know what I must do.'

Bethan and Gelert looked at one another silently. 'Truly, our Lady is heading for even deeper trouble, but all we can do is to stay with her' was the thought that was on each of their minds.

As they rode, Nest's mind was in turmoil. She knew that she was clutching at straws seeking advice from her mother. What could her old mother tell her that she could not tell herself? After all she was twenty- nine years old, had borne five children, and had been asked for her advice by the King himself. What help could her mother be? However, such had been the devastating effect of recent happenings in her life, and her terror of the consequences, that her mother was her only hope.

The party had just entered the forest near Hendy Gwyn (Whitland), and the track was straight and wide. Nest had heard the sound of a hunting horn not far away, so she decided to urge her horse Beauclerc into a canter. She had just turned her head to see if Bethan and Gelert were keeping up, when her horse caught a forefoot against an exposed tree root, and fell heavily. Nest was catapulted from her saddle, hit her head against a tree, and knew no more.

At once Bethan and Gelert were at her side

'Thank God, she still breathes - but very shallowly. I cannot see much damage to her head,' said an appalled Gelert.

'Quick, you must ride as fast as you can to the abbey at Hendy Gwyn. You must bring men with a litter. She is with child and the shock of the fall may yet kill her. Goodness knows if the accident will cause her to lose her baby anyway. I will stay with her to do what I can.'

Many hours later, after night had fallen, Gerald was approaching Hendy Gwyn Abbey, accompanied by Gilbert and a party of Men at Arms. He was devastated at the thought of what he might find there.

He had arrived home at Carew after a heavy day, to find that his wife was missing. His Steward told him the Nest and her servants had suddenly decided to leave 'for Pembroke' soon after his own departure in that direction. Manifestly they had not arrived there, and the children's nurse, Bronwen, had been quick to tell him that her Lady Nest had been very agitated and not herself, and had ordered her to take full charge of the children as she might not be back for several days. Bethan and Gelert had gone with her, but had refused to comment on the sudden departure to the other servants.

While Gerald was still trying to make sense of the situation, and feeling a growing sense of unease, a horseman had arrived from Hendy Gwyn, bearing a message for him from the Abbot.

'My Lord Gerald,

Please be aware that your wife, the Lady Nest, was carried here this afternoon after a riding accident in the forest nearby.

She is still unconscious and barely hanging on to life. I regret to tell you that my Physician, who is attending her, tells me that she has lost the child she was carrying due to the accident.

I do urge you to make haste to come here quickly as I cannot promise that she will survive until morning, although we are doing all we can.

In haste,

Xavier, Abbot.'

Sick with worry, Gerald had left at once for Hendy Gwyn, hardly taking the time to accept the pouch of bread and cheese urged on him by his cook. What on earth had provoked Nest into such drastic action? What was she thinking and where was she going? Why had the normally sensible Bethan agreed to go with her? Nothing made sense.

True she had not been herself since she had come back from Ireland, but she had suffered at great deal at the hands of the odious Owain and opportunistic Muirchertach. How he longed to get his hands on both foul men. How he intended to punish them for what they had done to his wife.

What was all this about her losing her baby: she had not told him she was pregnant?

Although it was past midnight, the gate was wide open at Hendy Gwyn Abbey, and the monks rushed out to help him from his horse. The Abbot was standing near ready to greet him.

'Good Abbot, please take me to my wife, I beg you,' said Gerald, desperate with fear. 'I cannot thank you enough for all you have done. Where is she? Is she still alive?'

'She is alive yet, my Lord' replied the Abbot, leading him into the Abbey. 'She is lying in the sanctuary. She has not spoken since she arrived. My Physician still fears for her life.'

Gerald found Nest still lying unconscious, her face as deathly white as the spotless sheets of the bed in which she was lying. Bethan was at one side wiping her brow, and the Physician stood with a bowl of leeches ready to bleed her. Incongruously, Gelert was standing near, holding a drawn sword.

'God be praised you are here, my Lord. I need to bleed her, and her foolish maid servant has instructed this oaf of a giant here to cut me down if I do.'

Gerald pushed everyone aside, and knelt down beside her. Taking her hand he said,

'My poor dearest, whatever has brought you to this? Please do not leave me. Please open your eyes and speak to me.'

To everyone's surprise and joy, Nest opened her eyes and tried to smile. 'Gerald! My baby, my baby, what has happened to him?'

Tears running down his face, Gerald repeatedly kissed her hands.

'Thank God you are back with us my darling. I could not bear to lose you. You are my life, my joy! Never mind what terrible demons you have in your mind: together we can banish them. I am so sorry my sweetheart that I was not aware how badly you were suffering. I have let you down, but I am here now and there is nothing that you can tell me which can possibly come between us. Sadly, you have lost the baby. I am so sorry. It is a new, innocent life lost, but you at least are alive, and we will get you well.'

Turning to the doctor he said,

'Good Physician, I know you only intend the best, but my wife needs no leeches. Please make speed and bring her hot mutton broth to put colour in her cheeks.'

In her heart Nest had not really accepted that she was carrying a baby. It was very, very sad - but Gerald still loved her and all would be well.

chapter forty-four

Gerald was looking grave, even alarmed. Nest knew that he was not easily unsettled in so obvious a way. Something serious must be afoot. His Steward, Hubert, was standing at his side, holding a piece of parchment.

'Is there something wrong my Lord?' she said, speaking formally because it was a public place?

There was an element in Gerald's manner, which Nest found disturbing. He looked away as he replied.

'His Majesty the King is paying us the honour of a visit next week.'

Nest was thrown into confusion. Surely this unexpected Royal visit would stir up trouble that she had hoped to avoid. However, despite herself, she felt a quiver of excitement that she would be seeing Henry again: he still had that unwelcome effect on her. She knew that her body was betraying her and she made herself think about how Gerald must be feeling.

He was certainly upset at the news. He had eventually forgiven and understood those moments of madness so many years ago. She could not believe that she had been so selfish as to stay those two nights with Henry when his throne had been in danger. Although Gerald had made himself understand, he certainly did not wish to be reminded of it.

She knew that she was very lucky that it was Gerald she was married to, loving, forgiving Gerald. Many another Norman husband would have killed her, if he dare, the King being involved, and Society would have accepted that he had a right to do it. Also, it was only two years since Owain had abducted her, putting another terrible strain on their marriage. The baby had been Owain's, she felt certain of that. However, Gerald had said nothing about this although she was sure he would have realised the baby could not be his. She knew she was very lucky to have Gerald, and she was determined not to risk her marriage again.

'We must talk about this development in private, my Lord.' She pleaded to him with her eyes. With a glance at Hubert she added, 'Such an important visit must be planned for.'

Once in the privacy of the Solar she tried to get him to discuss with her some plan to avoid the dangers of the visit.

'I am so worried about Henry coming here, and what it might do to us. Perhaps I can develop some convincing malady and go to stay with my mother in Dinefwr?'

'You know he will not believe that, and I am convinced that he will use this visit as an excuse to bed you. What can I do: he is the King and will bed whom he likes? Besides that, I fear that you will not be unwilling, knowing the bonds that there have been between you in the past.'

Pulling herself together, Nest put her arms around her unhappy husband.

'My sweet, you are my dear, wonderful, loving husband and I will not allow Henry to come between us. I will not deny that a woman's first love always has some sort of attraction to her, but I will not allow that to make you unhappy or to spoil our wonderful marriage.'

'But he is the King!'

Drawing herself up, and looking gravely into his eyes, she said, 'and I am Princess Nest and not to be taken at whim like some servant girl.'

Despite everything she said, and although she was sure that Gerald knew that she was being sincere, she was not able to convince him that all would be well.

Preparations went on apace for the visit. Large quantities of extra food were obtained for the needs of the King and his party. The castle was cleaned and decorated with flags and bunting, and Gerald ordered his men to fix wooden walkways on the outside of the new stone walls, and to paint them with lime-wash. The castle now looked very imposing, gleaming from afar in the sunlight.

A banquet was to be held in the King's honour, and many of the new local Magnates, like the mayors of Pembroke, Arberth and Havenford, were sent invitations. There was a buzz of excitement both within and without the castle walls. Nest knew that many of the Knights' ladies would be gossiping about her since they knew that she used to be the King's mistress.

'What are they saying about me Bethan, now that the King is coming?'

'What idle women who have nothing better to do always talk about, my Lady.'

'I do not intend to grant any favours to the King, Bethan. Tell them all that.'

'My Lady, I am so worried about you. The King is all-powerful and takes what women he likes. Since you once bore him a child and were formerly his mistress, he may very well be coming here with expectations,'

'Well, he will be disappointed. I am resolved to defy him.'

'My Lady, please think carefully. If he is defied he will be certain to take some violent action, either against Lord Gerald or your own self.'

However, Nest had decided to be resolute. She had after all helped Henry to save his throne. He must feel some gratitude for that.

When the Royal Party arrived, at first all went smoothly. He admired the castle and the arrangements for his visit. He was very friendly to Gerald and spoke of advancement for him. When he greeted Nest he was gracious but did not say or do anything untoward. The formal banquet that evening went very well, and Henry said he was delighted to be in Pembroke, which had always been dear to his heart. Nest started to hope that her fears were groundless. She was a little concerned, however, that he had not brought the

Queen with him, saying that her health did not permit long journeys.

Such banquets did not always include dancing, as many Normans preferred watching entertainment like jongleurs and fools, so Nest had made sure not to arrange any. However, at the feast, where Nest sat on Henry's left hand and Gerald on his right, The King suddenly said, 'I trust that you have arranged for us all to dance, Lord Gerald. I really enjoy dancing.'

Gerald smiled wanly. 'By all means your Majesty. There can be dancing soon after dinner.'

Of course when the dance started the King immediately took Nest's hand and led her to take up position for the first dance set. The complicated routine meant that he was actually dancing with Nest for only part of the time. However that, together with the waiting time between dances, was quite adequate for him to talk to her, albeit in snatches.

'I have been looking forward to this visit for years.'

'I have missed you very much, as I hope you have me?'

'No doubt you will be able to slip away to my room later on?'

Nest's replies had to be equally short.

'I have missed you too Henry.'

'Gerald has suffered enough - I have tried hard to retain his affections.'

'Please, if you love me, do not try to force me to your bed'

'If you love me, please leave me in peace.'

The King's conversation now became much harsher, with less effort to keep it private from the other dancers.

'You forget yourself, my Lady. Remember I am the King.'

'I shall expect you in my room tonight. If you do not appear, I shall send my Squire to fetch you.'

'I hope Lord Gerald knows where his true interest lies.'

It was not until the feast was over, the King withdrawn to bed, and Gerald and Nest were back in their temporary quarters (the King had been given the Solar), that Gerald was able to discover what was distressing her.

'He insists that I go to his room. I refused to go and then he grew angry and said he would send his Squire to you to fetch me. He said he hoped you would know where your true interest lies. My love this is my worst nightmare. I just cannot go. We are truly happy now. I do not want any other man. We have put our troubles behind us. I cannot be summoned to his bed like this.'

Gerald put his arms around her and drew her to him.

'I too, am blissfully happy in our marriage. You are the most wonderful wife and friend that a man could possibly hope for. I was deeply hurt by that time so long ago when you felt that you had to go to Henry to help him save his throne. I was wounded to the heart, but I understood. There was some unfinished business between you. He had been foolish enough to put you aside and yet, as King, he still needed you. After that I knew you had decided to commit yourself to me and I was content. As for the business with that ruffian Owain, we live in violent times and unfortunately many a wife has been raped by such as he, and husband and wife have had to come to terms with it. I could only take comfort that you and the children survived.'

'I do not want Henry. I could not bear it. When his Squire comes I shall refuse to go with him. The King will have to accept it. He surely owes my feelings some respect since I helped him save his throne.'

'I fear things will not be as easy as that. Thwarting the will of Kings is always dangerous. I have been lucky to have you for so long. You are my wife, I shall defy him for you.'

Further discussion as to the wisdom of that action was prevented by the arrival at the solar door of the King's Squire. He came to the point at once.

'I am here by order of his Majesty the King to ask for the immediate presence of the Princess Nesta in his chambers. He has matters of importance to discuss with her.'

'Please, give my duty to his Majesty the King and tell him that the hour is late and that my wife has retired for the night. In any case, it would not be seemly for a married woman to visit the King's apartments at night, alone.'

The Squire was aghast.

'My Lord, such a reply to his Majesty the King would be most unwise. Shall I not say that Princess Nesta is unwell - that would be less harsh.'

A frightened Nest appeared behind him in her nightgown.

'My husband is trying to protect me, as I am unwilling to go. Please give my entreaties to His Majesty, and beg him in the name of everything that we ever meant to each other, to spare this damage to my marriage. Please entreat him to forgive me. I hold his opinion of me in the highest regard. I beg of you, kind Squire, not to mention my husband's words. It will be better if he knows the reply is from me.'

To their surprise, the King himself now stepped from the shadows.

'I see it is necessary to remind you both that I am your King, and my wishes will be obeyed by everyone in my Kingdom. No one defies the King, except that he risks his life. Guards! Arrest Lord Gerald on a charge of treason and take him away to the cells. He is dismissed from the post of Lord of Pembroke. Bernard de Deols shall take over here in the meantime, while I consider the future. Take Princess Nesta and lock her in her room. She will go to a convent. I would not touch you now, Lady, if you were the last woman in the land.'

The vanguard of the King's party had just entered the deep defile in Crichan Forest as they ascended the trail towards the pass into Norman controlled Brecheiniog. There were cliffs rising through dense woodland on either side of the road. Close to the right of the track a stream in high spate was competing with it for space, and rushing back down to the lowlands from which they had just climbed.

The sun was now excluded from the narrow ravine by the height of the cliffs, and to Gerald it already seemed much colder. Only a few days ago he had been happy at home in Carew with his beautiful wife and devoted children, and they had been planning wonderful things to do, now that spring had come. There had only been two years between Nest's escape from her abduction and this latest disaster, and it had taken her accident on the way to Dinefwr to bring him to his senses and make him appreciate how lucky he was to get her back.

Then, in the twinkle of an eye, it had all been taken away from him. Here he was, being led away on his horse as a traitor, by the King. Poor Nest, who had had so much to endure, was to be thrown into a nunnery, and their children were to be brought up as orphans in Dinefwr. His appointment at Pembroke had been stripped from him and given to Bernard de Deols. His own fate was unclear. Such was the King's wrath at Nest's rejection of him that Gerald even wondered if he might be put to death on trumped up charges.

Gerald's soldier's eye had appreciated, as soon as they had entered the gorge, how spread out and vulnerable were the hundred or so Men-at-Arms and the dozen Knights that made up the King's party. The track was so narrow here that there was only room for two men to ride side by side, the result being that the entourage was spread along the trail for half a mile. The length of the column was further increased by the baggage wagons having to be helped through the frequent ruts in the road. Obviously, similar thoughts must have been occupying Earl Hugh, who was in the vanguard, in charge of the column, because Gerald saw that he had called a halt and was picking his way back to consult the King. Gerald noted that the King was now only a few yards in front of him. Perhaps a third of the Men-at Arms were bringing up the rear behind the baggage train, which was immediately behind Gerald.

As Earl Hugh discussed with the King how to give more protection to him in this dangerous place, many of the horses reared in alarm as trumpets blasted close by, accompanied by a rain of arrows. Gerald saw that many riders near the King fell at once. Simultaneously, Earl Hugh's terrified horse bolted across the stream away from the conflict. Many of the remaining Men-at-Arms followed Earl Hugh, thinking that he was leading a withdrawal.

Gerald could see that two large parties of Welsh soldiers had emerged from the woods, and were cutting the Norman column into three parts the better to destroy it. The King himself now stood virtually alone, with only his page and two Men-at-Arms for protection. Instinctively seeing where his duty lay, Gerald seized back his reins from the bemused soldier leading him, grabbed the man's sword and then urged his horse alongside the King. He was only just in time to cut down a Welshman trying to lead the King away.

'Follow me, Sire. We must regroup with Earl Hugh on the far side of the stream'.

Arrows swishing all around them, the King hastily followed Gerald to the comparative safety of the wooded slope on the other side. Seeing this lead, the surviving Normans followed their example all along the line, and started to make their way, in the shelter of the trees, to join Gerald, the King and Earl Hugh. The baggage trains were already lost, but in a few minutes upwards of ninety Knights and Men-at-Arms rallied around the royal party.

The Welsh guerrillas, overconfident of their strength, now came out of the woods further down the stream, and made a frontal assault, uphill, against the Normans. Seizing his chance, Gerald left a small force to guard the King, and led a cavalry charge downhill against the dismounted Welshmen. Most were killed or wounded and the rest routed in disarray.

Gerald called off the pursuit of the survivors and at once returned to the King.

'Sire, I submit that we are still in grave danger. It is likely that there are more Welsh troops in this area. It is vital that we cross the pass into territory under Norman control before nightfall.'

The badly rattled King, who a few minutes ago thought that he was as good as dead or else a prisoner, was slowly pulling himself together.

'Congratulations, Lord Gerald. I really thought that my hour had come.' He smiled woefully, 'I was fortunate indeed to have you in my party, for whatever reason. It seems that I have misjudged you.'

'Thank you, Sire. I hope I know my duty. May I now urge you to allow me to organise our remaining men to give us the best chance of escape from this very dangerous situation?'

'By all means, My Lord. We can talk later about your situation. Let us make haste as you suggest.'

Gerald now reorganised matters so that the Knights were around the King in the centre of the column. The vanguard and the rearguard were made up of Men-at-Arms. Further dismounted soldiers made their way on foot through the woods, where this was possible, on either side of the column, to give early warning of any further assault. Despite the fact that they could now only proceed at walking pace, progress was not much slower than before, as they were no longer delayed by the baggage wagons.

Several times in the next few hours, the men guarding the sides of the column, reported seeing Welsh troops shadowing them, but no further attack materialised. Just before nightfall, the relieved Normans finally emerged at the far end of the pass. There they were met by a column of troops sent by Bernard de Neufmarché to escort the King to his castle at Brecon.

Later, at table in the Great Hall, the King insisted that Gerald sat at his right hand and personally helped him to the best pieces of meat. When all horns were charged with wine, the King rose to address the company.

'This very day we have seen that the workings of The Almighty are truly mysterious and wonderful. Only two days ago, God, seeking the preservation of his anointed King, so clouded my mind and judgement that I carried off as a traitor my beloved servant Lord Gerald, and brought him close by me through the dangerous pass in the Crichan Forest. Here we were ambushed by the Welsh, who would have seized me and probably killed me but for the speedy action of my dear friend here beside me. He, true Knight and clever soldier that he is, saved my person from the enemy and drove them off in defeat and confusion, then brought us all safely to Brecon. I call on you all to join me in drinking to him, and in thanking Almighty God in his wisdom. Gerald, you are restored with all honour to your post at Pembroke.'

It was the middle of the night, and Nest lay in her bed in the Solar wondering how she could cope with the loss of Gerald. This latest terrible blow, sent her by a truly malignant fate, had arrived late the previous evening.

She had been discussing with Bethan, the sudden, dreadful order by the King to take Gerald away charged with treason, and his typical dog in the manger ordinance that she, Nest, would be locked up in a nunnery. As usual, Bethan was full of hopeful advice, supported by Gelert and even the usually rather dizzy Bronwen.

'The King is not used to being gainsaid, my Lady, and this is how Norman Kings behave when they are. However, after a few days, weeks or even months, he will see that he has acted against his own best interest. He will have lost the services of Lord Gerald, his strong shield here in the west, and more to the point he will see that his actions have permanently alienated the true love of his life. You are no ordinary woman to him. You are the one he should have made his Queen. If a mere servant girl can dare to judge a King, I would say that he always hopes that he will win you over one day. Putting you in a nunnery, and depriving you of your children, is not the way to help his cause. Even a Norman King will eventually realise that.'

Bronwen put in her bit in support.

'Bethan is right, my Lady, I could never take to someone who took away my children. I am sure he will see he has done the wrong thing after a while and put matters right.'

Nest began to feel a little happier about matters. No one had arranged to put her in a nunnery yet, and the King had not actually harmed Gerald so far. Perhaps her simple, yet sensible, servants had got to the heart of the matter. As soon as Henry had time to think about things, he might very well change his mind. Henry had replaced Gerald temporarily by one of his Knights, Bernard de Deols, but he, having been a close associate of Gerald, seemed fortunately reluctant to think about a nunnery for her. She had even been allowed to retain the use of the solar for the time being. Perhaps he would allow her to slip quietly back to Carew, there to await the eventual release of Gerald.

At this point Gerald's former secretary, Hait, arrived at the door. Nest was aware that Hait was besotted with her, and she and Gerald sometimes had discussed whether his obvious devotion had yet reached the stage of being an embarrassment. Gerald had joked that it was patently obvious that most men could not help being in love with her, such was her beauty, and he could hardly ban all the male sex from the castle.

But now, she now had so much on her mind that she could not cope with Hait, so she felt like being less than gracious when he hurried in to speak to her.

'My Lady, I must talk to you on a private matter. So, could I see you on your own, please.'

Such was the urgency of Hait's manner that Nest reluctantly dismissed her servants to see what it was all about.

'My Lady, I have some very bad news. It seems that a pedlar has arrived at the castle and, even at this moment, is being questioned by Bernard de Deols.'

Nest had a sudden sense of dread.

'What bad news? Tell me plainly at once.'

'The pedlar is saying that the King's party was ambushed two days ago near Brecon by your brother's men, and that your husband, Gerald de Windsor, was killed while protecting the King.'

Nest was instantly distraught. 'My husband - dead? Killed by my brother? It cannot be so; it must not be so!

'Take me to this pedlar, I must talk to him myself.'

However, when Nest rushed into Bernard de Deols' office, where he was still questioning the pedlar, she found dreadful and detailed confirmation of Gerald's death.

'I was descending the bwlch* on the way to Caerfyrddin (Carmarthen) when I saw a file of men, bearing the King's standard, coming up towards me a fair way off. I was just wondering if I dare try to sell them something, when there was a tumult, and the Normans were attacked from the woods. Many fell dead. I hid in the trees for hours, and later worked my way round the crags to reach the little settlement of Llandovery by another route. There I was told that the attackers were Gruffydd's men, and heard that they had intended to kill the King. However, Gerald de Windsor had saved the King's life, and he was fatally injured doing so. He was taken to Brecon but died on the way. I am so sorry, my Lady.'

She had somehow staggered back to the solar and for many hours had been stricken by the deepest sorrow. The noise of her cries and heart-rending sobs had reached all the rooms around her. Nor was she alone in her grief. Many throughout the castle, men and women, grieved with her. Gerald, stern though he could be, was loved and respected by all around him. From the powerful Knights of his entourage down to the lowliest servant girl, nearly everyone was very saddened and shocked by the unexpected news. He had always been caring and fair minded, always concerned to look after the interests of his staff. His sudden arrest had shaken everyone, but it had been widely expected that the King would soon restore Gerald to his position once his pride had healed.

* *Bwlch is Welsh for mountain pass.*

207

Everyone knew of the close bond between Gerald and Nest, so the sounds of her anguish surprised no one, and expressed what many of them felt themselves.

Only one person secretly rejoiced in the news - Hait. He was besotted with Nest and deeply envious of Gerald. Every time he had witnessed the little public intimacies between the couple, the loving look, the gentle passing touch, Hait's obsession with Nest had grown, and his loathing for Gerald and his access to her person, had increased. Now all was quiet in the castle, and Hait, lying on his palliasse in his little office along the corridor, felt that his chance had come. He must go to her. He knew that Bethan was temporarily sleeping elsewhere with the children.

He crept softly to her door and listened. He could only hear the noise of regular breathing. He tried the door. It was unlocked. He went in very quietly. By the light of the rush-light in the corridor he could see Nest sprawling on the bed, sleeping the sleep of one exhausted by her suffering. His heart filled with compassion, and desire. She surely needed solace now. He gently lay down beside her and put his arm around her. She shifted in her sleep and murmured, 'Gerald is it you'?

Hait whispered, 'my Lady, it is I, Hait. I feel for you in your distress and have come to comfort you. I feel your hurt as if it is my own. Let me stay at your side in case you need me.'

Slowly coming to full consciousness, Nest was aware that Hait was in bed with her, stroking her. This was all too much. He had gone right out on a limb. She could not cope with this nonsense in the midst of her misery. Instead of shouting for the guard, her first thought was that the besotted man must be ejected from her room before his presence was noticed. She got out of the other side of the bed, and very quietly gave Hait her views.

'Leave my room at once or I will be forced to call for Gelert. I know you mean well, but I cannot cope with you creeping in here causing me even more distress. Go away at once or I will arouse the castle. Bernard de Deols would slay you for this intrusion.'

'I am sorry to worry you so, my Lady. I heard you crying and it went to my heart because you have always been very dear to me.'

Nest seized his arm, and none too gently propelled Hait out of the door.

'Go quietly and tell no one of your folly or I will be forced to dismiss you. You have been very foolish, but I try to believe that you acted out of concern for me. Go back to your room immediately and do not do anything like this again.'

Hait reluctantly allowed himself to be ejected and went back to his room. However castles have eyes and ears, and news of his visit to Nest's room reached many people by morning. *

Various writers in their apparent zeal to blacken Nest's name have stated that Hait was able to seduce her while she was grief stricken at the news of Gerald's death. Some have even said that she bore a child as a result and arrangements had to be made for the child's upbringing.

Others allege that she connived at her abduction by Owain. Some have wildly claimed that she had as many as twenty children as a result of numerous amorous liaisons. In this book I have tried to stick as closely as possible to the historical record. It is plain that this very beautiful woman was intelligent, wise and highly principled, and that her advice was sought by the King himself. I think that this book's version of the source of the rumours about Hait is much more likely to be correct.

The records show only the following children, which, taking into account two marriages, and her relationship with the King (and the absence of birth control) cannot to be said to be excessive. Henry, (son of the King); William, Maurice, David, and Angharad (by Gerald) and Robert (by Stephen) - six in all. Two other children, whom I have called John and Llinos, were children from the previous relationship of Gerald and a 'concubine', and were adopted and brought up as her own by Nest on her marriage to Gerald.

Wales does not recognise many great women in her history, and her treatment of Nest perhaps illustrates why this is so. I am convinced that Nest, who was the 'Queen Bee' who gave birth to the founders of many of the great families of both Britain and Ireland, should be credited with her true value and importance. She is a woman of whom Wales can be justifiably proud.

Nest had gathered her children round the breakfast table for a
discussion. Bethan and Bronwen were with her

She had removed herself and her family from Pembroke after the terrible
news and gone back to live in Carew. She had resolved to pull herself
together as much as she possibly could for the children's sake. De Deols had
made no attempt to stop her. Bethan had told her about the gossip concerning
Hait's unwanted attempts at consolation, and in her state of grief she could
not cope with such nonsense. The giant in her world had fallen and she had
no room in her mind for lesser men.

She knew that she was in a state of shock and not functioning properly.
She had not yet really accepted the death of Gerald, and she knew that her
grieving would be long and deep when she did. In the meantime her family
was in danger after Henry's dictates, and she must do what she could to
protect them and help them come to terms with their situation. There was no
one else now to make the little speech she knew had to be made, so she
resolved to make it herself, even though she felt she might not get through it
without breaking down.

She took little four year old Angharad on her knee and gathered the rest
around. John was now fifteen and it was obvious that he had already been
told about what had happened. Nest was touched to find him standing beside
her with his arm lightly resting across her shoulders. He would have to be
the man of the family now, and he was already trying to play his part. Llinos,
aged eleven, was acting the little mother and telling everyone to listen. As
she looked around her, she suddenly felt the weight of responsibility that
now fell on her as sole remaining parent. Six bright intelligent faces were
waiting for her to speak. How was she going to tell them that they had lost
their father? William was now ten, Maurice eight and David six.

'Some of you know or guess what has happened, others do not, so I must
tell you all that I know. Your father, who you must always remember as being
a brave, noble and most honourable man ...

'Mummy, what is honourable?' - this from precise, eight year old
Maurice.

'It means he always tried to do the right thing. Well, his Majesty the King
came to Pembroke on a visit and somehow thought your Daddy did a bad
thing, and took him away to London to punish him ...

'I shall kill the King one day for doing that,' said ten year old William.

'You must not talk like that,' said John sternly, 'or else the King will put
you in the Tower of London.'

'Quiet, children! Please listen to what I have to tell you. It is hard for me to say it, so you must be silent while I try.' They all went quiet then and waited intently.

'On the way to London some men tried to kill the King, but your Daddy saved him, very bravely, but in doing so he got hurt.'

'Hurt, Mummy?' cried Angharad. 'How is he hurt? Will he be better soon?'

'I am very sorry children,' said Nest choking back the tears. 'A man has come to the castle who watched it all, and he told me that Daddy was badly hurt and then he died. I am not quite sure yet if it is true, but I am afraid it might be.'

Llinos and Angharad burst into tears and sought comfort in Nest's arms, while she in her turn tried to gather all six children to her bosom. John, playing his new role, tried to comfort Nest.

'I will help you Mother, with anything that has to be done. De Deols told me himself about father, and told me that I was nearly a man now and that I must be strong for you.'

'You are all wonderful children, and your Daddy would be proud of you. The King made a mistake about your Daddy, and I am sure he is sorry now.'

William asked fearfully, 'what will happen to us all now Mummy? A boy told me that you are going to be taken away from us, and that we children are to be separated and brought up with families in other castles.'

'I am sure nothing like that will happen. Your father was a great man and at the end he saved the King's life. I hope we will be allowed to stay here at Carew, where I will do my best to bring you all up just as your father intended. If, for some reason, the King will not let us stay here, then I shall try to take you all to your grandmother's house in Dinefwr.'

'I like it here,' said David, 'I do not want to go to Dinefwr. We do not know the children there and anyway, they all speak only Welsh.'

'I shall try to stay here because it is the home that your father has made for us, but we do not know yet exactly what has happened. Anyway, you must remember that your father was a very good, loving man and must not believe any bad things that people might say about him.'

Seeking to find some way to help the children (and herself) to cope with their terrible loss, she said, 'I want you all to stand now and close your eyes. I want us all to ask God to send your dear father back to us if he possibly can.'

When the children were ready, she said, 'Dear God in Heaven, people have told us that dear Lord Gerald has been badly wounded and has died. Please, dear God, if you possibly can, make it not so, and send him back to us as we all need him very badly. Amen'

When she said it, she felt that she was speaking just like a child, and that maybe she was encouraging hopes in them that were sure to be dashed. Perhaps because she needed him so much, she had spoken irresponsibly. As she opened her eyes, Llinos was saying excitedly, 'your prayer has really worked Mummy, just like magic!' and Angharad was running away from her shouting 'Daddy! Daddy!'

It really was like magic. Gerald was standing in the doorway, grinning like an idiot, and all six children, quicker off the mark than she was, were rushing to greet him. She wanted to join them, but her silly legs would not work and she found herself on the floor with Gerald holding her head up and everyone else gathered round very concerned. She managed a faint smile and murmured, 'miracles do happen Gerald.'

The sun was now high in the sky and the horses had nearly reached the point on the Ridgeway where their destination would come into view. It was a glorious day, warm but not yet too hot. Nest felt that she had never been so happy. The whole family was making a trip to the seaside, and she was blissfully proud of them all. A year had passed since Henry's momentous visit, but it seemed much longer. Those dark days when everything seemed at risk were now far away and all was well again.

She rode on 'Beauclerc' at the head of the group alongside Gerald on 'Windsor,' and behind them on ponies were Llinos, William, Maurice and David. Behind them, rode Gelert, Bethan and Bronwen on Welsh cobs. John, on his new horse 'Rufus,' had been given a position of trust bringing up the rear, where he could watch out for any of the other children having problems with their horses. She had queried whether David was really old enough for such a long trip as he was only seven, but Gerald had said he was sure he could cope with it, telling Nest quietly later that he could always ride back behind him if he did get tired.

This was the last day when they would all be together. Tomorrow, John, now aged sixteen, and as was normal for a well-born Norman boy, would be leaving his family to join the service of Bernard de Neufmarché at Brecon Castle. There he would be in effect a trainee Norman Knight, refining the skills required, many of them already commenced with Gerald. He had been looking forward to the day when this would happen, thus marking his transition from a boy to a man. However, now that his departure was so close, he had suddenly wanted to be a boy again and enjoy a day out with his family - just one last time. It was he who suggested the trip to the fishing village of Dinbych (Tenby), and asked his father to take a day off from his duties at Pembroke to accompany them.

Nest had been quite surprised when Gerald had agreed so readily, family outings being rare events. She made a point of telling him how pleased she was, that they were all going out together on John's last day.

The children had all learned to ride as soon as they were old enough, Nest insisting that the girls did too, just as she had at their age. They had their own ponies now, and were competent riders, that is except five year old Angharad, who was riding today behind her mother. Next year, she too would have a pony.

'I can see the sea,' shouted Llinos ecstatically. 'There it is, over there. I am the cleverest.'

'Oh no,' said David, not to be outdone, 'I saw it ages ago so I am really the cleverest. Anyway, what you can see is only a cloud. The real sea is out of sight at the moment, behind that tree.'

Nest, knowing from previous experience that this type of children's argument was likely to be sterile, decided on a more positive line.

'Can you all remember what it is like in Dinbych. It is ages since we last went, and I think Angharad has not been at all. Who can tell us what there is for children to do there?'

'There is lots of sand,' shouted Maurice. 'You can make castles out of it with your hands ...

'Yes, and make moats around them and fill them up with water,' added William.

'I like paddling in the water best,' said David, 'and trying to catch little fish in the rock pools.'

'I like borrowing a boat to row out to sea' said John. 'Oh, let's do that Dad, and maybe do some fishing.'

'That seems a good idea, John,' called back Gerald from the head of the column, just beginning to relax into the day.

'I think Angharad may have been to Dinbych once, my Lady,' mentioned Bethan. 'I think I remember her going when she was small.'

'Yes!' joined in Bronwen with a rare flash of intelligence, 'she must have been, or else David, who is only two years older, would not remember so much about it - oh sorry, my Lady, I did not intend to be rude.'

'I think you may both be right. Let us see if she remembers it when she gets there.'

'When are we going to eat? Is there any food in Dinbych?' enquired Maurice, getting the priorities right.

'Well I have talked to Bethan about it, and I think you might get something Maurice, but not perhaps what you are expecting,' stated his mother.

'Oh not fish!' said John scornfully. 'I remember fish last time and it was horrible.'

'If you are going to be a Knight, you will have to get used to living off the country, and being prepared to eat almost anything,' insisted Gerald, detecting an unsuitable attitude for an aspiring Knight. 'During the siege of Pembroke when all the food had gone, many men kept going by eating cow pats. I would have too, if it had gone on any longer.'

'Ugh,' said Angharad, 'I think John will change his mind and become a priest if you tell him any more stories like that, father.'

As they approached the fishing village, they could see that there were two glorious long sandy beaches glistening in the sun, either side of a small rocky promontory. The village consisted of thirty or so rather mean houses sheltering in the lee of the little headland, which also provided protection for the dozen or so fishing boats drawn up on the sand awaiting the next tide. A line of poles and ropes was festooned with nets drying in the gentle breeze.

'Look, Father,' said John, there seems to be a rather superior sort of grog

214

shop by the harbour. I do not remember that being there before.'

'I am certainly not going in any grog shop and neither are the children,' insisted Nest very firmly. 'My Lord, I propose that the servants and I spread some blankets on some dry sand a little way up the beach away from the stench of fish. We can use that as a base for the children's activities.' Then she went up to Gerald, who was now dismounted, reviewing the scene as if considering its military possibilities, and putting her arm around his waist, led him gently away from the others.

'Forget your responsibilities for a few hours my love, and let us have a relaxed, happy day with the children and each other. Our life has surely taught us that we must make the best use we can of the few times we have together.'

Gerald relaxed and smiling drew her to him and gave her a very public kiss.

'You are right as always, my darling. Let us all have some fun. Come, everybody, let us get organised! Maurice is hungry so we had better do something about it. I want John, Llinos, William and Maurice to gather as much dry wood as they can find, so that we can make a fire near our base. See that drift wood lying about just above the tide line, that will be fine, we need lots of that. You will find larger quantities farther along the beach away from the village. When you have brought a big stock here, we will build a cooking fire.

'Now Gelert, I want you to go with David and Angharad to buy some fish from the fishermen. If you are wise you will persuade one of the wives to gut and fillet it. In the meantime Bethan and Bronwen can unpack the food and equipment they have brought with them.'

There followed a period of blissful activity. The wood gatherers worked their way up the shoreline arguing amongst themselves whether any particular piece of flotsam was likely to be combustible, while the fish purchasers tried to strike bargains with the guttural Flemish fishermen, and then paid a penny or two to get the fish prepared for cooking. In the meanwhile Nest, Bethan and Bronwen organised the 'kitchen'. They had brought items such as cooking pans, flour, milk, honey and salt with them in the horses' packs and even a good supply of fresh water in case the local supply was dubious.

It was quite a while before the wood gatherers and fish buyers returned, but when they did, Gerald amazed the servants by insisting on constructing and lighting the cooking fire himself.

'You have not brought much really dry wood so it will be best if I do the fire myself to avoid any delay.' Nest grinned her almost forgotten, famous grin. Gerald had decided to enjoy himself.

He had sent Gelert to find two or three large flat stones, and when the fire was going well he used the embers to heat the stones. He then took the bowl of well mixed flour, water, milk and salt, which Bethan had prepared, and poured it in small piles on the heated surfaces. 'There, Bronwen, look after these dampers. Now have you got the fish ready Bethan?'

The fish were pierced with metal skewers and held over the fire to cook.

'If you rest each end of the skewers on raised stones then you might avoid burning your hands having to hold them,' advised Gerald, remembering nearly forgotten skills from his campaigning days.

As the beach picnic got itself organised, it attracted the attention of many of the village children, who gathered nearby to observe this new attraction. At first they were overawed by the presence of the Norman Lord and his wife and stood afar off, but Angharad and David, and then the older children, started to encourage them by going over to talk to them. There were, of course, language problems, since the villagers were nearly all Flemings, but it was not long before the youngest ones started to play tag, and the older ones began to kick a makeshift ball around.

'My Lady,' said Bethan primly, 'shall I chase those filthy urchins away? It is not seemly that they play with better folk's children.'

Before Nest could decide on an answer, things were interrupted by the arrival of Waldo, who appeared to be the owner of the new grog shop. He was a man of medium height, in his late thirties, of broad stocky build. He was well dressed, but in a practical manner. He had a look of purpose and intelligence. Gerald had seen him before, but not in that role.

'Welcome to Tenby my Lord. You will no doubt remember me. I am the leader of the Flemings you have settled in the east of your territory. I have established this new grog shop as part of my business development, and would be delighted to offer you any refreshments that you might desire.'

'Thank you for your offer. I am sure my wife and I would be glad of some ale. My servants, too, would no doubt be grateful for the same. But you surprise me. As the acknowledged leader of the Eastern Flemings, why are you involving yourself personally in the doings of a grog shop?'

Waldo smiled. 'It seems you do not know the ways of my race, Lord Gerald. In Flanders we were all businessmen, high and low. That is how we made our wealth. Now we are cast up on a strange shore, we are all trying to rebuild our lives in the only way we know. This village obviously needed a grog shop and I am here to get it going. When it is established, I shall appoint a keeper, and he will pay me a proportion of the profits. I have established my main residence in Wizo's Tun*, as I am sure you know. However I cannot live on air there, leader of the Eastern Flemings or not, and I am setting up various enterprises in the area to bring some money in,' he smiled, 'to keep my wife in gold and furs.'

'It all seems very admirable' said Nest, determined to approve of Waldo's

---

* *Now known as Wiston, a village or 'tun' founded by another Flemish chief who rejoiced in the name of 'Wizo the Fleming'!*

business skills. 'It is certainly very different from the ways of both Norman and Welsh Lords, but just what is needed to start up from nothing in a new country. What say you my Lord?'

Gerald smiled. 'I see you have found yourself a champion in the form of my wife, Waldo. However, this is purely a private family trip for the benefit of my children. We shall accept and, of course, pay for our refreshments, and then must ask you to retire and let us enjoy our privacy. If you are a family man you will understand. I look forward to meeting you again officially another day, to discuss your business plans.'

Nest was intrigued by this contrast between Fleming and Norman, and resolved to find out more about what Waldo and his race were doing, and how it was affecting the established population.

Gerald was having similar thoughts as he quaffed his ale. There was no doubt the vigour and enterprise of Waldo and his people was beginning to enrich the land of Penfro, but he could see that the original settlers, a mélange of Scandinavians, Irish, Welsh, Normans and Saxons, might very well feel threatened by them.

Waldo had obviously told the village children to leave the Norman Lord and his family in peace, so for the rest of the afternoon they all did what they wanted. John borrowed a small boat from the fishermen and rowed it round the bay taking the older children for rides one by one. Llinos, William and Maurice made a sand castle with their hands, filling up the moat with water carried laboriously from the edge of the sea, using a pan borrowed from a reluctant Bethan. Nest made mud pies with Angharad. Gerald played with his driftwood fire, employing a rather surly Gelert to bring further supplies after the children had given up on that chore. Bethan and Bronwen, relieved of their cooking and child minding, pulled up their skirts and paddled in the sea, shrieking each time their clothes got wet.

They all had a wonderful day and everyone was sad, when the sun sinking in the west, warned Gerald it was time to start for home.

As they mounted their horses and started to make their way up the beach, Gerald saw a group of armed horsemen, probably Flemings, leading a bound prisoner towards Waldo, who had come out of the tavern to meet them. Gerald asked his party to pause, and Gelert drew his sword. Nest sighed. Even today, on their last family outing together, the outside world would not leave them alone.

After a short discussion with the armed men, Waldo walked over to Gerald to tell him what was going on.

'My Lord, my Lady, I am sorry to intrude on your privacy yet again. I employ some horsemen to patrol the boundary of my land with the Welshry, as I have had trouble with Cadwgan's people coming over to steal our sheep and cattle. At dawn they surprised a man asleep in a barn and have brought him to me. My Lady, I am sorry to say that he claims to be your brother.'

Both Gerald and Nest had been stunned by the unexpected arrest of Nest's brother, Gruffudd, by Waldo's men.

Ever since the Montgomerys' failed rebellion eleven years ago in 1101, Nest had known that her brother had been awaiting his chance to recover his father's lands in Deheubarth. He had always been somewhere around, either trying to raise troops in Ireland, or back here in Wales quietly contacting his own people, awaiting some chance to throw the Normans out.

From time to time Nest had received secret letters from her brother, wishing her well and asking about the children. On one occasion, some years ago, Gerald had gone off, heavily disguised, for a meeting with Gruffudd in a tavern. He had told Nest later, that the two of them had confirmed the unofficial arrangement between them that while Nest was still married to Gerald, Gruffudd would not attack Pembroke or the enclave around it in Southern Penfo. For his part Gerald promised he would not actively hunt for Gruffudd, as he moved through Gerald's area on the way to the rest of Deheubarth.

Matters had become a little strained when Gruffudd's men had ambushed the King's party in Crichan Forest last year. Gerald had saved the King from capture and had killed many of Gruffudd's men. Nest had persuaded her brother to meet Gerald again secretly, and she had gone herself to help keep the peace. Once Gruffudd realised that Gerald had been there unwillingly, as a captive, and was simply fulfilling his oath of loyalty to the King in fighting off the ambush, he had become a little less belligerent. Eventually the unofficial truce between them was confirmed.

All had been well since. Now suddenly because the zeal of Waldo's Flemings, Gruffudd had been arrested and been handed over to Gerald officially. It was all very awkward.

Gerald dare not release Gruffudd openly in front of the Flemings because they owed little loyalty to him personally, and word might get back to the King, who now regarded Gruffudd as a dangerous insurgent after Crichan Forest.

Seeing that Gerald was on a family outing, with only Gelert as escort, Waldo had offered to deliver Gruffudd to Pembroke later that evening, once Gerald had returned there. Gerald could think of nothing else but to accept this offer.

On the way back, Gerald and Nest tried to keep up the holiday atmosphere for the sake of the children, but once at Pembroke they were glad to hand over the children to Bethan and Bronwen so that they could withdraw to the solar to discuss the situation.

However it seemed that no sooner were they in the solar, than Bernard de Deols, now quite happily relegated to second in command, was at the door to announce that Waldo's men had delivered Gruffudd, and that he had him under lock and key in the guardroom. De Deols was well aware of the unofficial arrangement between Gerald and Gruffudd.

'I realise that this is very awkward for you, Gerald, and for you, my Lady. I would like you to know that I will support you in any reasonable solution to the problem. I mean, anything that is not going to result in me being put in the Tower of London.' He smiled a little weakly.

'This is a very difficult one Bernard. Everyone knows that Gruffudd is here. How am I going to save his skin without losing my own?'

Nest's eyes were blazing. 'It is my brother we are talking about. There can be no question about him being handed over to the King. We just give him a rope and let him down over the battlements. I will not agree to any other solution.'

'Leave this to me, my love, I will go and see Gruffudd and work something out.'

'Remember, his life must not be risked in any way. He is the last hope for my people, and he is very dear to me.'

'You shall visit him yourself once I have been to see him.'

When Gerald was let into Gruffudd's cell by the guard, he found his prisoner to be less than charitable.

'What game are you playing, brother in law? Do you mean to hand me over to the King to be hanged?'

'And what sort of an idiot are you Gruffudd, to be caught alone, asleep in a Flemish barn?' How am I going to protect you now that Waldo has handed you over officially? The King arrested me for treason last year, and would be delighted to do so again if I let you go.'

His voice softened a little. 'By the way, have they fed you? I can order some food while we try to think of a way out of the problem.'

Once Gruffudd had a chunk of bread and cheese in one hand and a flagon of ale in the other, he seemed to brighten a little.

'This problem needs a Welshman's guile to solve it. If you let me go, or if I am allowed to escape, you will be in serious trouble once the King finds out. On the other hand, although even Henry would not expect you to hang your own brother in law, you will have to send me under escort to Rhyd y Gors. It seems a fair probability that the Castellan there, William Fitzbaldwin, would have few compunctions in summarily hanging me, to save the trouble of sending me to London.'

'That sounds a good outline of the situation. What then am I to do?'

'Well, there might be a way-

When Nest eventually was allowed to go in to see her brother, he was delighted to see her, but to her surprise did not have the appearance of a man facing imminent hanging.

Next day Gerald despatched Gruffudd to Rhyd y Gors, escorted by Bernard de Deols with a troop of cavalry. His sister bade him a tearful farewell. His last request to Gerald was that the party should call at Whitland Abbey so that a priest could hear his confession, as he thought that William Fitzbaldwin might not be so obliging to a man who had ambushed the King only last year.

As the party rode out of the castle yard, Gruffudd turned and waved to his sister. 'See you in Paradise, sister,' he shouted, which Bethan thought in bad taste.

Later that evening, many hours later, a very frustrated Bernard de Deols returned to Pembroke with an exhausted troop of men at arms.

'What has happened, why are you back here today? You should be spending the night at Rhyd y Gors,' asked Gerald.

'He has escaped, outwitted us. He asked to see a priest at Whitland Abbey and spent some time with him in a cell.

'The priest eventually came out, and we locked the door while we took some refreshment with the monks. However, we left an armed guard on the door. Later, when we went to collect Prince Gruffudd we found the priest bound and gagged on the cell floor. It seems that Prince Gruffudd hit him over the head and switched clothes with him. Goodness knows what the King will say when he gets to hear of it. We have spent the last few hours scouring Whitland Forest but could not find any trace of him.'

Later back in the solar, Nest pulled Gerald to her and offered her lips to him for a kiss.

'Oh I have a clever, clever husband, and I love him so much.'

chapter fifty

Gerald has his revenge
September, AD 1116

Gerald was riding with a company of his Flemish soldiers, perhaps a hundred men. They were following the valley of the Teifi, intending to swing south and eventually head home. He had made dozens of such patrols in the last few weeks ever since he had heard that the King unbelievably had pardoned his arch enemy, Prince Owain. Owain was reported to be heading home to claim his inheritance, his father having been murdered by Uncle Meredydd. Such are the fickle ways of Kings.*

Gerald had never forgiven Owain for the brutal abduction and rape of his beloved Nest, and the news of Owain's planned return had inflamed the desire for revenge in him to such an extent that she had warned him that it was becoming an obsession. He was beginning to feel his age and brooded that the time left for revenge was running out.

Looking back over his shoulder, he could not but be impressed by what he saw. His Flemings had become fine soldiers able to fight both on foot or horseback, able to cover many miles of rough country in a day. The new settlers had arrived in considerable numbers from the flooded lands of Flanders since they had had the go ahead from the King, and Gerald had quickly profited from their talents.

As the King had said in his original letter, they represented a cross section of the society of their land of origin; some had been farmers, some merchants, some shop keepers, others soldiers. Many had arrived with skills needed in the new settlements in Penfro, such as carpentry, boat building, roofing, stonemasonry and general building abilities. Their loss to Flanders was Gerald's, and Penfro's gain. Many had skills far in advance of anything available in the original population, and the whole area under Gerald's control had seen a huge amount of development since their arrival.

However despite his pride in his little army, Gerald was feeling gloomy. He was now fifty, an old man in his time, and he wondered how long he would be able to carry on leading his troops over such rough terrain in his increasingly desperate search for his enemy.

To Nest and to others, he called these regular forays, 'patrols'. He said that he was keeping the settled area under his control free from incursions by the Welsh, who certainly increasingly resented and envied the burgeoning population and wealth of an ever more alien and foreign-speaking land that used to be theirs.

Nest, however, was not deceived: she knew her man well. In his heart Gerald was now seriously obsessed with a feeling of injustice. This previously fair-minded and enlightened man had started to be swayed more and more by the feeling that that ruffian Prince Owain was going to get away with the foul rape of his lovely wife. In spite of determined efforts on his part to suppress these feelings, he could not help thinking that Owain had polluted her, and she would not be truly his again until he had killed the rapist with his own hands.

At the beginning, after the abduction, Henry had taken personal charge of the hue and cry to capture Owain. Gerald, of course, had thought this was only right, even though he believed the King's motives might have been a little mixed: how does one carry off the ex-mistress of the King and expect to get away with it?

After Nest's escape, however, the heat seemed to go out of the hunt, except that organised by Gerald himself. Then news had come that Owain had been captured, betrayed for money by his own people, and that he was in Gloucester Castle awaiting trial. Gerald had rejoiced and relaxed.

Then came the unbelievable news that, somehow, Owain had got on good terms with the King and had been invited to go on a campaign with him in Normandy. Kings were known to be fickle but this was incredible. How could there be such a change in Owain's fortunes, and what did it say of Norman justice?

After the abduction, Nest, understandably, had had great difficulty in coping with Gerald's state of mind. He wanted to rejoice in having her back, a loving wife as before, but he kept on thinking of Nest and Owain together, of what he had done to her, of him penetrating her for weeks on end. Perhaps she had grown to like it? She had tried to heal her husband's mental state by telling him endlessly how much she loved him and how much she loathed Owain. He had started to try to forget what had happened, but then there came this seeming treachery of the King, which had opened up the wounds again. She had smothered him in love and devotion and it had worked up to a point, but both Nest and Gerald knew that things would not be as they had been until Owain was killed.

Gerald's reverie was interrupted by the approach of a Flemish priest on a pony. He was dirty, exhausted and very distressed. He appeared greatly heartened to find that he had chanced upon a company of soldiers of his own race.

'Greetings, Father, what can I do for you, and why are you travelling alone in so wild an area?'

'You are Lord Gerald, are you not? Blessings to God, and the Holy Virgin, that I have fallen in with you. Terrible things have happened today not three hours ago.'

'What terrible things, Father? Drink some ale from my flask. Then tell me slowly and carefully what has happened.'

Pulling himself together, the priest took a swig from Gerald's leather bottle and tried to give a clear account of events.

'I was accompanying Bishop Guldenmans on a visit to meet the Bishop of St. Davids and other clerics in West Wales, when we fell in with a party of Welsh soldiers led by one Owain, formerly Prince of Powys.'

'What then, good priest?'

'We dismounted and began to talk. It was obvious to me that Owain and his men had been drinking mead heavily. They were very wild in their speech and unpredictable. My Lord Bishop was a little slow in recognising our danger, trusting too much in our status as men of the cloth. He started to remonstrate with Prince Owain about the evils of drunkenness, especially in a Prince. Owain now became threatening and violent, striking the Bishop with his whip and calling him a 'scurvy Fleming', who had no right to come to Wales. The Bishop still tried to reason with him, telling him that Holy Church judged him more severely than other men, unwisely referring to the shameful abduction of your wife, Princess Nest.'

'Did he indeed? What came next?'

'Owain now lost all control and went berserk, telling his men to kill we Flemings who, he said, were greedy invaders of the sacred land of Wales. He drew his own sword and cut down the Holy Bishop. I saw other priests seized and killed. Still for some reason being mounted, I dug in my heels and galloped to dense trees where I desperately tried to change direction so that they could not find me. Finally I found a deep thicket, where I hid my horse and myself and waited for two hours.'

For a while I could hear them shouting drunkenly, then finally they seemed to give up searching and the sound of their voices receded. Then I went off quietly in the other direction and prayed that I would find some friendly person in this terrible land to guide me to St. David's.'

'Good Priest, you should know that I am here searching for that same foul Owain, as I have daily, for many weeks. The man is a monster and must be brought to book for his many crimes. Your account of the murder of Bishop Guldenmans is dreadful confirmation of his wickedness. He cannot be very far away, and if I press on ahead, I shall have a good chance of catching him.'

Gerald's men were now milling around him, having gathered the gist of what had happened. The murder of a Bishop, especially of their own race, was a terrible thing, which must be avenged immediately.

'Men, you have heard what has happened. We must push on at once in the direction of Aberteifi. That is the route Owain is likely to be following. He and his party are drunk, so we may be able to overtake them before dark.'

'Pray, do not leave me here, Lord Gerald. I might come across Prince Owain again and my life would be forfeit,' quavered the Priest.

'I suggest that you join the rear of my Company, Father, but do not expect me to show mercy to this murderer of Bishops and abductor of my wife. You will find me deaf to such entreaties.'

At a word from Gerald, the soldiers made off at a canter, following the line of the valley. Before long Gerald picked up the tracks of a large party that were easy to follow. But, after about an hour of rapid progress and no sign of Owain's men, Gerald began to wonder if, indeed, he would catch up with him before dark, now only two hours off.

Suddenly, one of his men, slightly ahead, signalled that he could hear something. As Gerald came up with him on a bluff he, too, could hear the sounds of a large party of horsemen splashing through a stream, laughing and shouting in Welsh.

Gerald indicated that everyone should dismount and should tie their horses to trees. Then, stringing their bows as they went, Gerald led his archers in line over the brow of the next hill. Down below, in plain view, only a few yards ahead, Owain's men were bathing themselves and their horses in the stream. Gerald heard Owain telling his men to make a good job of washing off any bloodstains. He did not want any evidence on view when they arrived to claim his father's court. Owain himself was dismounted on the near side of the stream, and had taken off all his clothes and was washing them in the river.

Gerald and his men crept to the edge of the trees, and then, stepping out of cover, they released a volley of arrows into the Welshmen at close range. Many of them had left their weapons on the bank when they went into the river. They were now defenceless against this sudden onslaught. Some fell at once into the water, others, unwounded, struggled desperately to cross to the other side to make their escape.

Gerald's first arrow hit Owain in the shoulder. Surprised and in pain, he tried to reach his sword lying nearby on the bank. Gerald dropped his bow and rushed headlong down the slope, drawing his sword as he ran. As Owain bent to grab his own weapon, Gerald, holding his sword with both hands, brought it down with all his strength, across Owain's shoulders and neck. Owain fell, dying, with the arrow still imbedded in one shoulder and with Gerald's sword imbedded in the other.

One of Owain's men, still unwounded, came up to attack the now weapon-less Gerald, but was at once shot down at close range by one of the Flemings.

The surviving Welsh had now reached the other side of the river and fled up the far bank followed by a hail of arrows, which brought down still more of them.

Unbelievably, Owain, despite his ghastly wounds, was still alive.

'She needs a real man, you pansy,' he taunted.

Thus strengthened for what he had to do, Gerald steadied his foot against Owain's shoulder and succeeded in pulling out his sword. Before he was forced to give him the coup de grace, Owain gave a sigh and died. Gerald, his stomach retching, turned away. He had never liked the goriness of hand to hand combat, and the satisfaction of revenge hardly made up for it.

His second in command brought him back down to earth.

'Shall we follow the rest of Owain's men, my Lord?'

'No, let them flee. There has been enough death today. We will leave them to bury their own dead, but Owain's body must be tied across his horse, and we will take it to Pembroke.'

Gerald had suffered no casualties such had been the element of surprise. As he rode back home, he wondered what Nest would feel about the news.

This part of the story is glossed over for the sake of the narrative and would be hard to believe if it were not true! Following Nest's return to Gerald, Owain had a number of escapades in keeping from the clutches of the King. He sought sanctuary in Ynys Mon (Anglesey), but was eventually betrayed to the Normans, taken to Gloucester Castle (where Duke Robert was still languishing) and later was brought into the presence of the King. Henry seems amazingly to have been so taken by Owain that he was freed from prison, pardoned, and even taken on campaign in Normandy with him! However he learned that his uncle had murdered his father (Cadwgan), so he set off (apparently with the King's approval) to claim his inheritance. Nearing the end of his long journey, he fell in with a travelling Bishop and chose to murder him! The rest we know.

I do not wish to upset the citizens of my adopted land, but my researches show that there were an amazing number of murders, abductions and castrations among the ruling Princes in Wales at that time so that Cadwgan's murder by Meredydd was by no means unusual! As an example, the records show that at least six members of the Powys dynasty were murdered, blinded, or castrated by other members of the dynasty between AD 1100-1125.

225

The Day that Nest prayed
would never come
October 12th AD, 1116

Once Owain was dead, it was if a hidden weight had been lifted from Gerald's shoulders. He became a different man. He took time with the children, and he and Nest went back to their custom of going for a walk beside the millpond. They often sat on his cloak to watch the sun go down, and greatly daring for him, they once made love there, as they had in the old days. On that occasion, Bethan had later found mud on the back of her dress, and had had the temerity to mention it.

'My Lady, do you not think you would be wise to comport yourself more decorously, you might be talked about?'

Nest should have slapped her face, but instead she laughed.

'Oh Bethan, what a prude you are these days. Go and get some fun, you will be an old woman long enough.'

Suddenly the stars shone more brightly each night, the sun seemed warmer, the children more delightful and the autumn tints on the trees more beautiful than ever. Nest was blissful.

As a family they had now lived at Carew for sixteen years. All those years of planning and hard work had made for them a wonderful home. The gardens were full of flowers and many of the trees they had planted were a fair size, especially the fruit trees, which were laden with apples, plums, and pears at this time of the year.

The water mill was well established, and Gerald's miller was bringing in a good source of income, people coming from all over the Norman enclave to have their corn ground. Gerald was usually away all day at Pembroke Castle so did not have the opportunity to keep an eye on the miller, but Nest was there, and she was pretty sure that the man was a rogue, keeping part of the proceeds for himself. However, Gerald's mood had become so loving and serene, that Nest did not wish to spoil it by reporting her suspicions.

About five years ago, Nest's mother had arrived on her annual visit from Dinefwr, bringing with her ten bee skips and a beekeeper to look after them. The bees had fascinated both Nest and the children from the start, and Gerald had started to share their interest.

Many evenings Nest would delay their meal so that she, Gerald, and some of the younger children could creep down quietly to the apiary and lie by the hives watching the bees. She had learned a lot from the beekeeper, and rejoiced in sharing her knowledge with Gerald.

'See how the late foragers are returning heavily laden with their nectar, and how each one is checked by the sentinel bees waiting at the entrance.'

'I wonder how they know which are friends and which are foes. Does your new knowledge of the bee world extend that far?' he teased, amused at his wife's enthusiasm, yet interested just the same.

'I have wondered that too, and asked Bleddyn the keeper if he knew. He says he believes they have a strong sense of smell and can tell if the bees have the scent of their own colony. Neighbouring skips would have a different smell and be rejected by the soldiers. But there is more than that to interest you, my love. Bleddyn says that each colony is like one of our castles. Each skip has its own Lord or King to whom they all defer, and who has courtiers to groom and feed him. Most of the bees go out each day as foragers, as we have seen, to bring back nectar. Some bees make the wax combs to store the nectar while it is ripening into honey: others feed the young grubs, which are growing into adults. It is a whole world of interest.'

'It seems then, very cruel that they have to be killed each autumn to get their honey,' stated David.

'I wish it were not so,' replied his mother. 'There is much to admire in them. However if we drive the bees away with smoke and are thus able to steal the honey, they would die anyway without their stores and their children would be dead because of the smoke. Perhaps your clever father will put his mind to thinking of a better way?'*

Occasionally, if it was an important Saint's day, Gerald would give time off to most of the staff in Pembroke Castle, leaving only the duty guard, and everyone would pour out of the castle to enjoy themselves. Some would go to the market, some to the taverns to get drunk and others to sit by the river. Some of the Knights had learned angling skills from the Irish, and would spend such days sitting on the bank, dangling their lines in the water, escorted by their bored wives. These ladies then got into trouble by gossiping loudly with their neighbours, causing their husbands to remonstrate with them for frightening away the fish.

Gerald's own way of using his day off, since the death of Owain, was to take the whole family off down the river in the family boat. This depended on the tide being right. If high tide was in the morning, there would be enough water by the milldam to float the heavy boat, and they could then descend the Carew River with the tidal current in their favour. They would

---

* *Modern methods of bee keeping did not start to evolve until late Victorian times. In Nest's day, bees were kept in wickerwork 'skips', protected from the weather by a layer of tar. Fresh swarms were caught, and given a new 'skip' each spring. At the end of the season, the bees in the heaviest 'skips' were killed to obtain the honeycomb. Honey was not usually 'extracted', but the whole honeycomb eaten, so care had to be taken not to eat the 'brood', (young bees in the form of grubs, which did not taste very nice!) Honey was very important as a sweetener as sugar cane was not known at that time.*

The 'King' was actually the 'Queen', but that was not known until long after Shakespeare's day. (see Henry V, Act Two)

follow the river system down to the new tavern at Burton Ferry, where they would drink some ale, sitting at the trestle table overlooking the river. This was much more pleasant than sitting in the dark, smoky tavern. The plan would be to wait for the tide to change, and then use it to carry them back to Carew.

Apart from the family, plus Gelert and Bethan, Gerald normally took along two other male servants, who had learned to row while serving at Pembroke. With so many 'passengers' in the heavy boat, and only three or four oarsmen (including fifteen year old William who loved to row), it was much easier always to plan to go with the tidal current, than to try to fight it.

There were variants on the plan. Sometimes when they descended the Carew River to where it joined the main estuary of the Cleddau, instead of turning left, downstream towards the Haven and the open sea, they would turn right, upstream, and work their way close to the bank to avoid the full effect of the current. Gerald liked to go that way, as he could then check on progress on the new fort he was building at 'The Narrows', a narrow point where the main river ran through a gorge.

Last year Magnus, the Viking King of the Isle of Man, he who had carried off the nymphomaniac, Princess Siobhan, had made an audacious attack on the small town of Havenford, high up the Western Cleddau. He set fire to the town and carried off many women and much treasure.

To get there he had sailed right past the approach to the Norman's main base at Pembroke, just under Gerald's nose so to speak. After he had sacked Havenford, he had sailed back down again and made off out to sea before Gerald had had time to organise any response. The Danes had not done anything like that since Arnulph and Gerald had built Pembroke Castle twenty-five years ago, so it had been a tremendous shock for it to happen now.

He had therefore decided to stretch a heavy chain across the river at The Narrows and to guard it with a small fort. The chain was now in place, and the fort nearly finished. Gerald liked to mix business with pleasure by using a family outing to see if work was going well.

However, on this particular day, late in October, and with the likelihood that the weather would soon break and thus put paid to such expeditions for this season, the children had been given the choice, and they had all asked to row down to the ferry at Burton. The attraction of Burton was that the estuary was more open there, and there was more to see and do.

The boys hoped that they would be allowed to drink ale bought from the tavern, and Angharad, now aged nine, hoped to find interesting creatures in the rock pools at low tide. Bethan had brought her usual supplies of bread and cheese, and had excelled herself this time by also bringing curd tart and lardy cake. Lunch at Burton Ferry was therefore judged to be a great success.

When Gelert announced that the tide had now turned and that they would soon be able to re-float the boat, Nest felt a little sad.

'Is it not a pity that winter will soon be upon us, my love. I am sure there is no more perfect place on God's earth than this when the weather is good.'

She took his arm as they walked over the slippery, seaweed covered rocks at the water's edge. It was just as well that she did not know it was for the last time.

'When I first came here so sad and lonely all those years ago, and saw that stern Norman Lord waiting for me on the quay, I had no idea I was going to be so happy here.' She grinned and squeezed his arm. 'I think you are a fraud - just my loving, wonderful, big fraud. A big pussycat really!'

Gerald still found such overt affection a little embarrassing, but loved it none the less.

'I am glad the King never got round to sending me to manage some grim fortress in Normandy. Many of my contemporaries have been moved several times. I am very content with my little piece of Wales.'

'Do you like equally your other little Welsh piece?' she enquired flirtatiously.

'Mother, must you embarrass us so? The servants may hear you.' This was from eleven year old David, who liked his parents to behave decorously.

The boat was now afloat and steadied in the water by two of the servants.

Gelert picked up the children one by one, and waded out to the boat carrying them so that they did not get wet. Nest still liked the bit when Gerald swung her up in his strong arms to put her on board, and Bethan made much of it when it was her turn for Gelert to carry her.

As soon as every one was on board, together with the picnic gear, the four oarsmen rowed out into the channel with Gerald at the steering oar. The river narrows to a hundred yards wide just above Burton, near the fort, so Nest could point out to the children various things of interest on the banks on either side.

'Can you see the giant heron waiting so quietly on that rock, Angharad? He is keeping very still so that the fish do not take fright as the current swirls them past him.'

'I cannot see him Mother. Oh, yes I can, he has suddenly spread his wings and flapped up the river,' Angharad shouted.

'He has flown off somewhere quieter where little girls will not spoil his sport by shouting so loudly,' teased William.

'Be quiet, everyone,' insisted Gerald. 'Look over there, I think a seal has just dived. Watch him coming up again, with a fish in his mouth.'

'My Lady, I think there is going to be a storm,' said Bethan, staring at the darkening sky. 'I think I heard the rumble of thunder too.'

'We should be back again at Carew within half an hour, so let us hope the rain holds off until then.'

By the time they had passed Lawrenny, and were just swinging past the

Black Mixen rock into the Carew River, the heavens opened and the rain poured down on them, soaking everyone in minutes. The thunder was also now approaching rapidly. Nest drew Angharad close to her to shelter her with her cloak.

'Never mind sweetheart, we will soon be home and you will be able to get dry in front of the big fire in the solar.'

The oarsmen, rain pouring down their faces, increased their speed so as to get home as quickly as possible.

'I do not care,' puffed William. He was determined not to let this cold, wet end spoil their day out.

'That's the spirit William,' encouraged his father. 'I see you have the makings of a Knight, and you should do well when you go away next year.'

Just as the milldam at Carew came in sight through the rain there was a tremendous crash and those looking in that direction saw lightning hit a tree on the bank no more than a hundred yards away. The tree was split down the middle and part of it toppled heavily to the ground.

Nest and Gerald exchanged glances. They had better get home as quickly as possible. The children looked scared.

Gerald brought the boat alongside the little jetty at the dam, and leaving two men to secure it, Gelert and Gerald got everyone out of the boat with great despatch, and they all hurried up the path to the top of the dam in the pouring rain. The tremendous claps of thunder were still very close, and Nest felt that they were all very exposed.

The half-mile path back to Carew Castle ran alongside the lake, and steep little waves were crashing onto the banks. Nest, Bethan and Angharad's dresses were clinging to them like dish clothes and their hair was plastered down on their heads.

They all hurried along, hoping to get out of the appalling weather very soon. As they ran, Nest pulling Angharad along by her arm, there was another terrible crash, and lightning hit the path a short distance in front of them. They stopped in their tracks, not knowing what to do.

'I think we had better go back to that tree behind us and shelter there for a few moments,' shouted Gerald. 'The storm will soon pass over.'

Nest was not at all sure this was a good idea, but did not like to argue against Gerald's judgement. Certainly they could not continue along the path for the moment as it was too exposed.

Once they were under the massive beech tree, they were sheltered from the worst effects of the storm. Although it was early autumn, there were still enough leaves on the tree to keep off most of the rain. In a few moments the rapidly moving thundercloud would pass over and they would be able to complete their journey to the Castle.

The rain stopped suddenly, and with it the wind. The air became still and the sun was shining in the distance.

Gerald decided to give the order to make a move. 'Come on everyone, let us make a dash for it while it is fine. Go on, as fast as you can. Gelert and I will bring up the rear. There is still a nasty black cloud directly over us.'

Nest, Angharad and Bethan set off at once, all eager to reach home, followed by the boys and the two oarsmen. Gerald and Gelert were just about to leave the shelter of the tree to join them, when there was another devastating crash. Nest looked back as she ran, and saw a branch fall and both men knocked to the ground. Sick with horror she ran back to the tree. As she approached, Gelert staggered shakily to his feet, but Gerald was not moving. He just lay there, with one arm outstretched. It was just as if he was sleeping. There was no sign that the fallen branch had actually hit him.

Nest knelt by his side and squeezed his arm.

'Wake up my love. Please wake up and open your eyes.'

Bethan too was kneeling by her now and had dipped her kerchief in the lake to mop his brow. Still he did not stir. She was sure he was not breathing. Nest was desperate and did not know what to do.

'I think he was stunned by the lightning bolt. We must try to wake him up,' she said, shaking Gerald as hard as she could.

Gelert had recovered now and was feeling Gerald's pulse. Nest suddenly remembered doing those things all those years ago, while with her father's physician. She too, held his wrist and sought ever more hopelessly for signs of a heartbeat. She remembered other things too and put her lips over Gerald's mouth just as she had seen the Moor do. She tried and tried again to inflate his lungs.

The children were gathering round, fearfully, and there were people running to them from the Castle.

'My Lady, I am so, so sorry, but I am sure he has gone.'

Nest turned to look at Bethan, wild-eyed.

'He cannot leave me now! He has only just started to live!'

BOOK THREE

NEST AND STEPHEN

Nest was sitting with her back to a tree overlooking the lake. It was that tree, and she often went there when the weather allowed. It made her feel closer to Gerald.

As she watched the clouds drift across the sky, she tried to examine her feelings about her husband's death. She had of course been devastated when it had happened and had tried desperately to think what her father's doctor would have done in those first vital moments after the lightning strike. It had all been to no avail of course. When her attempts at resuscitation had manifestly failed, Bethan had eventually forced her to leave him.

His funeral had been a magnificent affair, and everyone had said wonderful things about Gerald. All of it was true, of course. He was everything that the best Normans aspired to be. However, Nest felt that she was acting a part and that soon the play would be over and the principal player would be back at her side discussing it.

But, he was dead and there was no escaping facing up to it. It was now several months and she still missed him dreadfully and she would continue to do so for the rest of her life.

Strangely, she had not really grieved this time. She felt that she had done that already - that terrible time when they told her that he was dead in the Crichan Forest. She had then wept and sobbed a terrible grief that had echoed through the whole Castle. When he came back that time it had been like a reincarnation that she did not truly believe in. She had lost him then, and had grieved. The extra few weeks of time with him were like a dreamlike bonus, which would enrich the rest of her life, and help to make up for the many sufferings, which she had had to endure in the past - from Henry, from Owain, even from Gerald.

Some nights, the bad dreams had come, the ones when her father was killed yet again, each time in some horribly different way, or her brothers, or all of them. The dreams then always took the same path: she was the only one of her line left and all the burden of responsibility to save Cymru from the loathsome Normans was on her twelve year old shoulders. She would then call desperately to Gerald to help her. Dreams do not worry about such details as why she would be calling out for Norman Gerald to help her save Wales from the Normans. She would wake up, her bedding soaked with perspiration.

Well, perhaps she had been right to call to him. The dream was right after all. Gerald and she had done rather well, she mused, as she pushed her back against the tree sensuously. Gerald, loving her, had created a new entity around Pembroke, where men and women knew they could live their lives in safety, where justice was not only for the rich, and where the terrible Vikings dare not set foot while he was Lord of Penfro.

All people, Cymro, Scandinavian and Fleming were treated the same by Gerald.

Nest told herself that all the work that he had done was not lost. Most of his achievements would live after him. Of course there was a new Lord of Penfro, but the world that Gerald had created carried on, with the mixture of all the races, the new towns, the new castles, roads and bridges. Penfro would never be the same after Gerald. Sadly, it would never be truly Welsh again, she thought. But the other side of the coin was that she believed that it would be left in peace by future warring Welsh Princes, as there were now so many sturdy Flemings settled there as to be a very hard nut to crack.

There she was, thinking that way again. She was not thinking completely as a Welsh Princess anymore. She was thinking in what she had decided was a 'Geraldine' way, a mixture of the best of Welsh and Norman. She and Gerald had raised a family of remarkable children whom she was sure would soon be very important in Wales. They would go on to help shape Wales for the new age. Perhaps the battle lost at Brecon would be won anew by Nest, not in bed, as Bethan had once joked coarsely, but in her womb. Her children would be powerful and influential and achieve great things. *

* *Nest was indeed the 'Queen Bee', whose children founded great families such as the Fitzgeralds, the Barrys, and the Fitzstephens. Her son by Henry became Lord of Narberth (and might have been Henry 2nd, had his parents sorted out their differences).*

One of Nest's sons, David, became Bishop of St David's, and two more, William and Robert, did us all the rather dubious favour of conquering Ireland, leaving us involved there ever since. Her daughter Angharad married William de Barry. One of their sons Gerald Cambrensis, became a well-known writer and traveller, and made his home at Manorbier (from the Welsh 'Maenor-Pyr' - Pyr's Manor). His description of the area round the castle is a delight, except he was not keen on full stops!

'Manorbier is excellently well defended by towers and outworks, and is situated on the summit of a hill, extending on the western side towards the seaport, having on the northern and southern sides a fine fish pond under the walls, as conspicuous for its grand appearance as for the depth of its water, and a beautiful orchard on the same side, enclosed on the one part by a vineyard and the other by a wood, remarkable for the projection of its rocks and the height of its hazel trees. To the right of the promontory between the castle and the church, near the site of a very large lake and mill, a rivulet of never ending water flows through a valley, rendered sandy by the violence of the winds.'

'Queen Bee' Nest, was a force to be reckoned with in her own day, and her influence in the form of her descendants lives on today.

Now she had a letter. Bethan had just brought it to her, together with a rug against the chill, and a chiding for staying out on her own in the rain.

The letter was from Stephen, Lord of Aberteifi, (Cardigan). Nest knew Stephen, as she knew all the Norman Lords in Southern Cwmru. She did not particularly like him or dislike him: he seemed harmless enough. He was no Arnulph, nor a Robert Fitzhammon.

Before opening it, she guessed what it might be. Eligible widows were in high demand. They were 'ready trained' wives and mothers, and might be rich as well.

Cardigan Castle

'Dear Nest,

I am hoping you will allow me to pay you a visit.

A little time has now passed since your tragic loss, and as you know, I have been a widower for several years. I would in no way seek to replace your beloved Gerald, but I could offer a secure home for you and your children, and you would not be far from Carew so you could keep an eye on your estate.

I do not know how to write a love letter as you can see. However, I shall be visiting de Deols at Pembroke tomorrow morning and will call at Carew on the way back in the hope that you may see me.

Yours,
Stephen'

There, that was it. She had been expecting something like this. She ran up the path to the castle to get a little warmth into her body, She still did unladylike things sometimes if she wished to. After all who was to chide her now, save Bethan.

She sent for Bethan and they sat by the log fire in the solar to discuss the news. 'My Lady, the King will not let you stay unmarried for long. Your brother is still organising forces against him, and the King might start to fear that you could combine with your brother, now that Gerald is gone, and raise all Deheubath against him.'

'I think that too,' said Nest. ' It is even possible that Henry may have encouraged Stephen to approach me.'

'Could you not talk to some of the ladies at Penfro. They may have heard things we do not know here at Carew?'

'It is too late for that. Stephen is coming this afternoon. Anyway, what could they tell me except tittle-tattle? I am not close to any of them now since I moved to Carew.'

She missed having a man around, and it was cold at nights sometimes! The children needed a father, especially Maurice, who at fourteen certainly needed a firm hand.

When Stephen arrived she insisted on seeing him alone, to Bethan's chagrin. She was surprised how small and insignificant he seemed. However he was pleasant enough and said the right things about Gerald.

'He was a fine man and you must miss him sorely. It is unlikely that you will be able to find another man such as he. Please forgive me, I do hope you do not mind me tackling the subject of your remarriage so directly and so soon. We are neighbours, and now in the same situation as one another. I felt that I should suggest we met before other possible suitors arrived on the scene. I am certain, such is your beauty and reputation, that many men will wish to be considered'.

Nest laughed, the first time she had done so since Gerald died.

'You are direct indeed, Lord Stephen. Never have I had such a proposal! You really know how to sway a woman's heart!'

Stephen seemed to wilt. 'I know nothing of fine words to please a lady. I only wish to say that having been recently tragically widowed from so fine a man as Lord Gerald you might be happy to now consider a more business-like arrangement. I would not expect you to love me, and there would be many advantages to you. You would have a fine home in Cardigan Castle and as my wife you could expect a leading role in local society. I would be very happy to offer a home to your children, including the two by Lord Gerald's former relationship.'

'But, why should I remarry at all? I am perfectly happy to spend the rest of my days at Carew, which was settled on me, and my heirs, by the King.'

'I think, my Lady, that you may be deceiving yourself. In our Norman society, it is considered best for a widow to remarry quite soon, and I think pressure would soon be put on you to do so. In your case there are other considerations. As you are well aware, your brother Gruffudd is in active rebellion against the King, and there would be concern that he might persuade you to join him. I am afraid to say that you will probably not have any option. It is not a question of whether you remarry, but whom you marry.'

'You make the position brutally clear, Lord Stephen.'

'I am not very good in dealing with these matters, but to be fair I should say that you will receive other offers. There are several Norman Lords seeking wives. I know Walter Fitzhammon is one such...'

'I would never, never agree to marry him. He is a monster who had Welsh wounded speared to death at Brecon.'

Stephen shifted uncomfortably in his chair. 'Perhaps you would prefer me to withdraw, I do not feel my mission is welcome to you. I should not have presumed that you would be interested in my proposal.'

Nest smiled and touched Stephen's arm gently.

'No, please stay. Let us discuss your proposal. You are right. I will be expected to remarry, I know that now. Please tell me how you think my life would be, and that of my children and my servants. I need to understand everything that you are suggesting.'

Well she had done it! After Stephen had explained what her role would be like at Cardigan, she was amazed to find herself agreeing to marry him in two weeks time! After he had gone, she had slumped on a couch and tried to work out why she had done such a thing. It must be because she was still numb with shock after the loss of Gerald. She could not cope with the yawning chasm in her life and she could not resist this chance to fill it.

Bethan was appalled, as were her children.

'My Lady, you cannot choose a husband like a sack of turnips. Surely you should have met him a few times to see if you are suitable for each other.'

'Why not?' said Nest, as if in a trance. 'I have to marry someone, and he is small enough to control if I do not like something he does! I am not going to fall in love again now, Bethan, and as he says, Cardigan is not far away from Carew so I can still watch my estate. I shall also be able to see my mother at Dinefwr regularly.

And so it was two weeks later that the bells rang out in Aberteifi for the marriage of Princess Nest and Stephen, Castellan of Cardigan Castle.

chapter fifty-three

Nest reflects at leisure,
Aberteifi Castle
August, AD 1118

'He is completely loathsome, Bethan. He has these desires in our bed, which turn my stomach.'

Bronwen was nursing the new baby, Robert, and she had joined Nest and Bethan in the solar to listen to the latest news of Nest's husband, having made sure Lord Stephen was out on a visit to Llechryd.

To Bethan it seemed that her mistress had made a serious mistake with her new marriage, rushing into it without thought, and was now faced with the consequences. Her husband apparently wanted to do things in bed which revolted her.

'What can I do Bethan, my Lord is not normal? I became lonely for a man to share my bed a few months after Gerald died, and I thought I could get used to someone new. He would not be Gerald nor yet the King, but I hoped I could learn to love him. Last night I took a dagger to bed and held it at his throat to convince him of my loathing for him. I fear I have gone too far.'

'My Lady, it is difficult for Bronwen and I to advise you. For ordinary women like us we have to take potluck with our men. Whatever they want to do in bed we have to go along with it or risk a beating, or worse. Fortunately, my Gelert has normal straightforward needs. The trouble with him is that he needs quite a lot, and I am not always ready to match him several times a night, when I have worked hard during the day.'

'My Iolo is different again. His body is often not equal to his desires so he expects me to spend ages arousing him. If I fail, he beats me or comes back drunk the next night. My Lady, the needs of men are difficult for us women to cope with. They all seem to be different and we just have to get used to the needs of our own man.'

'I shall never get used to what he wants to do, nor will I try.'

'I can see that you as a great lady might have some hope of modifying Lord Stephen's behaviour, but when we ordinary women marry a man we have promised in church to provide for his bodily lusts.'

'Tonight he is threatening to bring some woman from the town, whom, he says, knows how to please him. He says she shall instruct me as to what I am to do.'

Gelert now appeared. It seemed that he had heard everything, to Bethan's embarrassment. However, far from showing any concern about her account of his excessive desires, this normally taciturn man was struggling in the grip of something more serious. He threw himself on his knees in front of Nest and proclaimed his own solution to the obnoxious Lord Stephen.

'My Lady, please forgive me for interrupting your discussion. I have my own ideas as to what should be done. As you know my life is forfeit to you. At the battle I would have died had you not saved me. Of all the soldiers lying wounded unto death there, you chose and saved me. Lord Fitzhammon's men made short work of the rest after we were gone.'

Nest and Bethan shuddered: they remembered all too well what it was like at the battle.

'My life is yours. I have had twenty-five extra years, married to my Bethan and serving you.'

Nest was touched. 'Dear Gelert, you have amply repaid any debt you think you owe me by twenty-five years of devoted service. Do get up off your knees.'

Gelert was not so easily swayed from his purpose. For the first time in his life he ignored Nest's wishes and stayed where he was.

'My Lady let me strike Lord Stephen down? They will kill me but then you will be free of this man you hate so much. I will not say that we planned it. I will say he owes me money, or has killed my kinsman. I will never betray you.'

The new girl, Carys, hurried into the solar with David and Angharad.

'My Lady, Lord Stephen has arrived from Llechryd, and they are lowering the drawbridge to let him in.' How very fortunate, thought Nest, that Stephen is so excessively security conscious and often keeps the drawbridge closed even in time of peace. I always can hear when he is coming back.

'We shall talk of this later Gelert. In the meantime do nothing. I am very grateful for your loyalty. Please remember that I am no monster. I do not seek to kill husbands, even though I often wish this one would just disappear. Some other solution will have to be found for the problem. Bethan needs you Gelert, and your life must not be wasted.'

Stephen, when he reached the solar, scarcely greeted his wife, as he changed from his riding clothes, contenting himself with a vague threat to 'discuss matters of import' with her after dinner.

The Steward saw Nest before the meal and made a great matter as to what dishes should be served.

'My lady, I have had to make some decisions myself because when I came to see you to plan the meal, I was told you were busy with your domestic servants. I should tell you that Lord Stephen is very particular about all the arrangements for each day, and told me I should see you each morning so that plans can be made for all activities in the castle. Also, I should inform you that the other ladies of the castle are much put out because you give them no attention.'

Stephen's steward, Guy de Falaise, was in effect, second in command of the castle under Stephen, and took himself and his role very seriously. Nest thought he was self-opinionated and high and mighty, making much play of his claim that his father had come over with The Conqueror. His name 'de Falaise' meant his family was from the same town in Normandy as the mighty William.

Nest and her family had lived a very insulated life at Carew. Her 'castle' was really just a fortified house, with no Steward or other Knights and their ladies to worry about. She had gone rarely to Pembroke where Gerald did have a Steward, so she did not have to concern herself about the running of Pembroke, or occupying and arranging the lives of the women of the Castle. Her world had become that of her children and her husband, and her company had mostly been her Welsh-speaking servants and companions.

All of this would not do now she was Lord Stephen's wife. She was expected to run the whole domestic side of the castle in conjunction with Guy de Falaise. In particular she was supposed to organise the ladies in mammoth feats of sewing and embroidery, to decorate the Great Hall or simply to provide clothes for themselves and the children.

Consorting with Welsh-speaking servants was regarded very poorly. None of the other ladies had anything more than a mistress/servant relationship with their maids, especially Welsh-speaking ones, who should be kept an eye on, as potential traitors.

Nest knew that Stephen was very dissatisfied with his new wife on many more counts than his unrequited perversions, but unaware that he had decided that she was going to have to be knocked into shape in a very literal way, Princess or no. It was this very night that he had decided to bring all matters to a head.

Dinner itself was uneventful, but Nest could not help feeling that the ladies present were more than a little offhand with her. They seemed not to be including her in the conversation, but always laughed excessively at any of Stephen's unkind observations about people in other castles. Her own attempts at conversation made little progress, and she formed the impression that they all knew something that she had not been told of. Her sense of unease grew, and not for the first time she bitterly regretted her hasty decision to marry again.

After dinner, once back in the solar, Stephen seemed very impatient while Bethan was helping her mistress get ready for bed.

'If you brush my Lady's hair any more, Bethan, I swear her hair will fall out. Now hurry away, I cannot bear your fussing.'

Nest kept quiet during this tirade, being content to give Bethan a warm smile as she left.

Stephen now crossed the room, and stood above her as she sat on the bed.

Without any warning, he seized her by her hair, and started to shake her head violently while screaming abuse.

'You proud Welsh baggage, you think you are so high and mighty. Well it is time to sort things out with you. I have had enough of your likes and dislikes. You are my wife and you will accept whatever I want to do to you.'

Recovering from her surprise, Nest struggled free from him and kicked him hard in the stomach.

'You vile, little man, do you think you can use me like a rag doll? I have survived and surmounted much more than this. You had better treat me properly or the King will hear of it.'

Staggering to the corner of the room, Stephen picked up his horse-whip and brandished it in front of his wife's nose.

'Now you will learn your lesson, my Lady. When I have finished you will be glad to do all my bidding.'

Raising his voice he shouted, 'let the whole castle hear how the proud Princess Nest decided to become a good Norman wife.'

With this he struck her viciously across her head and shoulders leaving an ugly weal across her cheek. She could not help gasping, on account of the searing pain.

Instead of cowing her, the fact that Stephen was prepared not only to beat her, but also to mark her face, possessed Nest with a mindless fury that knew no limits. Asking God to forgive her, she seized the wooden crucifix from its recess in the wall, and just as Stephen was preparing another slash with the whip, she flung herself across the room, and hit him, using her full force with the heavy cross. He fell at once like a stricken ox. Caring not whether he was alive or dead, she drew her concealed dagger, and kneeling at his side she lightly and carefully scored two large crosses on his cheeks.

'Hit me again my Lord, and I will surely plant this dagger in your heart.'

The noise of the commotion caused other residents of the castle to overcome their reserve and pour into the room, followed by Gelert and Bethan. By this time Stephen had staggered to his feet and lurched across the room to peer in the mirror at his bloody face, and Nest was dabbing with a damp cloth at the ugly weal he had inflicted on her.

Everyone stared at the signs of violence, not knowing what to say. De Falaise was the first to speak.

'My Lord, we heard the noise of a struggle and thought there must be some intruders. Whatever has happened here?'

'Your concern is a credit to you,' snapped Stephen. 'Now get out of here and leave my wife and I to settle our differences.'

Reluctantly they all left the room. 'You too Bethan,' urged Nest.' I have matters to resolve with my Lord Stephen.'

When they were alone, Nest said quietly,

'Any more of this and I shall kill you, and the King shall know why. I hope you are convinced of that now. You mistake me, sir. A woman who has had to cope with the likes of Owain Prince of Powys and Robert Fitzhammon is not going to be fazed by a miserable little worm like you.

'I propose a fresh start. You want a wife to run your castle and to arrange any social happenings that arise. I need a peaceful home where I receive the respect due to my rank. I remind you that my status in society is superior to yours and to have me on your arm must be of great benefit socially. If you agree to treat me properly and with respect, I shall stay with you and perform all the public duties of a Norman wife. Also, I will not appeal to the King, unless provoked again, but neither will I sleep in your perverted bed.'

Stephen was a coward at heart, and his resolve to bring his spitfire of a wife to heel was fatally weakened by his certainty that Nest could maim him, or kill him, while he slept, and was quite capable of doing so. However, there was more to it than that. He suspected that the King still kept a warm place in his heart for Nest and that somehow messages still passed between them. He dare not take action against her.

Another factor was that he was aware that his Overlord, Robert Fitzgilbert, obviously held Nest in high esteem, and made much of her on his frequent visits, and would be likely to take Nest's side should she make any complaint against him. It was uncomfortably obvious to him now that Nest had the will, and probably the power, to unseat him from his very pleasant position as Constable of Cardigan Castle. No, the game was just not worth the candle. Trouble with Nest was going to involve, at the very least, public humiliation for him in the eyes of his subordinates. He could easily find his pleasures elsewhere, as he had before.

As he examined the ugly scores on his face, he decided to take the easy way out. He liked being Castellan, and he now had a baby son to carry on his line. No, he would meet Nest halfway, and let the world continue to be jealous of him having such a beautiful wife. Pouring a glass of wine, he offered it to her as if nothing had happened.

'I think tomorrow will be a better day. Let us ride out together and look at the castle I am building for Lord Robert Fitzgilbert at Cilgerran. I think you might be interested.'

Looking at him steadily, Nest replied, 'I would like that, my Lord. I have a soothing pink unguent here. Please keep steady while I apply it to your face.'

244

chapter fifty-four

Nest makes a decision
November, AD 1120

Predictably, Stephen reacted badly when the letter arrived from Henry. Always jealous of the bond between Nest and the King, he had intercepted the letter when it arrived, and was in a towering rage by the time he felt compelled to let her read it.

Nest could see at once that it was from Henry. Ignoring Stephen's mounting anger, she snatched it from him.

Rouen Castle, Normandy

'My dear Nesta,

You will know that it was a source of great sadness to me that reasons of state compelled me to marry another. I had hoped that our son Henry could have been legitimised by a marriage between us, but I was not able to persuade the Council, whose support I needed, for such a plan. This you know already or have guessed.

It is all many years ago and in the meantime you have had two marriages to very fortunate Norman Lords.

However, the consequences of my mistake still continue, complicated by the death of the Queen two years ago, which means that I now have no hope of more, legitimate, sons.

To come to the point, I have to make some very important decisions, and your ideas would be much appreciated. These matters concern the very bedrock of the Anglo-Norman Kingdom, and it is gravely urgent that I come to the right conclusions. I have always had a high respect for your advice, which has helped me a great deal in the past.

I therefore request that you attend on me at the Court in Rouen, as soon as is practicable.

Therefore, assuming your consent, I am despatching my ship, the 'Raven,' with this letter. The Captain, whom you know, has orders to wait in Aberteifi Port until you are ready.

I am writing separately to your husband making my wishes clear. I am sure he will be wise enough to accede to my request. I do not require, or expect, him to accompany you. His presence will be much more useful in Ceredigion.

With luck your ship should be here within a week.

Yours, always,
Henry Rex.'

'You could always forbid me to go as Gerald did,' said Nest maliciously, knowing full well that her husband's mettle was not up to denying a King anything.

'I am not a fool like Gerald. However, it is obvious to me that your encouragement of the King's interest in you has put him up to this. Why else would he think of it? I know that you detest my bed and that you fancy trying that of your first lover.'

'I certainly hate your bed and anything your perverted mind would like to do in it. I think I have reminded you of it with my dagger a few times and would do so again. I am glad Henry wants me to go to him and I do not deny that a few nights with him would be very welcome.'

'You are a whore and a slut, Princess or not,' yelled Stephen, striking her face hard.'

'I hope that leaves a mark, as I would like to show Henry some evidence of how you treat me, you vile little man.'

Stephen stormed out of the room, white with fury. He was a coward at heart. Gelert, unseen in the shadows just outside the door, sheathed his sword and breathed a sigh of relief. Both he and his mistress' hated husband would live a little longer.

chapter fifty-five

It was very strange. After twenty years, the 'Raven', with the same Captain who had taken her to Wales, was now entering the estuary of the River Seine, taking her back to Henry.

Her hands firmly gripping the gunwale to counter the roll of the ship, and accompanied by the faithful Bethan, Nest was joined by the now elderly Captain Thomas.

'There you are Captain. What good advice will you offer me, now that I have heeded the request of the King to return to him?'

Thomas was struck by a number of emotions inconvenient to his position as Ship's Master to the King, and had to take his time in replying. Nest, now forty, was unbelievably beautiful. When he had taken her to Penfro, he had thought her powerfully attractive in her youthful vulnerability, but now she was absolutely stunning. As she turned to speak to him with her golden hair streaming in the wind, her laughing deep green eyes seemed to be penetrating to the depth of his being, but not in a dangerous way. She was aware of her power over him, as over so many other men, but he knew that she would never use her power to harm him. His admiration was safe with her. He thought at that moment that, if she asked him, he would do absolutely anything for her, and to have lost so much control almost frightened him.

Sensing deep feelings she made it easier for him.

'You gave me very good advice when you took me to Pembroke. I was a young girl, newly deprived of my baby and sent rejected by the King to marry a stranger. I deeply appreciated your fatherly support and will always be grateful to you.'

'You will know that I have a deep regard for you, my Lady, and will always be yours to command.'

'You seem to be close to the workings of the King's mind, Master Thomas. Without in any way being disloyal, can you tell me why Henry has asked me back?'

'Quite simply, he needs your advice. He has some big decisions to make and he trusts you to act in his best interest. You are the mother of his eldest son, for whom he has a warm regard, but more than that, I believe that he still loves you.'

'Loves me! How can you say that Master Thomas? He packed me off to Wales so that he could marry Good Queen Maud. He has had many women. I am but a rather troublesome member of the small legion who have shared his bed.'

Bethan decided to put a word in.

'My Lady, I believe you should listen to Master Thomas. He will surely wish to give you his best advice.'

Suddenly contrite, Nest flashed Thomas her warmest smile, which nearly unmanned him.

'Accepting for a moment your rather surprising view of Henry's regard for me, why ever does he need to bring me, a woman, all the way from Wales, when he has a host of Counsellors to advise him close about him?'

'He does not trust them, my Lady, not in the matter of the succession. Each one has an axe to grind.'

'Please explain to me plainly, Master Thomas so that I am better prepared when I reach Rouen.'

'What I can say must be for your ears only, my Lady.'

Bethan tutted a little but moved along the deck out of earshot.

Captain Thomas lowered his voice and continued, 'William the Atheling, the heir to the throne, the King's only legitimate son, is wild and dissolute. He has built up his own rival Court around him consisting of some of the most drunken and wayward sons of the Magnates. He has offered them all lands, fame and wealth as soon as his father dies. He has no respect for his father and openly mocks him when he is carousing with his friends, even urging him to die soon so that he can be King.'

'This must be very distressing for the King. Can he not discipline him in some way?'

'Henry is regarded by many as being a very hard and stern man, but William, saving your presence my Lady, was the only one born on the right side of the blanket.'

Nest flushed a little but controlled herself: she wanted to know the situation in Rouen, and Captain Thomas despite his gaffes was the one to tell her.

'Do go on Master Thomas, you are being most helpful.'

'Since his lady wife, the Queen, died two years ago, he has no hope of more sons, and seems strangely weak in controlling William, despite advice from various members of the Council.'

'This is not uncommon behaviour in both fathers and mothers. They keep hoping that by ignoring crass actions by their sons that they will eventually improve, despite strong evidence to the contrary. Poor Henry! However, I do not have the least idea how my being in Rouen is going to help the King?'

'It is not my place to hazard guesses as to His Majesty's intentions. I am certain though, that he would not have sent his ship for you if he did not think that you could help.'

'I will not embarrass you by asking your opinion as to whether he just feels rather lonely and needs a new bed mate. I shall soon find out about that suspicion. Thank you, Master Thomas, you have been very helpful, as always.

'Now, tell me what the Court is like at Rouen and who are the most important Magnates there?'

Nest was surprised to find that the Court at Rouen was in many ways similar to that in Westminster. Many of the great lords had lands on both sides of the Channel and tended to find it in their interests to cross from one country to the other whenever the King moved. She therefore recognised many faces.

Both Courts were of course French speaking, and nearly all the Magnates were Norman. However, what was conspicuously absent, was the Saxon influence. In Westminster, she had got used to the fact that all the lower orders with which she had daily contact - maids, cooks, syces, equerries, guards, doorkeepers, butlers, candle-makers, and all the rest, were almost always Saxon, except Bethan and Gelert of course. She had become used to this rather bizarre manifestation of one nation's subjection to another. Now it was powerfully brought home to her in the capital of Normandy where everyone, high and low, was Norman. It also reminded her of why her brother, and so many of her own countrymen, were striving to drive the Normans out of Wales, much of her country too being ruled and dominated by this aggressive and dominant race.

She reminded herself of that brave and reckless little twelve year old who had been brought to the Norman Court swearing to Bethan that she would never forget that she was a Welsh Princess. Where was that Princess now? Had she somehow forgotten who she was, after taking a Norman King for a lover and two Norman Lords as husbands? She shivered at the thought and decided to always keep a place in her heart for her brother, and all he stood for.

She had been met at the port by the aged Count Robert de Meulan who had greeted her warmly on behalf of the King. His duty was to escort her to her rooms at Rouen Castle, where she could rest after her journey, and later prepare herself to be presented at Court that very evening.

Bethan had made a great fuss in helping her chose just the right apparel from the large trunk, which Gelert had supervised being carried from the ship.

'You must look your very best, my Lady. You must make sure that the French ladies are humbled by the beauty of a Welsh Princess.'

When, at the appointed hour, clad in her most flattering light blue dress, with her hair meticulously brushed and braided under a silver circlet, and attended by Bethan and Gelert, she had swept up to the door of the Great Hall, she looked completely stunning. Count Robert was there to meet her, smiling his pleasure at having the duty of escorting such an exquisite creature.

He offered her his arm, and whispered that the King would be giving her a formal audience seated on his throne, and that then he would take her through the crowds of courtiers to be presented.

As she moved forward on Count Robert's arm towards the throne at the other end of the hall, everyone turned to look at her. Here was a new, striking and beautiful face. One so comely might be a serious contender for influence in the Court.

Henry looked very regal and grave seated on his throne, but his face lit up with pleasure as the Lord Chamberlain announced her.

'Princess Nesta of Deheubarth, your Majesty, wife of Stephen, Lord of Cardigan.

Nest curtsied prettily, and was glad that she had been well coached all those years ago about how to behave in Court.

'You are most welcome to my Court, Princess Nesta. We would have it known that we hold you and your Nation in our very highest regard. We trust that you travelled well. The seas around your Country can be very stormy.' He then added drily, 'I am sorry that Lord Stephen has been unable to accompany you.'

'You are most gracious, your Majesty. Captain Thomas looked after me very well, as always. I am delighted to be in Rouen. Thank you for sending your ship for me.'

The King now rose and offered Nest his arm.

'Perhaps you would be kind enough to accompany me as I progress round the Court. I will introduce you to some persons of note.'

Nest grinned, her famous grin, which touched Henry to the core. Where had all the years gone since first she had looked at him like that?

'I remember that you used those words to me once before, your Majesty,' she answered lightly squeezing his arm.'

Henry felt himself warming at her touch. After all the women he had known, he still stirred at this sign that she might welcome his advances later. Something after previous experiences with her he had learned not to take for granted!

The faces were different than they were the last time that Henry had taken her round the Court on his arm, all those twenty odd years ago, but the response on the ladies' faces was the same. Some were admiring her for her beauty: some hated her for it and looked for flaws and faults. All wondered what difference she might make to their lives since she was obviously highly favoured by the King.

Nest looked into their eyes as she was introduced and speculated which ones had shared his bed. However, she did not much care. She had always known that there were many other women on the fringes of his life. What she did know was that he had never preferred any other woman to her.

'What are you thinking about?' he murmured, shooting her a knowing glance.

'I was wondering which ones you have bedded,' she grinned.

'I thought so. However, I shall not satisfy your curiosity, but you cannot avoid seeing some of the consequences.'

He stopped in front of a young man of about seventeen.

'Princess Nesta, let me introduce Robert, my son.'

Nest knew that he had about twenty children by various women, but this was the first one that she had met. She was pleased, yet surprised, that Henry acknowledged them openly in Court. Her hopes were now raised that she would be allowed to meet her own son, Henry. The King had long ago agreed that this would happen one day, and one of her motives for coming to Rouen was that this might be the occasion.

'As if reading her thoughts, Henry said, 'our son has often asked to be allowed to meet you. He has been on a campaign for me in the Vexin. I am hoping he will be back here later this evening. If so, I will send him to your rooms so that you can see each other. He is a very fine young man and a great credit to us both. It has long grieved my heart that reasons of state separated you from him. All that shall be put right now.'

Nest's mind was a whirl. The loss to her of her baby all those years ago had been a terrible wrench to her, and Henry's rather casual statement that she was now to meet him again was quite a shock, now that it was really going to happen.

She could not imagine what he would look like. A bit like his father, she presumed. He was now twenty and apparently trusted to go on campaigns on the King's behalf. He would be a capable soldier, battle trained and hardened by his experiences. When Nest last saw him he was a baby, and he would have no memory of her. Although she was going to be allowed at long last to meet him, he would now be a different person. She realised sadly, that the baby who had been taken away was lost to her for ever, and this young man when she saw him would be no substitute, however fine a young man he had proved to be.

They had completed a full circle of the hall, but Henry's statement that she would be seeing her long lost son that very evening meant that she was not able to respond properly to every new face. They probably think that I am cool and haughty, she thought. She would have to put that impression right later.

Henry led her to her place beside him, at his right hand at the head of the great table. She was being treated almost as if she were already his consort. Recovering herself, and now picking up more signs from those around her, she realised that they were all being very deferential. What a change from the court at Cardigan!

On her right side, she found she had the company of the Earl of Salisbury, who had become Henry's Chief Advisor. He was an elderly, rather pompous man, and Nest thought him overdressed, contrasting with the stark simplicity of the King's own black gown.

Glancing down the table she felt a quiver of shock and abhorrence. Only a few places away, she recognised Robert Fitzhammon, the man who had ordered the castration of her brother Cynan, and had killed all her wounded countrymen after her father's last battle. As a fiery twelve-year old, she had sworn to somehow punish him for those ghastly crimes. Now, seeing him sitting close, still apparently basking in the King's regard, her old feelings came back powerfully for a moment, and she longed to ask Henry to send him on a dangerous campaign where he would be in the forefront of the battle. Now she blamed Fitzhammon for those feelings too, very nearly making her into someone she did not want to be, cruel and vengeful.

Fitzhammon seemed to be avoiding her gaze, but for a second, as he turned to speak to his neighbour, their eyes met. Although he was several yards away, he shivered as he looked into those deep green eyes. For the second time in his life he felt as if someone were walking over his grave. Although a brave man in normal life, he resolved to keep well away from Nest in future. His feelings were not improved when Henry called down the table to him.

'Ah, Fitzhammon. My son Henry is due back from the Vexin this evening. I want you to take his place there. A dangerous assignment, but a chance to earn a little glory.'

Nest felt as if Henry had been reading her mind. Surely it was purely a coincidence that, following her murderous but secret thoughts, Henry was now sending Fitzhammon off to battle. It was to that same dangerous campaign that he had also sent their son.

Henry was very attentive to her at dinner, often serving her himself from platters brought by the servants. He had said nothing about why he had sent for her, other than that he wished to consult her later 'on matters of state.' Nest could not tell from this what he really required of her. However, her life had been so empty lately that she found herself revelling at the chance to enjoy herself. Bethan, waiting nearby, thought she had never looked so beautiful, or so full of life.

Nest noted that the Norman Court under Henry was much more orderly than it had been under William Rufus. Drunken revelling was frowned on, as was loud or boastful speech. When she commented on this to the Earl of Salisbury, he told her that Lords who misbehaved at Court ran the risk being sent on unwelcome expeditions to quell trouble on the French border. She wondered again what Fitzhammon had done to deserve his new posting.

The long meal eventually drew to its end and Henry rose from his chair, causing everyone else to rise too, and escorted Nest out of the hall. Everyone 'above the salt' followed too. *

* *At Norman meals the position of the valuable jar of salt marked the boundary between persons of note and the places occupied by lesser members of the Court.*

At the door Henry turned to her with a smile and said 'No doubt we shall meet later, after our son has been to see you.'

Once back in her room, Bethan was full of questions. 'What had the King said?' and 'would he be wanting her to share his bed?'

'Enough idle chatter, Bethan, I am just glad to be away from Aberteifi for a while. It seems that the King wishes to consult me about some matters, but I know not what.'

'Is it body or mind he wishes to consult,' said Bethan unwisely and immediately wished she had not.

Nest's eyes flashed.

'You are sometimes very impertinent, Bethan. Do not presume too much on my good nature. If you wish to be invited on future expeditions with me, please keep your bawdy thoughts to yourself.'

Further conversation was interrupted by the arrival of someone at the door. Bethan thought it was the King, but Nest knew better and composed herself to meet her firstborn.

It was Gelert who brought him in.

'This gentleman says he is Henry Fitzhenry and he insists on an audience with you, although I have told him you are due to retire for the night, my Lady.'

Her first thought was that he looked like the King, but perhaps with a slight look of her side of the family too. He just stood there awkwardly, not knowing what to say.

Her own reserve melted in a second and she gathered him in her arms. 'Henry, my son, I have waited for this moment for so many, many years. I last saw you a baby and now you are a fine young man.'

'Mother, I have asked the King so many questions about you, even when I was quite small. I have always wanted to know why I could not see you. He always said that I would see you one day but would never tell me when.'

'And what answers did your father give you, and what did he say about me?'

'He always said that you were a very beautiful Welsh princess, and that you loved me very much, and that it was a torment to him that you had to be sent away from me. Lately, he has said more things and hinted that I would see you soon, perhaps often. He has always favoured me highly.'

Bethan, with a few nudges to Gelert, asked permission to withdraw so that Nest could talk to her son more freely. They had not been waiting outside the door long when a page arrived saying that the Earl of Salisbury wished to see young Henry urgently, as he was about to retire for the night, and had not yet received his report about the state of affairs in the Vexin. Reluctantly, Nest parted from her son and contented herself by discussing it all with Bethan.

Later that night Henry the King came to her just as she had known he

253

would. She had told Gelert, when she retired, to take care whom he cut down with his sword, so the first that she knew of Henry's arrival was when she found him sitting on her bed, with Bethan slipping out of the room, smiling.

'I seem to be here, Nesta' he said, taking her hand. 'Am I welcome? You have the reputation of not being afraid to refuse Kings.'

'Nest raised herself sleepily on her pillow.

'I shall not deny you tonight, Henry. I confess that when I was lying in a cold bed in Aberteifi, with only a dagger for company, I often remembered those wild, reckless nights in the Tower of London, and earlier ones when I was a young girl at Westminster.'

'Yes! I miss all those days and nights, and more than that I miss what we had together, so long ago. I know now that I made a mistake when I sent you away to Wales. I was wrong not to make you my Queen, wrong to deny our son Henry as my heir.'

'These are weighty confessions my Lord,' breathed Nest. 'You look cold. Would you not tell me your thoughts more comfortably under the covers with me?'

Bethan, in the next room, smiled to herself and softly closed the door. She was happy that Nest was herself again for a little while.

254

chapteR fifty-seven

Rouen, the following morning
October, AD 1120

Bethan bustled in with hot water and freshly ironed clothes. Opening the shutters, she realised that her mistress, still in bed, had been crying. There was no sign of the King. Normally so confident and self-assured, Nest's appearance reminded Bethan more of the frightened little girl captured in Brecheiniog than a Princess at the height of her beauty.

At the sight of Bethan's sympathetic face, far from trying to regain her composure, Nest burst into a fresh flood of tears. Reverting from servant to older friend and companion, Bethan rushed to comfort her.

'My Lady, whatever is the matter? I looked to see you blissful this morning.' Then, more quietly, she added, 'has the King harmed you in some way?'

Nest allowed her to hold her tightly while she cried her eyes out.

'Do not distress yourself, Cariad.' *

'Tell me what is wrong, You know all your secrets are safe with me.'

'I feel so lonely, Bethan. That is not a feeling new to me since I married Stephen, but now I feel lonelier still because I am a stranger to myself. I feel that I have become a whore. I thought that the King had sent for me because he had some deep problem to resolve, just as he did in the Tower of London those many years ago. But all he needed was my body, and he did not even take much trouble with that.' After some more deep sobs, she added hopelessly, 'I wish I could go back in time and be that happy Princess, safe with my beloved Gerald again. Am I not truly pathetic?'

Bethan paused for thought. She realised that her Mistress needed more than hugs. She needed to understand herself.

'My Lady, I think that I know you as well as anyone. It has been my privilege to be at your side through many years.'

The sobs were stopping.

'Of course you understand me dearest Bethan. You are a true friend and companion. I am very lucky.' More sobs followed.

'I see you, Cariad, as a beautiful, intelligent, most caring and loveable woman. With Lord Gerald you found peace, safety and companionable love. You were lucky enough to find a true, understanding friend as well as a husband. That is very unusual. You were happy with him.' She hesitated.

'But I do not think you found passion, and I think you need passion.' She paused, thinking she was getting into deep water, Nest was above all a Princess of the Royal House of Dinefwr.

'Go on,' said her mistress quietly. Bethan took a deep breath.

* *'Cariad' is Welsh for 'sweet one', 'darling', or 'lover'.*

255

'As I said, Princess you may be, but you are also a very passionate woman whose body has the need of a skilful lover. That is why you recklessly spent several days and nights in the Tower all those years ago. Any ordinary woman would have gone without the passion to avoid the consequences.'

'Any more Bethan?'

'Four years ago you tragically lost your strong, safe Gerald, who understood you and loved you whatever you did, and you, perhaps unwisely, married Lord Stephen who has made you very unhappy. He does not share your bed and cares not that your body has a deep hunger for love. May I say more, my Lady, or do I displease you?'

'Do continue.'

'I think that apart from expecting to advise the King, you were also expecting him to give you satisfaction in bed and he has apparently let you down in that regard.'

Nest's face flushed with anger, and Bethan thought that her Mistress had become angry enough to beat her for the first time in her life, but then her face softened and she grasped Bethan's hand.

'You are right as always, Bethan, but it is hard for me to accept it. My body hungers for love and sometimes betrays me now that I do not have anyone to warm me at night. I find it very difficult. Sometimes when one of Stephen's Knights pays me attention, I wish I could be like some strumpet and let him pull me into a dark corner and do what he will with me. I am becoming a whore at heart, Bethan, instead of a Princess.

'When Henry asked me to come to Rouen I confess the first reaction was a warm feeling between my legs. It seems that that is how Henry himself perceives me. The satisfaction that he apparently needed was the use of my body, and unfortunately my advice came a poor second. I feel I am no better than a whore.'

'You are a woman, Cariad, and a warm and complex one.'

To both women's surprise, the King's voice came from the shadows. He had come into the room, unnoticed, a few moments earlier and decided to listen a while.

'It is very sad that you have to tell your secrets to servants, Nesta, however loyal. Now leave us Bethan, and keep your mouth shut about the intimacies of Princesses, if you know what is good for you.'

Bethan curtsied hurriedly and fled from the room feeling that life had suddenly become dangerous.

The King sat on Nest's bed and took her hand it his.

'I am so sorry about last night. I confess that I am exhausted by all the problems of State and I was not equal to the demands of bedding you. King or not, I remind you that I am just a man, Nesta, and sometimes as with you, my body lets me down. Bethan has done us both a favour, for now I know how miserable your life is in Cardigan, and how wrong I was to allow you to marry Stephen. Tell me all that grieves you my darling.'

'It is kind of you to be so concerned. My burden is a minor one compared to the ones you bear. However, if you really want to know what my marriage is like I will put it to you plainly. I sleep alone, Henry, for my vile husband has unnatural desires. He is perverted and I have to keep a dagger in my bed, which he knows I would stick into him if he tried to rape me.'

Discarding his clothes and getting into bed beside her, Henry held her close and wanted to put matters right, in every way. Being a logical man, he thought he should first reassure her about how much he valued her for her advice.

'I need to talk to you about Prince William,' he started.

'Oh Henry,' she laughed, 'you have made love to dozens of women but I do not believe you understand them very well.' She kissed his mouth warmly and deeply and progressed to his ears and shoulders.

'Make love to me like you did when I was a young girl. Our discussion will follow naturally, later.'

'I may be a King but I think my powers in bed are fading. I am losing confidence that I shall be able to satisfy a passionate woman like you. I am usually all right with women of the Court, because I do not care what they think. I do not worry whether I can perform, but with you I do care and already my manhood is shrinking.'

Nest was immediately contrite and full of feeling for him. Hugging him to her, she put her head on his chest.

'Of course I want you to make love to me, but I am content that you are with me. This is not some contest or challenge. It is you, with me, being together in any way we want to be. I know you to be a wonderful lover Henry. You do not have to prove it. I believe you to be under many pressures and I am not here to put more pressure on you. I am happy to be snuggled up beside you.

'Let us play a game of pretend. Let us say that you are a callow youth with no experience of women, and that I am an older seductress intent on overcoming your reluctance. You must try your best not to respond to me. You must force yourself not to touch me. I will do all the touching.'

Henry was happy to relax into the new game: it sounded far more agreeable than proving yet again that his powers were fading.

Nest started by kissing and caressing his feet and lower legs, and progressed via his knees and his flanks to his neck and shoulders. Henry feeling himself beginning to respond reached out for her, but she laughingly pushed him away, saying that he still was not allowed to touch her. She then progressed to his more private regions, taking his member in her hands and kissing it lightly until it grew bigger, then putting it in her mouth. She started to move her head up and down, greatly stimulating him, so that he found himself rampant with desire for her. Finally, he could control himself no longer, and rather than coming in her mouth, he flung her on her back and entered her.

'Gently, slowly, Henry,' she whispered, fearing that he would expend himself too soon. Nest herself was greatly aroused by her fellatio and suddenly exploded in the most amazing orgasm that she had ever experienced. This had the effect of setting off Henry who came at once, so powerfully that he was shaken to his depths.

He hugged her delightedly, stroking and kissing her hair, and she his. Finally they both fell contentedly asleep while Bethan had the sense to keep them from any interruption for several hours.

When they awoke Nest sent for cake and wine and they sat up in bed while she fed him. It was just as it had been when they had consumed cake and wine in the hunting lodge all those years ago.

When she saw that he was properly awake, she said, 'now tell me of those mighty matters of State which you have honoured me by thinking I might help you with.' She accompanied these words by stuffing a further large piece of cake in his mouth, which effectively stopped him replying until he could sort out his thoughts.

When finally his mouth was empty enough again, he said, 'I find it hard to explain how I feel about you. It is like when you came to help me work out what to do about the Montgomerys' insurrection and Robert landing at Portsmouth. I somehow feel safe when you are with me. All my concerns about the succession, and the machinations of the Great Lords, seem greatly reduced when you are here to share them. Does that seem a little pathetic in a King?'

'By no means. I believe it to be the true basis for the relationship between a woman and a man. Tell me all about it. I am all ears so long as you put your arm round me again and I can cuddle up to you.'

'Well, apart from missing you in my bed, I asked you to come to Rouen because I have serious problems about which I have no one to talk to in safety.'

She poured them more wine, and when they had drunk it she said, 'tell me anything, and I will do my best to think it through with you.'

'I grow older, my beloved, and I fear that the succession to my crown is not safe. The Great Lords know that I have only one legitimate son and that he is dissolute and unworthy of the throne. The Anglo-Norman Kingdom is difficult to rule and needs a sure, safe successor, who will make a strong King.'

'Young men are often wild, Henry, but they usually settle down and become wiser if responsibility is settled on them.'

'What you say is often true, but not in the case of William, I fear. He actually puts it about that he despises my counselling, and me. It is obvious that he thinks only of his dissolute pleasures.'

258

'You may yet have other legitimate sons, Henry, and you could persuade the Great Council to adopt one as your heir.'

'I remind you that the Queen died two years ago, and anyway, such a son would not have time to grow up before I died. There are not enough years left. The Great Lords would take advantage of a young boy and there would be rebellion and anarchy. My greatest concern now is to make sure of a safe succession to my throne so that my life's work is not destroyed on my death.

'No, Nest! The answer is more and more clear to me. Our son, Henry, is a fine young man. He is intelligent, strong and compassionate. He has a good head on his shoulders. You saw him yesterday: you know what he is like. He is a mixture of the best of both of us. I know now, that my only hope is to make him legitimate, and my heir.'

Nest now knew the real reason why she had been sent for. Henry wanted to make her his Queen and their son the heir to the throne. However, he had not yet quite spelt it all out. The thought was thrilling, but must be carefully and calmly considered.

'Let us think hard about your plan. Tell me exactly what you propose and I will play the Devil's Advocate and point out the difficulties.'

Pulling her close to his side, he said, 'it is simple in concept but difficult in the detail. You must be my Queen and Henry must be adopted as my legitimate heir.'

'Your long experience of women has not improved your sense of romance, Henry. Even Kings are supposed to do a little wooing!'

Henry remembered what it had been like all those long years ago when he and she had been at the hunting lodge, and he had surprised her by jumping out of bed and kneeling down at her side. He wrestled with a ring on his finger and holding it in his palm took her hand in his.

'Dearest Nesta, you are the one true love of my life. With you as my Queen I can conquer the world. With you at my side I would be the happiest of men. With our son as my heir, England would be safe from anarchy. Please Nesta, accept my hand in marriage and make it all come true.' Henry slipped the heavy ring onto her third finger and kissed her hand.

Nest thrilled with pleasure and tried to close her mind to the problems just for a little while.

'Oh Henry, I do love you, I do so hope we can make it succeed. You tell me we are returning to England tomorrow. Let us savour this moment until we arrive there, and by then we will have decided on the best way forward.'

William's followers were milling round the quayside where the White Ship lay ready for sea. Servants held lanterns, while pot boys from the harbour taverns supplied yet more flagons of wine for the already inebriated courtiers. The ship's captain, Master Jack, followed the drunken Prince round the groups of raucous young men, while Prince William slapped their backs, telling them to drink more so that they would survive the rigours of the voyage the better. Master Jack had been drinking, but not yet enough to prevent him worrying about the state of wind and tide.

'Sir we must all embark ready to sail. The King's party is coming along the quay, and Captain Thomas will cast off as soon as all are aboard. The tide is dropping and we must leave soon, so as to clear the rocks near the harbour entrance.'

'Sod the rocks! Sod my royal father! I will go when I am ready, Master Jack. Come take a few swigs of this brandy. That will warm you for the voyage and stop you following me round worriting like an old hen.'

The King and his party paused when they reached the dishevelled Prince and his drunken friends.

'My son, Captain Thomas urges me to sail as soon as we are on board as the tide is dropping. I urge you to do likewise. I would also advise you to stop your crew drinking else they will be incapable of carrying out their duties. At your insistence, I have let you borrow the 'White Ship', which is my pride and joy. I would like to see her arrive safe and sound in Portsmouth without risk.'

The Prince threw his arms around Master Jack.

'Your precious ship is in safe hands with the good Captain. Have no fear, father!'

''I think I would be happier William, if your brother Henry was on board to keep an eye on things.'

'Oh no, father. I will not fall for that one. I do not want your spy of a son keeping an eye on me. Anyway,' he sniggered, 'he would have to worry that he might fall overboard if I started to think he was too high in your favour, especially as he was born on the wrong side of the blanket. No, you keep Henry, but send my sister Edith and some of her pretty friends. Richard can come too: he is much more fun.'

Following a blast of trumpets, the King's ship, the 'Raven', cast off from the quay, and her crew cautiously rowed the vessel past the White Ship. Captain Thomas then steered for the harbour entrance to pick up the offshore breeze coming over the hills behind the harbour.

Meanwhile, the 'White Ship''s own departure was further delayed to allow Prince William's sister to board, together with a party of her female friends and their servants. The drunken Prince and his party greeted the arrival of the women bawdily, and yet more wine was consumed to celebrate.

Finally, the very unsteady Captain Jack ordered the mooring ropes to be cast off, since arrival of the women had caused the Prince to lose interest temporarily in the departure of the vessel.

The crew struggled to get their oars ready, but the effects of the drink hampered their efforts and some oars got tangled up with their neighbours, causing the ship to drift away from the quay almost broadside on.

With much shouting from the Captain and the boatswain, the White Ship finally reached the harbour entrance the right way round, but hardly under full control. To add to the Captain's difficulties, the Prince suddenly freed himself from the arms of a lady in waiting, and shouted to the crew that they should raise the mainsail, as he wished to catch up with the King's ship. He gave his orders without any reference to the Captain, who was too befuddled to do anything about it immediately. The wind now caught the half-raised sail, sending the ship at speed to the west, close by the shore.

'Pull the cursed sail down again,' he bellowed, suddenly shaken out of his torpor. 'I cannot keep her on course. Pull it down I say,' he screamed desperately. 'We cannot clear the rocks. Pull, larboard oars!' he shouted. 'I cannot hold her.'

The Prince raised his head from a pretty face to see the white gleam of breaking waves close at hand. For a moment it seemed all would be well, and the vessel would just clear the outermost rocks, but then the wind strengthened and backed a little, forcing the ship to change course yet closer to the rocks.

Suddenly there was a jolt, a shuddering of the whole hull, then a long rending crash, bringing the ship to a violent halt and throwing everyone to the bottom of the boat. Immediately the still partially raised sail pushed the ship over to larboard, and water poured in, filling the vessel in seconds.

The boatswain and Captain Jack, still dry on the raised steering deck, pulled the ship's boat alongside. The Captain seeing the Prince nearby, clinging to the rigging, moved along to the end of the deck and reaching down, managed to grab him by an arm. Helped by the boatswain, the Prince was hauled to the temporary safety of the stern deck and then put in the boat alongside, aided by other members of the crew. With the Captain, Prince, Boatswain and four of the crew, the boat was well loaded, so Captain Jack resolved not to allow anyone else on board, and ordered the crew to cast off and row back to the harbour.

Many of the remaining unfortunates in the stricken ship had by now succeeded in climbing up onto the side of the wreck and were shouting desperately for the boat to put back to pick them up.

'Keep rowing men, we cannot take all that lot, they would swamp the boat. We must save the Prince, England's hope for the future. When we have done that we will send a fishing boat to pick up the rest.'

The half-drowned Prince shouted to the Captain, 'I can hear my sister's cries. We must go back for her. Turn round I say.'

'Your Highness, this is a small boat. It does not have room for any more. If we go back, a hundred people will swamp the boat. We can send help to them when we reach the harbour.'

A further grinding crash from the receding ship, and still louder cries, signalled that she had slid a little deeper into the sea.

'Go back immediately!' ordered William, 'or it will be the worse for you if you ignore my orders and my sister is drowned.'

Very reluctantly, Captain Jack had the boat turned round and rowed back to the ship. As it came alongside, dozens of terrified men and women jumped down into the boat causing the near side to be pushed under the water. At once it was overwhelmed and within seconds they were all in the sea, seeking something to cling to.

On board the 'Raven', oblivious to the tragic scene still only a couple of miles away, the King sat under the shelter with Nest and the rest of his party. The wind had picked up as soon as they had cleared the shore and the ship, now under sail alone, was making good progress out into the Channel. Servants were passing round mulled wine, warmed with difficulty over a small fire in an iron box in the bows, so placed, that the smoke blew away forward, away from the royal party.

Nest cuddled up to the King, claiming she was cold, while their son Henry sat close by, enjoying the intimacy of a family for the first time since he was a baby.

'What do you think of seeing your father and mother together for the first time?' she asked.

'I like it Mother. I like it very much.'

'You are a little quiet my Lord,' she said to the King. 'Do you not like the sea?'

'Indeed, I love the sea and it does not make me sick. However I have had a strange feeling of foreboding since we sailed. I would have expected that hothead William to have overtaken us by now.'

'Maybe he has already done so in the dark, my Lord, especially if Captain Jack's course is a little careless,' said Henry to his father, trying to reassure him.

'I will endeavour to improve my mood. I am sure I am not being rational.' To Nest he whispered, 'and you, my love have agreed to my offer of marriage and that has made me very happy.'

'It has been very strange for me all these years my Lord, my father.' said young Henry. 'My guardian told me at an early age that my father was the

King. Indeed, I remember sitting on your knee when quite young.'

'And what were you told about your mother?' put in Nest, rather mischievously.

'I was told that my mother was a Welsh Princess, but they never seemed to be able to tell me when I would see you, or why I was not with you. My guardian, Raoul de Nevers, was a kindly man. He took great trouble with my upbringing, but I always knew he was not my real father, nor his wife my real mother.'

'My son I must apologise to you for your upbringing being so strange, and that your wonderful mother was kept from seeing you. At the time, I was advised that the separation was necessary for the good of the State.' Nest grimaced in the lamplight.

'But now, I know that I should have followed my heart and married your mother and made you legitimate. Seeing me here with you and your mother, you may not be too surprised to learn that I am going to try to put matters right at long last, if twenty years late. I will be meeting our saintly Archbishop Anselm on our return to seek his support, and conferring with the Magnates of this realm to convince them to accept my wishes. William is not the right man to be my successor, and I want you dear Nesta at my side to advise me for the remainder of my reign.'

chapter fifty-nine

The Earl's Hunting Lodge,
Boarhunt, Hampshire

It was like the old days. Nest and Henry were lying naked by the fire, drinking wine and eating cake. They were going to make love, but not until they were recovered from their voyage.

The Earl had kindly provided his hunting lodge at Boarhunt for the use of the King, when he had landed at Portsmouth after the night crossing. Henry was in no rush to get back to London. He needed time to plan his meeting with the Archbishop and the Magnates very carefully. Nest would help him to do that. Besides he now was of the opinion that the White Ship had missed the tide and would not arrive for a further twelve hours. These were all very good reasons for spending the day dallying with Nest.

They were both tired, but the general effect of the privacy of the room, the wine, the romantic fire and the proximity of their naked bodies soon overcame the need to sleep, and Nest found she had started to kiss his shoulders and cheeks. Henry was still worried about his declining powers but soon forgot that when her kisses spread to the lower parts of his body. She had just climbed on top of him experimentally, when there was an urgent banging on the door. It was their son, who had announced last night that he intended to go riding that morning.

'My Lord the King, my Lady Mother, I must speak to you at once, there is a matter of great importance. I am very sorry.'

'This had better be important,' growled Henry, his manhood rapidly declining, as they both hurriedly donned gowns.

'I am sure he knows the need for us to rest after our journey. He would not disturb us unless there was good cause,' whispered Nest, trying to protect her son from his father's disappointment.

Nest let him in and he entered accompanied by an exhausted looking messenger.

'What is all this about' she said, 'I sure that you know your father needs to rest after his journey.'

'I beg you, please sit down father, and you, mother. This man has brought bad news and I wish there had been someone other than I to tell you of it.'

'Whatever is it? Has there been some rebellion? Tell me at once!' Seeing his son still hesitating, the King turned to the messenger. 'You, man, spit it out! Tell me this bad news that you bring.'

The man fell on his knees before the King.

'My Lord, the Captain of the Port of Barfleur has sent me on a fast vessel. I came straight from Portsmouth having been told you were here. I wish I could bring better news, but the truth unvarnished is that the White Ship has been wrecked just outside Barfleur, and all on board lost, except for a galley boy who floated ashore clinging to a spar.'

The King went white, half rose from his chair and then fell back again. 'And my son William, what news of him?'

'I am so sorry, my Lord King, but his body was found on the rocks, with many others, after the Captain of the Port organised a torchlight search by fishermen in a fleet of boats. The body of Princess Edith has also been found.'

Nest felt a surge of overwhelming emotions. She was desperately sorry for Henry, losing two of his children so suddenly in such a violent way. Despite this, she also saw that, with William dead, Henry had even more need to legitimise his remaining son, Henry, by marrying her. It seemed as if she was going to be Henry's Queen at last after all these years. Surely the Archbishop and the great Magnates would now be convinced of the need to save the succession. She tried hard to put these unbidden thoughts aside. Henry would need comfort and support now. She struggled to keep her reactions in check and rose from her chair and ran to the King to comfort him.

The King was ashen white and staring fixedly at the ceiling as if in a trance. As Nest put her arms around him, he rose from his chair and pushed her away.

'No, no! Do not touch me! This is God's punishment on me, because I thought to renounce William as my successor. I am being punished for my adultery with you and for plotting to secure my own comfort and pleasure. It is God's will that my Kingdom shall be plunged into anarchy on my death and I must accept it.'

The King's recently appointed Chief Advisor, the Earl of Salisbury, had now entered the room, having heard the news from others.

'My Lord. You have had terrible tidings from France. You are deeply shocked at the loss of your son and heir. I urge you to take time to grieve and do nothing hastily. I advise you to seek the views of the Archbishop, before reaching any firm conclusions about God's will.'

265

chapter sixty

Nest could hardly bear it. The Raven was just abeam of St Govan's Head, with the King's Flag still flying in the wind, the very same flagstaff which twenty years ago she had passed on the way to marry Gerald. It was in many ways the same as before. Again the King had rejected her, this time because he thought the death of his son in the White Ship must be a punishment sent by God. Last time he was going to marry the saintly Matilda 'for reasons of state', this time he was going to marry the young Adelaide of Louvain in a desperate attempt to produce another legitimate son. It was all so unnecessary and so hard to bear. Bethan was at her side as always and the elderly Captain Thomas not far away. She would have to talk to them: there was no one else.

Twenty years ago she was still very young, and though her breasts craved for the baby who had been taken away from her by the King, her life was still before her, and the hope of making a new marriage with Gerald. How wonderful he had been after the initial uncertainties. Now she faced the ignominious prospect of going back to Stephen after the destruction of her suddenly raised hopes of being Queen. How he would gloat when he found out what had taken place. How was she going to endure spending the rest of her life with him?

'I just do not understand how it has all gone wrong Bethan. I met my wonderful firstborn son, and the King told me that his legitimate son William was weak, dissolute and unfit to succeed him, and he wanted our son Henry to succeed instead. His plan was to persuade Archbishop Anselm to get me a divorce from the odious Stephen so that I could be Queen of England. He was sure that he could make it happen. Then, God intervenes, and William is suddenly removed as heir, and apparently the way forward is simpler. However the King does not see it like that but somehow thinks the drowning of his awful son means that he has offended against God. Several of the Magnates urged him to see it differently, but he was a man stricken by guilt and he sent me away'.

Captain Thomas had moved nearer, and spoke before Bethan had composed her thoughts. 'I do not know why his Majesty rejected you, my Lady, just when the death of Prince William removed an obstacle to the succession. I do know that grief can generate many strange feelings in a man. It may be that the King somehow felt it was his fault that Prince William had turned out so badly. I feel very deeply for you my Lady and do not know what I can say or do which might improve matters. It is sometimes very hard to understand the work of God. It is only with time that we can see the full picture'.

'I appreciate your deep feelings Master Thomas, but I cannot see how this tragic death, and the King's irrational reaction to it, can possibly be a good thing ordained by God'.

'I confess I do not understand myself my Lady. Surely with you at his side as his Queen, and the succession assured in the form of your fine son, England would be a safer, better place. However, God might take a broader view, and intend that the suffering of the Saxon people of England under the alien Norman yoke should come to an end, and that this can only happen through a violent civil war, Norman against Norman. I know this does not help you my Lady', he finished lamely.

Nest tried to smile, and touched his arm. 'I will try to see things your way, Master Thomas. It is easy to forget that you Saxons are still dispossessed of your birthright after more than fifty years. I also forget the sufferings of my own land, and the struggle of my dear brother to bring freedom to my people. I shall find it very hard to forget that I was so nearly Queen, and my son nearly heir to the throne. However if I am to remain sane, and be true to myself, I must now help my brother to seize any chance to give the land of Cymru back to her own people. I must also help my children to grow up to understand the needs of their native land. Thank you Master Thomas, you have helped me see what I must do with the rest of my life'.

267

Nest was sitting on a rock on Mwnt Beach. Bethan was silently close by, leaving her mistress to her reverie. Gelert was up the path on the top of the cliff watching the horses and looking out for the unlikely arrival of someone from Cardigan Castle. Stephen was on a three-day visit to Pembroke so the activity at the castle would be reduced.

It was a hot day. The sun already heated up the sands and rocks in the tiny bay. Nest was wondering whether she should find some shade under the nearby cliff, but thought she should be clearly visible from the sea. She was waiting for her rebel brother Gruffudd, who had promised to meet her there at eleven. It was already past noon, so she was beginning to think he would not be coming. Perhaps he had spotted a Norman ship and was lying low.

It now seemed a very long time, but it was only really six years, since finally her life seemed to be coming to a climax with Henry wanting to make her Queen and their son, young Henry, his heir. She had thought she would be finished with the unspeakable Stephen, and back at Westminster, where she might at last have had some influence over what happened to her poor people. However, it was not to be and she was here again at Cardigan, trying to make some sense out of her life.

One comfort for her was that her son Henry had been given a roving assignment by the King to hunt down pirates still operating in the Irish Sea. He had been given command of three fast ships and a hundred heavily armed men and his patrols had already greatly reduced the pirates' activities. He was mostly in North Wales, but seemed to manage to find excuses from time to time to sail down to Cardigan to see his mother. Stephen resented his visits and tended to take himself off to Cilgerran when he called. Through him, Nest kept up to date with what was going on in London, especially the activities of the King, as Henry junior was required to submit reports every four months in person to him.

It saddened her to learn that now Henry had continually to worry about the succession. Despite having married the young Adelaide of Louvain, there was no sign of a baby son to succeed him. Only last year he had recalled his daughter Matilda from Germany, on the death of her husband the Emperor Henry Vth, and made the Magnates swear to accept her as Queen should he die without a male heir. They had done so, but without conviction. Nest wished she could have made everything right for him. It was so sad it had all gone wrong.

Nest still looked young, and several of Stephen's Knights obviously would have liked to have to have taken her to bed, as everyone knew she did not sleep with Stephen. It would have been easy to fall into that trap, and

Nest at first had often been tempted, but never quite succumbed. She had known that some better role was waiting for her than that. A loving relationship was more important to her than the satisfaction of mere bodily needs.

Bethan was nudging her arm. A fishing boat was pulling into the little bay. It was Gruffudd being rowed by four of his men. She worried, as she knew how reckless he could be and marvelled that he had avoided capture by the Normans for so many years.

He must have spent too long in Ireland she thought as he greeted her with a bit of blarney.

'What would a pretty young girl like you be doing cast up all alone on such a savage shore as this?'

'Why, waiting for her fairy Prince - but you do not look like him,' she added, as she hugged him to her.

'Seriously, are you not thoroughly tired of living with Stephen? There is no reason for you to stay here any more. Your Gerald is long gone. I think you should come back with me to Ireland to help organise the forces that will, ere long, throw the Normans out of Wales. I need you there, Nest, and frankly your presence here is a problem for me. When I look for targets for my men to attack, Pembroke is now too full of Flemings to tackle successfully. Logically, I should go for Ceredigion, but you, my sister, are here. It is very difficult for me.'

'It is difficult for me too Gruffudd. My children are growing up. They are half Norman, and think of themselves as mostly Norman. I cannot just abandon them and fly away to Ireland, much as I want to see our people free. Angharad is now married ...

'Yes sister, to that Norman, de Barry!'

'and is likely to give me grandchildren soon. My youngest son Robert, is only nine, and needs to be with his father, unsatisfactory though that is for me. David is twenty-one and is being trained for the church. He has the ambition of being Bishop of St David's one day and with his faith and skills he may very well succeed. My heart is with our people, but my duty is with my children and future grandchildren. Surely you can understand that?'

'I cannot believe you are happy here with vile Stephen. Let me rid you of him. I can arrange for an archer to wait for him on top of Treffgarne Rocks next time he visits Pembroke. He would be an easy target for a longbow-man as he passes below through the gorge. Then you would be free of him and could marry a Welshman.'

'Someone like Owain's brother?' she laughed. 'I do not think so. We cannot usually go back in life, brother. I know because I have tried. My role is to rear my Welsh/Norman children to be worthy of my wonderful Gerald. I am not lost to you, because I love our people dearly, but my own way in life was chosen when I settled down contentedly with Gerald. You know I wish you well and hope that by your efforts, some part of Wales will some day be free of the Normans and be truly Welsh again.'

Gruffudd was sad as his men rowed him back to his hidden ship along the coast. He loved his sister and wanted her to be happy. Surely she must be miserable living with the unspeakable Stephen.

He need not have concerned himself too much. No sooner had her brother's boat pulled out of sight, than Gelert rushed down the steep path from the top of the cliff with the news that Stephen's Overlord, Richard Fitzgilbert, was approaching the cove alone on horseback.

Bethan pursed her lips with pretended disapproval as she hurriedly brushed her mistress's hair.

'You have cut it very fine this time my Lady. If Prince Gruffudd had delayed his departure much longer then the two men in your life would have met, with disastrous consequences.'

Nest was too happy to be cross with her.

'Would you have me be a nun Bethan. Lord Richard is a fine man and makes me laugh. With him for a lover I feel young again. He gives me strength to cope with my difficult life with Stephen, and I always know he would never let Stephen seriously mistreat me. Please be happy for me Bethan. I am an old woman of forty-six, yet so fine a man finds me desirable. I have lost Gerald, and also lost any chance of being Queen, but at least if I must stay in my Norman life and rear my near Norman children, I have a man who cares for me and who makes me happy.'

A s the sun rose on that ghastly dawn, Nest stood petrified on the battlements as the growing light revealed one horror after another.

The flames from the blazing town were still leaping high in the air illuminating pitiful survivors being hunted down by Gruffudd's soldiers. Their screams could be clearly heard from the castle.

As the light grew stronger, Nest could see that the river near the bridge was choked, bank to bank, with the bodies of Norman soldiers and camp followers who had died in yesterday's battle. The sluggish water was coloured deep red. Whether stained by the blood of the fallen or tinted by the glow of the sunrise Nest could not tell.

Gruffudd had sent word to her some days ago that his victorious army had everywhere vanquished the Normans except at Pembroke, and that the whole of Deheubarth would soon be his. He had warned her that his forces would shortly be approaching Aberteifi and that she would not be in any danger, provided that she remained within the castle walls. He said that the castle would not be stormed, as he did not wish to risk the life of his sister.

The town was regarded as mainly Norman and would be pillaged. The castle would be invested. He hoped to treat with Stephen at that point and would demand Nest's 'release', and she would be able to return to her own people in Dynefwr.

After some reflection, she had decided to show Gruffudd's letter to Stephen hoping that some lives might be saved because of it. However, after reading it he had laughed unpleasantly. He said that all the remaining Norman troops were concentrating on the town, including heavy cavalry, and such a force would slaughter the Welsh rabble. The lost areas in Deheubarth would soon be under Norman rule again.

Yesterday the Norman army had taken up position on the far bank of the river so that the flatter land there would allow full use of the cavalry. When the host had taken up battle array it looked as powerful as Stephen had said it was and Nest feared for her brother's life.

However when the allied Welsh and Irish army approached the town it did not behave in the undisciplined way that the Normans had come to expect. Gruffudd had had time to plan for this day in his many years in exile in Ireland and things would be different this time. With a growing sense of anxiety, the ladies on the battlements saw first a line of lightly armed soldiers who appeared suddenly a few hundred yards in front of the Norman cavalry. Instead of hurling themselves wildly at the waiting enemy, they stopped three hundred yards in front of them and started to drive pointed stakes into the ground, angled towards the Normans. A line of longbow-men now formed up quickly behind the hedge of stakes and methodically started to

271

release volley after volley into the tightly packed horsemen. Soon hundreds of horses and their riders were writhing on the ground.

Stephen responded to this deadly new warfare by sending his remaining cavalry to charge the archers, but the continuous line of stakes formed a deterring barrier and the cavalry were forced to swerve away at the last minute, chased by a further hail of arrows.

When the cavalry tried to outflank the position, they found that the main body of Grufudd's troops had moved up behind the longbow-men and driven lines of stakes to the side and to the rear, with more archers releasing a deadly fire. The Norman archers were completely outclassed as the Welsh longbow had a far greater range, being able to kill a man at several hundred yards.

Too late Stephen realised that the only way to deal with the Welsh was by an infantry assault. However, the mass of the remaining wheeling and confused Norman cavalry prevented proper deployment of the Men at Arms.

All this time, a murderous flood of deadly arrows struck the now panicking soldiery. Suddenly the Norman line broke and both infantry and Knights ran towards the river and all tried to cross the bridge at once.

At this point the Welsh troops appeared from behind the line of stakes and fell on the rear of the fleeing Normans, slaughtering them as they crowded to cross the bridge. Other Normans attempting to cross the river by the ford, were shot down by the longbow-men, or got out of their depth in the swirling current and were drowned, dragged down by their armour.

In less than an hour it was all over, with dead and dying lying in piles, even clogging the river in places. Some of the survivors were lucky enough to get through the castle gates before they closed, but as Gruffudd had promised Nest not to storm the castle, he put into operation a plan to prevent the bulk of the survivors reaching the gates. Even as the panicking Normans had started to escape over the bridge, a force of Welsh cavalry forded the river in a shallower section a few hundred yards above the bridge and galloped to cut off the route to the castle gates.

With access to the Castle denied, and pressed from the rear by the Welsh infantry hot on their heels, the remaining Normans fled along the river bank and were hunted down by the horsemen, or ran into the town and tried to hide in the houses.

As night fell Gruffudd's soldiers started to loot and ransack the houses, setting fire to them in the process. As Normans and townspeople alike were smoked out of the dwellings they were hunted down and killed by the soldiery. The only people to be spared were Normans of high rank who might be worth ransoming, or ordinary people who claimed they were supporters of Gruffudd.

Nest's feelings were stretched several ways by the scenes of carnage. On the one hand her husband and his men were fighting for their lives to defend

272

the way of life which she had enjoyed for many years. Her children knew no other existence, and regarded themselves as more than half Norman. Ladies who were her friends, and who were with her now on the battlements, waited with desperate fear for the outcome of the battle, and their fate at the hands of the victorious Welsh.

On the other hand, her brother was leading her own people in the assault on the town, and she loved him and was deeply moved by the fight of her Nation to recover their lands and their pride. It appeared that this battle was bringing alien Norman control to an end and bringing the restoration of Deheubarth to Welsh rule.

Of course, this conflict in her heart was not new. It had existed since first she had come back to Penfro to marry Gerald. However, Gerald had had an easy relationship with Gruffudd, who had always taken care to spare Gerald's lands in his various assaults on Norman power, so that Nest had never before had to face the full depths of her dilemma.

Now it was different. Nest could see that Norman power was being swept away, perhaps forever. Strong, capable Henry had died last year leaving no legitimate son to succeed him. Civil war had broken out between Henry's daughter Matilda, whom Henry had tried to have accepted as his successor, and another Stephen, his nephew, who had seized the throne on Henry's death. The net effect of it all as far as Wales was concerned was the severing of all help and assistance for the now isolated and beleaguered Normans there. There was no chance of any new army arriving to sweep Gruffudd away. No one in England was interested in Wales. Every Magnate there, was too busy deciding which cause to support, Stephen's or Matilda's. *

'Poor Henry,' thought Nest. 'All his work to build a strong Anglo-Norman Kingdom is being destroyed. He should have married me: young Henry would have been a very capable King.' How very sad it was.

No orders or assistance being forthcoming from the Lord of Pembroke, or his Liege Lord, Richard Fitzgilbert, Stephen had taken on himself the task of co-ordinating the last battle against the Welsh. He was now at her side, sword in hand, looking tired and strained.

Nest was glad that her lover, Richard Fitzgilbert was not there: he would be safer elsewhere. Nest had persuaded him to escort a party of high born Norman ladies across hostile territory to safety in England last week, when she had first received her brother's secret message about an imminent assault on Cardigan. She had correctly calculated that he would not be back in time

---

* *Henry died bizarrely, aged 67, from eating 'a surfeit of lampreys', his favourite seafood. Perhaps he had food poisoning. Matilda was out of the country when the King died, and his nephew Stephen of Blois seized the throne. Matilda eventually returned and a long civil war ensued. England would have been spared a long period of suffering if Henry had married Nest and had made their son Henry legitimate.*

for the battle. She missed him though, and hoped that she had done the right thing in deceiving him about the oncoming attack.

Sir Robert Fitzmartin, the Lord of Newport, was here though. Both Stephen and Sir Robert had been lucky to have been able to get back into the castle after the debacle at the bridge yesterday. Now Stephen was looking for someone to let out his frustrations on, who better than his Welsh wife?

'Proud of your brother are you? See how his savages hunt down men in the streets? It will be our turn next. I do hope his wild men have been told to look out for you when they climb over the battlements or Heaven help you.'

Nest said nothing: there was nothing to say to this defeated man whom she had loathed for years.

'You will be rid of me soon. You will be able to go back to Dynefwr and whore there to your heart's content.'

'You are a bitter, perverted, unloving man Stephen. My heart bleeds for those poor people in the town and I long for the fighting to finish. I grieve for my friends who are waiting, here in the castle, terrified, for their fate.

'One way or another, our life here is coming to an end and I will not spare you from what I think for that reason.

'I have loathed sharing your bed. You have no desire to make a woman happy. Your idea of what a wife is for, is sadistic pain and perversion. I wish I had never married you.'

These words were flung at Stephen with little regard as to who heard them, and humiliated he was driven to respond in the only way he knew, by striking her with his fist.

Sir Robert intervened to prevent further scenes of domestic violence.

'Please, restrain yourself, Stephen. We must all comport ourselves well in front of our men. We are not dead yet and we must give hope and encouragement to all around us.'

As Nest struggled to her feet, further deplorable scenes were prevented by the arrival of a breathless Bethan.

'My Lord, my Lady, the Solar is on fire and I cannot reach Richard and young Gerald, whom I fear may be trapped there.'

Glancing towards the main tower Nest could see that Welsh fire arrows had ignited the wooden roof, and that flames were starting to lick through the solar windows on the third floor.

Putting aside their violent quarrel, Nest cried, 'Quick Stephen, we must go speedily to save them. We need men with buckets of water to quench the flames.'

' I cannot concern myself with the fate of children now. I am at risk of losing the castle. You must organise servants to help you.'

'You base brute! My grandchildren may be burning. May you rot in Hell!' she spat.

Urgently Bethan tugged at her arm. 'Quick my Lady, we must try to save them ourselves.'

Throwing a final look of pure hatred, Nest ran with Bethan towards the entrance to the tower shouting to all and sundry to come and help her.

More smoke and flames were now pouring out of the third floor, and already the lower floors were smoke-filled.

As the two women rushed into the ground floor kitchen, they immediately started to cough.

'My Lady, let us soak towels and serving cloths in water and hold them over our faces. That is the only way we can hope to get up the stairs.'

While Bethan quickly soaked towels, Nest tore down two curtains and soaked those to wrap round their dresses.

'They may save our dresses catching fire.'

At this moment, two menservants who had already tried to get up the stairs came staggering down, and lurched through the kitchen choking and gagging.

'It is hopeless my Lady, we cannot get up there.'

'Recover yourselves as quickly as possible and cover your faces with wet clothes and follow us up with buckets of water.'

Both women now started to force themselves up the stairs, the smoke swirling down around them. The wet clothes did help a great deal, but enough of the noxious fumes were reaching their noses, causing them to cough and splutter.

The next floor, the dining room, was so thick with smoke that Nest could hardly see to the other side. She was encouraged to find that Gelert had now joined them.

'Thank God you are here, Gelert, you are a true friend. I am so worried that Gerald and Richard may be upstairs. Let us get up there quickly before it is impossible.'

Choking and gasping, they struggled up the last staircase with Nest in the lead. A wall of heat and denser smoke met them at the solar door. The roof over the middle of the room was burning, with small pieces of blazing wood dropping to the floor igniting the straw. Nest could not see if the boys were there or not.

'Gerald, Richard are you there?' she tried to shout. She thought she could hear a plaintive reply from the far corner.

'I think they are in the corner by the window,' Gelert shouted. 'I will try to get them'

'Keep low to the ground, Gelert. It will be less hot there.'

The roof fire was roaring away now, and Nest was sure the whole of the blazing structure was about to come down.

'Let us crawl round the edge of the room. The roof will soon fall.'

Judging their moment, Nest led the other two on all fours round the room. The heat was intense and patches of the straw were suddenly starting to burn.

She could now see the two little boys lying on the floor near a window, whimpering with fear.

'Nan is here, we will get you out, you must be brave. Get Richard, Gelert and I will take young Gerald. Let's get out of here at once. There is not a second to spare.'

She grasped Gerald and started to half carry and half drag the boy back towards the door. Bethan tried to help her while Gelert picked up Richard. Nest started to feel dizzy and unreal. She must force herself to get to the stairs with Gerald. She must think only about that. It suddenly seemed much harder and she realised that Bethan was not helping her any more. As in a dream she looked back and saw that Bethan's dress was on fire and Gelert had left Richard and was trying to roll Bethan on the ground to put out the flames. It was a nightmare: someone had to be saved. She might be able to get Gerald out. She must close her mind to the horrors behind and save Gerald. Gelert was a tower of strength. If Bethan and Richard could be saved, he would do it.

She had reached the head of the stairs. She was so tired and dreamy. All she could think of was rescuing Gerald. She struggled down the first flight. Gerald was supporting himself now and it was easier. She must make sure he was safe and then she would go back to help Gelert. Where were the other servants? Did no one else care?

As if in a trance, she realised she had reached the entrance to the tower. She and Gerald were safe. More servants were coming in with buckets of water, led by Sir Robert Fitzmartin. Willing hands took the boy from her.

'My God, Nest, you shame us all. You could have died up there.'

'I must go back. My grandson Richard was still in the Solar when I left and Gelert was trying to save him, and his wife. Let us go back together, but you will not survive without wet towels to help your breathing. Soak your clothes too or they may catch fire.'

While Sir Robert and the servants tried to find towels and blankets, Nest took a few gasps of fresh air and quickly drenched her blanket and towel. She was already starting back up the stairs before the others were ready.

She met Gelert carrying Bethan at the top of the first flight. He had horrible burns on his face, and his jerkin was charred and smouldering. He had torn away Bethan's burning dress and had rolled her in his blanket.

'Please God she is still alive, my Lady. Forgive me! I had to leave the boy. I have failed you. I will go back now. I ...'

He slumped to the ground, and two menservants started to drag him to safety.

'Take them both down and tend carefully to their burns. Come Sir Robert and pray Heaven that Richard has not yet perished.'

When they reached the Solar, the heat was even worse than before. Part of the roof had fallen in and the blazing timbers had started to burn through the floor. Nest could not see Richard. Had he gone back to the far window? The only hope of getting back there was on the other side of the room where the floor was still unaffected by the falling roof.

'Stop Nest, I do not think he is there. He must have gone down or -'

Sir Robert's words were lost in the roar of the blazing roof and he could only watch as she recklessly started round the far wall. As he moved to drag her back, a blazing beam fell between them cutting off her escape.

She crawled, half ran to the end of the room, her blankets smouldering. The window gave relief to her lungs, but most of the room was ablaze now. She was going to die. Thank God Richard was not still here or he would be dying too.

She could see that Sir Robert's men were throwing buckets of water onto the flames, but it was all too late, too late. A blazing beam fell a few feet away and more of the floor was on fire. She did not want to burn. She was still beautiful and desirable. She must not burn. There was no way back to the door. There was only the window. She leaned out of it. She could feel the heat of the approaching flames on her back. She must jump. Far below, she could see servants toiling to the tower door with buckets. She shouted to them to catch her. She must jump: her dress was on fire. She must not burn. She stood for a second on the windowsill, her dress ablaze. There was no help. No one would catch her. She jumped.

As she fell it was if she fell through all eternity. She did not feel the impact, which broke her back. She thought only of which one did she really love? Was it Henry and his skilled passion, or was it Gerald and his quiet friendly love. She smiled inside. Of course it was Gerald that she wanted. Gerald was the real one. Kind, loving, gentle Gerald!

'I love you Gerald. Please be there for me.'

Bethan found her. She knew that she was dead. 'My Lady, I too have failed you. Why was not I here when you fell.' She knelt and prayed for the beautiful, loving, wonderful woman she had served for most of her life.

277

EPILOGUE

epilogue

The Battle of Aberteifi marked the end of Norman rule in South Wales for many years. Only Pembroke held out against Gruffudd's army.

After the death of Henry in 1135, England was rent by civil war between his daughter Matilda, whom he had desperately tried to persuade the Magnates to support as his successor, and Stephen, his nephew, who seized the throne on his death. The war was caused by Henry having no legitimate son to inherit the crown. Many of the Magnates could not accept that a woman would be strong enough to hold the Anglo-Norman kingdom together in such difficult times, although quite a few had promised to do so before Henry's death.

If Henry had married Nest and their son had been accepted as legitimate, (the Archbishop and the Magnates being no doubt willing to agree to this to avoid an imminent problem with the succession), there would have been no civil war and his dynasty would have continued. His failure to do so resulted in the destruction of much of his life's work, together with many years of anarchy. It seems obvious that when the King named Nest's child after himself, that he intended to marry Nest and for their son to inherit the throne. This book tries to give some ideas as to why this never happened.

Many historians and popular legend have been unkind to Nest. I think that she was a brave, highly principled woman, of strong character, and that she tried within the many constraints on her, to influence the powerful men in her life for the good of both Wales and England. She was both very beautiful and highly sexed, and it is hardly surprising that sometimes her feelings betrayed her principles. She was also very intelligent and there is evidence that the men in her life respected her advice. Some of our dry academics have difficulty in coping with a woman such as Nest, since she does not fit into any of the convenient slots that they have prepared for famous women: whore, blue stocking, dumb beauty etc.

Certainly her genes must have been excellent, since many of her descendents achieved great things. One son, David, became Bishop of St.Davids. Her grandson, Gerald of Wales, became famous for his travel books, like 'The Journey through Wales' and 'A description of Wales.' He was also one of the period's greatest writers in Latin. He visited Rome three times and studied both in Paris and in England. He lived in Manorbier, which he describes beautifully.

Although he was born after Nest's death, he refers to the family memory of her with affection and respect.

Two of Nest's sons, William Fitzgerald, and Robert Fitzstephen, landed in Ireland and commenced its conquest, starting Britain's long and often tragic involvement with that island. There are many other connections, and

Nest has been described as the 'Queen Bee', from whom many of Britain and Ireland's great families have sprung. Sadly though, Henry Fitzhenry, Nest and Henry's lovechild, from whom great things might have sprung, died rather bizarrely fighting pirates in Anglesey.

One of the most interesting things that I found when researching the book, is that Nest is of that Welsh family line which eventually married into the House of Tudor, providing England with such strong rulers as Henry the Eighth and Elizabeth the First. I have provided a family tree showing these connections.

Welsh history does not contain many famous women. Wales should take Nest to her heart and be proud of her.

TABLE SHOWING NEST`S ROYAL LINKS

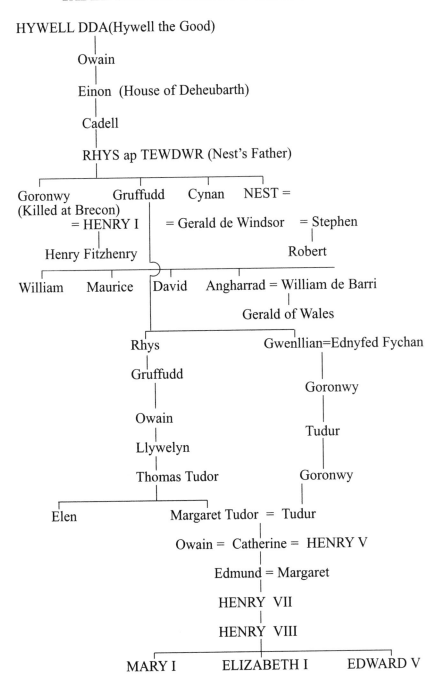

HYWELL DDA(Hywell the Good)

Owain

Einon (House of Deheubarth)

Cadell

RHYS ap TEWDWR (Nest's Father)

Goronwy   Gruffudd   Cynan   NEST =
(Killed at Brecon)
     = HENRY I   = Gerald de Windsor   = Stephen

Henry Fitzhenry   Robert

William   Maurice   David   Angharrad = William de Barri

Gerald of Wales

Rhys   Gwenllian=Ednyfed Fychan

Gruffudd   Goronwy

Owain   Tudur

Llywelyn   Goronwy

Thomas Tudor

Elen   Margaret Tudor = Tudur

Owain = Catherine = HENRY V

Edmund = Margaret

HENRY VII

HENRY VIII

MARY I   ELIZABETH I   EDWARD V

LIST OF SOURCES

History of England Beyond Wales, *Edward Laws*, 1888
Kings and Queens of England, *Antonia Fraser*, 1975
Anglo-Saxon Chronicles, 12th c.
The Chronicles of the Princes, 12th c.
History of Wales, *John Davies*, 1990
Age of Conquest, *R. R. Davies*, 1987
Oxford History of England, Domesday Book to Magna Carta
History of Carew, *William George Spurrell*, 1920
The Pawns of Kings, *Margaret Mackinley*, 1981
Makers of the Realm, *Arthur Bryant*, 1955
Portrait of Pembrokeshire, *Dilwyn Miles*, 1984
Short History of Pembroke Castle, 1976
History of Pembrokeshire, *James Phillips*, 1909
South Pembrokeshire, *Mary Beatrice Mirehouse*, 1910

If you are interested generally in the history of the period, Antonia Fraser's book 'Kings and Queens of England' gives a good background. If you can find a copy of 'Makers of the Realm' by Arthur Bryant, it is quite fascinating and it includes one of the rare favourable references by historians to Nest.